Praise for *Rose Addams*

"An intimate look at a woman entering her third act on life's stage. Rose reflects on her role as wife and mother and how she will improvise in a very complicated and unpredictable world."
—SENATOR PAMELA WALLIN

"Margie Taylor loves Rose Addams. Loves her despite Rose's blind spots and anxieties. Or *because* of them. In this compulsively readable novel, Taylor shines a witty and compassionate light on the world of a woman navigating her sixth decade—a daring project, given how little literature has bothered. As Taylor deftly nudges her heroine past personal crises that test her convictions about motherhood, marriage and propriety, she lets Rose (and us readers) glimpse a new, deeper kind of self-knowledge that only comes with age."
—MARGUERITE PIGEON, author of *The Endless Garment* and *Some Extremely Boring Drives*

"Readers will smile to recognize family members, friends, and themselves in this gentle skewering of a middle-class, middle-aged Vancouver woman and her circle. Hints of Jane Austen, Barbara Pym and Elizabeth Strout enliven a perspicacious account of friendships, generation gaps, unsuitable attachments, and the indignities of encroaching age. Margie Taylor has created, in Rose Addams, an avatar for women of a certain age who struggle to learn a new generation's perspectives and mores, but when crises arise, are heroically present with their experience and fierce commitment to the vulnerable of society."
—KAREN HOFMANN, award-winning author of *A Brief View from the Coastal Suite* and *Echolocation*

"Margie Taylor writes with great empathy and sharp insight. Readers will root for the characters in this compelling story."
—LISA GUENTHER, author of *Friendly Fire*

"A beautifully crafted work, *Rose Addams* features vivid characters facing real-world problems in a narrative that reads like a thriller. I had a hard time putting this one down."
—KEN MCGOOGAN, author of *Fatal Passage* and *Lady Franklin's Revenge*

"In a style reminiscent of Carol Shields and Bonnie Burnard, Margie Taylor has crafted a warm-hearted tale from the life of Rose Addams. Rose, as her husband Charles points out, is a woman 'compelled to insert herself into every situation.' Not quite a busybody, not quite a fixer (sometimes the opposite), Rose tries her best to be useful and kind and keep up with the times. No easy task when presented with the abrupt appearance of a young man who stayed at their home briefly when he was a child, a daughter in a personal crisis, new and peculiar behaviour from Rose's husband, and various surprise announcements from her long-term friends and their mismatched (according to Rose) romantic partners. Rose's strong character and her knack for jumping to (incorrect) assumptions make for a highly engaging, frequently funny, story that is, ultimately, about the changing nature of all of our relationships as we age."
—BARB HOWARD, author of *Happy Sands* and *Western Taxidermy*

Rose Addams

Rose Addams

a novel

Margie Taylor

NeWest Press

Library and Archives Canada Cataloguing in Publication

Title: Rose Addams / Margie Taylor.
Names: Taylor, Margie, author.
Identifiers: Canadiana (print) 20220402094 | Canadiana (ebook) 20220402132 |
    ISBN 9781774390696 (softcover) | ISBN 9781774390702 (EPUB)
Classification: LCC PS8589.A90725 R57 2023 | DDC C813/.54—dc23

Board Editor: Eva Radford
Cover and interior design: Michel Vrana
Author photo: Kim Culbert https://www.kimculbert.com/

NeWest Press wishes to acknowledge that the land on which we operate is Treaty 6 territory and a traditional meeting ground and home for many Indigenous Peoples, including Cree, Saulteaux, Niitsitapi (Blackfoot), Métis, and Nakota Sioux.

NeWest Press acknowledges the Canada Council for the Arts, the Alberta Foundation for the Arts, and the Edmonton Arts Council for support of our publishing program. We acknowledge the financial support of the Government of Canada through the Canada Book Fund for our publishing activities.

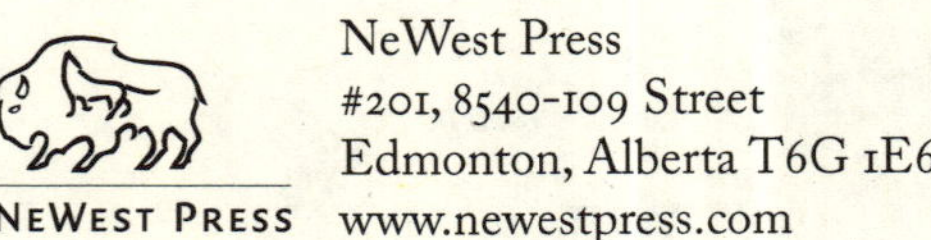

NeWest Press
#201, 8540-109 Street
Edmonton, Alberta T6G 1E6
www.newestpress.com

No bison were harmed in the making of this book.

Printed and bound in Canada
22 23 24 25 5 4 3 2 1

1.

THE GUY IS STILL THERE, HUNCHED ON THE SIDE-
walk a few feet from the entrance to the store. Dark hoodie, torn
jeans. Cardboard sign with Homeless Please Give written in crayon.
Rose *does* give, when she has spare change. Which isn't as often as
it used to be because, really, who carries cash anymore? He never
looks up, but he acknowledges contributions by nodding and pressing his hands together in thanks.

"Namaste."

She likes that. It's what her yoga teacher always said at the end
of a class; Rose assumed it meant "thanks" but it means more than
that. According to Wikipedia, it means "I bow to the divine in you."
Which is nice.

She puts the car into reverse gear and wonders if she should
give Charles a call before setting off, let him know she's on her
way. He likes to be kept in the loop. Charles is her husband of
four decades—forty years exactly next May. He is her friend, her
defender, and her support system, and, when she's not wanting to
strangle him, she admires his spirited approach to life and his sense
of humour. She might have done so much worse; she'd never tell
him that, of course, but she often thinks it.

Backing out of her parking space, she makes sure to check behind her for stray shopping carts. He's still there, the homeless guy. The first time he said namaste she wanted to ask if he did yoga, but most likely he'd just picked it up somewhere and liked the sound of it. Homeless people don't do yoga, do they? Where would they do it? And yoga lessons cost the earth. Morgan takes them three times a week at some studio in Toronto—twenty dollars a pop, if you can believe it. Still, if it helps her focus on her studies, it's probably worth it. And Ian is paying for it, she says.

Ian. Now *there's* a lovely man. And *such* a good family. Not rich or anything like that, just good, solid people who put their efforts into raising a good, solid son. It's sad when you think of it, the difference good parenting makes. There's Ian, Morgan's fiancé, graduating with distinction from Brown, practically running a film company. And there's that poor young man, standing outside a grocery store, relying on the kindness of strangers. A drug addict probably. A lifetime of poor choices learned from parents who made equally poor choices. The apple doesn't fall far from the tree.

He'd do better if he smiled, made eye contact. Even said good morning. It's hard to ignore someone when they smile at you and say hello. Which is all they can do these days. They aren't allowed to ask you directly for money. When did that change? Must have been a bylaw that came into effect when she wasn't paying attention. This guy, anyway, isn't the one who followed her home the other week. That one panhandles outside the liquor store in the village, a short walk from their house. He came right to her door and knocked and asked for a handout, if you can believe it. How did he even find her? She gave him ten dollars and a peanut-butter sandwich and he left. So far, he hasn't come back.

The blast of a car horn directly behind her prompts her to slam down on the brake pedal. She checks her rear-view mirror, makes the nod-and-hands-together prayer gesture to the driver of an SUV backing up behind her. *Sorry. My bad.* The driver, a young guy in sunglasses and a beanie, doesn't notice. He has his speakers on maximum volume; even with the window closed, the boom-boom-boom is deafening.

It's a miracle there aren't more accidents in these lots. People coming and going, no rules about whose turn it is. The polite ones wait till the coast is clear but nobody is polite any more. We've become a nation of pushy, entitled road hogs demanding the right-of-way.

And it's all the fault of the internet—

Another toot from yet another car, this one coming towards her and cutting into the space beside her. What the hell? When did the simple act of leaving a shopping mall turn into an exercise in military withdrawal? Half these drivers shouldn't be on the road, of course. Too old, too preoccupied.

This time it's the other driver, a woman, giving the apologetic smile. Okay, so it was her fault. And she's sorry. There, you see, Rose? Not everybody's an idiot.

Feeling better, she shifts into drive and creeps out of the lot, casting a final glance in the direction of the homeless guy. Oh no, is that a *dog* with him? Has he adopted a *dog*? She hates when homeless guys have dogs. She gets it, of course: they need company just like anyone else. But dogs are domesticated. They're pets. They're not used to living in the wild. And the streets of this city are as wild as you get. The Wild West, that's where we're at. "Bang Bang (My Baby Shot Me Down)". "I Fought the Law".

You don't hear a lot of songs about guns any more. There used to be tons: "I Shot the Sheriff", "Don't Take Your Guns to Town", "Happiness is a Warm Gun". Well, that probably doesn't count, the Beatles were being ironic. And now John and George are dead and Paul's gotta be, what, 103? Is Ringo still alive? They're all dying, all our heroes. Who's the one who died last week? Somebody she really liked. Oh my god—Aretha Franklin. The Queen of Soul. What did she die of? Cancer? She'll Google it when she gets home.

If she gets home. The traffic is ridiculous. Road works everywhere and something going on up ahead, an accident or something.

Blue flashing lights and cars merging into a single lane. She has a sudden urge to check her phone. No reason to, it hasn't buzzed or beeped or anything and she isn't expecting a call. It's just that she hasn't checked it since leaving the store and maybe she should call Charles and now that traffic's come to a halt it just feels right to pick up her phone and check it out. She won't—it's against the law. But she really *really* wants to. It's an addiction—there was a psychology professor being interviewed on the radio and he said it's like gambling and it's at least partly responsible for an increase in suicide rates among teens. Thank god there were no cell phones around when her kids were in their teens. No social media, none of that stuff. It must be hell, raising teenagers these days, she can't even imagine.

Just as the traffic ahead of her begins to move, her phone rings. Carefully, keeping her eyes on the road, she feels for her phone and puts it on speaker.

"Hello?"

"Mom?"

"Hey, hon, how are you?"

"Where are you? Are you in the car? You shouldn't answer the phone if you're in the car—"

"It's okay, I've got it on speaker. And the car's barely moving. How are you? Are you at school?"

"You know it's a big fine if they catch you. It's like $540!"

"Yes, I know."

"And four demerit points. Why don't you connect it to your car? Jason can show you. He did it for Dad, right? Got Bluetooth installed. You should get him to do it for you."

"I don't want it," Rose says. "I don't want people calling me when I'm driving."

"Then why pick up?"

It's a reasonable question, but it only serves to irritate her. "Is this why you called, to lecture me about the phone?"

"No, I want to talk to you about the wedding."

The wedding. Rose has been wanting to talk about the wedding for weeks, ever since Morgan reluctantly confided that she and the lovely Ian were getting married in December, the day after she—Morgan—completes her PhD. "Don't make a big thing of it," she said at the time. "It's not a big deal. We've been living together for three years, remember."

So here's the thing: Rose is the least likely person in the world to make a big deal about her daughter's wedding. She and Charles decided on a Friday to get married the following Wednesday; they invited twenty close friends, found a Unitarian minister, and hosted a riotous night at a hotel bar in lieu of a wedding reception. It was months before it even dawned on her that they hadn't had a cake. She is hardly a bridezilla. The fact that she was delighted when Morgan dropped her bombshell over Christmas doesn't make her a monster. And it was, after all, a bombshell, Morgan being close to forty and never once as far as her parents knew having shown the slightest interest in becoming a wife.

At any rate, since the announcement, Morgan has clammed up like—well, like a clam. No wedding talk, no shopping for dresses, no info about who's invited, or where it's taking place. It's too early, she keeps saying (which it isn't); I've got other things on my mind (which she does: she's been working on her dissertation for over three years and is *this* close to being done.) And Ian is working on a film—something for Netflix, Rose thinks, although the nature of his job is a mystery. Morgan says he's an executive producer, which sounds important, but when he was visiting at Christmas he shrugged it off.

"I'm the whip-cracker," he said. "The one everybody loves to hate."

Rose can't imagine anyone hating Ian. He is possibly the kindest, most even-natured man she's ever met. And he obviously loves her daughter.

Fighting the urge to grab the phone and hold it to her ear, Rose says, "That's wonderful, hon! Yes, let's talk. Have you decided on a venue? Should I come out?" There's a pause and for a moment she thinks they've lost the connection.

Then Morgan says, "I'll wait till you're out of the car. Call me, okay?"

2.

CHARLES WAS WAITING FOR HER WHEN SHE STRUG-
gled into the kitchen with three bags of groceries, her purse, and a
pair of runners that had been sitting on the back seat for the past
six weeks. They were supposed to be part of her new fitness regime.
At the beginning of the summer she caught a program about the
benefits of walking. One hundred and fifty minutes a week could
cut the risk of stroke, heart disease, and type 2 diabetes by 20 to 50
percent. "Keep a pair of runners with you in your car," the doctor
said. "Any time you have an extra ten minutes during the day, pull
over, put on your runners, and go for a walk. You'll lose weight, feel
more alert—and you'll sleep better, too."

The very next morning she dug her Nikes out of the back of
the closet and, feeling healthier already, put them in the car. At first
she kept them on the passenger seat, where she'd be able to grab
them at a moment's notice. After a few days she moved them to the
floor, and at the end of the second week she dumped them on the
back seat. Where they stayed, glowering at her, and making her feel
guilty every time she opened the car door.

Okay, fine. Not everybody has the luxury of taking ten minutes
out of a busy day to pull over suddenly and go walking. All right

for the doctor; he had tons of money, most likely, and he was a man on top of it—he likely didn't have a husband hanging around the house waiting for his dinner.

Well, to be fair, neither did Rose. Charles had never been one of those helpless where-do-we-keep-the-butter types who can't operate the toaster without setting off the smoke alarm. He was nothing like her friend Eileen's husband. *Ex*-husband, to be exact. Jermyn Cortland. What the hell kind of name is *Jermyn* anyway? He was a successful plastic surgeon with a high-profile clientele in a fashionable part of the city and he couldn't boil an egg. Rose's favourite story about Jermyn was the time Eileen went down to California to visit her mother. She took the kids and left Jermyn on his own, having first prepared three weeks' worth of home-cooked meals that she left in the freezer. When she got home, he hadn't eaten even one of them; he *said* it was because he didn't know how to operate the stove.

If it had been Rose she'd have dumped him on the spot. Eileen stuck it out for five more years before kicking him out and in the end it had nothing to do with his domestic incompetence: he was having an affair with his receptionist. (Eye-roll alert: of *course* he was.)

But no, Charles was nothing like that. He knew how to cook; he did his share of the housework; he changed diapers when the kids were babies. He might have been a domestic idiot years ago, before she met him, but his first wife spent five years knocking him into shape. Rose was deeply grateful to Liz for taking the good-looking young ruffian that he was and moulding him into someone Rose could stand to live with. She'd never told Liz that; maybe she should. Maybe, if she ever saw her again, she would.

She set the groceries on the kitchen counter and dumped her runners on the shelf near the back door. They would stay there, most likely, until she got another burst of motivation in the new year.

Charles started emptying the bags and putting things away. "Good," he said, "you remembered my orange juice."

The orange juice was for his hypoglycemia; he'd been diagnosed in June and warned not to let his blood sugar get low. Since then he made sure to eat several small meals during the day and kept orange juice on hand for those moments when he felt low.

"What's this?" He was holding up a package of Uncle Lee's Legends of China green tea and frowning at the picture of a panda on the front.

"You can see what it is," Rose said. "It's green tea. It's organic." Seeing his face she added, "It's good for you, Charles. You drink too much coffee. We both do."

"I've given up red meat and butter and ice cream. I'm not giving up coffee." But he put it up on the shelf. Where it would likely sit, along with the Organic Assam Breakfast Tea, the Tetley strawberry tea, and the Earl Grey tea leaves "picked from Rainforest Alliance Certified tea estates around the world." All of them gifts from Morgan over the years, designed to make her parents, if not smarter, then at least healthier.

Which reminded her. "I got a call from Morgan while I was in the car," she said. "She wants to talk about the wedding. Can you finish putting these things away and I'll give her a call."

For once, Morgan answered right away. "Hey."

"Is everything all right?" Rose said. "You sounded upset when you called."

"Well, I've been better. I guess." This is never what a mother wants to hear. Before Rose could say anything, Morgan added, "The wedding's off."

"Off? You mean . . . are you saying you and Ian aren't getting married?"

"*I'm* not. I can't speak for Ian."

"I don't understand, honey. What do you mean? Are you getting cold feet? You can put it off, you know. It doesn't have to be in December. Maybe wait till after Christmas, give yourself some time to get things organized."

"Mom! There's not going to be a wedding. I'm not marrying Ian. I wouldn't marry him if you tied me up and walked me down the aisle at gunpoint."

An odd image, and also a little unwieldy. But Rose got the point. "Do you want to tell me what's happened?"

"Not really."

Patience, Rose thought. She's upset, obviously. She waited for Morgan to continue and when she didn't she decided to try another tack. "I bought some green tea today. I was reading this article about the health benefits of drinking green tea. They say it can help prevent cancer. Something to do with polyphenols . . ."

"So you're not interested that my life is falling apart."

"Oh, honey, of course I'm interested. I just thought . . . you said you didn't want to talk about it."

"I don't. But I need you to give a shit."

"I *do*, Morgan. I just don't know what to say. I mean—is Ian around? Are you still seeing each other?" There was no answer. Rose wondered if Morgan was crying. Charles was watching her, wanting to know what was going on. She shook her head, mouthed the words, "They've broken up."

It was his turn to shake his head. "What?"

Rose put her hand over the phone. "They've broken up. She says the wedding's off."

"Let me talk to her," he said, reaching for the phone.

"Morgan? Do you want to talk to Dad? He's right here, he'd like to talk to you."

Another pause, and now she was sure her daughter was crying. Finally she said something about calling them back and Rose said, "I love you," but Morgan had already hung up.

"She didn't want to talk to me?"

"She's upset," Rose said. "I'm pretty sure she was crying. Oh, dear, what do you think happened? I always thought they had such a good relationship. They seemed good together, don't you think?"

Charles didn't answer right away, and Rose wondered if he knew something she didn't. Her husband was good at keeping secrets. Liz had told her that, once, a very long time ago. "He's a very private person," is the way she put it. "He seems hail-fellow-well-met, but he's very English. Very secretive."

Rose didn't see Charles that way at all. To her he was an open book. The first time they'd gone out they'd shared so many details of their private lives they joked they'd have to keep dating just to avoid being blackmailed. Over the years, though, Rose came to realize that Liz was right. Charles was full of secrets—you could never really know him.

And Morgan was just like her father. She and Ian had been together for almost a year before she even mentioned him. Up until then there were vague comments about going places with "a friend," who could have been anyone. It wasn't until Rose and Charles were planning a trip back East that Morgan let it be known that she and the "friend" were living together.

"You'll like him," she said. "He works in film but he's not like most of them. He's actually pretty down-to-earth." Morgan had worked in film for a few years before going back to school to get her master's. She had a distinctly jaded view of movie people. "I think I'm a snob," was the way she put it. "I like *educated* people. Most people in film aren't all that smart. They know about film, and that's it." Rose said Ian was certainly educated, and Morgan said yes he was but he was the exception.

Anyway, Morgan was right about Ian—when they met him in Toronto they liked him immediately. He flattered Rose by not only asking about her job, but by following up with further questions. Few people had much more to say about Rose's work at the library after being told she was the director of Information Services. They generally mumbled something like, "Oh, that's nice," and went on to ask about the library's policy on overdue books. She often told Charles that if she'd simply stayed at the librarian level people would show more interest. "They'd ask me about books," she'd said, "and pay attention to my recommendations. The way things are, though, I don't even have time to read." With Ian, however, she ended up having a brief but satisfying discussion about the advent of digital technology and the challenges involved in the "virtual stacks."

Even Charles, who could be very protective when it came to his daughter, left the restaurant singing Ian's praises. "You can see what she sees in him," he said, as they drove along the Danforth in the back seat of an Uber. (Ian had an account and politely but firmly refused to let them pay for it.) "He's smart and successful without showing off. He wears his learning lightly."

"He has lovely manners," Rose said. "And he's drop-dead cute, don't you think?"

"I'll let you be the judge of that. I try not to comment on men's cuteness."

"Well, he is. I have a good feeling about those two. This might be it."

That night she lay awake long after Charles had fallen asleep, staring into the half-light of the hotel room. Morgan and Ian— what a great couple they'd make. The children would be gorgeous. If they had any. Her daughter was great with kids but not in any rush to have one of her own. But now she'd landed someone as perfect as Ian . . . .

Landed. Was she really using a word like that? In this day and age? The idea that a man was a kind of trophy, a deep-sea bass you had to hook and reel in? Did she really think that at some profound, subterranean level?

She turned over on her side, away from Charles's snoring. Years ago, when he used to drink, his snores would shake the house. The kids complained it kept them awake, and they slept one floor up. Now that he kept to the occasional gin and tonic it was more of a gentle wheezing, like a leaf blower over on the next block. Tonight, though, feeling celebratory, they'd shared a bottle of retsina and followed it up with two shots of ouzo. She was going to have a nasty hangover in the morning. And Charles was snorting like a bull moose in heat.

It didn't matter. Rose never slept well in hotel rooms anyway. She got up and threw on the luxurious white cotton bathrobe provided by the hotel. She didn't need it—it wasn't cold, but what was the point of paying $350 a night for a hotel room if you didn't make use of the amenities? Funny how you can never find these robes in the stores, she thought. The hotels must have a monopoly or something. When they were first together Charles would regularly help himself to towels, bedroom slippers . . . once he "borrowed" a pillow because he said it was so much better than anything they had at home.

Thankfully, those days were long gone. He'd reformed, a little. Plus, the hotels have ways to get their own back now if you walk off with their stuff. This place has one of those cute little signs on the dressing table inviting guests to please make use of the hotel's robes, and should you become so attached to the fluffy cover-ups that you decide to take one home they'll be happy to add an extra $150 to your bill.

The long, low window seat in their hotel room offered a spectacular view of the Toronto skyline. The CN tower glowed red, blue, and gold in the twilight, and the last faint traces of orange sunset glow dusted the western sky. They were on the tenth floor; if they were higher she'd be able to see Lake Ontario, maybe the cottage lights on Toronto Island. But this was as high as she'd go when it came to hotels. What if there was a fire? *She* could walk down more than ten floors, but she wasn't sure Charles was up to it. His knees were giving him trouble. A replacement was in the works for one of them, but that was a year away, at least.

Giving in to an impulse, she reached for her phone and sent Morgan a text: *Great to see you tonight, hon, and lovely to meet your friend LOL!* She didn't expect a reply but in less than a minute her phone beeped:

Great to see u too!! Dad's looking good u both are. What did u think of him? The friend that is ☺

He seems lovely. Hope to see more of him.

He is and u will! Nite Mom ☺

She put the phone down and settled back against the cushion of the window seat. There'd been only a few times over the years when she thought her life was perfect but this was one of them. Morgan in a relationship with a smart, good-looking man; Jason going from strength to strength at that law firm downtown.

Jason. My god. There was a time when she thought if she could just keep him out of jail and off drugs till he was eighteen she'd have done her duty. Whoever would have guessed her harum-scarum son would grow into this responsible, upstanding, community-minded citizen? Seriously. He was thinking of running for city council, could you believe it? Jason, who once worshipped Kurt Cobain and was kicked out of the gifted program for being disruptive!

Her father always said, don't pat yourself on the back if your children are successful or beat yourself up if they aren't. *Well, Dad, you'd have loved my kids. They've turned out fantastic. And yes, I'm going to say it: Charles and I did something right.*

On that note, feeling virtuous and at peace, she headed back to bed, elbowed Charles in the ribs to get him to turn on his side, and went to sleep.

3.

It was the day before labour day weekend and the traffic was bad. To be expected, really. Rose was on her way to work, thinking about the dinner party tomorrow night. The one they gave every year. Charles did most of the cooking; Rose just made sure to stay out of his way while he did so. The kitchen could be a stressful place when her husband was in chef mode.

By the time she pulled into the underground parkade, it was almost 8:30. She turned off the engine and reached behind her to grab her purse from the back seat. It was then she noticed someone lurking about fifty feet away. It was difficult to make out if it was a man or a woman; he, or she, was enveloped in a long dark overcoat and appeared to be wearing a hoodie. Rose sat there, purse in hand, wondering if it was safe to open the door and get out. There was no reason why she shouldn't, and nothing seemed particularly menacing about the stranger. It was simply odd to see someone standing there at this time of the morning. A panhandler would wait by the exit, wouldn't he?

This is ridiculous, she thought. I'm turning into one of those frightened old biddies who think everyone is out to rob them. Or worse. Don't panic. It's probably just a coincidence. Get yourself to the elevator and don't look back. She got out of the car and headed towards the elevators. She heard footsteps. Whoever it was was following her.

"Mrs. Addams?"

She stopped and turned around. It was the guy in the hoodie. She recognized him—the homeless guy, the one who hung around the grocery store, just outside the entrance. No dog this time, but it was him, she was sure of it. She wanted to ask how he knew her name but thought better of it. Don't engage, she thought. Just stay calm and get near enough to the elevator to press the button.

He was standing close to her now, close enough that she could have smelled cigarette smoke on him. Or beer. But there was nothing like that. Well, it was a little early for drinking, wasn't it, even for a homeless person?

"I didn't mean to scare you," he said. He smiled but it would have been better if he hadn't; he was missing a front tooth. She'd never noticed it before but then he didn't usually smile—he generally acknowledged contributions with a nod, his hands pressed together in thanks. "I just wanted to say hello."

Her phone was in her purse. She'd have to take her eyes off him in order to retrieve it, and she didn't want to do that. Willing herself to stay calm, she attempted to smile in return. "Well, hello . . . I'd better go now. Have a good day."

"You don't remember me, do you? I'm Ryan."

"Ryan?"

"My mom babysat for you. Remember? When I was a kid. I even lived with you for a while."

"Oh my god. Ryan! How—how are you? Gosh, it's been . . . well, it's been years."

"A long time, yeah. I didn't know it was you, either, and then I heard you talking with a lady outside the store. She called you Rose and then I realized it was you. I wanted to say hi but then you left so I didn't."

"How did you know . . . how did you know where I worked?"

"I see you upstairs in the library. I go there a lot. I like to sit by the window and read. It's good, they don't hassle you so long as you're quiet. You don't need a library card. You can just pick a book and read it. You gotta get there early, though, if you want to get a seat by the window. Especially when it's cold out. A lot of people go there just to get out of the cold."

Rose knew all this, of course. Over the years she'd seen the library evolve into a safe cultural space for large sections of the community; she'd done her part to help make that happen. Two years ago she'd headed a task force looking into hiring a full-time social worker to support vulnerable citizens. In the end, there wasn't the money and their recommendations went nowhere, but still, the intention was there. Since then, unfortunately, she hadn't had many opportunities for one-on-one contact with, well, with people like Ryan. She was busy, after all, and her office was up on the seventh floor. No one went there but staff.

"So, how are you?" Ryan asked. "How are Morgan and Jason doing? And Mr. Addams—I mean Dr. Addams. He's a professor, right?"

"They're all fine, Ryan. Everybody's good." She was getting anxious. She was already late, and if she didn't find a way to wind things up soon she'd miss her Friday morning conference call with the district board. "Ryan, I'm sorry, but I have to get to work."

"Oh, yeah, no problem. I just wanted to say hi."

She reached into her purse and brought out her wallet. "Here, let me give you something."

She had a twenty-dollar bill and two tens. With only a slight hesitation, she handed him the twenty; he placed it carefully in his coat pocket and thanked her.

"Hey," he said, "you know what would be great? Do you have your phone on you?"

Was he going to rob her? Take her phone and run off with it? Was that the whole point of this meet-up? "Um, I'm not sure . . ."

"I just thought maybe you could take a picture of us, and when I get settled you could send it to me. I'd just like to have it, you know?"

"Oh, right. Sure . . . That's a great idea." Rose pulled her phone out of her purse, and turned so that they were facing in the same direction. He was slightly taller; he bent down so she could get them both in the picture.

"Say cheese," he said, and she did. "Can I see it?" She held the phone out to him and swiped at the photo to make it bigger. He was pleased. "That's really great! Will you show it to your kids?"

"Do you want me to?"

"Yeah, I would."

"Then I will. How's your mother, Ryan? I haven't seen her in . . . well, since you were a little boy."

He seemed uncomfortable with the question. "She's okay, I guess. I don't see her a lot." The elevator doors opened; Rose stepped in and Ryan joined her. "Can you press the first floor for me? I've got a book I'm reading and I think I'll finish it today."

He sounded cheerful enough but she felt a pang at the thought of his life, what it must be like standing on street corners, relying on the goodwill of passers by. Using the library to shelter from the world. "Where are you living? You do have somewhere to stay, don't you?"

"Oh, yeah. Sure."

"Do you have a room somewhere, or . . ."

"It's all right, Mrs. Addams. I'm okay."

The elevator came to a stop. Ryan stepped out into the lobby and Rose followed him. "You have a good day now. Say hi to your kids for me, okay?" He turned and headed past the information desk towards the fiction stacks. As early as it was, several of the chairs by the window were already occupied. Funny she never noticed them before.

"You know," Marie said, "every time I talk to you lately something new and bizarre has happened in your life."

"That's not true." Rose took a bite of her sandwich and switched the phone to her other hand. She was calling Marie from her favourite place in the library, the rooftop garden on the ninth floor. On a day like today, under a cloudless sky, it was the perfect place to sit and watch the world go by.

Marie insisted. "Remember the crow that attacked you in the park?"

"That was a year ago, and I'm not sure he was attacking me, exactly. It's more like he was aiming for a tree branch and hit me by mistake."

"And then there was the homeless guy who followed you home, and now there's another one stalking you in the parking lot. You should write a book."

"Right. Set me up with your agent. Anyway, he wasn't stalking me. He just wanted to say hello."

"So tell me about this guy. How is it that you know him? You said his mother worked for you?"

"We hired her as a nanny, back when the kids were small. She took off and we ended up taking care of her son for more than a year."

"My god," Marie said, "that's amazing!"

It *was* amazing. And sad. Rose looked down at the movement of people, moving quickly during their lunch hour. They had homes, and jobs, didn't they? "It was years ago. Before I knew you. I haven't thought about either of them for a long time." She took another bite of her sandwich. "Do you think I should do something?"

"Like what?"

"I don't know. Help him somehow? Maybe find him a job? I'm pretty sure he doesn't have a place to live. I see him all the time outside Whole Foods. He wouldn't be out there if he had a place to go. Would he?"

"I don't know. Did you ask him?"

"I did, but he didn't really give me an answer."

"It sounds harsh, but it's really not your responsibility. You know that, don't you?"

"Yeah, I know. It's just that he lived with us. And his mother was a piece of work. What would you do if you were me? You're a writer—you're always on the lookout for stories. And this is a story, right? Wouldn't you want to follow it up?"

"I write children's stories," Marie said. "Talking bears and flying unicorns and elves that live under rainbows. I stay away from stalkers."

4.

IT WAS THE YEAR THE ROOF FELL IN. MORGAN WAS four-and-a-half and Jason was about to turn three. Rose and Charles took the children to Seattle that Memorial Day weekend, hoping to get away from the wind and rain in Vancouver. Seattle turned out to be just as wet, but at least they could shelter in a comfortable hotel room and use the kiddie pool and hot tub.

They came home two days later to find water leaking through the ceiling drywall onto their bedroom carpet. When the roofer came to check out the damage, he said a section of shingles had been torn off in the wind. It had likely been leaking for weeks, he said, leaving a puddle the size of a small lake in the attic.

"Too bad you didn't call me earlier," he said as he wrote up the estimate. "That whole section of roof is going to need to be replaced."

"Sounds expensive," Charles said, hoping it wasn't.

The roofer shrugged. "Depends how good a job you want done. You get what you pay for, right?" He went on to talk about mould issues and how there could be structural problems if the wood was rotten. Rose and Charles sat there and nodded and got more and more quiet. The house was less than ten years old—how could there be so many issues? As the roofer began to go on about "cowboy" builders back in the 1970s, the phone rang. It was Dee, the woman who ran the kids' daycare.

"I got a job! A real one, Rose. I'm going to be managing a clothing store in Kerrisdale!"

This was bad news. Every morning Rose and Charles took it in turns to drive the children halfway across town in order to drop them off with Dee. It was a long way to go, but she was one of the few daycare providers who agreed to keep them after six, if necessary. And she came with excellent references.

"Congratulations," Rose said and tried to mean it. "When do you start?"

"Well, officially, I start next month but I need to go in for training on Monday." And then, as an afterthought, she added, "Sorry, Rose. I hate to leave you in the lurch. But you'll find someone, I'm sure."

Well, Rose couldn't blame her. The woman had a baby and a three-year-old. Given the choice between taking care of three youngsters and an infant and heading out the door each day to work with grown-ups, Rose would have made the same decision. She *had* made the same decision, as it happened. She had to ask, though: "What are you going to do about your kids?"

"Oh, my sister's coming to stay with us. She and her boyfriend split up so she's moving in. She'll take care of the kids while I work."

"Do you think your sister would take care of mine, too?"

"Well . . ." Dee hesitated. "To be honest, I don't think she could cope. Your kids are great, Rose, but they're kind of a handful, you know?"

And on that note, they parted company.

Talking it over with Charles after the roofer had gone, Rose was indignant. "My kids are a handful, she says! A *handful*. As if hers are angels or something. They're lively, that's all. They don't sit there like lumps chewing on their hair."

"Chewing on their hair?"

"You know what I mean. They're *intelligent*. They're *exploring* the world. They're doing what children are meant to be doing. Not sitting there drooling and staring into the void."

Charles suggested there might be something in between. "You have to admit," he said, "our two are kind of hell on wheels." He saw the look on her face and hastened to add, "I love our kids, Rose. I'm just saying they can be a lot of work."

"So what do you suggest? As of Monday we don't have a baby-sitter. And I am *not* giving up my job."

"I don't want you to. I have a better idea. We should hire a nanny."

"A nanny? You mean a live-in nanny? Where would she live? We don't have a spare room."

"The kids can share a room. We'll put a desk and double bed in Jason's room, and the nanny can have that. And you won't have to get them up and dressed in the morning. They can sleep in if they need to. It'll be perfect."

Rose wasn't sold on the idea of sharing her home with a stranger, but the idea of not having to get the kids up and dressed and out the door by 7:30 every morning was appealing. Maybe the girl would be willing to do a little babysitting, too, in the evenings. Not a lot—she wasn't going to treat her like some people treated their nannies, like a kind of indentured servant. She and Charles were too egalitarian for that. But it would be lovely to be able to go out now and then, on nights when the nanny was staying in anyway, and know that the children were being taken care of. The more she thought about it, the more sense it made. No more fighting traffic to get to the sitter's on the dot of 5:30; no more staying up late to get the next day's lunch and snacks prepared.

Charles was sure it wouldn't take more than a week to find someone. "Once we get an ad in the paper, the responses will start pouring in."

It was more of a trickle. By the end of the first week three people had answered the ad. Charles had to attend an out-of-town conference on Saturday, leaving Rose to conduct interviews on her own. "I trust your judgment," he said. "Just pick someone who's like us. Only better."

The first woman was in her sixties, which Rose thought could be a good thing. It might be good for the children, having an older person in their lives; her own parents were dead, and Charles' mother lived in England.

"I love kids," the woman said, "and I miss my grandkids. They live with their mother. Somewhere in upstate New York, last I heard. You wouldn't need any housework done, would you? My knees are bad. The doctor says I shouldn't do any bending. Or lifting. I put my back out last year and it's still not right. I take painkillers for it. You gotta be careful, though, you can get addicted, eh?"

The second interviewee arrived forty-five minutes late. "I got lost," she said. "You didn't say what stop to get off. I figured I'd ask at a coffee shop but I couldn't find one."

Rose apologized for giving poor directions and offered the girl a drink.

"I'll have a cappuccino, please."

"I'm sorry, I only have regular coffee."

"The drip kind? No thanks, I'll just have water."

It wasn't an auspicious start and it didn't get better. The girl was fresh out of high school and was mainly looking for cheap room and board. It was either take a job as a nanny or move in with her boyfriend.

"He wants me to live with him," she said, "but I've only known him a couple of weeks. It's, like, kind of too soon, you know what I mean? And his friends are kind of weird. They do a lot of drugs. *He* doesn't, don't worry. He's been clean for almost a year. And he loves kids."

By the time Cynthia ("call me Cyndi") turned up and was prepared to start on Monday, Rose was pathetically grateful. "Welcome!" she said, fighting an impulse to give the woman a hug. Instead she held out her hand and Cyndi allowed hers to be grasped, very briefly. "This is Morgan." Rose was inwardly thankful that she'd thought to braid her daughter's hair and change her out of the garish purple dress she'd been insisting on wearing all week.

"Hey, Morgan, how are you?" Cyndi said.

As she often could be in those days, Morgan was suddenly shy. She clung to Rose and pressed her face against her thigh, refusing to look up. Rose started to apologize— "She takes a while with new people—" when Cyndi unexpectedly knelt down and placed a manicured hand on her daughter's shoulder.

"I like your sweater, Morgan," she said. "Is it new?"

Morgan nodded.

"When I've finished talking with Mommy, will you take me to your room and show me your things?" Another nod.

Jason, who was never shy, demanded to be part of the action. "Come see my things, too!"

"I sure will, hon," she said. "Now, why don't you and your sister go to your room and get ready to show me your things. Is that okay with you?" To Rose's astonishment, her children left the room immediately, without a backward glance.

Rose had a list of questions prepared for the interview but she never got around to asking them. Cyndi was chatty and personable. At the end of half an hour they had talked about everything under the sun except references, experience, and expectations.

"I like her," she told Charles, "and I think she's a bit of a witch. She had the kids and me under her spell the moment she walked in. I mean, they love her! I think they'd follow her anywhere."

"Like the Pied Piper," he said.

"Yes, but hopefully with a better outcome."

5.

Pied Piper or not, things went smoothly for the first little while. Morgan and Jason became deeply attached to Cyndi. She seemed able to get them to do anything. She got Jason to give up his bottle overnight, something Rose had been trying to do for weeks, and she trained Morgan to pick up her toys at the end of the day and put them away where they belonged. Her kids were picky eaters but under the nanny's supervision they scarfed down broccoli, spinach, and green beans like they were candy. Not even Cyndi could get them to eat Brussels sprouts, but you can't have everything.

Her friends were jealous. "You're so lucky," one said. "You have the world's best nanny. Mine can't ever even turn up on time, and three days out of five I get a call at work to get home early as she has a doctor's appointment or something."

Another friend had a live-in nanny but the woman was a train wreck. She left a trail of dirty dishes around the house from her late-night snacks, and spent her evenings sobbing on the phone to her mother. "She's homesick," the friend said. "We had an agreement that she could call long-distance from time to time. Her mom's in New Zealand. I'm afraid to look at my phone bill."

"Why don't you get rid of her?" Rose said.

"Oh, I couldn't. She's good with the kids and to be honest, I couldn't face going through the whole interviewing process again. You are just so lucky, Rose, to have Cyndi. She's the real deal, isn't she?"

Was she? As time passed, Rose wasn't so sure. For one thing, for someone who seemed so open and ingenuous, Cyndi was remarkably secretive. Any time the conversation turned to her past working experience, she found a way to change the subject. She did this so effortlessly Rose was hardly aware she was doing it. Now and then she let things slip—small things, inconsequential, really, but the kind of things Rose would think about later.

There was the Colorado snow globe, for one thing, a souvenir of the city of Denver. Cyndi kept it on a shelf in her bedroom and allowed the children, as a special treat, to shake it, very carefully, and delight in the flakes of snow descending on the miniature city. Morgan was especially fascinated with the skyscrapers; she was convinced there were tiny children living in them, carrying out a scaled-down version of her own life in their Lilliputian towers.

One morning, when Rose was getting ready to leave for work, she mentioned to Cyndi that one of the women she worked with was heading to Colorado for a week. "She and her husband are staying in Denver," Rose said. "She's wondering if she'll need a winter jacket. What was it like when you were there?"

Cyndi was digging through Morgan's dresser, looking for her swimming goggles—she had recently started taking the children to the pool twice a week. Without looking up, she said, "I was never in Denver."

"Oh, I'm sorry. I just assumed you'd worked there. Because of the snow globe and all."

"No, I've never been there." Cyndi stood up, goggles in hand.

Rose had the distinct impression was lying, but why would she? It was impossible to tell what Cyndi was thinking. Rose apologized once more, called goodbye to the children, and left for work. Once she was in the car, she began to calm down. Charles was right: she overthought these things. Cyndi was just a very private person. She probably had to be, what with always living in other people's houses and not having her own personal space.

But then came Christmas and Cyndi's agreed-upon two-week vacation to go home and visit her family. Rose deliberately kept the holidays full of activity, in order to distract the children. They'd been devastated to learn that Cyndi wouldn't be with them at Christmas.

"Will Santa bring her anything if she's not here?" Morgan asked. "Will she get any presents?"

"Of course she will," Rose said. "Santa goes to Montreal, too, you know. He goes everywhere."

"What about the pony I made her?" Morgan had made a papier-mâché horse during the Saturday morning Art for Kids at the library. She named it Princess and wanted to give it to her nanny.

"She'll get it when she gets back, sweetheart. You can give it to her then."

"But it won't be Christmas then."

"No, but it'll be better than Christmas. She won't be expecting it so it'll be a special surprise." Morgan was mollified—somewhat.

The next few days, although hectic, were a kind of respite. Rose was in charge of her family again, and she liked it. Not enough to give up work, obviously, but it was pleasant for the four of them to have the house to themselves.

On the twenty-sixth, they gathered at Eileen and Jermyn's for their annual Boxing Day brunch. It was a noisy, chaotic event as usual. The house rattled with the squeals of overheated children, and popular Christmas music played at top volume on an audiotape loop. When Brenda Lee began to belt out "Rockin' Around the Christmas Tree" for the fourth time, Charles suggested switching to something a little less raucous, but Eileen wouldn't hear of it. And Rose agreed. "It's for the kids! 'Tis the season to be jolly, remember?"

Charles mumbled something about the kids being permanently scarred, but he let it go and retreated to the downstairs study, where Jermyn and a few other men were drinking beer and watching TV.

It wasn't until near the end, when Rose was rounding up her tribe and preparing to leave, that Eileen happened to mention she'd run into Cyndi on Christmas Eve, outside the entrance to The Bay. "I shouldn't say I ran into her," she said. "I saw her but she didn't see me. I was going to say hello but I dropped a parcel, and by the time I picked it up again she was gone."

Rose said it wasn't possible—Cyndi was in Montreal. "She left last weekend," she said. "She's gone to stay with her mother."

"Well, that's weird," Eileen said, "because it was definitely her. She was wearing that checked jacket she wears. You know, the one with the red collar. It was her all right. I remember thinking it was odd because she had a kid with her. A little boy, I think, but I can't be sure."

"She lied!" Rose said to Charles in the car on the way home. Charles was driving and the children were asleep in the back. Which meant they'd be up half the night when they got back, cranky and irritable after all the excitement. "She didn't go to Montreal after all. Can you believe it?"

"Maybe she had a change of plans," Charles said. He was driving more slowly than usual, concentrating on navigating through the snow that was beginning to drift across the highway. He'd had a couple of drinks but refused to let Rose drive, insisting he drove better when he was a bit drunk, said it made him focus on his driving. "Or maybe she went and came back early."

"If she was in town on the twenty-fourth that would mean she spent three days in Montreal, at the most. She wouldn't go that far to spend just three days. It's expensive." Charles changed lanes to get past a snowplow, whose blue lights were flashing on and off ahead of them. Rose waited till they were back in the slow lane to add, "It's weird, don't you think? Why would she say she was leaving to visit her family and then not go?"

"Maybe she had a fight with her mother and came back. And she's too embarrassed to tell us. You know how private she is. I say just forget it—it's none of our business what she does with her time off. She's been taking care of the kids for almost six months. As far as I can see, she's done a terrific job. Let it go, okay?"

Cyndi turned up, as promised, on the fifth of January. But she wasn't alone. A small, curly-haired child trailed her into the hallway, waiting on the mat while Cyndi introduced him. He wore a T-shirt, a parka a couple of sizes too big, and a pair of jeans rolled up at the bottom. His sneakers were scuffed and missing their laces. "This is Ryan. You don't mind, do you? He's a really easy kid. You won't even know he's here. Ryan, come say hello to Mrs. Addams."

Before Rose could respond, the child came over and wrapped his arms around her. The pressure of those thin little arms demolished any resistance she might have felt.

Cyndi laughed. "He's a hugger," she said.

The child looked up at Rose with dark, brooding eyes, and she was reminded of those paintings of elfin children with enormous eyes that were so popular back in the sixties.

"Is it all right?" Cyndi said, a note of anxiety creeping into her voice. "I know it's a shock and all that, but can he stay here? Just for a while?"

"Of course," Rose said, taking the child by the hand. "Come on, Ryan, let's go figure out where you're going to sleep."

It took some prying, but Rose eventually got the details out of Cyndi. She and her partner, Greg, had been living in Colorado when Ryan was born. Cyndi, who didn't have a green card, eventually came back to Canada to find work, leaving Ryan with his father. Now Greg was heading up north to work on an oil rig and couldn't have Ryan with him.

And she was right about one thing: Ryan was a very easy child. Almost too easy, Rose thought. He seemed to have learned early on that the best way to manage around grown-ups was to keep a low profile. He spoke when spoken to and appeared to enjoy playing with other children, but he was wary around adults, especially his mother.

"I don't think he's frightened of her, exactly," Rose told Charles, "but he acts like he's not sure how to behave around her."

"This is to be expected," Charles responded. "He doesn't know her very well, does he? He hasn't seen her in over a year; she's probably more like a stranger than anything."

As for Cyndi, she treated Ryan exactly like she treated Morgan and Jason, no better and no worse. It was as if she saw no difference between the children she was being paid to care for and her own flesh and blood. And Ryan, like the other kids, called her Cyndi. When Rose commented on this, Cyndi said she'd told him to call her by her first name. "I don't like being called Mommy," she said. "It makes me feel old."

Two months after turning up with the boy, Cyndi disappeared. She left a hastily scribbled note Scotch-taped to the fridge, addressed to Rose. "I'm sorry," it read, "but I can't do this. Ryan's better off with you and Charles. You can call his dad to come and get him. I left the number by the phone. Cyndi."

They tried to track her down at first, but it was as though she'd disappeared from the planet. Charles tried calling the number Cyndi left; all he got was a recorded not-in-service message. He wanted to call the police, but Rose resisted; she knew how it would go once the authorities got involved. A social worker would turn up at their door, little Ryan would be taken away and placed "in care," and a family of strangers—maybe several families of strangers— would become his temporary guardians.

"He knows us," she told Charles. "He's happy here. Or at least, as happy as he can be. I can't bear the thought of turning him over to someone we don't know. It would break my heart."

Charles, who wasn't completely sold on the police idea in the first place, gave in. It's not like Ryan was troublesome; he was a sweet boy when it came right down to it. And he didn't appear to miss his mother once she was gone. When he asked about her they told him she'd gone away for a while, but she'd be back soon, and that seemed to satisfy him. At least, he didn't ask about her after that.

6.

ROSE DECIDED NOT TO TELL CHARLES ABOUT MEET-ing up with Ryan in the parking lot of the library, at least not until she figured out what, if anything, she was going to do about him. Charles might get upset that she'd put herself in some kind of danger. She hadn't, of course; whatever Ryan was up to he didn't seem threatening. More than likely, he was on drugs—that would make sense, given his background. Or what she knew of it.

By the time she got home (an hour late, thanks to a last-minute budget meeting), Charles was in the kitchen, preparing to make supper. She slipped off her shoes, sat herself down on a kitchen stool, and brought up the subject of Morgan.

"Do you think I should go out there?"

"To Toronto? To do what?"

"I don't know. Just to be there, I guess. She sounds really upset. Working away on her dissertation . . . and now this."

"Rose, I wouldn't go unless she asked you. What would you do there, anyway? She has friends there. She's got support." He was right, of course. And maybe it wasn't permanent. Maybe it really was just a fight. "You know, I saw this coming." He saw the look on her face and hurried to add, "Don't get mad. But it's not a complete surprise. I wondered if he'd be able to stick to his promise."

"What promise? What are you talking about?"

Charles opened the fridge door and took out a carton of eggs. Waiting for an answer, she watched as he got a bowl down from the cupboard and retrieved a fork from the utensil drawer.

"What are you doing?"

"Making an omelette," he said. "Do you want some?" He started cracking eggs into the bowl. When he'd broken four and was about to crack a fifth one, she put her hand out to stop him.

"How big an omelette are you making!"

He looked surprised, stared at the egg in his hand as if he didn't quite know how it got there.

"Why don't you sit down?" she said. "I can make it. You look tired."

Charles nodded. "Yeah. I guess I am. Sorry."

Rose began whisking the eggs with the fork. The silence was uncomfortable; she sensed he was embarrassed, caught doing something stupid. Wanting to change the subject, she turned back to the issue of the wedding. "What did you mean when you said you saw it coming? Did Morgan say something to you?"

Charles watched quietly as she added a dash of pepper and snipped a leaf of basil into tiny pieces. Salt would be good but they didn't use it any more—everything that made food taste good was bad for you now. There was her grandfather who lived to be ninety-three on a steady diet of butter, bacon, fried bread, and cigarettes. Butter was back, though, and margarine was out. Be grateful for small mercies.

Rose set the bowl aside and began vigorously grating some cheddar. She cut a pat of butter, dumped it into the skillet, and turned on the heat. "If you don't want to tell me, fine."

"It was when she was back here for Christmas. We went for a walk and she said he'd been seeing this girl."

"What girl? Was he having an *affair*?"

Rose couldn't believe Ian would be having an affair. He wasn't the type. Charles said no, not an affair. Just an old girlfriend he'd started seeing again.

"They were meeting up for coffee now and then. That kind of thing. Morgan was kind of worried about it, that's all. She said she'd met this girl a couple of times and she didn't trust her. *I* said, do you trust *Ian*? And she said yes, she did, and he'd made a promise he wouldn't see her again. And then she said he'd asked her to marry him."

"She told you that? Before they told both of us?"

Seeing his mistake, Charles tried to backtrack. "I don't think she meant to. It just came out. The thing is, she hadn't said yes to him yet. She wanted to talk about it first."

"With you."

"Well, with both of us. She just happened to mention it to me first when we were out walking."

Rose added a teaspoonful of milk, gave the eggs another whisk, and poured the mix into the sizzling butter. She turned around, eyes blazing. "She's always done that, hasn't she? Talked to you before she talks to me. I remember when she was little she'd wait till you got home from work to tell you about her day. She told me bupkis."

Charles got up from the counter and came over to the stove. "Here, let me take over. You sit." He took the spatula from her and began lifting the edges of the omelette. You had to be careful with this stove, it was always either too hot or not hot enough. The pan was a problem—non-stick is what you need but Rose had thrown out her old Teflon pan when the coating started to flake and replaced it with cast iron. Which is supposed to work as well but it doesn't. He sprinkled a fistful of the grated cheese over the eggs, folded the omelette over, and then, with his usual expertise, slid it onto a plate.

"Voila!"

"Perfect," Rose said. "As always."

"It's not a competition, Rose."

It damn well is, she thought. But she kept it to herself.

Halfway through the meal, Charles set down his fork. "I've got something to tell you."

Oh god, here it comes. He's having an affair, too. Bracing herself, she asked, "What is it?"

"I'm done. I've left the university. I've retired."

The relief was so intense she almost burst out laughing. And then, "What? What do you mean, retired? You've quit?"

"I've quit. Let the bells ring out, let the banners fly." He didn't sound celebratory; he didn't look it, either. He looked exhausted.

"Did something happen?" she said. "Did Blake say something? Or do something?"

Arnold Blake was the new vice-president of Academic Affairs. He was brought in to replace Pete McMartin who'd held the position for almost three decades. In doing so he beat out several in-house applicants with brilliant academic records who expected they would get the promotion.

Charles wasn't one of them. He had as much paperwork as he could stand being History Chair. Or so he said. And if he thought they might approach him about it, he didn't say anything to Rose. In the end they didn't, and he appeared happy to carry on with managing the day-to-day challenges of the department. But there was tension between Blake and Charles almost from the beginning.

"He's been brought in to clean house," Charles told her when Blake was hired. "It's all about the bottom line with this administration. Cut back on tenured faculty, fill the gaps with part-timers and grad students, and put the savings into administration. They've been trying to do it for years but Pete wouldn't play it their way. Blake has no such scruples. The man is a cipher."

So if Charles had admitted that the new VP was the reason behind his retirement, Rose would not have been surprised. You can only bang your head against a brick wall for so long; at some point you need to simply walk away. But now he said no, it had nothing to do with Blake. It was something else, he said. Something stupid, Rose thought, when you got right down to it.

A young woman, a freshman, had come by his office wanting to know if she'd get at least a B-plus in his fall semester class. "She said her dad told her she can't stay in college if she doesn't get at least a B-plus, so she needed to know what she was getting before she registered."

"What did you tell her?" Rose asked.

"I told her I'm a teacher, not a fortune teller. I said I had no idea what grade she'd get, but if she were coming to university with that kind of attitude she'd do better to stay home and save her parents' money. And then I sat down and wrote an email to the faculty president. I told him I'm taking time off for medical reasons. But I'm not going back."

"Don't you think we should talk about this?"

"We *are* talking about it. That's what we're doing right now. I'm telling you I've made a decision and there's not much more to be said."

Rose felt there was a great deal more to be said, and she would have said it if her phone hadn't rung just then. It was Morgan, calling to say she was coming home.

"Now?" Rose didn't mean to sound unwelcoming but she was surprised. It was the end of August and Morgan was due to present her thesis in just over three months. She'd made it very clear they weren't to expect to see her before then. "I can't afford to take time off," Morgan had said. "There's too much riding on this." Now she told Rose she'd booked a flight from Toronto to Vancouver, a red-eye getting in at 7:00 Tuesday morning. Rose took a deep breath. "It'll be great to see you, sweetie… How long are you staying?"

"I'm not sure. But you can pick me up, right?"

Rose thought about the nightmare commute she'd have, getting to the airport at that time. And the fact that no matter how well she managed the traffic she'd be at least an hour late getting into work. Assuming the flight, of course, was on time.

"Of course, hon, I'll be glad to."

Charles piped up, "I'll pick her up."

Rose sighed with relief. She had always been the airport chauffeur in the family, but if he wasn't working, for once, he would have time to do it. "You're really not going into work?"

He glared at her. "I was serious, Rose. What did you think—it was all a dream?"

"I guess I just don't get it. It doesn't seem like you. Making a decision like that without talking to anyone . . ."

"I should have consulted you," he said. "I'm sorry. The thing is, when it hit me—when I thought about spending one more semester, one more day, even, standing in front of a class of first-year students, I just couldn't stomach it. I loved teaching for years, you know. And then I didn't."

"You were a good teacher," she said, as if he needed reminding. "I've run into people at parties who used to be your students and they said it was your class that inspired them. Taught them how to think. Made them better people, basically."

"Good. I'm glad. And now it's somebody else's turn. Your omelette's getting cold. Let's eat."

7.

THE ADDAMS' LABOUR DAY DINNER PARTY WAS A tradition with their friends. The seating never varied: Charles sat at one end of the table, Rose at the other. Garnet Simpkins, who taught fourth-year English, always chose to sit in the middle, with Rose on his left and whatever young woman he was seeing on his right, firmly within reach. Jeff Lindstrom always sat next to Rose, on her left. This was his choice, not hers. Jeff was married to Marie, who was a successful writer of children's stories and had been Rose's second-best friend for years. Over time, however—especially after Eileen Cortland left town—Marie was elevated to the rank of BFF, as the kids say.

They met when Rose was first working at the library. One of Rose's tasks back then was to set up readings for local authors. As much as Rose loved to read, this was not her favourite assignment. Authors could be prickly, even children's authors, *especially* children's authors, who frequently laboured under the not-ill-founded misapprehension that they were not being respected.

Marie, however, was a delight. She scurried in ten minutes before the reading, bearing armfuls of books, and immediately apologized for being late. When Rose assured her she wasn't late,

Marie launched into a hilarious description of her difficulties leaving the house. "I couldn't find my other shoe," she said, "if you can believe it. I mean, I have more than one shoe, obviously, but I wanted my lucky shoes. I always read better when I'm wearing them."

Rose glanced down at Marie's feet. She was wearing a perfectly ordinary pair of black slip-on pumps, the kind Rose favoured if she had to spend a day walking the library stacks. There was nothing remarkable about them. "Did you find them?" she asked.

"No, I didn't. I had to make do with these, which is too bad and probably means things aren't going to go well. My lucky shoes are bright red like Dorothy's—you know, *The Wizard of Oz*? I wear them when I read to children. They get focused on the shoes and keep quiet while I read. Do you think I have time to pee? Jeff told me to go before I left but I was already late from looking for the shoes so I didn't have time. Nice to meet you, by the way. Love your hair!"

Rose was self-conscious about her hair at the time. It was naturally curly and after a decade of straightening treatments that left it feeling—and possibly looking—like bleached hay she'd decided to grow it out and let it follow its natural bent. Charles had said she looked like a Chia Pet. "A *sexy* Chia pet," he added, trying to make amends. But the damage was done.

"It's too thick," she told Marie. "I'd love to have hair like yours." Marie's hair was short, straight, and cut in a classic bob, the kind that would be made famous a few years later by Uma Thurman in *Pulp Fiction*.

"My hair is the most boring thing about me," Marie said, piling her books onto the table Rose had set up in the children's section. "It refuses to curl—I gave up on it years ago. It's funny, isn't it, the way we women go on about our hair? The best compliment you can give another woman is to say she has great hair. It's different with men. All they care about is whether they *have* hair or not. I never knew a man to say he thought another man had great hair. I'd worry if he did, to be honest."

In spite of Marie's forebodings, the reading went well. So well, in fact, the children and their parents clamoured for another reading the following week. Marie's stories were funny and heartfelt without being cloying. They reminded Rose of her favourite tales by Roald Dahl. When she mentioned that to Marie after the reading, the woman practically hugged her.

"He's my favourite author! *James and the Giant Peach* is the reason I became a writer. I love that he had this no-holds-barred approach when it came to writing for children. First he has James' parents killed by a rhinoceros, and then the aunts are killed when the peach rolls on top of them. Children love it. Their parents might get upset but the kids think it's great. Whenever I have second thoughts about killing off a character or making my heroine do something really terrible, I think, what would Roald Dahl do? And then I go ahead and do it."

After the second reading the following week, Marie suggested they go for a drink. "I could talk to you all night, Rose, but I can't do it standing up. Let's go somewhere quiet and get to know each other. What do you say?"

That was almost thirty years ago. Since then, Marie had written more than a dozen children's books, and each of them sold more copies than the last. The National Film Board made a documentary about her called *The Pram in the Hall*, based on Cyril Connelly's famous pronouncement about children being death to writers. Marie hated the title, almost as much as she hated Cyril Connelly, but she got why the NFB chose it. She had made a decision not to have children and, although she loved Rose's kids, never regretted it.

"I would have made a lousy mom," she once told Rose. "I'd have spent every spare moment trying to find a hiding place to write my stories, and resenting every moment that I couldn't. I'm not a multitasker, I'm far too selfish."

As she set the table for the dinner party, Rose thought how much she would have much preferred to have Marie beside her, but people always want to alternate, male–female, male–female. Whenever she tried to mix it up, seating herself in the middle of the table, for instance, and pulling Marie down next to her, someone always corrected her and had things put back to normal. And so she was stuck with Garnet on one side and Jeff on the other. At least Garnet was interesting; Jeff, who worked as an accountant for an insurance broker, was dry and pedantic, but he'd been with Marie for thirty-three years and, for whatever reason, it seemed to work. Maybe because they were so different—people stay together for all kinds of reasons. This left Marie sitting next to Richard Maclean, who was only there because his sister Bernadette was always invited. And he and his sister were joined at the hip.

In the last twenty years there had scarcely been a dinner party that didn't include Bernadette. She was the grad department secretary and was as much of a fixture on campus as the stone statue of the founder gracing the lawn in front of the student union. Charles, Garnet, and most of their colleagues sincerely believed the framework of the university would crumble if Bernie weren't there to hold it together, practically single-handed. She worshipped her professors and they, in turn, paid her homage whenever they had the opportunity.

The female faculty, especially the younger ones, were never quite as effusive. They suspected her of harbouring secret wanton desires within that well-endowed bosom of hers; their lunches were sometimes enlivened by stories, probably apocryphal, of Bernie's past sexual history. It wasn't hard to imagine—she had the face and figure of a woman who would have been considered a sexpot in her youth. Still might be, if you took away the pendulous double chin and the dusting of foliage across her upper lip.

As for Richard—well, Rose and Marie frequently speculated on that. He was certainly gay but whether or not he had an actual life apart from Bernadette, who knew? He was charming and could be quite funny at times, but his personal life, if he had one, was a mystery.

"It's a shame," Marie said, after one of their dinners. "I mean, it's the twenty-first century. *Everyone* is gay these days. Or bi. Do they still call it that? Is *bi* still a word?"

Rose wasn't sure but she agreed it seemed odd that Richard would keep his homosexuality under wraps. I mean really, who *cared?* Still, she'd be interested to know if the poor man had *any* kind of a sex life. "Do you think Bernie knows?"

"Oh, she must," Marie said. "All those trips they take together. Sharing a hotel room, having dinner together every night. He probably goes off on his own once she goes to bed. It would make it more bearable, don't you think?"

Richard and his sister travelled a lot. Every year they spent weeks touring various European cities, dutifully checking out museums and art galleries and posting photos on social media. Lately they'd discovered the joys of cruising—not *that* kind, Rose reminded herself, thinking of Richard. Although maybe that was part of it. He was in very good shape, after all, and he must want some kind of social life apart from acting as his sister's companion. She wished she had the nerve to just come out and ask him. Maybe one of these days, if they were left alone for a few minutes, she could find a way to just casually bring it up: "Say, Richard, did you see that same-sex marriage just became legal in Finland?" Or maybe not.

When Eileen and Jermyn were still together, they were always part of the group, although he generally had little to say and always wanted to leave early. To get back to his mistress, most likely. After they split, Eileen continued to turn up now and then, but she found it uncomfortable, being a singleton in the middle of couples. Rose reminded her that Bernie was single and she didn't mind, but she, of course, had Richard, which was a little like having a date. Eventually, Eileen stopped coming, making excuses that she was busy, or not well.

Three years ago she sold her condo, moved to Arizona and took up golf. Now they exchanged Christmas cards and called each other on their birthdays. Rose missed her a lot when she first moved away, but she'd gotten used to thinking of Marie as her closest friend. If only she wouldn't insist on sharing everything with Jeff. Couples like Jeff and Marie told each other everything. They had one of those horrible no-secrets-between-us relationships. If you wanted to be sure Marie didn't tell Jeff something you had to practically tie her down and make her swear on her mother's grave not to tell. Bad analogy. Marie's mother died just two months ago. They had been thick as thieves and Marie was completely heartbroken.

"I'll never get over it," she told Rose. "I'll miss her till I die. She was eighty-five and she had a wonderful life, but I just can't believe she's gone."

"There's never a good time to lose your mom," Rose said. It's what she always said when someone's mother died, because it is true. Her own mother died when Rose was a teenager. She had MS and didn't have a wonderful life, but Rose tried hard to empathize with her friends. And sometimes she even succeeded.

8.

CHARLES ALWAYS DID THE COOKING WHEN THEY had guests. He said it was to give Rose a break, but the truth is he welcomed a chance to show off. On this particular night he'd come up with grilled salmon in a honey, garlic, and brown sugar marinade; herb-roasted potatoes; and sautéed mushrooms.

They were halfway through the main course when Marie brought up the subject of student debt. "Did you read the article in this month's *Atlantic*? Parents are draining their retirement savings to send their kids to college. Sacrificing themselves to give their children an education."

"It has ever been thus," Garnet said. He always adopted a Shakespearean tone when he was drinking. "The job, alas, of the parent is to lay down his life for that of the child. And do the little buggers appreciate it? Do they hell! 'How sharper than a serpent's tooth to have a thankless child.'"

"You don't know that they're thankless," Rose said, trying not to sound as irritated as she felt. "And it wasn't always that way. I went to university on federal loans and grants and came out owing less than two thousand dollars. After four years!"

"Yes, but wasn't that an awful lot of money back then?" This from Garnet's latest conquest, a grad student well into her twenties but still a good thirty years younger than anyone else at the table. "I mean, it was probably like twenty thousand would be today. Wasn't it?"

Rose, who'd temporarily forgotten the young woman's name, ignored her and continued. "You have to realize there's a lot more at stake for these kids than there was for us. What does it cost to go to school now—ten thousand a year?"

Marie said it was higher than that depending on where you went. "My great-nephew is planning to go to Acadia. It's something like eight thousand but that's not counting living expenses. I think they worked it out he's going to end up paying about eighteen thousand dollars a year!"

"And he's a domestic," Jeff said. "The fees are higher for foreign students."

Charles agreed. "I have international students who are having to come up with forty thousand just for the tuition. It's ridiculous. And it's exploitive."

Garnet said he wouldn't have a problem with tuition costs if they put the money back into salaries.

His girlfriend, *Lauren*—the name suddenly came to Rose— looked surprised. "Don't they?" she asked. "I mean, isn't that why tuition keeps going up—to keep up with what they pay the professors?"

"Forgive her," Garnet said, taking her hand and giving it an affectionate squeeze. "When it comes to economics, Lauren is a bit of a neophyte."

Lauren pulled her hand away, rather sharply Rose thought, and repeated her question. "Well, isn't it? I mean, why else would they keep going up?"

"It's student aid that's hiking the fees," Garnet said. "The more students can borrow the more universities can charge. So it's a win-win for the banks and the schools—and not so much for the students. Or their parents."

Jeff disagreed. Being an accountant, he always took umbrage when other people talked money. "Universities base tuition on what their wealthiest students can pay. And the wealthy students don't need loans."

"Lucky for them," Lauren said, finishing the last of her wine and holding out her glass for a refill. "I owe something like forty thousand—and I've still got two years to go."

Garnet chuckled. "We must find you a sugar daddy, my dear. Someone rich enough to pay off all that debt."

The young woman glared at him. "Is that meant to be a joke?" she said. "Because it's not fucking funny." She turned to Rose. "Can you point me to the washroom? I think I'm going to be sick."

Garnet attempted a joke—"Was it something I said?"—and reached out to take her hand.

She brushed him away. "Don't fuss. I hate it when you do that."

As she left the room Garnet whispered to Rose to go after her. "She's not well at the moment," he said. "I may have to take her home."

Obediently, Rose got up and followed Lauren out of the room. She knocked on the bathroom door. "Are you okay?" There was no answer. Tentatively, she tried the handle. The door was locked and she knocked again. "Lauren? Is everything all right?" She heard the toilet flush and Lauren opened the door, looking somewhat worse for wear. Her dark eyebrows stood out like brackets against her pale forehead; small beads of moisture had formed at the corners of her mouth. A faint smell of vomit hung in the air, mixed with the citrusy, faintly floral scent emanating from her hair.

"Sorry about that—I'm pregnant." She said it without emotion, like an inescapable fact, and Rose took it as such. Irresponsible of Garnet, though. He had three grown children, two grandchildren, and another on the way—surely he knew how to use a condom. As if she were reading Rose's mind, Lauren hastened to add, "It's not Garnet's. We don't actually, you know, do it. We're just friends."

"Really?" It was none of her business but she was dying to ask, what *did* they do? As long as she'd known Garnet, which was almost as long as she'd known Charles, he'd been a notorious swordsman. His first wife, Maeve, left him because he couldn't keep it in his pants—her words—although he'd always avoided making moves on the student population.

"You don't want to go there," Charles told him at the time. "All it takes is one pissed-off undergrad to get you in some serious hot water. Look what's happened in the Creative Writing department. Reputations in shreds all across the board. Hell hath no fury."

Jeff had made a joke, a very poor one, about it being the reason they called it *creative* writing and Marie snapped at him, which was highly unusual. "That's extremely inappropriate," she'd said. "These men have been playing sexual power games for far too long. It's about time they got their dicks caught in a vise."

Rose pretended to be shocked: "Marie! You're a children's writer!"

"Which is why I said 'dick.'"

And now here Garnet was, dating a student. Well, not *his* student. Lauren was getting her master's degree in Women's Studies and Garnet taught English. Still, he'd better be careful. As Charles had said, look what happened in the Creative Writing department. Although, if Lauren was telling the truth, maybe they really were just friends. Maybe age had finally caught up with him. Thinking of her own sex life, Rose allowed herself to feel just a little smug. Not everyone was as lucky as she and Charles.

"Maybe you shouldn't be drinking," she said, trying not to sound like a busybody. "I just mean, if you're pregnant and all . . ."

"Oh, it's okay. I'm not having it. I'm having an abortion. Garnet's arranged it."

Rose wasn't sure what she should say to this, so said nothing.

"He's been really good about it, actually. He's even offered to pay for it. You wouldn't happen to have any ginger, would you? When I was little, my mom would give me a piece of candied ginger to suck on when I'd been sick. It made the taste go away."

Rose said she had powdered ginger but Lauren said thanks, but no, she didn't think it would do the trick. "Do you think we could go outside for a minute? I need some fresh air."

Rose walked her to the back door and out onto the patio. It was a warm night. The sweet, pungent scent of honeysuckle mingled with the faint spice of someone barbecuing down the block. The tail end of summer . . . the nights drawing in.

Lauren pulled out a single cigarette and a lighter from a pocket in her dress. "Do you mind if I smoke? I won't if you'd rather I didn't . . ."

"Go ahead," Rose said. "I like the smell of cigarettes, to be honest. They remind me of my misspent youth."

"Did you used to smoke?"

"No, but my boyfriends did. Charles was the first man I went out with who didn't."

Lauren lit her cigarette, took a deep drag, and surveyed the garden. "It's nice out here. Those blue and purple flowers—what are they called?"

"Hydrangeas. They grow well here, with all the rain we get."

"They're really pretty. I like flowers but I don't have a green thumb." She took another puff and stared moodily out into the darkness. "Garnet's been trying to get me to quit," she said.

"Smoking?"

"Uh-huh. I know you think he's a jerk but he's been good for me. I was really a mess when I met him."

"What makes you think I think he's a jerk?"

"Oh, it's pretty obvious. You're stuck with him because he and your husband are friends, but you don't like him very much. It's okay. I don't either. But right now I kind of need him."

"Because of—" She didn't like to come right out and say it, so she just said, "Because of what's going on?"

Lauren shook her head. "No, it's not that. I could go home to my parents if I had to, my folks would take care of it. They did once before and I guess they'd do it again. I just don't want to give them the pleasure. They love it when I fuck up."

"I can't believe that," Rose said. "You're their daughter, they only want what's best for you."

To her surprise, the young woman started to laugh.

"What's so funny?"

"I'm sorry. But, oh my god, you're exactly like Garnet described you."

Determined to keep her voice steady, Rose said, "And how did he describe me?"

"He said you were like one of those old-fashioned TV moms. You know, always there for your kids, never letting anything get you down. He called you Mother of the Year."

Rose stood up. "I need to get back to my guests," she said. "Feel free to come in when you're ready. Or not."

She was trembling with anger and trying very hard not to show it. How dare this little bitch make fun of her! In her own home, her own back yard! And Garnet—talking about her like that, after all these years. He'd hardly seen his own kids since he and Maeve broke up. What the hell did he know about parenting?

As she walked back into the house, Lauren called out, "Wait!" and hurried to catch up with her. "I'm sorry—are you mad?"

Rose said nothing.

"He meant it as a compliment," she said, putting her arm around Rose's waist and giving it a squeeze. "I shouldn't have laughed. I'm out of control these days, I don't know what's the matter with me."

"Well, for one thing, you're pregnant." Rose wasn't quite ready to forgive her, but she did see that the young woman was penitent.

"Was it like that for you when you were pregnant? Your emotions and all, were they pretty crazy?"

"It was a rollercoaster. Up one minute, down the next. In the beginning, anyway. After the fourth month it got a lot better." Stupid thing to say, she thought. This girl wouldn't be experiencing her fourth month. Rose glanced down at Lauren's stomach—no sign of a bulge. She had to ask. "How far along are you?"

"Not far. Eight weeks, maybe."

"So, are you sure? I mean, you might not be pregnant—you might just be late."

"No, I'm sure. I've been there before. Here, I mean. I've been pregnant before." Lauren finished her cigarette and looked for somewhere to put it out. Seeing no sign of an ashtray, she stubbed the ash end on the sole of her shoe and dropped it into her pocket. "Do me a favour, okay? Don't tell Garnet about the cigarette."

"It'll be our little secret," Rose whispered.

She meant it as irony but Lauren smiled and said, with obvious sincerity, "I like you, Rose. Garnet's right: you're a good person."

Charles looked up as she and Lauren came back to the dining room. "Welcome back," he said. "We thought we'd lost you."

"We were just having a chat," Rose said, taking her place at the other end of the table.

She saw Garnet's brow furrow in consternation—he was always very protective of his women, as long as they *were* his women. He didn't like them to share things with his colleagues. Or his colleagues' wives. "Should my ears have been burning?" he asked, making it sound like he didn't care one way or another.

Rose knew he did. "Not particularly," she said, and left it at that. Lauren reached past him to get the wine bottle, and said nothing. Abortion or no abortion, Rose was pretty sure this particular relationship wasn't long for this world.

9.

ROSE WAS ABOUT TO SUGGEST DESSERT WHEN Charles pushed himself up from the table, held up his glass, and cleared his throat. He'd had maybe one drink too many this evening and he was slightly unsteady on his feet.

"I have an announcement to make."

For the second time in twenty-four hours, Rose had an *oh, god* moment. He wasn't going to talk about Morgan, was he? Her daughter was a private person; she'd hate having her personal life discussed at the dinner table.

"As of yesterday," Charles continued, "I am officially an ex-professor of European History 101, Contemporary Global Issues. My friends, I have retired. Raise your glasses, please!"

Lauren obediently lifted her glass—the others simply stared, first at Charles, and then at Rose.

"You've retired?" Marie said. "You're kidding, right? Rose, is he kidding?"

"No," Rose said, "he's not. He told me last night."

"How could you let him do that? He's the head of the department!"

"It's nothing to do with me—he didn't even ask me about it."

Marie's husband, Jeff, who was seventy-five and should have retired ages ago, shook his head. "This is ridiculous, Charles. You're far too young to retire. You've got years of good teaching ahead of you."

Bernadette simply looked stunned. "I don't believe it," she said. "You never said a thing. We spoke yesterday . . . I can't believe you didn't tell me." Richard patted her plump, freckled hand.

Rose leaned across Garnet and Lauren, wanting to reassure her. "He didn't tell anyone, Bernie," she said. "I was as surprised as you are."

Charles was still standing. "I said, raise your glasses, everyone. I want to make a toast."

Garnet spoke up. "Charles, for god's sake, sit down. We're not toasting to your retirement—I demand an explanation."

"You can demand all you want, but right now I have the floor and I want you to raise your glasses." Reluctantly, one after the other, they all lifted their glasses. "To freedom!"

"To freedom." It was a rather dismal toast, apart from Lauren who repeated it with gusto, and Richard who said, "Good for you, Charles. Onward and upward, right?"

"Exactly." He drained his glass and sat down, looking pretty damned pleased with himself.

As host, or co-host, of this gathering, Rose felt she should say something to lighten the mood. Bernadette looked ready to cry, and Garnet was making no secret of the fact that he, of all people, should have been told ahead of time. He was just as fed up as Charles with life at the university. Rose was sure he would have been completely on board if Charles had spoken to him about it. Especially if he'd asked his advice. Garnet was six years older than Charles and had been teaching longer. He saw himself as a kind of mentoring figure and Charles went along with it, out of respect for the friendship. This time, though, Charles had made an important, life-altering decision without consulting Garnet. Even Rose thought that was strange.

"Who wants dessert?" she said, determined to sound bright and cheerful. "We've got Charles' famous lemon-buttermilk pound cake, freshly made this morning."

Charles was the only taker. "I'll have a slice, my love, extra large. And put some ice cream on it, will you? I'm celebrating tonight."

Rose looked around the table. "Nobody else? Bernie, you'll have some, won't you?"

Bernadette shook her head. "I couldn't. Thank you, Rose, but I simply couldn't. I'm too upset."

"Really, Bernie? Charles made it especially for you."

"Well . . . all right, then. Just a small piece. With a little ice cream, too, I guess."

"I'll have a piece," Jeff said. "Wouldn't want to see it go to waste."

"Good point," Richard said. "Seeing as Charles went to the trouble."

"Cake for everybody," Charles said, sounding a little like a king distributing largesse to his subjects.

Rose started clearing the plates. She was trying not to be angry with Charles for putting a damper on the evening. He must have known it wouldn't go down well, making an announcement out of the blue like that. It wasn't just Bernie. Garnet and Marie were subdued; even Jeff, who was normally oblivious to the undercurrents of social intercourse, was folding and refolding his napkin as if he didn't know what to do with his hands.

Lauren stood up. "Here," she said, "let me help you." Rose was grateful for the offer. Charles often gave her a hand with the washing-up but tonight he appeared to be enjoying his temporary role as guest of honour.

Ignoring the fact that the others weren't terribly interested, he laid out his plans for the next few months, given that he wouldn't be teaching. He had a book he wanted to write, he said, which was news to Rose. The subject, however, wasn't. "I think the time has come for another look at Myra Hindley."

"The murderess?" Marie asked. "The one who killed all those children?"

"Oh, Charles, you're not!" Rose exclaimed. But she knew that Hindley and her deplorable husband had been something of an obsession for Charles on and off for years. He'd written an article about them and had it published in a British historical journal, but this was the first time he'd mentioned putting any of it into a book.

"I've been thinking about 'the banality of evil,'" he said, "what Hannah Arendt wrote when she covered the Eichmann trial. She said he wasn't a monster—she called him 'terrifyingly normal.' He committed evil deeds without evil intention."

Sounding more than a little peeved, Garnet cut him off. "We know all that. Any first-year history student can cite Arendt chapter and verse."

Did Charles realize how angry Garnet was? Probably not, Rose thought. He was too wrapped up in enjoying himself. "Yes, we know that," he said, "but here we are, seventy years on, still talking about an axis of evil. As if we're Biblical prophets threatening death and destruction to the enemies of Jehovah. Good and bad, dark and light. We still don't get it. Which is why we're losing the battle."

Lauren stopped in the process of gathering up the napkins and stared at him. "Are you saying there is no good and bad? You don't think Osama Bin Laden was a terrible person?"

Charles smiled. "I didn't know the man, but from what I could gather he wasn't an ogre. He was an intelligent man who, for reasons relating to his history, his culture, all sorts of reasons, embraced fanaticism. As did Hitler. Although I don't think Hitler was as smart. He believed Nostradamus predicted the downfall of Britain. And he talked to his dogs."

Richard, who was fond of dogs, said lots of people talked to their pets, didn't they?

"Yes," Charles said, "but Hitler believed they talked back."

Rose was distractedly scraping food off the plates and into the green bin, for composting. This was fairly new for her. She'd been in the habit of putting all foodstuffs into the green bin until Morgan caught her trying to stuff the remains of the Christmas turkey into a pail that was already overflowing with fried onions, coffee grounds, and the parsnips that Charles loved but nobody else would eat.

"Mother, what are you doing? You can't put in an entire turkey—it's too big and attracts rats. It has to go in the garbage."

"Well, that seems like a waste."

"I know, but they say not to do it."

It seemed to Rose that they were always changing the rules on her—you just get used to one thing and they tell you something different. She felt guilty about the turkey, anyway. You were supposed to make soup with it and she did when the kids were young, but now that it was just Charles and her it seemed a lot of work to go to when you could buy perfectly good homemade soups at the store. Well, not homemade, but as good as.

In the dining room, Charles was back to talking about Hindley and Ian Brady, her loathsome partner in crime. "I remember when they went on trial," he said. "I was in university at the time and some of us skipped class the day the trial started. We were hoping to get a seat in the courtroom."

Marie sounded fascinated. "Really? And did you?"

"We were out of luck. The place was packed with news reporters and victims' families. There were hundreds of policemen guarding the entrance to the courthouse. We didn't even get a look-see at Hindley and Brady going into the building. They took them in through a side door and kept them behind a screen for protection. Just as well for them . . . there were people who'd have killed them on sight, if they'd had a chance."

Rose had heard the story before and wished they would change the subject. It was a terrible story, and definitely not something you wanted to dwell on at dinner. Why on earth Charles had to bring it up was beyond her.

Lauren came into the kitchen bearing napkins and utensils. As she rinsed them under the tap, she confided to Rose that she had kept her mouth shut during all of this as she didn't want to reveal her ignorance. "I have no idea who they're talking about," she said, "but I feel like I should."

Rose started to give her the shorthand version of the story, but Lauren cut her off. "It's okay," she said quickly, "I'll Google it." She placed the knives and forks in the dishwasher and then asked about coffee. "Should we make a pot? Everyone's still drinking but I think I'd like a cup to sober up. And Garnet's driving so he should probably have some. I'll make it if you like."

"I always leave the coffee to Charles," Rose said. "This machine is really complicated. Do you know how to work it?"

Lauren gave Rose one of those looks the young-and-tech-savvy reserve for old fogeys who can't be expected to walk and chew gum at the same time. She assured Rose she'd be able to figure it out and set about spooning coffee beans into the grinder. "I'll make it extra strong, if you don't mind. I think we could all use a caffeine fix after your husband's announcement. Do you think he's making a mistake? I mean about retiring, not the book."

As a matter of fact, Rose did think it was a mistake, but she wasn't about to get into it with this young woman who was probably not even thirty if she was a day. Younger than Morgan. And sleeping, or not sleeping, with her husband's best friend. "Oh, I don't know. I haven't really had time to think about it." Rose left Lauren in charge of the coffee and headed back into the dining room to check on her guests.

"They say she died a devout Catholic," Marie was saying. Rose sighed. They were still talking about Hindley. "Lord Longford fought for her release and they made a movie about it."

"Oh, I saw that," Bernie commented. "Jim Broadbent was in it. He's such a good actor."

"Well, Brady's dead now, too," Charles said.

"Really?" Bernie asked. "What did he die of? Did somebody finally strangle him? Such a terrible man."

"Old age, I think. He was seventy-nine."

"I keep thinking of that poor woman," Marie said. "Keith Bennett's mother. She made it her life's work to find out where her son was buried and she died not knowing."

"All right," Rose said brightly, "who wants coffee?"

"I think she was crazy," Jeff went on relentlessly. "They put Brady in an insane asylum but they should have had her in one, too."

"I don't think she was," Charles said. "If she'd been mad, or if she'd gone mad afterwards, people might have been able to forgive her. But from everything I've read, she was exactly what she always said she was: completely sane."

"What *I* can't work out," Garnet said, "was what she saw in Brady. By all accounts she was infatuated with the man. Completely obsessed. He must've had something going for him, but damned if I know what it was."

Rose gave up and went back into the kitchen. Lauren had finished loading the dishwasher and was tidying up. Marie came in a few minutes later and hesitated. She wanted to talk but was uncertain, seeing Lauren. The younger woman, taking the hint, said she was going to step outside for a smoke.

"Sorry for not coming in to help," Marie said. "I just find the whole discussion so fascinating. Do you think he's going to do it? Write that book?"

"I hope not. Although, if he doesn't he's going to be awfully bored. He has no hobbies, unless you count watching the news and reading. What's he going to do—hang around the house all day? *I* won't be here—I *like* my job. I'm not giving it up."

"Good for you," Marie said. "And why would you? You have a great job and you do it well. So, what do you think of little Miss Muffet?"

"Lauren? She's okay. Actually, I think she's probably too good for Garnet. She's really quite sweet."

"She's pregnant, isn't she?"

"Did he say something?"

"Didn't have to. It was pretty obvious when she got up and left the table. It was either that or the flu. It wasn't the salmon—which was delicious, by the way."

Well, it wasn't like betraying a secret. Lauren didn't say not to tell anyone and as Marie said, it was probably pretty obvious.

"Is she having the baby?"

"No, apparently not. She says Garnet is arranging for an abortion. And . . ."

Now she *was* about to betray a secret. But it was about Garnet, whom she didn't care for all that much, and it was too good to keep to herself. Rose glanced at the door. Lauren was still outside; the others were continuing to discuss Hindley. She shut the door separating the kitchen from the dining room, just to be safe.

"She says they never do it." Marie looked puzzled so she added, "*It.* Garnet and Lauren don't have sex."

"You're kidding. She said that?"

"Uh-huh."

Marie gave this some thought. "*She* must do it—she's pregnant, after all. So it's Garnet that doesn't?"

"Or can't." It was wicked to be gossiping like this about one of their friends but it felt quite delightful.

"Or can't. Well, well, well, isn't that interesting. So who's the father?"

"She didn't say. And don't give me that look. It's none of my business. Or yours, so don't go asking her, all right?"

"As if I would!"

"You would, if you had the chance, you know you would. And don't say anything to Jeff about all this, okay?"

Charles called from the other room. "Where's that cake, Wife?"

He's drunk, she thought. Rats. He'd want sex tonight and she was suddenly very, very tired. "Coming, Husband!"

While Marie sliced the pound cake and set it out on a plate, Rose loaded up a tray with coffee, cream, and sugar. "I talked with Morgan today," she said.

"Oh, really? How is she?" Marie was a great fan of Rose's kids. She had acted as an unofficial godmother to them both since Morgan was eight. "How's the dissertation? She must be almost done."

"She's called off the wedding."

"No! I don't believe it. Really? The wedding's off?"

"Off. They've broken up and she sounds royally pissed."

"You don't think it's just a fight? A lover's quarrel or something?"

"I don't think so. From what I could tell it sounds pretty definite."

"Oh, Rose, I am sorry. Sorry for them and sorry for us. I was really looking forward to that wedding. Everybody else I know is either dying or getting divorced."

"I know, I was too. Do me a favour? Don't say anything until I talk to her again. I'm almost one hundred percent certain it's off but, well, you never know."

"Right. Fingers crossed."

10.

SUNDAY MORNING ROSE WENT UPSTAIRS TO MAKE UP the bed in Morgan's old room. Why, she wondered, was her daughter coming back right at this moment? Two weeks ago she said she was panicking about finishing the introduction to her thesis, which her advisor had told her to write last, at the same time as the conclusion. Maybe she'd managed to finish it after all and was waiting to hear back from the professor. It made sense that she might want a break for a few days, especially with things the way they were with Ian.

When she finished fluffing the pillows she stood back and admired her handiwork. Not the bed, particularly, but the whole room. It had undergone several facelifts over the years, as Morgan grew older and her tastes changed. There was the time when she was fourteen and they had just moved into the house and she begged her mother to paint the entire room—walls, ceiling, even the door of the closet—a deep midnight blue so she could imagine she was sleeping outdoors under the stars. A few years later they discovered that the silver glow-in-the-dark stars they stuck onto the ceiling were permanent; you could still see their outlines through the classic white-on-white paint Morgan chose her last year of high school.

Still, it was a far cry from Jason's choice at the time, which was to paint his room black. The only colour, such as it was, came from a four-by-six-foot poster of *Goodfellas*, his favourite movie of all time.

Five years ago, when Morgan quit her film job and moved back home, she and Rose transformed this room into a restful almost Zen-like hideaway: the walls were a muted shade of lavender, and they substituted the heavy curtains with sheers. They replaced the old lambskin rug with a hand-knotted Himalayan runner Rose picked up at a flea market, and they opted for organic sheets and pillowcases that cost the earth. ("Polyester is a derivative of crude oil and plastic," Morgan told her. "It's terribly bad for your skin.") It was Rose's idea to get rid of the IKEA bookshelves, which were falling apart anyway, and replace them with baskets that could hold Morgan's books and be stored under the bed. They found a couple of big comfy floor pillows she could use when she meditated and put a dimmer switch on the overhead lights. The stuffed toys weren't going anywhere, of course, nor were the framed pictures of Morgan and her friends, but they hauled out the TV and placed it in her brother's old room.

"I don't even watch TV," Morgan told her. "I don't know anyone who does."

"I watch TV," Rose said.

"Yes, Mother, of course you do."

Whatever that meant.

She came downstairs to find Charles on the phone with Jason, who had rung up to say hi and was only just learning about his father's retirement. From what she could glean from Charles' side of the conversation, her son wasn't completely sold on the idea. He was needing some convincing. Charles said goodbye and put the phone down. "He's coming over," he said.

"Now? Has he eaten?"

"He didn't say."

"Should I make something? I could make up a batch of pancakes."

It had been their Sunday go-to when the kids were young. Batches of pancakes with real maple syrup, chocolate chips added for Morgan, blueberries for everyone else. Now she only made them on special occasions. Charles preferred porridge and she almost never ate breakfast. The last time she made them was New Year's Day, before Morgan and Ian flew back to Toronto. Ian was lavish in his praise of her cooking skills. His own mother never cooked, he said; everything came out of a can.

"But she worked, didn't she?" Rose said, wanting to be generous towards the woman who'd produced this lovely young man.

"*You* worked, Mom," Morgan said. "You still had time to make breakfast."

Only on the weekends, Rose thought, but kept it to herself. Praise from one's children is a rare enough thing, especially when the child is a daughter. No need to spoil the moment by stirring up memories of rushed mornings, lunches left unmade, and all the times they had pizza for dinner when Rose was too tired to cook.

She got the flour and baking powder down from the cupboard, retrieved milk and a carton of eggs from the fridge. The carton felt unusually light.

"Damn! We had that omelette on Friday—I forgot. There're only two eggs left."

"Isn't that enough?"

"I always use three. You wouldn't want to go out to the store, would you?"

"For one egg? Call Jason and ask him to pick some up on his way over."

She hated to do that. She said it was because he was busy, but there was something else: he might mention it to Lee that he had to stop off on the way to pick up eggs for his mom. Lee would roll her eyes (Rose could just see her) and say something like, really? Again? As if Rose was always relying on her son to supply her with groceries. Which she wasn't.

"It's okay. I can make them with two, I'll just make a smaller batch. Is Lee coming with him, do you know?"

"I don't think so," Charles answered. "Jason said she'd gone for a run."

Thank you, Lord, for small mercies. Her son's girlfriend had a way of making Rose feel just a little ridiculous. Less competent, not as articulate. When Lee was around, Rose always dropped a dish or said something silly. For the umpteenth time she asked herself why her son, who'd grown up to be so sane, so sensible, had stopped seeing his long-time girlfriend, Sophie, and taken up with such a difficult, controlling . . . *woman*. Rose liked everything about Sophie, who wanted to have children and would have made a terrific mother, and she hated everything about Lee, who said she loathed children and had her tubes tied seven years ago, when she was only twenty-three.

Marie didn't like the new girlfriend, either, and was skeptical when Rose told her. "Will they even do it at that age? I bet she just told Jason that to trap him into marriage. She'll get pregnant and Jason, of course, will do the right thing because he's Jason." In her view, Lee was inauthentic. "She's posing as a real person but it's all ego. And she's manipulative. I can see why she makes you uncomfortable—under that perfect exterior she's extremely judgmental."

Jason didn't see any of this. He thought she was wonderful. She was so *accomplished*, he said, so good at her job, which was working as a nurse health coach. She had trained as a nurse and worked in the ER for several years before leaving to work as a health consultant. When Rose asked her what exactly she did as a consultant, Lee replied that she was a "facilitator for change." Which, in Rose's opinion, was one of those phrases that said nothing while seeming to say a lot.

According to Jason, Lee's co-workers loved her; everyone said she was going to be running the company five years from now, maybe sooner. Unfortunately, not everyone appreciated her wonderfulness. Her supervisor at her last nursing job had been really mean to her, for some reason. Didn't like her at all. Jason was sure she was jealous; the woman was shorter than Lee, not nearly as pretty, and didn't have anywhere near the people skills Lee had. He knew this because Lee had told him. Of course.

The problem, as far as Rose was concerned, was that other members of her family more or less agreed with this. Charles thought

Lee was smart and stylish, which she was, and it didn't hurt that she sucked up to him on almost every occasion.

"Honestly, Charles," she told him, coming as close to batting her eyelashes as one could in the twenty-first century, "you explain things *so* well. If I'd had a teacher like you when I was in college, I'd have understood *so* much more."

Oh, come on, Rose wanted to say. Was he really swallowing that hogwash?

Marie said she wasn't surprised. "Men will believe anything if comes in attractive packaging. Although, personally, I don't think she's all that attractive. She just knows how to make the most of what she's got."

But even Morgan, who'd adored Sophie and had once said that the best thing about her younger brother was his girlfriend, seemed okay with Sophie's replacement. "I don't know why you're so worked up about it," was the way she put it. "She's friendly enough. And she's definitely taken Jason out of his comfort zone. I mean, she's got him wearing a watch again, did you notice?"

Rose didn't see why wearing a watch was important.

"It makes him stand out from the crowd," Morgan said. "Shows he's a responsible person, not one of those guys who has to have his phone in his hand just so he knows when to come home for dinner. And that's another thing: she's liberated him from his smartphone. Remember how Sophie used to complain he was always checking his phone? They'd be out to dinner or at a movie and he'd be looking at it every five minutes. It drove her crazy. Last time I saw him he didn't even have it on him, if you can believe it."

"But don't you think she's just a little, I don't know, controlling?"

"She has strong opinions, but so do I. So do you, Mom. We all do. You shouldn't hold that against her."

"Well, I guess I just miss Sophie."

"I know. I get it. But Jason's moved on and so has she. And you need to move on, too."

Even Marie advised Rose to keep her feelings to herself when she was around Jason. "He's going to figure it out, one of these days," she said. "She'll do or say something and he'll see her for who she is. But in the meantime, you absolutely can't let him know you don't like her. If he has to choose, he'll choose her. You know that, don't you?"

She did.

"And if they have children—"

"Stop! Don't go there," Rose said.

"I know, it's a horrible thought. But if they do, and you don't get along with her, you'll never see your grandkids. Look at Garnet. He hasn't seen those children in over two years."

"Yes, but that's more complicated."

Marie agreed. It was definitely complicated. Garnet's daughter-in-law had accused him of exposing himself to her three-year-old. Garnet's story was that he'd been over for dinner, drank too much, and passed out in the spare room. Some time in the night he got up to use the bathroom, forgetting to put on his pants before leaving the room. When he came out he stumbled into the children's room by mistake, switched on the overhead light to see where he was, and woke his granddaughter. Who, seeing an elderly man hovering over her bed, wearing only an unbuttoned dress shirt, quite naturally let out a howl that brought her parents running. Garnet hadn't seen his grandchildren or his daughter-in-law since.

11.

JASON PULLED INTO THE DRIVEWAY JUST AS ROSE was sliding a plate of freshly cooked pancakes into the oven to keep warm. She went to the door to greet him and was relieved to see Charles was right: Lee wasn't with him. That being the case, she could afford to be generous. "Hi!" she called out. "Where's Lee? I made extra pancakes just in case." *Now who's being inauthentic?*

Her son strode up the sidewalk towards her, looking every inch the successful young lawyer in casual weekend wear. Morgan was right; before Lee, this would have meant a sweatshirt, baggy jeans, and sneakers. This morning he wore a new white t-shirt under a camel-tan topcoat, and had added a dark blue wool scarf. He still wore jeans and sneakers, but the jeans were fitted and slightly tapered and the shoes were spotlessly white. Lately he'd taken to letting a heavy stubble sprout on his chin and upper lip, accentuating his jawline and enhancing his masculinity. *Was it all right to say this about your son?* Everything was a minefield these days—you had to be so careful.

"Pancakes! Perfect! Thanks, Mom. Is Dad around?"

"He's in the kitchen, waiting for you. We didn't want to start before you got here."

"Great. I'm starving."

Jason waited until he had wolfed down his first serving of pancakes before turning to his father and putting the question: "So, you're retiring, Dad. Kind of sudden, isn't it?"

"I've been considering it for a while," Charles said. "I actually thought about it last year when the faculty association was pushing for certification."

"You didn't want to unionize? That surprises me. I always see you as a leftie kind of guy."

"I am. But I make a good salary, and I didn't want to put people's work at risk by going on strike. I just didn't see the need for it, but a lot of the younger instructors—well, they saw it differently. I thought, Charlie, old boy, maybe it's time to move on."

"I didn't know any of this," Rose said. "You didn't say anything about it to me."

"There was no need. The union vote fell through and it wasn't an issue."

"So you didn't retire then, Dad, but you've packed it in now when the threat of a union is finished."

"I don't think it's finished. I think it's just on hold for the moment. Once enough of us old fogeys are gone it'll come up again, I'm sure of it. And maybe it's a good thing. It's just not for me."

Rose was unconvinced. "You said it was because of that student who came about wanting a B-plus!" It was just like Charles to tell her one thing and then something completely different to the kids. She got up to get the rest of the pancakes out of the oven, forgot to use an oven mitt, and burned her fingers. The plate crashed to the floor and broke in half. "Damn!"

"Are you okay?" Jason hurried over to where she stood, sucking her fingers and glaring at the mess on the floor. "Ten-second rule," he said, and began picking up the pancakes and putting them on the counter. Rose said she'd make some more but Charles and Jason both insisted these would be fine. Damn ceramic tile flooring— she hadn't wanted it in the first place. So cold on the feet and so unforgiving if you dropped something. But the guy they hired to do the kitchen reno looked at her like she was mentally challenged when she told him she wanted to keep the old linoleum.

"You don't mean that," he said. When she said, yes, she did, he drew himself up to his full height—he was an inch or two shorter than her—and tried his best to look imposing. "Mrs. Addams, you're telling me you're gonna go ahead and spend twenty-three thousand dollars—"

"Before tax," she added.

"You're gonna spend twenty-three thousand dollars before tax to install top quality cupboards, a granite countertop, high-end appliances—and you're gonna keep the lino? You ever hear about putting lipstick on a pig?"

She told him she thought that was a little harsh. "Maybe we could just take up the old linoleum and put down some new lino? What do you think?"

"I don't do linoleum, ma'am." And that was that.

Rose ran her burnt fingers under cold water, while Jason dropped the broken plate into the garbage and they returned to the table.

Jason helped himself to the syrup and picked up where he'd left off. "So I guess the thing I'm wondering—and you can tell me if it's none of my business—can you afford to retire? You just turned sixty-four. You're in good health, you both are—"

Rose tapped briefly on the table. "Touch wood."

"Yeah, well, with any luck you'll live a long time. Look at Grandma—she's almost a hundred, right? You could have another forty years on the planet—"

"God forbid," Charles said.

Jason looked surprised. "Don't you want to live to a ripe old age?"

"Not particularly. If I get to three score and ten I'll be fine."

"What's that?"

"Seventy," Rose said. "It's what the Bible says we should have, if we're lucky."

"Seventy's nothing." Jason speared another pancake. "I read somewhere there's somebody alive today who'll live to be a hundred and fifty, can you believe it?"

"Again," Charles said, "God forbid."

"What would you do with all that time?" Rose said. "The thought of carrying on when all your friends are gone, there's nobody who remembers you as a girl. When my grandmother was eighty, she said there was nobody left who called her 'Ethel.' I found that really sad. I still do."

She was quiet for a moment, thinking about Grandma Morgan. The Holy Terror, her father always called her. The one who always flipped up Rose's skirt to make sure she was wearing a slip. The one who put the fear of God into her boyfriends. But the one person who thought she was smart enough to go on to college and made sure that she did. *Thanks, Grandma*, she thought. *I owe you.*

Jason was eager to get back on track. Conversations in this household had a way of straying off topic; you had to be vigilant if you wanted to keep to the matter at hand. "Anyway," he said, "I'm just asking if you've thought of everything. If you've thought about money and all. You need to have enough to get through the next whatever amount of years. Can you afford it?"

Charles pushed himself away from the table. "Good pancakes," he told Rose. "I'm done."

"Dad?"

"You're right," Charles said. "It's none of your business."

The words hung there in the stillness of the kitchen for a good long moment after he left. Jason was startled. His father hadn't spoken to him in anger since he was a teenager. "Mom? Is Dad okay? I didn't mean to make him mad—I'm sorry."

"It's all right," she said, knowing it wasn't. Something was going on; Charles was usually so easygoing—there were no taboo subjects, nothing that couldn't be discussed. He was open to everything and anything. He never judged. "He didn't mean it. He's just tired. We had a late night last night. He probably drank too much.

Don't worry about it, hon, I bet he's sorry already for talking to you like that."

"I'm just worried about him, is all, you know? I mean, he always said he was going to work till he dropped. I remember him telling me he'd never retire."

She nodded. "I know. And you have every right to ask, Jason. We're a family—we care about each other. It's as much your business as anyone's."

"What kind of pension does he have? Lee says if you don't have a defined-benefit pension plan you're basically screwed. She says you need something like a quarter million in savings just to stay on top."

"I didn't know Lee majored in economics. I thought she was a nurse." Rose heard the edge in her voice and forced herself to smile. "I'm joking, hon. I didn't know Lee paid attention to—well, to things like that."

As usual when it came to Lee, Jason was oblivious. "She reads a lot, Mom, you'd be surprised."

"Really? That *is* kind of surprising. When I told her Michael Ondaatje was coming to town, she said she'd never heard of him." *And* she thought Evelyn Waugh was a woman, but Rose decided to keep *that* to herself.

"She doesn't read fiction," Jason said, as if that explained everything. "She likes to read about, you know, the real world."

She would have liked to tell him fiction is the lie through which we tell the truth, but couldn't remember who said it. What was the point, anyway? Nothing his mother said was going to change the way he felt about his girlfriend. Time to change the subject. "I almost forgot—your sister's arriving Tuesday morning. Dad's picking her up at the airport."

"You're kidding! That's great—what's happening? Why's she coming home? Is Ian coming with her?"

"Well, no. At least, I don't think so. The thing is, they've broken up."

"Really?" He didn't sound surprised.

"The wedding's off," she added.

"Was it ever on?"

"What do you mean?"

Jason shrugged, then got up to rinse his plate before putting it in the dishwasher. "I don't know. It just never seemed like a thing to me, you know? Morgan didn't want to talk about it, she wasn't sending out save the dates or anything. Lee said she was pretty sure it wasn't going to happen—"

"I'm sick to death of hearing what Lee says! She's got more opinions than—than a racehorse has hay!"

Jason looked at her, and then they both burst out laughing. "A racehorse has hay? Where'd you get that one?"

"Oh, I don't know, I guess I'm tired, too. It was a long night. Sorry, Jason, I didn't mean to bite your head off."

He picked up his keys from the kitchen counter and glanced at his watch. "I should get back," he said. "We're meeting up with some friends later and I need to do some prep for Tuesday. That's great about Morgan coming. I'll text her. How long's she here for, do you know?"

"Oh, not long, I don't think. She's got her dissertation coming up in November so she'll probably want to get back pretty soon."

Jason gave his mother a hug. "Tell Dad I'm sorry, okay? He's worked hard, he should do whatever he wants—he deserves it."

12.

SHE STOOD AT THE DOOR AND WATCHED HER SON get in his car and drive away. He was so good about coming around to see them, keeping in touch even when he was up to his ears in work. He didn't deserve to be snapped at like that. Especially when he never snapped back. He was like his father that way: even-tempered and calm without being a wimp.

Except that this morning, Charles *had* snapped. Was it possible he wasn't as sold on this whole retirement thing as he professed? Or was it something else? She remembered a conversation she had with Liz shortly after their divorce was final. Liz had called Rose and suggested they meet for lunch at the bistro on forth. A no-hard-feelings kind of lunch, although neither of them used those words.

Their conversation was stilted at first. They sipped their water and studied the menu. When the waiter came by they ordered wine and the pasta special. For a few minutes they made small talk, while Rose wondered about the purpose of the meeting. She was pretty sure Liz had something she wanted to say, but she was at a loss to think what it might be. The elephant in the room, of course, was Charles. Liz was the first to bring him up.

"I think it's fair to warn you," she began, "he has a lot of demons."

"Demons?" Rose almost laughed, it was such a preposterous thought.

But Liz was serious. "When you don't know him all that well, you think he's the most well-adjusted fellow in the world. And most of the time he is. But he has a dark side, and you can live with him for years and not see it." Seeing the alarm in Rose's eyes, she hurried to add, "He's not dangerous or anything, I don't mean that. What I'm saying is that he presents well. He's learned to show the side of his nature that pleases people. That gets him where he wants to be."

"Fair enough. But we all have parts of our personality we keep tamped down—it's not that unusual."

Liz paused, as if she was trying to think of a better way to say what she wanted Rose to hear. "Are you aware he once tried to kill himself?"

Rose wasn't aware of this; she wasn't sure she wanted to hear it.

"It was before we were married. Before we were even going out. I knew who he was, but I didn't really know him. There were a group of them, all in their senior year. They kind of ran the university: they were on student council, they won all the sports events. They were the big men on campus, you know?"

Yes, she did know. Charles had told her, mentioning it as a kind of joke, the things he and his friends got up to. Nothing really serious, nothing that would have got them expelled. The one time they got caught they were let off with a reprimand. The campus administrators seemed as much in awe of them as were the rest of the students.

"There was an incident," Liz said, "at a party. I wasn't there—like I say it was before I knew him—but there were a lot of people and things got out of hand. This kid, he was a freshman, he jumped out of a seventh-storey window. They said he jumped but later there were people who said he was pushed. He didn't die, believe it or not, but he broke his neck and was paralyzed. The police came and arrested a bunch of guys and it came out that some of them were handing out drugs. LSD, mescaline. That kind of thing. The kid who jumped out the window, he'd taken something, or someone put something in his drink. Nobody knew for sure, it was all pretty confusing." She paused and took a sip of wine.

"Was Charles . . . was he the one with the drugs?" Rose asked. It seemed unlikely—he was such a straight arrow in some ways. As far as she knew, he'd never even smoked pot.

To her relief, Liz said no, he wasn't involved in any of that. "The thing is, this kid who jumped out of the window, Charles knew him. He was a friend of Donnie, Charles' younger brother. Charles had been kind of looking after him that semester . . . showing him around, letting him hang out with him and his friends. The boy was shy and didn't know anybody—Donnie didn't go to college, he and Jean got married right after school and immigrated to South Africa, so the kid didn't have anyone to hang out with. Charles felt protective about him. And it was Charles who invited him to the party. He wouldn't have been there if Charles hadn't told him to come."

Rose felt obliged to defend him. It was a tragic accident but the people to blame were the ones with the drugs. "But it wasn't Charles' fault, what happened, was it?"

"No, of course not. It wasn't his fault. But the boy's parents blamed him for it. And so did his mom—Charles' mom—she was terribly upset about it. Mostly because she thought it made her look bad. She said he'd got in with a bad crowd, said he'd always been trouble, always caused trouble for his family. She really laid into him."

"That's terrible."

"Yes, well, that's Gladys. Be glad she's a few thousand miles away—you don't have to deal with her. Anyway, after that he started seeing a psychiatrist who prescribed Valium for depression. Charles got drunk one night, swallowed half a bottle of pills, and ended up in hospital having his stomach pumped."

"Oh my god, that's terrible!"

"He never talked about it. I only know because I got to know one of his college friends after we were married. *He* told me the whole story. Why, I don't know. I think he was jealous—he had a bit of a thing for me."

It occurred to Rose that Charles wouldn't appreciate Liz telling her this. He wouldn't want her to know there'd been a time, even briefly, when he wasn't calm, upbeat, at peace with the world, and completely in control of the situation.

"Why are you telling me this?" she asked.

Liz didn't answer right away. She poked at her pasta, pushing the pieces of chicken around on her plate. It really wasn't very good pasta, when it came right down to it. The chicken was always a little tough, and *al dente* took on an entirely new meaning when it came to their noodles. Why, Rose wondered, had they met here so often in the past? And, again, why were they meeting right now? She couldn't help thinking that Liz had an ulterior motive: was she really as "over" Charles as she professed? Did she really have Rose's best interests at heart?

Finally, Liz just said she thought it was something Rose should know. Not that Charles was likely to go crazy again. That's how she put it, as if his youthful bout of depression was so alien to anything she'd experienced it had to be labeled as crazy. "If I had known," she said, "I don't think I'd have married him. I'm not good with that kind of thing. My mother suffered from depression all her life. It was a nightmare. I grew up terrified I was going to come home from school and find her dead on the sofa. I never wanted to marry someone who might do that." She took a sip of wine and added, "It's why I don't want kids. I can't take the chance that my mother's genes could be passed down to my children. It would be irresponsible of me and I just couldn't handle it."

Before she could stop herself, Rose began to laugh. "That's crazy, Liz. I mean, just because your mom had trouble with depression doesn't mean your children would. Look at you—you're fine, right? You're her daughter and you don't suffer from it. I think you're overreacting."

It was the wrong thing to say. Liz put down her fork, picked up her purse, and took out her credit card. "I can't do this," she said. "I thought I could but I was wrong. I'll pay for this on the way out."

Rose started to object but Liz was already on her feet, preparing to leave. She stood for a moment, looking as if she might cry. "Liz, I'm sorry, I didn't mean to upset you," Rose said.

"I hope you and Charles are very happy together," Liz said. "I thought he was happy with me, but I was wrong. Maybe he'll be able to be himself with you. I hope so. And I wish you well. I do. But this was a mistake. I won't call you again."

Rose watched as Liz walked to the front of the restaurant and waited to pay. She looked fragile, somehow, her pale blonde hair tied back in a ponytail, her slim figure silhouetted against the sunlit restaurant glass.

That was the last time they met. Liz sold the house and moved back to the UK. A few years later Rose learned that she had remarried and moved to Scotland. And just three years ago, the Addamses began receiving Christmas cards from "Liz, Dave, and the girls." The "girls" were her dogs apparently—she had Corgis.

"Like the Queen," Charles said.

Rose responded, "Isn't that typical," and then had no idea why she said it.

13.

THE PLANE WAS LATE GETTING IN. BY THE TIME Charles and Morgan arrived back at the house, Rose had left for work. She left a note on Morgan's pillow:

"Welcome home, sweetie! Bagels and cream cheese in the fridge—get Dad to show you how to work the new coffee machine. Look forward to seeing you tonight!"

Once she was on the road she regretted writing that, about the coffee. Did it sound like she thought her daughter was stupid? Dammit, she was always doing this, second-guessing herself when it came to Morgan. But the coffeemaker *was* complicated; neither she nor Charles would ever have bought one so sophisticated. They'd been making do with the Bodum for years and would still be doing so if Jason hadn't given this one to Rose as a Mother's Day gift.

"It's from both of us," he said. "*Consumer Reports* gave it a five-star rating. Lee says it's going to rock your world."

If Lee thought a coffee machine could rock her world she was an idiot. But Rose kept this to herself and focused on learning how to operate it. Or rather, Charles, who loved new gadgets, figured it out and then showed her. There was no denying it made fantastic coffee, once you knew how to work it.

"Which you need to have a degree in coffee-ology to do," she said. "Plus it cost the earth."

"How do you know that?" Charles asked.

"I Googled it."

"You're not supposed to Google presents. It shows a lack of class."

"Well, that's me. A peasant through and through."

She parked the car, took the elevator up to the first floor, and got off; she wanted to check out the reading area. The chairs by windows were already occupied. It took her a moment to pick him out, but he was there, in the far corner, head bent over a book. She waited to see if he'd look up—if he did she could wave and smile like she just happened to be passing, but he was absorbed in what he was reading and didn't look up. She was shy about approaching him. What was she going to say, after all? *How are you doing, Ryan? Still homeless?*

She should reach out, see if he needs any help. Nobody begs outside grocery stores if they don't need help. Too bad about his teeth. She remembered Cyndi was always giving the kids sweets. Rose tried to persuade her not to: "Sugar ruins your teeth," she'd say. "It's like poison." Cyndi would shrug, "Kids need a little treat now and then." Maybe it wasn't sugar that had done the damage. Drugs were bad for your teeth—something about drying up all the saliva. She could take him to the dentist, pay for a cleaning and checkup. Would her plan cover that? She could say he was a family member. He was, once. Sort of.

Ryan had been living with them for a year when Greg, his father, turned up on their doorstep one evening. Nice enough guy. A bit rough around the edges but that was to be expected, considering he'd been working on the rigs up north. He introduced himself politely, apologized for dropping in on them without any warning, and said he'd only recently learned about the situation. Over a cup of coffee he explained he had no idea Cyndi had gone off like that and didn't know where she was. Still, when it came right down to it, he wasn't surprised.

"She's not a bad person," he told them. "You probably don't think much of her, after what she's done, and I don't blame you, but she means well. She just can't handle certain things. Like, you know." He nodded towards his son, who was eyeing him warily from a corner of the room. "She's good with kids, and I'm pretty sure she loves Ryan but she's got a lotta anxiety about it. And when things get to her she takes off. When I didn't hear from her for a while I tried to find her. She never gave me your address; I didn't know where she was working. Finally I called her mother in Montreal. She told me Cyndi had turned up about six months ago without Ryan, stayed for a week or so, and then left. She's the one who gave me your address—she didn't have your phone number or I would've called. Anyway, like I say, I appreciate you taking care of the little guy. How much do I owe you?"

It was out of the question, of course, taking money for keeping Ryan. Rose wouldn't hear of it and neither would Charles. They were uncertain, though, about letting his father take him, especially considering the boy hardly remembered him. He hadn't seen him in over a year, a long time for a child. From Ryan's point of view, it was practically handing him over to a stranger. His father seemed to understand that it would be unsettling for the boy. He said he had a job in Spokane starting on Monday, so he needed to leave the next morning.

"It's a good job," he said. "It doesn't pay as much as working on the rigs but it's better, especially for a kid. I'll have an apartment and regular hours. Ryan can go to school and settle in and make friends. We'll be a proper family, right, Ryan? Would you like that?"

Ryan said nothing. Rose was about to object when Greg opened the carryall he'd brought with him and brought out a small, brown, stuffed monkey.

"Remember this guy, Ryan? Curious George. I found him behind the sofa after you left. I've been keeping him for you."

Ryan's face lit up. He came over to his father, accepted the toy, and clutched it to his chest. For once, his expression registered sheer, unadulterated pleasure.

"It was his favourite toy," Greg said. "He had it since he was a baby. I would've sent it to him but like I say, I didn't have an address."

He and Ryan left soon after. Rose invited them to stay for dinner but Greg said he wanted to get an early start in the morning.

"If you can show me where his things are, I'll pack them up," he said. "The place I'm staying at has a pool. We can get in a swim before bed. Would you like that, Ryan?"

This time Ryan nodded eagerly. He had Curious George, all was right with the world. It was obvious he was leaving with more than he'd had when he arrived. Rose had bought shirts, shoes, sweatpants, pyjamas, and toys, wanting to "even things up" as she put it. Seeing this, Greg tried once more to get them to take some money, but again she and Charles refused.

"We loved having him," Rose said.

And Charles added, "We'll miss you, Ryan. Drop us a line now and then, okay?"

Ryan nodded and then, without being prodded, he gave each of them a hug. The children were already in bed but Rose got them up to say goodbye. In a kind of stage whisper, Jason asked his mother if he could give Ryan something. When she said, "Of course," he ran back to his room and returned with his favourite troll doll, the one with the orange hair.

"Are you sure?" she asked.

He nodded and handed the little toy to Ryan with all the gravitas a four-year-old could muster.

"Well, that's real nice of you," Greg said. "Say thank you, now, Ryan."

"Thank you," Ryan said. And then, clasping the troll doll in one hand and Curious George in the other, he followed his father out to the car.

The four of them stood in the doorway, waiting while Greg buckled Ryan into the back seat, got in, and backed out of the driveway. Just before driving away, he rolled down the window on the driver's side and waved.

"Thanks again, people. I'll take good care of him, I promise."

Somehow, although they had little enough to go on, they believed him.

14.

CHARLES WAS SETTING THE KITCHEN TABLE WHEN Rose walked in. "Morgan," he said, "has gone for a run to unwind from the flight. She shouldn't be long. How was your day?"

"The usual. Meetings and more meetings. You know what they're like."

"I do. And I have to tell you, I'm glad to be done with them."

She was still getting her head around that, Charles being done with meetings. Not working anymore. What would they talk about, she wondered? The weather?

A tall, slender figure appeared through the glass of the patio door. Seeing Morgan as she bent over to untie her runners, Rose experienced a familiar surge of pleasure: her daughter, her first child. "*She is clothed with strength and dignity, and laughs without fear of the future.*" That Proverbs quote is Morgan—that's always how she sees her.

Morgan came through the door, brushing wet strands of her dark fringe away from her forehead, and set a spray of long-stemmed lavender on the kitchen counter.

"Hey, Mom, look what I found along the trail! I thought it would make my room smell nice. It's soaking wet, though, just like me."

"Give us a hug!" Rose exclaimed. They embraced, quickly, and Rose noticed two new piercings. In the ears, though, so not necessary to comment. "You've cut your hair. It looks lovely. You haven't had it short like that in years."

"I wanted a change. Kim's bachelorette party is next weekend. I told her I couldn't afford to come back for it but now that I'm here I've got no excuse. The wedding's in two weeks so I guess I'll be going to that, too. You remember Kim, right?"

Rose tried to think back—a high-school friend of Morgan's, a petite, soft-spoken girl who always called her Mrs. Addams. "She's the Oriental one, right?"

"*Asian*, Mother. Nobody says Oriental anymore."

"Is there something wrong with it?"

"It's a remnant of colonialism."

"It's not a slur. It just means of the Orient. Like we're Occidental, of the Occident."

"Moving *on*." Morgan smiled. "I'm starving. Do you want me to serve it out?"

Charles took a lasagna out of the oven and set it on the table. "You have a seat," he said, digging through the utensil drawer. "You're a guest, for tonight, anyway. You just let us wait on you. And you, too, Mom—you've been working all day. You sit down and I'll do the honours."

Mom. He only called her that when the kids were around. She hated it and used to tell him so: I'm not your mom, remember? It's what his own father did—his parents always called each other Mum and Dad. How could you have a sex life if you talked to each other like that? Charles said it wasn't an issue: his parents had been sleeping in separate bedrooms since his younger brother was born.

"They liked it that way," he said. "They liked having their own space. It probably made it easier for Mum when Dad died, being used to sleeping alone."

Rose told him his parents were very strange. "Is it because they were English, do you think?"

"Not really. They were just strange, period."

Once they were seated, Rose pursued the Asian–Oriental argument. "Are you saying it's racist, or just that it's out-dated?"

"It makes them sound exotic—like Kim's some kind of Eastern stereotype or something."

"Well, I don't see how Asian is any less of a stereotype. It's just a different word for the same thing."

Morgan sighed and rolled her eyes skyward. "Can we please talk about something else? Dad tells me he's retiring. How come you didn't tell me?"

"I didn't know! Your father only told me on Friday."

"Well, I think it's a terrible idea."

"And so do I. But he doesn't seem to care what I think."

"I'm right here, you know." Charles said it as if it were a joke, but Morgan wasn't amused.

"Why would you do that, Dad? You love teaching, you know you do."

"Past tense, dear. I *used* to love teaching."

"So what's changed?"

"I don't know. The students, I suppose. I'm tired of students who don't want to think. Who don't want to be challenged. I'm tired of being told I have to moderate my language in class because if I swear or make a bad joke they won't feel 'safe.' Why *should* they feel safe? *I* didn't feel safe when I was going to school—I felt I was in the presence of people who knew things, things I didn't, and I felt thoroughly intimidated. *Safe* didn't come into it."

Now it was Rose's turn to smile. "I don't think you've ever felt intimidated in your life. The things you told me about when you were at school in England, you and your friends ran the place—you had all the undergrads running around doing errands for you. And the girls were throwing themselves at you."

"Maybe in my final year. We did have it pretty much our way then. But I didn't come on campus expecting the world to welcome me with open arms. These kids are so entitled. That girl—that young woman who came to my office, she was just more up front about it. They all think they deserve at least a B-plus; you give them anything less and they run crying to the dean about it. And god forbid you fail them. You'll have their parents on the phone threatening to have you fired!"

None of this was new to Rose; she'd been hearing Charles and his colleagues rant about millennials since—well, since there were millennials. When Charles got started on the topic, he was pretty well unstoppable. And now he was onto the next batch of students, the one called Generation Z. "From what I can see, they're worse than the millennials. They've grown up in a digital world where they've never had to wait for anything. It's all available online, all the time."

Morgan made an attempt to interject. "That isn't their fault—"

"These students take it for granted that every course will be tailored to fit their needs. They expect to have their grades delivered seconds after they hand in their papers." He turned to Rose. "You remember that seminar I went to last spring? The one Arnold set up and insisted every department head attend?" When Rose nodded, he turned back to Morgan. "Engaging Generation Z. That's what they called it. An entire day spent on bullshit: collaborative learning . . . online gaming . . . using social media to make our classes more interesting. Complete and utter bullshit!"

Morgan tried to suggest that it was not completely bullshit but Charles wasn't listening. "It's not enough," he said, "to just stand up there and teach anymore. And who knows? Maybe it never was. Anyway, I'm done. The old order changeth and the rest of us can just get out of the way."

After a moment, Morgan said, "Well, I still think it's too bad, you retiring and all. What'll you do with your free time? Take up golf?" She meant it as a joke. Charles was famous for claiming that golf wasn't a sport, it was something you took up when you were too old and broken-down to do anything else.

"Actually, I'm planning to write a book."

Before Morgan could follow this up, Rose jumped in and changed the subject. "Tell us about the dissertation, hon," she said. "How's it going? Have you written your conclusion?"

"I'm thinking about dropping it."

Charles stared at her, his fork halfway to his mouth. "What?"

"I'm thinking about quitting. Dropping out of the program." She speared a lettuce leaf and continued eating, like she hadn't just dropped a verbal bombshell in the middle of the lasagna.

Charles kept staring as if he wasn't altogether sure his daughter was in her right mind. Rose was having a similar reaction, but she felt it was important to keep a steady hand on the tiller, so to speak. "Is this, dropping out of the program, is it because of the wedding?" she asked. "I mean, because of you and Ian . . .?"

"It has nothing to do with Ian and me."

"So it's just a coincidence that you and he break up and you're thinking of walking away from something you've been working on for . . . how long?"

"Three years, six months, and thirteen days. No, it's not a coincidence, actually. My life is falling apart, like I said. Do we have any wine?"

"There's a couple of bottles of red in the dining room cabinet," Rose said.

When Morgan left the room to get it, she and Charles looked at each other.

"Is she serious?" he said. "I thought this was the most important thing in her life."

"It is, next to Ian. At least, it was. And now she's dropped them both. Or thinking about it. Did she say anything to you about this when you picked her up this morning?"

Charles shook his head. "Not a word. I asked her about Ian and she said there was nothing to talk about—it was a mutual decision and she hoped he'd have a very happy life. But she didn't say anything about the thesis. I just assumed she was taking a break and she'd go back and finish it."

"What did she bring with her? Did she have any luggage?"

"Two bags and a carry-on backpack."

"She had two suitcases and you thought she was here to take a break? Honestly, Charles, you can be so dense sometimes."

Morgan returned with a bottle of Beaujolais—the expensive one. Rose began to say something but stopped herself. Her daughter's life was falling apart; now was not the time to be stingy.

15.

THE SOUND OF THE FRONT DOOR SHUTTING WOKE her from a dream. She and Morgan were sitting on a park bench near the house they lived in when the kids were small, watching children play on the swings. Morgan is apologizing for throwing up during dinner. She tells her it's not the food that's the problem. "I'm pregnant. Didn't you know? And I'm having an abortion."

The clock on the bedside table read 3:15. It must be Morgan. Good, she was home. She and her friends had taken a cab downtown and had arranged for an Uber to bring them back. They were so responsible, these young people. Didn't drive drunk, always made sure to use contraception. She thought of Lauren—well, almost always.

"Mom? Are you awake?"

Morgan was standing in the doorway, silhouetted by the faint light from the hallway. Rose sat up in bed, hoping for a mother–daughter chat. The kind they had back when Morgan was living at home, before she went off to college. Those were the times when she really felt things were the way they were supposed to be: sitting together in the dark, sharing the events of the day. How lucky I am, she'd think. How great to have the gift of a daughter.

There was never any need to worry about waking Charles; he was dead to the world. It was amazing, really, the way he was able to fall asleep the minute his head hit the pillow. He said it was because he had a clear conscience, implying that she, who took ages to fall asleep, didn't. She said it had nothing to do with his conscience; it was all about the gin and orange juice he drank while watching the news.

"Come in, hon. Come talk to me."

Morgan entered the room, accompanied by the aroma of her night out with the girls: cigarettes, beer, and just a whiff of something stronger. Pot? Did they call it that any more? It was that when she was younger, as in, "Are you kids smoking pot in there?" Now it was weed, she thought. And it had been a very long time since she'd indulged.

"Hey, Mom, how are you doing?"

"I'm good. Did you have a good night?"

"It was a shit show, actually."

Rose sat up straighter, prepared for the worst. "Really? What happened?"

"Oh, nothing much. It was pretty lame, to be honest. Caitlin got into a fight with a cop. Deena passed out on the sidewalk. And Kim ended up trying to hook up with the Uber driver on the way back from the bar."

"Isn't Kim the one that's getting married?"

"She is. But Sam told her she should have sex with a stranger before she gets married, and then it dawned on her that from now on she's always only going to have sex with Kevin for the rest of her life. And so she tried to get the driver to come up to her apartment."

"And did he?"

"He said it was against his professional ethics. But I think he just wasn't into her."

"But she loves Kevin, doesn't she?"

"Yeah, she does. But that's not the point. I told her Sam was right, she should have a fling before she settles down with Kevin. But not with a stranger—god, that's so dangerous. You could catch something. I said she should have sex with her ex, the guy she was dating before she met Kevin. And then she got all sentimental and teary and drunk-texted him—"

"Who? Kevin?"

"No, Brendan. The one she used to date. And her phone rang and it was him and Caitlin grabbed it and threw it out the window and so we had to pull over and look for it. Oh, god. What a night."

"Did you find the phone?"

"Are you kidding? No! It was pitch black out and we were in the middle of nowhere. And then Crystal had to pee so she went off into this field and managed to pee on her dress and the driver didn't want to let her back in the car because of the pee. So *that* was a hassle. Like I say, it was a complete shit show and I honest to god hope I never see any of them once the wedding's over."

"But they're your best friends. You don't really think that, do you?'

"We were friends in high school, Mom. That was almost *twenty* years ago. People change. No, actually, the problem is people don't change. Deena always drank too much and Sam always bossed everybody around. Caitlin was always a bitch, and now that she's pregnant she's even worse. Kim's sweet, though. Caitlin should buy her a new phone. She won't and Kim won't make her."

Morgan got to her feet and stretched. "I'm going to bed. If I'm not up by noon can you wake me?" She stood looking down to Charles sleeping, snoring ever so softly. "Is Dad okay, do you think?"

"Oh, he always makes that noise when he sleeps. It's not sleep apnea, but the doctor said he might need one of those nasal strips. It doesn't bother me and as long as it doesn't bother him. Why, has he been keeping you awake?"

"I don't mean that. I mean, is he okay in general? He just seems . . . different these days."

"He's fine. I'd be the one to know if your father wasn't okay—I'm around him all the time."

"I know, Mom. Don't get defensive."

She started to say she wasn't getting defensive, but Morgan bent down, kissed her goodnight, and left the room. Rose settled back in bed but she was awake now, and she knew wasn't going to fall back to sleep. The dream came back to her: it was Lauren in the dream, not Morgan. She was wearing the dress she wore at dinner the other night, a sheer, lacy, long-sleeved number cut a few inches above the knee. As if Kate Middleton were out on the town and decided to show a little leg. Marie had thought she was overdressed and Rose agreed. But maybe they were both a little jealous that neither of them could get away with something like that. Not these days, anyway.

What was Lauren doing with Garnet? She was very pretty; she probably had young men eating out of her hand. That line about them being friends—why would a young woman need an old fart like Garnet for a friend? And the way he put his arm around her, that look on his face when he introduced her to the group. *She* might think they were just friends but *he* certainly didn't. Watch out, Romeo, she thought—Marie's right: you'll end up with your dick in a vice.

I'm having an abortion.

She'd said it so easily. Rose had never been able to do that; she still couldn't. There were good reasons at the time not to have the baby. She was unmarried and still in school. Her mother had died a few months earlier, her father was grieving, and she was not in love with the father of the child. Mistake. Mistake. Mistake. That was the only word that fit: the pregnancy was a mistake and there was only one way to fix it.

She couldn't possibly have gone to Dr. Short. He'd been their family doctor since before she was born, he brought her into this world. Rose was sure he would die of shock. Worse than that: he'd tell her father. A friend recommended a doctor who was younger than Dr. Short, but not so young as to not have dealt with this many, many times. When he gave her the news—"Yes, you're pregnant. Eight or nine weeks, I'd say"—she burst into tears. "It's not the end of the world," he said, looking faintly disgusted.

"It is!" she cried. "It's absolutely the end of the world."

There was a crucifix on the wall of his waiting room. Either because of that, or simply because he heard the desperation in her voice, he said he hoped she wasn't thinking of doing anything "evil."

And she quickly answered, "No, of course not." Because she wasn't. It was against the law, right? And a sin.

It was an aunt who suggested it. She knew someone who knew someone and, within a week of promising the doctor she was not about to do anything evil, she was on her first plane trip, heading west. Off to do just that. Something evil.

Which it wasn't, of course. She knew that now, she'd known it all her adult life. A woman's right to choose. Our bodies, ourselves. She'd marched in protest against the laws that criminalized abortion. She stood up in front of everyone at a rally and admitted she'd had an abortion. One of the hardest things she'd ever done. She would never be that brave again.

It was the right, the only, thing to do. But the guilt lingered. If you say that you end up claimed by the anti-choicers, the ones who believe the life of a foetus is always more valuable, more worth claiming an existence, than that of the woman who's carrying it. And you let down the pro-choice people who fought for a woman's right to choose. So you can't ever say it.

Give me another life, she thought, and I'll do it differently. Just one more time, please. Is that too much to ask?

It was. It is.

It started to rain. Rose sat up in bed when she heard it slapping against the window, causing the blinds to rattle against the glass. She got up, closed the window, and stood for a moment, staring out into the gloom. She thought of Ryan, out there, sleeping in an alley somewhere, or under a bridge. It made her ill to think of it.

16.

The rain continued for the next four days. It fell in sheets, melancholy and unrelenting, accompanied by heavy winds and rolling thunder. The city across the bridge was lost in cloud; the mountains disappeared altogether. It was disorienting and claustrophobic. Rose navigated to work with her windshield wipers on high speed, hunched over the steering wheel, struggling against the illusion that the city was being submerged. The weather channel said a front of low pressure was stalled over the region, driven by the jet stream. They were hopeful, they said, it would clear up by Friday.

Tuesday morning, Charles stood in the doorway of the kitchen, nursing his second cup of coffee. He said he'd been up since five. Unshaven, still in his bathrobe, he wore the lost, slightly bewildered expression she remembered from the days he tried to assemble the children's toys.

"Where're you off to?"

"Work," she said. "Where else would I be going? Are you all right?" She waited.

"I guess so," he said. "Do you have meetings tonight?"

"No. Unless something comes up. Do you want me to pick up something for dinner?"

Another long pause while he mulled this over. For Christ sake, she thought, I'm trying to get out the door. He took forever to make up his mind lately. Not about anything important. My god, he had made the decision to retire in half a minute. But inconsequential things flummoxed him. Like, did he want orange juice or apple cider? Brown bread or white? The light on or off?

She took a deep breath and tried again. "Hon? Are you okay? Are you feeling all right?"

"Don't fuss, Rose. I'm fine. I'm going to work on my book."

"Your book?"

"The Myra Hindley book. I need to start going through my old clippings—start doing the research. I've got lots to do—don't worry about me."

"Good." She picked up her car keys and gave him a quick kiss on the cheek. "I'm off. I'll call you if I'm going to be late."

On the way into work she thought about what Morgan had said, about her father seeming different these days. Was there something she wasn't seeing? Maybe she was too close to him to notice. The way Eileen had been thrown for a loop when it came out that Jermyn was fucking around. Rose had suspected for months, as had every other friend of Eileen's. When it came out, even Eileen's daughter said she wasn't surprised, saying. "Oh, Mother, you're such a *naif.*" Which wasn't very kind and certainly wasn't helpful. Well, that's what you get for sending your kids to expensive private schools. Say what you will about her relationship with Morgan, when the chips were down her daughter had her back. And vice versa.

But, Charles *did* seem a little unfocused lately. And dependent. He'd started expecting her to wait on him—make him a sandwich before she left for work and leave it covered on the kitchen counter. So he could have it for lunch. In almost forty years of marriage, Rose could count on one hand the number of times she made lunch for Charles, and they all occurred in the past week.

She stepped off the elevator, said good morning to her co-workers, and saw that Morgan had sent her a text: *Call me, ok, when you get into work.*

Julie Mitchell was waiting outside her office. This was never a good sign. Rose tried to think of what might have set her off this morning but came up blank. Sometimes the best defense was a full frontal assault of goodwill.

"Good morning, Julie," she chirped. "Crazy day out there. What is it about the rain that brings out all the crazy drivers?"

Julie followed Rose into her office, closed the door, and stood there, arms folded across her chest, glaring at her. Rose busied herself getting settled at her desk, switched on her computer, and gave in to the inevitable.

"What is it, Julie? Is there a problem?"

From somewhere on her person, Julie retrieved a piece of paper and thrust it in Rose's direction. "Did you write this?" she demanded.

It was an email Rose had sent out the day before; Julie had printed it out and used an orange Sharpie to highlight several sentences. "That's kind of a rhetorical question," Rose replied. "It came from my email so obviously I must have written it."

"And you didn't feel the need to consult with me first?"

Julie was working herself up to a first-class pissing contest; Rose could see that. Normally, her strategy would be to throw water on the flames, but this time she felt herself to be on firm ground. She was not going to back down, for once.

"I didn't, actually," she said. "I was letting staff know about the changes we've made in the upstairs study space. It's mostly about the computers and those are my domain, right? So, no, I didn't feel the need to consult with you first."

Domain was the wrong word to use; she knew that as soon as she said it and sure enough, Julie was off and running with it. "Well, computers may be your *domain* but access to our facilities is *my* domain. And the study room *is* part of our facilities, I believe? Unless I'm mistaken?"

Rose gave in. Julie would carry on until she did and Rose really didn't have the energy for these confrontations. "Yes, I suppose if you look at it that way . . ."

"I do."

"Right. Fair enough. So, you've underlined some of the wording here—did you want to change some of these things?"

Having won, Julie could afford to be generous. "No, it's fine," she said. "Sending out another email would just confuse the issue." She turned to leave, then paused. "The Outstanding Service Awards are coming up next month," she said.

"Yes, I know."

"I just thought I'd mention it." And she left.

What, Rose wondered, was that all about? She picked up her phone and called Morgan, who, without saying hello, demanded to know what was going on with her father.

"I'm sorry—going on? What do you mean?"

"I talked with Jason this morning," she said, "and he says Dad's writing a book about a murderer. Is it true? Is he really going to do it?"

"Oh, that." Rose was relieved. From the sound of her voice she'd thought Morgan was going to tell her Charles was about to jump off a bridge. Or something.

"Why would he want to be bothered with someone like that? I can't believe he'd want to waste his time on her."

"I don't know, Morgan . . . Something to do?"

"Well, I think it's beneath him."

"So do I, hon, but let's just let it go. I think he'll find something else to do, soon enough."

"You think so?"

"I do. I think it's unlikely that book will ever see the light of day."

"Well," Morgan said, "if it does, I hope he uses a pen name. I certainly don't want *my* name used in connection with it."

Rose hung up and noted the time on her phone: 8:56. She was less than a half hour into her day and she was exhausted. Julie, she could deal with; Charles was another matter. She wished she could be certain about that book. It had sounded like a spur-of-the-moment thing when he made the announcement at dinner. Rose was pretty sure, at the time, he was saying it to shock. She thought that, maybe, given a couple of days and a chance for sober contemplation, he might reconsider.

But what was he going to do? There were clubs he could join, organizations looking for volunteers; the bulletin boards in the library were a constantly curated agglomeration of opportunities for community-minded retirees. She had checked them out the other day but none of them seemed a good fit.

He could be a volunteer grandparent: dedicated to "fostering intergenerational understanding." Charles was good with children but it sounded like a lot of work. The Literacy Society wanted board members, but of course that meant meetings. And he was done with meetings. She tried to picture him driving older seniors to their doctors' appointments. They'd start talking politics, or make some comment about kids today, Charles would feel obliged to set them straight, things would get heated, and before you knew it he'd get a phone call thanking him for his time and suggesting he offer his services elsewhere.

Besides, men never listen to their wives. Charles wasn't going to go for anything she came up with. The solution, if there was one, was going to have to come from someone he trusted. Someone who isn't his wife. If she called now, she just might reach him in his office, before his classes started.

"Rose, my lovely, how good to hear from you." Garnet spoke as if they hadn't just seen each other a week ago at dinner. "How are you? And how is that adorable daughter of yours? I gather she's home for a visit. You must be pleased." As usual, he had a way of getting her back up, even when he was trying to be nice.

"Why is that?"

"I beg your pardon?"

"Why do you assume I'd be pleased that she's back home? I'd rather she stayed in school and finished her thesis."

"Oh. Well, yes, I can see that. But still—mothers and daughters, you know. A mother's treasure is her daughter."

It sounded like something he got off a wall plaque; it didn't need a response. "Garnet, I need to ask you something."

"I'm all ears, my dear. Fire away."

She pictured him sitting up straight in his office chair, his ears pricked with anticipation. He really was such an old gossip. Charles always said if you wanted something to make the rounds of the faculty, telling Garnet was faster and more efficient than putting it into an email. "I'm a little worried about Charles," she said. "But I have to ask you, please don't tell him I said so. He'd hate me talking about him like this, even to you."

Garnet's voice grew grave as he assured her he wouldn't say a word. "Is it his health? He did seem not quite himself at dinner. Making an announcement like that, out of the blue. I can only imagine how shocked you must have been. How are you, my dear? How are you coping?"

"I'm fine, Garnet. But I am a little worried about Charles. I think he's depressed. Or bored."

"But he's got a book to do, hasn't he? He's going to write about that awful Hindley woman."

"I think he's only looking at that as a way to keep himself busy. I can't believe his heart is in it."

"He should not have retired, Rose, you know that. It's not too late for him to change his mind. I'll speak to Bernie, she'll sort out the paperwork."

"No, don't do that! There's no point. He doesn't want to teach any more, I'm sure of it. He's not going to go back to teaching but he needs to do something. He needs a project. Something to focus on, something he cares about."

There was a pause; Rose could hear him shuffling papers in the background and wondered if he was paying attention. It would be like Garnet to go to Bernie anyway and have her "sort it out."

"Garnet?"

"Just a minute," he said. "Somewhere on my desk is a file folder—ah, here it is. 'Status Update on Commemorative Project.' This would be ideal for Charles. Maybe he's mentioned it to you. It was his idea, originally. Although that was almost a year ago—he's probably forgotten all about it. Does it ring a bell?"

It didn't. Garnet went on to explain. "The arts faculty is putting together a booklet for the hundredth anniversary of our first graduating class. Student activism in the twentieth century, focusing on our alumni. Charles suggested it at a joint faculty meeting and one of the chaps brought it up to Blake. Just in passing, you understand. Didn't really expect much of a response. Well, you know, Arnold keeps his cards close to his chest. Anyway, he jumped on it. Loved the idea. Said it would fit perfectly with the new marketing strategy. Depressing, isn't it? A university education is just another commodity. Ah, well, the benefactors must have their pound of flesh. The court awards it and the law doth give it—"

Once Garnet began quoting Shakespeare he could go on forever. "So about this project," Rose interjected, "you're saying it's going ahead?"

"Yes. Yes, it is. We have the funding now and Charles could take the lead on it. Strictly research, no committee meetings, everything done online or by telephone. I think this would be right up his alley."

Rose thought it sounded perfect, especially if it meant Charles wouldn't have to go on campus. "Will you talk to him, Garnet? Don't mention me—I want him to think it came strictly from you. I don't want him to think I leaned on you for a favour."

"Mum's the word, my dear. And you know you can lean on me any time. I'd like nothing better."

There was something about the way he said it that made her uncomfortable. Surely he wasn't coming on to her after all this time? Charles used to tease her that Garnet had feelings for her. "If anything ever happens to me," Charles once said, "Garnet will be on your doorstep the day after the funeral with a proposal of marriage. You can bank on it."

"If anything ever happens to you," she said, "I'll sell the house and move to Greece."

"You've thought about this," Charles said. "You have a plan."

"I do. And it doesn't include Garnet Simpkins."

She was about to hang up when Garnet said, "Actually, I have a bit of news: I'm about to become a father."

"You mean a grandfather—you're already a father, right? Actually, you're already a grandfather."

"Yes, of course. I misspoke. What I meant to say was I'm going to become a father *again*. The lovely Lauren—you met her the other night—she's pregnant. *We're* pregnant—that's how you say it nowadays, isn't it?"

"I thought," Rose said, and stopped. It sounded too crude to come out with it like that. She tried again: "Didn't she decide . . . I mean, she told me . . ."

"She's changed her mind. And I couldn't be more delighted."

"Really? Well . . . that's wonderful, Garnet! Congratulations."

"Thank you."

"Is it okay if I tell Charles?"

"Actually, Rose, if you don't mind, I'd like to tell him in person. We're meeting up on Saturday. I'll tell him then. And I'll bring up the project then, as well."

"Sure, Garnet." She hung up the phone and sent a text to Marie. *Huge news! Just spoke with Garnet. Lauren's having the baby and he's delighted!*

You're joking! Please tell me you're joking :O

Not a joke. Calling himself the father if u can believe it :O

OMG we have to talk! Lunch on the w/end?

17.

TWO DAYS LATER ROSE WOKE UP WITH A TERRIBLE head cold and was relieved to be able to call in sick and not have to make the commute. Charles made her a cup of tea with lemon then went upstairs to read. He was making his way through a library copy of *Hero of the Empire*, about the making of Winston Churchill. Rose had put it on hold for him last fall and it had only recently come available. Morgan went for a run, returning drenched to the skin in spite of her expensive Lululemon rain gear.

"How do people live like this?" she asked, wringing out her tights in the kitchen sink. "It's like we're in the middle of a monsoon."

"You've been living bag east for too long," Rose replied. "You've forgotten aboud life on the Wet Coast. Bake yourself some tea, why don't you?" Rose was curled up in an armchair by the stove, sipping her tea and thumbing through an old issue of *Vanity Fair*. Her head hurt and her nose was stuffed up, but it was deliciously soothing to be inside on a day like this, wrapped in the cozy fleece pajamas Charles had given her for Christmas. For years he bought her sexy, Victoria's Secret-style lingerie, which were really presents for him, not her. She was relieved when he switched to things she could actually sleep in.

Morgan wanted to know if they had green tea and Rose pointed to the shelf above the microwave. "Have you drunk any of this, Mom?"

"I keep beaning to, bud then I forget and bake myself a cup of Tetley's. Your father won't touch green tea. Whed I sugges it he acts like I'm trying to poison him. Maybe you should bake some of it with you when you go back to Toronto." She blew her nose, loudly.

Morgan filled the kettle with water and set it on the stove. "About that," she said. "We should talk. I guess you and Dad want me out of here."

"Don't be ridiculous," Rose began, and then had to stop in order to sneeze. "It's nod that and you know it. I just think you should finish whad you started. You were so gung-ho aboud getting your PhD so sure id was what you wanted. I don't understand whad happened."

"I don't know, Mom. It's complicated. And I really don't want to be judged."

"Go ahead," Rose said. "I promise nod to judge. Honest."

Morgan stood by the stove, waiting for the kettle to boil. "The thing is," she said, "I'm thirty-six."

"Yes, I doh," said Rose. "I was dere." She blew her nose again.

"You also have to promise not to interrupt. And you shouldn't, anyway. You sound awful."

"I promise. Sorry."

"I'm thirty-six and I've spent most of my life in school. I went from high school to university and then I went on to get my master's. After that I spent six years working in film and hated it."

Rose went to say something and then remembered her promise. She nodded. "Doh on."

"Four years ago I applied to the PhD program and got in. I didn't expect to—I didn't think my marks were good enough. But I got in and I was thrilled—I mean, it was like finally I was on the right path, you know? I was finally doing what I was meant to be doing all my life."

Rose sneezed again, several times, and Morgan frowned. "Are you sure you shouldn't be in bed? We can talk about this another time."

Rose shook her head, blew her nose and said, "Id's okay, doh on."

"I was thinking about it the other day, what you and Dad said when I got in. Do you remember?"

Rose was in no position to answer; she was going through tissues at an alarming rate.

"You said you were proud of me—like I'd finally made the right decision. Like I wasn't going to be the loser older sister with the Mr. Perfect younger brother."

"Oh, come od now," Rose croaked, "that's not fair! We never saw either of you that way. Where did you ged such an idea?"

Morgan took the kettle off the stove, filled a cup with hot water, plunked a teabag in, and set it on the counter. "It doesn't matter. The point is, that's how I felt at the time. I remember going for a walk with Dad the weekend before I left for Toronto. He was telling me what to expect—you know, how to kind of sell myself to a potential supervisor, and to make sure I found one that was really interested in my research—someone who could be counted on to be there if I needed him. Or her. Some of what he said I figured was maybe not all that relevant any more—he got his doctorate such a long time ago."

"Back in the darg ages." Rose blew her nose and murmured, "Before we had pencils."

"But I really remember two things: he said I'd better be passionate about doing this in the beginning because if I wasn't I was going to absolutely hate it by the time I was writing my dissertation. And the other thing he said was that the worst would be just near the end, when I'd finished all the research and was done writing. 'You're going to look at it then,' he said, 'and you're going to think the whole damn thing's been a fucking waste of time.'"

"He said thad?"

"Yes. Well, he didn't say 'fucking' but that's what he said. That I'd look at it and want to throw it into the nearest waste paper basket."

"And whad did he suggest?"

"He said to ignore every instinct I had to dump it and just keep going. 'Carry on,' he said. 'That's all you can do. And in the end you'll be glad you did.'"

"Good advice," said Rose.

"Yeah, probably. It's what everyone's always telling me—you've gone this far, just *finish* it." Morgan stared down into her teacup, as if the answers to life's challenges were hidden in its green, watery depths.

Rose wondered if "everyone" included Ian. Was that what precipitated the breakup? Maybe he'd been pushing her too hard. She blew her nose again and retrieved another tissue from the nearly empty box. Morgan was right: this probably wasn't the best time to have a serious, possibly life-changing, conversation.

"Maybe we should talk tonight—"

"The thing is," Morgan said, "Steve Jobs founded Apple when he was twenty-one. Isaac Newton created calculus when he was twenty-three. By the time Muhammad Ali was thirty he'd been the heavyweight champion of the world for eight years. I've. Done. Nothing. I've sat in school, and read books, and written papers. If I complete my PhD and manage to land a teaching position—which is a *huge* 'if', by the way—and *if* I eventually get tenure somewhere—which is an even bigger if—I'll spend the rest of my working life sitting in school, reading books, and writing papers. Which no one except some other academic will ever read. Assuming they get published. Which is the biggest *if* of all."

Rose began to protest but Morgan cut her off. "Mom, you promised. And you're too sick to talk anyway."

Rose nodded, feeling that Morgan was taking advantage of the situation. She *was* too sick to talk, which meant she was also too sick to argue. "Sorry. Doh odd."

"And I'm one of the lucky ones. Thanks to you and Dad, I'm not coming out of this with a massive student loan. I'm not like your friend Lauren, owing all that money and pregnant on top of it. Pregnant!" She said it with such horror Rose had to smile. "Anyway, when I started to think about it, I realized that it's like I've been on this academic trajectory for years. It was practically laid out for me in childhood. You and Dad both went to college, Dad *teaches* at college, you both assumed Jason and I would go to university—there was never any discussion about doing anything else. It was just *assumed*. We didn't really have a choice."

Rose managed a feeble, "Oh, come od now. That's not true."

"Think about it, Mom. If either of us had come to you after high school and said we wanted to be—oh, I don't know, bricklayers or something, would you have agreed?"

"Why would you want to be a bricklayer?"

"I wouldn't—I don't. That's just an example. But I might have wanted to be an artist. Or a musician. Or maybe go save the humpback whales."

A fit of sneezing kept Rose from responding. Seeing that her mother was running out of tissues, Morgan fetched a toilet paper roll from the bathroom and suggested she go back to bed.

When she was able to speak, Rose put her hand up. "Here's the thing. If you said you wanted to be an artist or play the piano or whadever, we'd've said, 'Go ahead.' But you didn't. And getting a degree could actually help you save whales."

"The point is . . ." Morgan took a deep breath. "The point is if I go ahead and finish my dissertation, I'll be expected to continue, maybe do a postdoc. And then I'll need to pull my resumé together so I can land a contract position somewhere. None of it excites me. If I let myself think about it, it depresses the hell out of me. The only way to fix it is to get off the bus, you know? Just . . . stop."

"Was that what breaking things off with Ian was about—getting off the bus?"

"Sort of. Ian was always my fall-back plan. You know, if things didn't work out and I didn't get a good teaching job, or if I got one and hated it, well, I'd be married. I could let him support me while I figured it out."

It sounded uncomfortably strategic. "Really? You thought of it like thad? I thought the two of you were id love."

"So did I. And then we were out one night and he said he was happy I'd given up film for academia. And I'm, like, 'Why?' and he said it was because if he ever found himself out of work he'd have this well-educated wife with a good job and benefits to support him until he found another gig."

Rose dabbed at her nose gingerly. It was feeling raw and sore and she didn't think she had the energy left to keep up her side of the discussion.

"I'm sorry, honey. I guess I dod see the problem."

"Don't you see? He was seeing me as *his* fall-back plan. We were both looking at the other person as a kind of security blanket. He was my contingency plan and I was his."

If she had been feeling better, if her head hadn't throbbing at the temples and her sinuses were clear, Rose might have said that every marriage comes with certain expectations. Marie always said having Jeff in accounting made it possible for her to devote herself to writing, especially in the beginning. And hadn't she seen Charles that way, to some extent, when she first met him? But she didn't have the energy for the speech, and she knew this wasn't what Morgan wanted to hear. It would sound calculating. She wanted to believe that all you need is love. And Morgan needed her to be supportive.

"Well, if you both feld that way," Rose said, "you probably made the ride decision."

Morgan stood up and pushed her hair back from her forehead. The short cut was beginning to grow out and no longer framed her face so perfectly. She had bought one of those fascinators to wear to Kim's wedding on Saturday, a whimsical fusion of pink feathers and sequins that would add a much-needed playful touch to the outfit she'd chosen: a black, sleeveless sheath dress more suited to a funeral. Wisely, Rose kept her thoughts to herself.

"Anyway, that's where I am right now. I've lost my passion and I think everything I've done is shit. So I can either carry on, like Dad said, or drop out and spend the rest of my life feeling like a failure."

"You won't be though. Wouldn't be. You wouldn't be a failure, sweedheart."

"Not to you, maybe. Or Dad. But to the people whose opinions count, I would."

Ignoring the implication that her opinion didn't count, Rose urged Morgan to give it some thought. "Dod rush into anything, that's my advice. Maybe ask for an extension to give yourself some time. Can you do that? Ask for extra time to finish?"

Morgan said she could and she had. Twice. "Now I just think, what's the point? Why put off the inevitable if I'm just going to wind up dropping it in the end?"

It was exhausting going around and around like this. No matter what Rose said Morgan was going to disagree. Still, she tried once more. "I just thing you've put all this time into working on your thesis, don't you think you should finish?"

"God, that's just like you! You always do this. You can't ever let me just express myself. You've got to tell me what to do."

She didn't expect Morgan to snap at her; she wasn't prepared for it. "I'm nod telling you what to do—"

"You are! You always do! It's why I don't tell you things. You treat me like a child."

"And you treat me like a mother!" Rose was exhausted from the conversation, sneezing, congested, and close to tears. She blew her nose, violently, and told herself to get a grip. Find a way to get things back on an even keel. "Look," she began.

"Let's drop it," Morgan said. "I shouldn't have brought it up in the first place. It's my problem and I'll deal with it."

They finished their tea in silence, listening to the rain drumming against the overhead skylight. When it rained like that, you thought it was never going to stop. It was like some post-apocalyptic dystopia where every day was the same as the next, and identical to the one before it.

Morgan took her teacup to the sink, rinsed it out and set it on the rack to dry. "Mom, I'm going upstairs to have a shower. Let me know if you need anything."

"I will. Thanks." She settled back in her chair, picked up the magazine, and pretended to read. After a few minutes she gave up and went back to thinking about the argument with Morgan. She hated to think of her daughter being unhappy, but it was more disturbing to think that sometime down the road she might regret her decision to break things off with Ian. Who really was such a lovely man.

And as for the PhD—all that time spent studying, doing research. Not to mention the money! She couldn't really be thinking of abandoning it just because of a temporary lack of confidence. Charles must talk to her. Morgan cared what her father thought. When she was too angry, or too stubborn, to be guided by anybody else, she would seek input from Charles. It drove Rose crazy, sometimes, the way she'd raise her hackles any time her mother made the slightest suggestion. As in, "Don't you think that top is a bit too tight?" Which had resulted in Rose getting the silent treatment for the rest of the night for implying (she hadn't, really) that Morgan was putting on weight. Whereas Charles had only to raise a critical eyebrow, and Morgan would head back into her bedroom and change. Yes, she decided, she'd get Charles to talk to her. If anyone could make her see the light, it was her dad.

18.

ROSE SLEPT FOR MOST OF THE REST OF THE DAY AND woke up feeling rested but disoriented. The room was dark. The bedside clock showed 7:45 and for a moment she wondered if she'd slept through till morning. She got up, threw on her dressing gown, and made her way downstairs.

The argument with Morgan came back to her; she was thankful it had gone no further. There'd been that time back in middle school when Morgan didn't talk to her for a month; Rose couldn't remember what the fight was about, originally, but it grew into a standoff where neither would give in, each believing the other owed her an apology. Rose gave in first. She simply couldn't stand being shut out of her daughter's life. And what was the point, really, of being right if you were going to be unhappy? That was the way Charles, fed up with being the go-between, put it. "You hate being at odds with her," he had said, "and you know she's not going to back down. She's even more stubborn than you are. You're the adult so act like it."

It was as close as he ever came to laying down the law, and Rose didn't much care for it, but she had to concede he was right: if she and Morgan were going to get over this particular speed bump, she would have to make the first move. So she had stopped at the high-end bakery on Broadway and picked up a half-dozen red velvet cupcakes as a peace offering. They were Morgan's favourite and they weren't cheap. In Rose's opinion, $3.50 for a cupcake was highway robbery, which is why she usually preferred to bake them from scratch. So laying out twenty-one dollars for six cupcakes was a true measure of sacrifice. Luckily, Morgan appreciated it.

"Aw, Mom, that was so sweet of you," she said, giving her mother a hug. "I'm sorry I was such a bitch."

And Rose, happy to be back in her daughter's good books, just hugged her back and said nothing about the bad language. One battle at a time, she figured.

Charles was in the living room, watching TV in his beloved recliner. There was no sign of Morgan. It always reminded Rose of *Slaughterhouse-Five*, that chair, the part where the aliens strap Billy Pilgrim to a yellow Barcalounger when they're transporting him to the planet Tralfamadore. It was a perfect image for the 1960s; her father had a chair like that and so did her Uncle Max. And just as her father had done, and her Uncle Max, Charles cherished his Barcalounger with a passion. Three years ago, Rose, in one of her periodic attempts to update the living room decor, suggested they get rid of it. It was old; the leather was cracked in places, and the stitching along the seams was coming unravelled.

"It looks like we can't afford anything better," she said.

Charles said he didn't care what it looked like—it was comfortable and it smelled the way good leather should smell. "We're talking about something of value," he said.

"To you."

"Yes, to me. I live here; it's my house, why shouldn't I have the things around me that I care about? This chair is the only thing I kept from my first marriage . . ."

"Yes, I know that."

"I gave up my roll-top desk, I gave up my set of copper cook-ware—hell, I gave up my house!"

"All right . . ."

"I will not give up that chair, Rose. I hope, in fact, to die in it."

"That can be arranged." She tried another tack. "What about moving it?"

"Moving it? Where?"

"To the basement?"

"You're suggesting that when I want to relax I head down to the sub-interior of the house and hide myself away, like some troglo-dytic tunnel-dweller. That's charming, that is."

"Oh, for god's sake, Charles, I'm just trying to come to a com-promise. Something we both can live with."

"I will never compromise. Strong men don't compromise—Andrew Carnegie said that, as I recall."

"But not to his wife, I bet."

It was a lost cause, getting rid of that chair. Rose wondered now why she'd made such a fuss about it. The television was on but the sound was muted. She and Charles always muted the ads. He considered them an affront to his intelligence, and she hated the fact that they were always so much louder than the regular programming. They did it to get your attention, of course. So the only solution was to turn the sound off. Which meant you had to keep watching the damn things in order to turn the sound up again when they were over. Either way, they had you.

Charles looked up and smiled. "Sleeping Beauty. How are you feeling?"

"Better, thanks. My headache's gone and I don't feel so stuffed up. I'll go in tomorrow—I'm not sick enough to stay home another day. Did you eat?"

He nodded. "I did. Morgan didn't want anything. She's gone to meet a friend."

"She has? Oh, good. I'm glad to hear that."

And she was. Partly because it seemed that every time she and her daughter spent more than a minute together they got into an argument. And partly because it worried her that Morgan spent so much time alone at the moment. Or with her parents, which amounted to practically the same thing.

"What are you watching?"

"A nature program. A documentary about bees."

"Are they in trouble?"

"Some," he said. "But not the honey bees. It seems they're thriving."

"Well, that's good news."

"Yes, but the verdict is out when it comes to the effects of climate change."

She took a seat across from him on the sofa. "We need to talk."

It was never the best way to start a conversation. Charles always assumed—and was generally correct—that he'd done or said something to upset her, and they needed to "sort things out." And when Rose got it into her head to "sort things out," she tended to go on about it until those things were thoroughly sorted. Or until Charles was too exhausted to carry on with the discussion and took himself off to bed, leaving her to work it out on her own. Either way, he could probably say good-bye to learning more about the bees.

"What's up?"

"I think you need to talk to Morgan," she said. "I'm worried about her."

"Why? She seems fine to me."

"I think she needs some advice. I tried and it went badly. If anyone's going to talk to her it has to be you. She'll listen to you . . . your opinion matters to her."

"Fine," Charles said, "if that's all you want, I'll talk to her tomorrow. But I don't think it'll do much good. If she and Ian are finished, it's their decision. I can't see what I could say that would change her mind." He reached for the remote.

"I'm not talking about her and Ian," Rose said. "And can you please not turn the sound back on just yet?"

Obediently, Charles placed the remote back in its holder.

"I want you to help her make up her mind about her Ph.D."

"Oh. That."

"Yes, that. If she's definitely not going back to school, or going back to Ian, what is she going to do? She says she wants to travel but she's made no plans. And she doesn't have any money even if she did. I think she's having a crisis of confidence. Did that ever happen to you, when you were working on your doctorate?"

"Every other week."

"And what did you do about it?"

"I kept going. I didn't really have a choice. My mum had told everyone who'd listen I was going to be a university professor. She'd tell random shop clerks, 'He's reading History. Of course, he'll be writing it soon. He's very talented.' If I'd quit I could never have told her—the shock would have killed her."

It would take more than that to kill Gladys, Rose thought, but she and Charles maintained the fiction that his mother was a frail old lady, perpetually at death's door and liable to cross over at a moment's notice. It was easier, and less painful for Charles, than having to admit his mother was a name-dropping shrew who was simply too mean to die.

"Well, then," Rose said, "you need to tell her that. She thinks everything was always easy for you. Popular athlete, straight-A student. And a teacher who was voted number one on campus by the student union."

"Who was?"

"You were."

"I was?" He seemed honestly puzzled.

"Yes, several times."

"Who told you that?"

"A bunch of people. Garnet for one. And Bernie. Good grief, Charles, you can't tell me you don't remember?"

"I guess I don't."

They were quiet for a moment, and it was then that she realized that the rain, which had been the counterpoint to every conversation for almost a week, had stopped. The moon had risen and was faintly visible behind the dark, low-level clouds. Nimbostratus: low clouds accompanied by moderate precipitation. One of a handful of trivia retained from grade ten geography. Cirrus, stratus, cumulus, nimbostratus. Cirrostratus, cirrocumulus, altocumulus, cumulonimbus, altostratus and . . . stratocumulus, that was the other one. Cooks shall create nifty chocolate cookies and carefully add salt. And Mr. Horlick and his yardstick, stabbing the blackboard each time he made a point. Went on vacation to the Caribbean and drowned the following year.

"Rose?" She turned her gaze from the window to see Charles watching her with interest.

"You were a million miles away," he said.

"Sorry." She ran a hand over the sofa cushions, smoothing them out. "Do you think we made a mistake? With the kids, I mean. Pushing them to go on to university."

"Did we push them? I don't think we did. They always expected to get a degree, didn't they?"

"Did they? Jason was always into music, remember? He taught himself to play the guitar. And his piano teacher said he had a real ear for music."

"Yes, and if you remember he wouldn't take the time to practice."

"Maybe we should have made him. We let him stop taking lessons just when he was getting good."

"So we should've pushed him to keep practicing and *not* pushed him to go to college, is that it?"

"I don't know. Maybe. I mean, you and I aren't musical so we probably didn't encourage it as much as we should have. We just assumed he'd do something else. And he did."

Charles shifted in his chair. Conversations like this made him uneasy, she knew. The past was the past—you did what you felt was right at the time. Self-recrimination was a waste of time. "If he was meant to be a musician nothing we could have said or done would have stopped him," he said. "And I've certainly never heard him complain that we forced him into anything."

"Morgan thinks it's our assumptions that shaped her future. We assumed our kids would go on to university and they did. We never considered any other route."

"Why would we? What else would she have done? Gone back-packing through Europe? Climbed Mount Everest?"

"Don't get angry. I'm just speculating. She might have become a poet. Marie says her writing shows an intuitive sensibility to the surrounding world."

"Marie thinks the sun shines out of Morgan's backside," Charles said. "She thinks our kids are perfect."

"Don't you?"

"Of course, but I'm their father. I'm allowed to be biased."

The news ticker crawling along the bottom of the screen was announcing breaking news: another shooting somewhere in the States. Three injured, one dead. Hopefully, not kids this time. Nope, sorry—a high school somewhere in Washington. Tomorrow her Twitter feed would be inundated with "thoughts and prayers" going out to the families. And nothing would change.

Rose turned her attention away from the television—it was too sad, all these children being murdered. "So what do you think?"

Charles was still watching the screen. "I think someone should start shooting the lawmakers who support the NRA," he said. "That'd be a start."

"No, I mean about Morgan."

"I think we should let her make her own decisions. I did. My father wanted me to play professional football; my mother assumed I'd be a doctor. I chose to teach. Kids make their own decisions. We're not as influential as we think. Trust me." He saw her face and realized it wasn't enough. "I'll talk to her, I promise."

"Tomorrow?"

"Soon."

"Talk to her tomorrow, Charles. She needs to make a decision. She's in limbo and it's driving me crazy."

19.

RYAN WAS MISSING. HE WASN'T IN THE LIBRARY IN his usual place, and he wasn't at the back using the computers. Rose tried to remember the last time she'd seen him outside the grocery store, with or without the dog. A week, maybe more. She couldn't shake the feeling that something had happened to him. After fretting about it off and on for most of the day, she decided to leave work early and go looking for him.

There were dozens of homeless shelters in the city, some just for men, some for youth, and some for women and families. At least four of the ones for men were operated by the Salvation Army. Assuming that Ryan would stay somewhere within walking distance, she started with Haven House on East Cordova. It was right downtown, just a fifteen-minute walk from the library. Ryan, she thought, could manage that easily.

The supervisor on duty at Haven House was friendly but firm: there were confidentiality issues, he said. He couldn't give out names. "Try the Gospel Mission on Hastings," he suggested. "They operate a daily soup kitchen. The person you're looking for might not stay there, but he might drop in for a bite to eat."

The young man she spoke to at the mission was willing to help but he, too, said his hands were tied. And names didn't mean much anyway. "Lots of our clients don't use their real names," he said. "They don't always want to be found."

"Even by their families?"

"Sometimes especially by their families."

Rose thanked him and turned to leave, but he followed her out onto the street. "Look," he said, "if you're really trying to find your friend, I can make a suggestion. You see that group over by the bus stop?" He indicated a handful of young men standing on the sidewalk, smoking. "They're some of our regulars. If you were to buy a pack of cigarettes and share them out, they'd likely be willing to help you out. They may not know this Ryan person but they might have an idea where to find him."

Rose thanked him and made her way across the street to a convenience store on the corner. "I'd like to buy some cigarettes," she told the kid behind the counter.

"What kind?"

"I'm not sure. I don't smoke."

"So why are you buying cigarettes?"

"That's a good question." She smiled, suddenly feeling a little nervous. She thought the kid might smile back but he didn't. "I'm buying them for a friend of mine," she said.

"What does he smoke?"

"I'm not sure."

A man had entered the store and was standing behind her, waiting to pay.

"What's the most popular brand?" Rose asked.

The kid stared at her like she'd asked him to name the capital of Uzbekistan.

She tried again. "What do you sell most of?"

"We sell a lot of Marlboros."

"Great, I'll have a package of those."

"Full, originals, or smooth?"

"Oh, I don't know . . ."

The man behind her gave an impatient cough; Rose turned around and apologized for holding up the line.

Mollified, he suggested she buy a pack of fulls. "I smoke those. If you're buying for a guy, he probably doesn't smoke smooths."

"Thank you!" She turned back to the kid and asked for a pack of Marlboro fulls.

"What size?"

"Size?"

"King size or regular?"

This time the man answered for her: "Give her a pack of regular."

The kid lifted the covering from the overhead rack and took down a pack of Marlboro fulls cigarettes.

"That'll be nineteen fifty," he said, ringing it up on the cash register.

"Really?" Rose was shocked. How could people afford to smoke when it cost that much? She handed the kid a twenty and waited for her change.

"It's the government," the man behind her said. "They tax the hell out of cigarettes."

"My sister used to roll her own," Rose said. "Now I see why."

"Best thing is just not to smoke," he said. "I quit all the time—easiest thing in the world. The hard part is not starting again."

She was shy about approaching the young men outside the hostel. She felt old and over-dressed. Why the hell hadn't she gone home and changed into something less . . . *bougie* before coming here? She looked like a social worker. Or worse: maybe they'd think she was a cop. They moved aside to make way for her as she approached; she smiled, making eye contact. Held out the cigarette package like a totem, a symbol of friendship: I come in peace.

"Would you like a cigarette?" This to the first man who smiled at her, older than the others, good-looking in a kind of Colin Farrell-gone-to-pot kind of way.

He didn't hesitate. "Sure thing. Thanks!"

Encouraged, she offered the package to the others, urged them to take a couple. They demurred at first, said they didn't want to take all her smokes. The first man tucked his cigarettes away in his coat pocket and asked if she wanted a light.

"Oh, yes. Thank you."

The package now contained no more than four or five cigarettes. She took one out, handed the package to the Colin Farrell guy, and placed the cigarette between her lips, holding it between her index and middle fingers. Did she look like someone who did this regularly? Probably not. It felt wrong. Made her think of the times she tried to smoke as a teenager, wanting to be cool. Her sister made fun of her, her smoking friends rolled their eyes. And she never managed to inhale without coughing.

He struck a match and held it to the tip of her cigarette, cupping his hand around the flame to keep it from going out. It was a surprisingly intimate gesture and made her self-conscious. She inhaled—too deeply. The heat seared her lungs, burned her throat. She coughed, several times.

"These are stronger than I'm used to," she said, when she could finally speak. Her eyes were watering—she couldn't imagine trying it again.

"Yeah, they're pretty strong," Colin said. (She couldn't stop thinking of him that way, now that she'd started.) "You're probably more used to Belmonts or one of them ladies' smokes." He was being kind. She'd given herself away and they all knew it.

It seemed like a good time to bring up the reason for her appearance among them. "I'm wondering if you can help me," she said. "I'm trying to find someone. I was hoping you might know him. Or have seen him somewhere?"

She could see it in their eyes: they were on their guard. No one spoke and so she smiled and tried again. "He's the son of . . . of a friend of mine. He came up to me the other day in the parking lot, I hadn't seen him in a long time, he said he just wanted to say hello . . ." She had the distinct feeling they weren't buying this. Maybe she should have made up a story—said it was her son. Or grandson. "His name is Ryan. I don't think he has a place to stay and I just wanted, you know, to help him. If

I could." She was getting nowhere. "I'm sorry. I didn't mean to be intrusive or anything. I just thought maybe one of you might have seen him around . . ."

"Where's he hang out?" This from one of the others, a kid with shaggy blonde hair who looked like he should still be in school. Middle school, in fact.

"I used to see him in front of the Whole Foods on Robson. And he likes to go to the library to read in the mornings."

Several of the men nodded and she wondered if they, too, found refuge in the library.

"You tried those places?"

She nodded. "He hasn't been outside the grocery store in a while. Or in the library. I'm kind of worried about him, to be honest."

The man who lit her cigarette—Colin—spoke up. "What'd you say his name was?"

"Ryan. It was Albertini when he was small but I don't know if he goes by that now. His dad's name was something different . . . he might use his dad's name."

"You got a picture?"

She shook her head. And then she remembered: yes, of course, the selfie she took in the parkade. She'd forgotten all about it. "Wait a minute, I do have something. I don't know how good it is . . ."

For a picture taken in a hurry in an underground parking lot, it was surprisingly good. She looked very uncomfortable, but there was nothing new in that—she hated having her picture taken and always looked awkward in photos. Ryan, on the other hand, looked better in the picture than he did in person. His skin looked healthier and the way he was smiling, you couldn't see his teeth. A stranger, looking at the picture, would assume they were related—mother and son. Or aunt and favourite nephew, perhaps.

They passed the phone around; one young man studied it longer than the others, before announcing he was pretty sure he knew this guy. "It's Pug," he said.

"Lemme see." His friend took the phone from him and studied it.

"Yeah, you're right. That's definitely Pug. You said his name was Ryan?"

"That's his name, yes. But you call him Pug?" It was an odd name, she thought, for someone with Ryan's build: tall, thin, slightly stooped. Maybe it was because of his eyes; they were brown and somewhat protruding. But they said no, it was because of his dog.

"He's got this little pug he walks for some old lady on Pender Street. It's not his dog but he takes care of it, walks it four or five days a week."

"Does he stay here, in the hostel?" she asked.

"Why? You lookin' for him for a reason?"

They were closing ranks, she could see that. Passing around the cigarettes had given her an opening but now they were suspicious: what did someone like her want with a guy like Pug? Once again, she explained about the meeting in the parking lot. How she had been left with a feeling that he'd approached her for a reason.

"I just thought maybe I could help. He said he likes to read. I work at the library. I was thinking there might be some part-time work there, helping the librarians."

She was making it up as she went along. The fact was, she had no influence when it came to hiring, and the most she could hope for was that he might find some work as a volunteer. This would mean convincing Julie, who was in charge of volunteers, to take him on. She couldn't make it seem like a personal favour—or rather, maybe she should. Julie liked having people in her debt. Rose hated the idea of being beholden to the woman but if it would get Ryan some work, she'd do it.

At any rate, the mention of a job seemed to do the trick. The young man who first recognized Ryan said that Pug came by now and then to play cards. "But he don't stay here. He's got a tent set up in MacLean Park. He comes by at lunchtime sometimes. Sometimes he has the dog with him and he gets one of us to take him while he goes in and eats. You could try then."

His friend had a better suggestion. "He walks the dog in Strathcona Park. They got a place where you can let the dogs off their leashes and he likes to do that, let the dog run around, eh?"

Rose knew the area. She and Charles had rented a house in Strathcona when they were first living together. A run-down row house that had likely succumbed to gentrification years ago—if it was still standing, it would be worth a fortune today.

"Do you know when he goes there?" she asked. "What time of day, I mean?"

"Early mornings, I think. He don't do it every day. But it's still your best bet."

"Thanks so much, you've been really helpful. I'll try that."

She turned to leave but the first man, the Colin Farrell man, stopped her.

"Don't forget your cigarettes," he said, holding out the pack.

"Oh, you can keep them," she said, "I don't smoke." She realized as soon as she said it that it was unnecessary after her shameful earlier performance.

But he was kind. "Good," he said. "I'm glad to hear it. Take care of yourself now."

He said it in a way that made her think he was flirting with her, just a little. But that was silly; men, even the ones who are homeless, do not flirt with a woman about to turn sixty.

20.

ROSE PARKED HER CAR OUTSIDE THE PARK GATE AND
changed into her runners. At the last minute that morning she'd
thought to bring them, and it was a good thing—the grass was
soaked and the mud was ankle deep. A sign posted by the entrance
reminded users to pick up after their dogs; a nearby bin marked
Dog Waste Only sported a roll of green poop bags. She hoped
people were using them.

Rose checked her phone: 11:45. She needed to be back home
by two o'clock in order to give Morgan the car. She had offered to
drive the bridesmaids to Kim's wedding at four. A few days earlier,
Rose had asked her if she was sorry not to be one of the bridesmaids herself, and Morgan gave her one of those looks.

"Really, Mom? Are you serious?"

"Well, I just thought . . . I mean, you and Kim have been friends
for such a long time . . ."

"Kim and Kevin have been living together for seven years.
They're getting married to get her parents off her back. As far as I'm
concerned, the wedding is a non-event. So trust me, I'm fine with
not being a bridesmaid."

The forecast was for sunny breaks later in the day and rain returning later in the week. Right now it was cool and overcast. She should have worn her winter jacket. And gloves. Hands buried in her pockets, she set off along the trail, mindful of puddles and keeping an eye out for dog walkers. A young Lab bounded towards her. She stopped and waited for him to approach, holding her hand down for inspection: *Easy, now. Don't jump on me. Please.* His owner gave a sharp whistle and the dog immediately sat, looking ridiculously pleased with himself.

"Good boy," she said, patting him on the head.

The dog's owner put him on a leash and gave him a treat. "He's friendly, just a little boisterous."

"How old is he?" Rose asked.

"Three and a half, but in his head he's still a pup. Aren't you, Chester? You're just a kid inside, right?" Chester seemed to agree; he leapt up and placed his front paws on the man's chest, doing his level best to lick his owner's chin. "All right, fella, calm down. Time to go home."

"Have you seen someone walking a pug here today?" Rose said.

"A pug? You mean Oscar?"

"I don't know the name of the dog. The person who walks him is named Ryan."

The man smiled. "I only know the names of the dogs. If Oscar's the one you're looking for, a young man walks him here, three, four times a week. I didn't see him today, though. Sorry. Have a good one."

Rose thanked him and moved on. Apart from Chester and his human, the park was pretty empty. A young woman about Morgan's age ran down the path towards her; she was wearing headphones and had a Weimaraner in tow. As she passed, Rose smiled but the young woman didn't make eye contact. Farther on, the path widened, revealing an open area about the size of a football field. Several dogs and their owners were making use of the park: a frenetic terrier rushed madly back and forth, a German shepherd raced to retrieve a Frisbee, and a large shaggy mutt of no clear extraction was letting off steam by barking at no one or nothing in particular. Rose kept to the perimeter and completed a circuit of the field. There was no sign of a pug and no one who looked like Ryan.

It wasn't until she'd lapped the field twice and was heading back that she negotiated a bend in the path and saw him coming towards her. He was walking with his head down, holding on to the dog's leash with one hand, his other hand jammed into the pocket of his familiar black hoodie. As he approached he moved to the side to let her pass.

"Ryan?"

He looked up, startled, and at first seemed not to recognize her.

"It's me," she said. "Rose. Remember?"

"Oh, hey. How are you?"

Now that he was looking directly at her, she saw that he was bruised on one side of his forehead. He had a cut on his lip that appeared to have been stitched, and one eye was swollen.

"I'm fine," she said, "but how are you? I haven't seen you for a while."

"I was in the hospital. I only just got out this morning."

"Oh my! Did you fall?"

"Not exactly." The little pug pulled at the leash, eager to get to the exercise area. Ryan bent down and ruffled his fur. "Hang on, Oscar, gimme a minute."

"Can I pet him?" she asked.

"Sure! He's friendly. You're friendly, aren't you, Oscar? You like getting petted."

Rose let Oscar sniff her hand, then stroked his soft, glossy coat. The dog was a little on the heavy side but was obviously well cared for.

"You like dogs?" Ryan said.

"I do. Nice ones, anyway. And this is a nice one, aren't you, Oscar?"

"I bring him here two, three times a week so's he can run around and play with the other dogs. Mrs. Larkin, his owner, she's a nice lady but she has trouble walking. She likes me to walk him and give him some exercise. You missed me this week, didn't you, buddy? You didn't get your walks."

"It's great that you do that. I hope she pays you."

"We do a trade. I walk Oscar and she teaches me piano."

"Really? That's wonderful. How's it going?"

"Okay, I guess. I'm a slow learner. But I like it."

He smiled and she noticed something different. "Your tooth," she said, "it's back!"

"Yeah, that was kind of a lucky thing. When I was in the hospital, they screwed it back in. It got knocked out a while back and I've been carrying it around in my pocket. They cleaned it up and fixed it. Pretty nice of them, I thought."

"Did they charge you for it?"

"No, they weren't going to. I offered to come in and clean floors or serve food—you know, to pay for it. But they said they had people to do that."

"Can I ask what happened, Ryan? Why did you end up in the hospital?"

"Aw, it was just one of those things, Mrs. Addams. I'm okay now."

He didn't want to talk about it but she felt she needed to know. If he was sick, if he needed medical treatment, she wanted to help.

"I'm sorry," she said, "I'm being nosy, aren't I? But I've been thinking about you since—well, since we met in the parkade. I was wondering how you're doing."

"Yeah. Well, thanks. That's nice of you. I should get going—yeah, okay, okay, buddy, we're going."

"Maybe I'll see you at the library?"

"Oh, sure. Probably."

"I was thinking there could be a job there for you, if you're interested." He said nothing and she was embarrassed. Did it sound like she was doling out charity? "I just thought, you like to read. And they're always looking for people to help out managing the stacks. They have volunteers who do it, usually, but I'm pretty sure they'd pay to have someone come in a few hours a week and help out with the books. Volunteers can be kind of unreliable. And of course they're getting old . . ."

"The books?"

"No, the volunteers."

"Oh. Yeah."

Oscar was straining at the leash and Ryan was preoccupied with holding him back. Was he even listening?

"If you're interested, I'll talk to Julie when I get back and see what she thinks. Is there somewhere I can reach you?"

He shrugged and smiled. "I'm kinda hard to get hold of. Maybe you could give me your number and I'll call you. Is that okay?"

"Of course."

Rose was delighted—this, at least, was progress. She retrieved a pen from her purse and wrote her cell phone number on the back of an envelope. Ryan studied it carefully, then tucked it into his coat pocket.

"So you'll call me, right?"

"Sure. Okay, I better go. It was nice to see you, Mrs. Addams. Take care, eh?"

She made a sudden decision as he headed up the path. "Ryan, wait!" He stopped and turned around. "Can you come for dinner on Thanksgiving? If you don't have other plans?"

That was a stupid thing to say, she thought. Why on earth would he have other plans? Still, it's what she'd say to a regular person, wasn't it? And he could possibly have other plans. It'd be prejudicial not to ask.

"Can I think about it?"

"Of course. Just call and let me know."

"Okay," he said. "I'll call you." And with that he and the pug headed up the path and disappeared around the bend.

Charles was waiting for her when she got home, and he was fuming. He waited until Morgan left to pick up the bridesmaids, and then let her have it.

"I can't believe you put him up to it!"

For a moment, Rose was confused. "What are you talking about? Put who up to what?"

"Garnet, of course. Asking me to chair that damn alumni project."

Oh, right, she thought. They'd had lunch, and Garnet had brought up the project.

"Why would you think I'd want to take that on? I left the college because I was sick to death of committees and budgets and working with academics. I have no desire to go back to any of it."

"All right, fine! You don't have to shout."

"I am not shouting. I can't believe you went over my head like that."

"Over your head? Charles, you're not my boss . . ."

"It's not funny, Rose. You can wipe that smirk off your face."

Well, it was funny, just a little. He was acting as if she'd betrayed him—given away state secrets or something. "I was just trying to help."

"Did I *ask* for your help? Did I say I *wanted* your help?"

There was really no answer to this. "So you turned him down," she said.

"Yes, I turned him down. And then I had to explain to him that I'm not depressed, actually, or even close to it."

"Who said you were depressed?"

"*You* did. According to Garnet you think I'm one gin and tonic away from slitting my wrists."

"That's ridiculous."

"Yes, it is. I've never been happier. As for the alumni project, it's a stupid idea—I don't know who suggested it in the first place."

"*You* did."

"I most certainly did not."

"You *did*. Garnet told me—he said the project was your idea."

"Well, if it was I must have meant it as a joke. And I definitely didn't intend to get involved in the damn thing."

"Why don't you give yourself time to think about it? You might feel differently in a month or so."

"I don't need time to think about it. It's a ridiculous suggestion. I have better things to do with my time than accept make-work projects from my friends."

"Better things like what? Exactly what *are* you going to do with your time, Charles?"

"I told you," he said, "I'm going to write a book."

The book? Really? As far as she knew he hadn't so much as sat down at the computer. According to Morgan, her father spent the morning reading. In the afternoon he walked down to the cafe in the village where he read the paper and drank too much coffee. Unless he was making notes on the back of the coffee shop napkins and stuffing them into his pockets, she saw no signs of a writer in the early stages of creation.

"So maybe you should get started."

"Maybe I should."

"So will you?"

"I will. There's plenty of time. I need to let the ideas percolate." He went to the fridge, took out a large bottle of tonic water and set it on the counter. "It's going to be a wonderful book, Rose. You know that, don't you?"

"Yes, of course it is," she muttered, not trusting herself to say anything further.

21.

Of course! Have you told Charles?

Not yet. Waiting for the right moment.

Let me know how it goes. What can I bring?

I'll get back to you. There's an issue.

???

Call me later.

The issue was with Lee. According to Jason, she wanted to have Thanksgiving dinner at their apartment. Their very small, very stylish apartment on the twenty-second floor of a downtown high-rise. It had a spectacular view of the mountains and could comfortably accommodate something like four people. Five, in a pinch. It would also mean taking the elevator, something Rose avoided when she could—although some elevators were simply unavoidable.

She tried not to be overly negative when she talked to Jason about it. "We'd never fit everyone around that little table of yours," she said. "And how is your Dad to cook the turkey there? Would you want him to cook it here and bring it over?"

"Lee was thinking we'd do it buffet style," he said. Seeing the look on her face, he added, "We don't always have to sit around the table. We can mix it up a little."

"Mix it up a little? Jason, it's *Thanksgiving*. You don't 'mix up' Thanksgiving. Your father would never go for it."

Which was when he confessed he'd already spoken to Charles and his dad was all for it. "He said he'd be happy to have someone else do the cooking for a change. I think he's getting tired of the responsibility."

When confronted on the issue, Charles tried to back down. "I didn't say I was all for it. At least, I don't think I did. I did say I thought it might be nice to let someone else do some of the cooking. Wouldn't you like to get out of all that cleaning up afterwards?"

"The cleaning up is part of it. It's part of the ritual!"

"I didn't know we had a ritual. Anyway, it's just a meal. I don't know why you're making such a fuss about it."

There were times when Rose wondered if she and her husband were even remotely on the same page. First he quits work on the spur of the moment, now he decides Thanksgiving is "just a meal." What was next—Christmas is "just a day"?

For once, Morgan sided with her mother. "I don't want to stand around Jason's place nibbling on stuffed mushrooms and turkey skewers. I want to sit around the table like always. I can help with the cooking, if you want."

"You . . . cook?"

"When I have to, yes. I'm not completely incompetent."

Not wishing to lose her as an ally, Rose hurried to assure Morgan that she was just taken aback, a little, by the offer but very pleased to hear it.

"We'll all pitch in," she said. "And I'll ask Lee to make something as well. Just to, you know, smooth things over."

"Good idea," Morgan said. "We don't want her feelings to be hurt."

Fat chance of that, Rose thought, but kept it to herself.

Lee took it surprisingly well, saying she'd simply been hoping to take a little of the burden away from Charles, given his situation. Rose said it wasn't a burden; neither she nor Charles looked at Thanksgiving that way, and sorry, but what "situation" was she referring to? Lee said she had the impression that Charles was having difficulty adjusting to retirement.

Rose was happy to set her straight. "He was a little bored in the beginning," she said, "but he's getting excited about a book he wants to write. He's very enthused about it." Enthused, was that a word? It sounded wrong when you said it. "It's keeping him busy," she added, lying through her teeth.

"That's wonderful," Lee said. "He's such a sweetheart. It's so important to keep your mind active, isn't it? At his stage of life?"

"Yes, well, he's not quite into geezerdom yet."

"No, of course not, but mental stimulation is so important, isn't it? We have to keep challenging our brains if we want to stay fit. I've been reading a wonderful book about detoxing the brain. I'll send you the link."

Steering the subject away from the demise of her husband's brain—and hers, which was obviously the subtext of the conversation—Rose suggested Lee should feel free to bring something for Thanksgiving dinner.

"Maybe something your mother cooked when you were growing up," she suggested.

"Oh, Mother never cooked, she was too busy ruling the world to spend time in the kitchen. We ate TV dinners mostly, or takeout." She laughed and added, "She was a terrible mother, which is why I never wanted to have children."

Well, that explained it. Rose put down the phone and wondered if she would be more sympathetic to Lee if she knew more of what Marie liked to call "her backstory." A moment later her phone dinged: Lee had sent a link to *Switch on Your Brain: The Key to Peak Happiness, Thinking, and Health.* On second thought, no, she wouldn't.

Once it was settled that dinner would be at their place, Rose decided to make it a gathering of the regulars. Marie and Jeff had already agreed to come, and Bernie called to say she was missing Charles now that he'd gone and quit on her—her words, exactly—and if Marie and Jeff and Bernie and Richard were going to be there, then there was no option but to include Garnet. And Lauren, since she was now living under his roof and preparing to have his child.

Except it wasn't his child, was it? Charles said it didn't matter who provided the sperm; the father was the one who raised the child. Or was planning to raise her. Because Lauren was convinced she was having a girl.

"Everybody says so," she said when Rose called to invite her to the dinner. "I'm carrying high, which they say means a girl."

You'd hardly know she was carrying at all, to look at her. Mind you, that's how it was with your first. Rose remembered being more than a little smug when she was pregnant with Morgan; she was well into her sixth month before she started to show. And then with Jason she was letting out her pants almost as soon as she knew she was pregnant.

"How are you feeling?" Rose said.

"Awful. I throw up half the day. That's another sign I'm having a girl."

"It is?"

"Definitely. They're not old wives' tales, you know, they're based on fact. The sicker you are the more likely you're having a girl."

Rose was surprised at Lauren saying "old wives' tales," but perhaps she was being too judgey. "I guess it's too early for the ultrasound to show much."

"I think she looks like a tadpole. But Garnet's impressed. He's got it framed and hanging in his office."

Garnet had accompanied Lauren to the clinic a few days earlier. Afterwards, they stopped by to show them the image of an amorphous little blob captured by the technician. It was touching, really, the protective way Garnet cradled the photo. He seemed overwhelmed by what nature had wrought.

"The miracle of conception," he said, gazing at the picture with the kind of reverence he usually reserved for a good bottle of Scotch. "It makes you think, doesn't it? What are we here for? Out, out, brief candle! Life is but a walking shadow . . ."

"To be or not to be," Rose interjected, before he could finish the quote.

"Mock me if you will, but you see before you a happy man. Nay, a contented man, which is even better. And it's all thanks to this darling girl."

The "darling girl" grimaced. "If we're going to stay together, you're going to have to stop saying nay."

Rose made a list of everything she needed to buy. And, more particularly, everything that *couldn't* be served. Nothing with tree nuts because of Charles' allergies; he could still eat peanuts, though, which surprised Rose until Charles informed her, with a hint of condescension, that peanuts are *legumes,* don'tcha know? He said it as if even a child should know the difference, but Rose refused to take it personally. Eight out of ten people would assume a peanut was a nut, if you asked them.

Anyway, it was hard to keep up with the allergy situation these days. When she was young there was one kid in her class who had an allergy to tomatoes, and everyone figured she was just spoiled. None of the others liked tomatoes either but they had to eat them. Nowadays, though, everybody had something. Bernie was allergic to red wine—something to do with the histamines—and her brother, Richard, couldn't have gluten. As for Lauren, she called to say she'd recently switched to a vegetarian diet so they weren't to take it personally if she didn't eat any turkey.

"It's better for the baby," she told Rose, who wasn't convinced.

"Shouldn't you be getting a lot of protein?" she said. "I mean, they say you need a balanced diet for your health and the baby's. You might be putting yourself in danger."

"You should see the list of supplements I'm taking," Lauren said. "Believe me, I've got it covered. And I'm still doing dairy, so I'm getting plenty of vitamin D. Honest, Rose, I'm perfectly healthy. And so's the baby."

"How's the nausea?"

"That's the one problem. I'm still throwing up two–three times a day and my appetite is lousy. So don't expect me to eat very much— I'll probably spend most of the night in the bathroom."

Well, *that's* something to look forward to, Rose thought. Perhaps she should have suggested Lauren stay home, but that would sound unfriendly. And she wanted her to come. It was important to have as many younger people at the dinner as possible, given that Ryan was coming. With Morgan, Jason, Lee, and Lauren in attendance, the age ratio would be nicely balanced. She wouldn't have to feel she was subjecting him to an evening of oldies. And anyway, she liked Lauren. Since meeting her that first time a few weeks ago, her feelings toward her had changed. She might be too young for Garnet but she was smart enough in her own way and nobody's fool, as Rose's grandmother might have said.

As she explained to Marie, "She's got his number, for sure, and she doesn't put up with any nonsense. I never thought I'd say this, but she may be finally getting Garnet to stand up and fly right, you know?"

Overlooking the clichés, Marie agreed. "She's something, that girl. Although I continue to wonder what the hell is she doing with him? Does he have some secret fortune stashed away that we don't know about?"

"I doubt it. Charles always says the only good thing about being a prof is that you get paid to sound like a know-it-all. Money doesn't come into it. At least it didn't in our case and it probably doesn't for Garnet."

22.

TWO WEEKS PASSED BEFORE SHE HEARD BACK FROM Ryan. He had resumed his sessions in the library, but his head was always bent over a book and she didn't want to disturb him. Occasionally she saw him outside the grocery store. He didn't look up—it seemed, in fact, that he was meditating there. The cardboard sign, Homeless Please Give, was gone, and anyway, now that they'd been introduced, if you will, it felt odd to continue to give him handouts.

When he did finally call, she almost didn't pick up. First of all, it was after 10:00 and nobody calls that late—at least nobody she knew. And secondly, she didn't recognize the number. It was only after the fourth ring that it suddenly occurred to her it might be Ryan. It was. He apologized for not calling earlier but said he had to wait until he could use somebody's phone.

"I can't talk long," he said. "The guy's waiting for a call. So, like, how are you?"

Rose tried to sound casual but pleased. Which she was. She was afraid she had scared him off, tracking him down in the park the way she did. His calling her like this was a good sign.

"I'm fine," she said. "I'm so glad you called. How's Oscar?"

"Oh, he's great. He really liked seeing you the other day."

Well, this is a little odd, she thought. "He did?"

"Yeah, he's got a good, you know, shit-detector when it comes to people. He likes you."

"Did he . . . did he tell you that?"

There was a pause. "Dogs don't talk, Mrs. Addams."

"No, of course not. I just meant . . ."

"You were thinking maybe I'm a nut job, eh?"

"Oh, no, I'm sorry!"

Ryan was laughing. "It's okay, no, really, it's funny. Hey, I have my problems but that's not one of them."

"I talked to Julie," she said. "You know, the woman at the library? I asked her about hiring you part time and she said she'd consider it. I mean, if you're interested."

"Oh. Thank you, Mrs. Addams. That was really nice of you. I'm a little busy right now, though. Sorry, hang on a minute."

Rose could hear someone in the background and after a moment Ryan came back on and said he had to go, the guy needed to use his phone.

"So, about dinner?" she asked, and made a mental note: for god's sake, remember to tell Charles. Don't spring this on him, whatever you do.

"Right. Yeah, I'll come."

"Wonderful! I can give you the address, if you've got a pen or pencil on you."

"Is it where you used to live?"

"No, we moved to the North Shore quite a while ago. Before Morgan started high school."

"Um, hang on a minute."

There was a pause; she heard him talking to someone nearby and in a moment he was back on the phone. "I got a pen," he said. "I'll write it on my hand."

She gave him the address and wondered if he'd think to copy it onto a piece of paper before taking a shower.

"Got it," he said. "What time should I come?"

"Around five. I can come and pick you up if you like."

"No, it's okay, I can get there."

"Okay, good. I'm glad you're coming. I'm looking forward to it."

"Me too. See you."

She started to add that there was a bus now that ran right past the door but he'd already hung up. Would he be able to figure that out? Rose hadn't taken a bus in years but street people took them all the time. Didn't they?

Saturday morning she woke in a panic thinking about Brussels sprouts. She'd left them till the last minute and now, the day before the dinner, would there be any left? The turkey had been ordered six weeks ago and was cooling its heels in the garage this very minute, but she was behind the eight ball with the sprouts. Luckily she'd picked up frozen cranberries last week, but she still hadn't bought bread cubes for the stuffing. If she had to, she could grab a couple of boxes of Stove Top; who, really, would be the wiser?

Forgoing her morning coffee, Rose put on a warm sweater and a pair of sweat pants and drove to the village market. It was crowded with last-minute shoppers like herself, mostly men out doing errands under their wives' supervision. Or so she assumed. She gathered a handful of pathetic Brussels sprouts that had been picked over and rejected in the vegetable section and made up for it with extra parsnips. And, glory be, there were enough dried bread cubes on hand to stuff a hundred turkeys. At the last minute she remembered Charles had asked her to be sure to pick up unbleached all-purpose flour. Morgan had put in a special order for pie, and pies were his specialty.

"Make two," she said, "so we have a choice."

"Will do," Charles said. "Do you have a preference?"

"Anything but pumpkin."

"Fair enough."

It was a huge concession on his part. When Charles first came to Canada he embraced everything about Thanksgiving and that included pumpkin. Never having tasted it before, he did his research and found that it was low in calories and loaded with vitamins and minerals. He told his children it was the perfect food, said he for one would be happy to eat it all year long. His children didn't buy it. Morgan said even the smell of it turned her stomach; for years she boycotted Starbucks from the end of August to the beginning of December, simply because of their pumpkin spice lattes.

On her way back from the store it occurred to her she still hadn't told Charles about Ryan. Now she wondered how he'd take it. Look how he'd attacked her over the alumni project. He was so unpredictable these days; how might he react to the news of a complete stranger, almost, turning up at the dinner table? The old Charles would have welcomed it. When it came to holiday gatherings, he usually liked a full house.

These days, though, he was different. Morgan was right: it was impossible to put her finger on it but Charles was just a bit "off," if that was the right word. You could still have a decent conversation with him, but you couldn't count on him to follow up.

She decided to tell him at dinner. Well, she'd have to, wouldn't she? And it would be easier with Morgan there to deflect . . . what? What exactly should she deflect? Too many questions from Charles, perhaps. Questions she'd rather not answer.

"Do you remember Ryan?"

They were eating Chinese. Rose had picked it up on her way home from the grocery store as a treat for Morgan and Charles. She wasn't a fan, particularly, mainly because she was paranoid about MSG, which gave her a headache and a tingling in her neck and cheeks. They *said* they didn't use it, but how would you know? Charles insisted it was perfectly safe, but he could eat a buffalo and not suffer ill effects. The man had a cast-iron stomach. Now she added, as if she'd only just thought of it, "The little boy who stayed with us when you and Jason were young. Remember him?"

"Ryan," Morgan said. "I remember him. He was really sweet. I told everybody he was my boyfriend."

"Really?" This was news to Rose. Morgan saw the look on her face and laughed.

"I was *six*, Mom. All the girls in my class had boyfriends. We chased them at recess."

Charles wanted to know if they caught them and Morgan said she didn't remember.

"I had a girlfriend when I was six," he said. "A pretty little blonde girl who lived next door. I used to try to grab her ribbon out of her hair—she hated that. She used to say, 'Charlie Addams, you are the most awful boy in the world.'" Smiling at the memory, he added, "I told my mum I was going to marry her when I grew up."

"What did your mom say?" Morgan asked.

"She told me I was going to *be* somebody when I grew up, and I'd know better than to tie myself to a charwoman's daughter." He laughed. "That was our 'good owd mam.'"

"*Anyway*," Rose continued, "I ran into Ryan the other day, in the library."

"That's amazing!" Morgan exclaimed. "How's he doing?"

"Well, I didn't get to talk to him for long, but I invited him to join us for dinner tomorrow."

"That's fantastic, Mom! I can't wait to see him."

Rose was looking at Charles, waiting for his reaction. "What do you think?" she asked. "Do you mind if Ryan comes for Thanksgiving?"

Her husband frowned. "This was a friend of Jason's?"

"No, Dad," Morgan said. "*Ryan*. His mom was our baby-sitter, remember? And then she took off and he lived with us for a while."

"A year," Rose said. "And then his father came and took him. And we never did hear from Cyndi, his mother." She turned to Charles. "You must remember. You liked him. When Cyndi left you agreed to keep him. You taught him to swim, remember?"

Charles nodded, slowly. "Right," he said. "I remember."

Rose was unconvinced, but she let it go. "I invited him for five. That's when everyone's coming. So we need to get the turkey out of the oven by four."

"If I get up at six," Charles said, "I can get the pies baked before getting the turkey in the oven at eleven. It'll be an early start for you, Morgan, I hope you're up to it."

"I think I can manage it," Morgan said. She had offered to make the stuffing, and help her mother peel the potatoes.

"So," Rose said, "you don't have a problem with Ryan joining us for Thanksgiving dinner?"

Charles smiled. "Not at all. There's always room for one more. What's he done since graduation, I wonder?"

"Graduation? I don't know . . ."

She caught Morgan looking at her father in dismay and hurried to change the subject.

23.

BY 5:00 ON THANKSGIVING DAY, THE COMPANY WAS assembled, all but Ryan, who had become in Rose's mind the guest of honour. Charles had managed to cook on and off for nine hours and not once set off the smoke alarm, and the house was filled with the aroma of sage and onion and freshly-baked pies. Lauren, who had told Rose she wasn't sure she'd be able to keep anything down, was now eyeing the spread with anticipation. She'd brought a side dish of honey-roasted carrots with mint and a bottle of kombucha for those, like her, who wouldn't be drinking.

"It's naturally fermented green tea," she explained, handing the bottle to Rose while Garnet took her coat. "It has no alcohol. And it's very healthy."

Garnet's contribution was a bottle of Scotch although he made a production of announcing that he, personally, would not be imbibing this evening. "As long as the mother of my child is abstaining, I will support her by keeping her company."

"You don't have to," Lauren said. "I honestly don't care if you have a drink."

But Garnet was firm. "O thou invisible spirit of wine, if thou hast no name to be known by, let us call thee devil."

Lauren rolled her eyes. "Fine. Whatever."

Jason and Lee arrived with a dish of sweet potatoes roasted in brown sugar and cinnamon, and nachos with chipotle and pomegranate seeds for a snack. Rose was relieved; she'd fully expected Lee to make something with kale or quinoa. Nothing wrong with either of those, of course, but they don't come under the heading of "festive."

Bernadette arrived and threw herself at Charles like a drowning seaman clutching a life preserver. Richard, who'd come bearing two bottles of white wine and a tray of cornbread muffins, handed his offerings to Rose and tried gently to uncouple them. Bernie was having none of it.

"Oh, Charles," she moaned. "Charles, Charles, Charles."

"Now, now," Charles said, patting her on the back. "It's going to be all right. You mustn't get yourself into a state."

"I can't help it," she said, her face buried in the shawl collar of Charles's cardigan sweater. "I'm sorry, but I can't."

With infinite delicacy, Charles managed to detach himself from her embrace. Helping her off with her coat, he said what he always said when he wanted to please her: "You're looking well, Bernie. Have you lost weight?"

This time, though, she wasn't buying it. "I've been putting *on* weight if anything. I've been eating like a horse. Haven't I, Richard? Haven't I been eating like a horse?"

Quietly, as if his sister wasn't standing right next to him, Richard affirmed that yes, Bernie was eating substantially. "She's depressed," he said. "She always overeats when she's depressed."

It was incumbent on someone to follow this up with a question; Rose, being the host, took the initiative. "That's too bad, Bernie. I'm sorry to hear it. What's the matter?"

Bernie dabbed at her nose with a Kleenex and made an unsuccessful effort to stop her lower lip from trembling. *Oh, god,* Rose thought, *here we go again. Please, not today, Bernie. Not on Thanksgiving.*

"Now, Bernie," she said, trying to sound patient and understanding. "You can tell us. What's troubling you?"

Bernie let out a strangled sob and shook her head. With a flick of her hand she indicated she was too overcome to speak and would leave it to Richard to speak on her behalf.

"She's going through the change," he said. "It's made her very emotional."

It was only by a superhuman act of restraint that Rose was able to keep a straight face. "Oh. Well, yes, that can happen. Maybe—maybe you need to see someone, Bernie. A doctor?"

Bernie nodded. Yes, maybe she would do that. Charles offered her his arm and led the way to the dining room. Rose waited by the door, struggling to compose herself. The change. Good grief. Bernie was older than Charles. Was it even possible?

Marie came out of the powder room and saw Rose standing in the hallway. "What's going on?" she said. "Was that Richard I heard?"

"Bernie's just dropped a bombshell. Wait for it—she's going through the change."

"The change? At her age?"

"That's what she says. It's not possible, is it? I mean, she's too old."

"My mother was in her late fifties when she went through it."

"Really?"

"She made my father's life a nightmare. That's when they split up."

"I thought it was his drinking."

"It was, but I think he drank because she drove him crazy. Who knows? She was terribly overweight, you know. Obesity can cause late menopause—something to do with fat producing estrogen and delaying the aging process."

"Well, that would make sense, I guess. I feel terrible. I almost burst out laughing. I thought she was just being, you know . . . Bernie."

"We'll have to be extra nice to her," Marie said. "It's tough enough to go through it when you're healthy. And she's not. Here, I'll take those."

She relieved Rose of the wine and muffins and turned to head into the dining room. "Coming?"

"I'm just waiting for Morgan. She went out to get a bottle of wine. And Ryan's not here yet either."

"Was Charles okay with it, when you told him?"

"He was fine. 'Always room for one more,' that's what he said. The weird thing is, I don't think he remembers Ryan. I think he thinks he's a former student or something."

"Did you tell him about him stalking you in the library?"

"No, I just said I ran into him in the library and invited him to dinner on the spur of the moment. Which is partly true. Sort of. Don't look at me like that. You tell Jeff everything, I know that. It just seemed like a lot of unnecessary information, and I didn't want him thinking there was anything to be nervous about. I didn't want Charles judging him."

"So he doesn't know Ryan is homeless and maybe has a drug problem?"

Rose shook her head. "No. Neither do the kids. I told Morgan the same thing. She's excited that he's coming—they were only a few months apart. And I haven't told Jason yet but I'm sure it'll be fine."

It was dark. Rose was getting anxious. She hoped Ryan hadn't decided not to come. He could possibly have agreed to the invitation just to be polite. Might he have gone ahead and showered and washed off the address, or written it on a scrap of paper and lost it? She did that all the time—not writing things on her hand but jotting them down on scraps and then losing the bits of paper. She should have insisted she'd go get him. Or have someone pick him up.

Just as she was thinking she'd hunt through her phone for the number he called from, the front door swung open to reveal Morgan, her cheeks ruddy from being out in the cold, her eyes glittering with excitement.

"I'm back, and I've brought a guest!" She turned and urged her unseen companion to come forward.

Rose smiled, and moved to greet him. "You came," she said. "I'm so glad."

Morgan was delighted. "He was standing on the sidewalk. I didn't recognize him at first, and then I thought, 'It's Ryan!' And he didn't know it was me. Did you, Ryan?"

Ryan stood in the doorway, looking a little uncomfortable with all the attention. He had exchanged the hoodie for a long, loose-fitting overcoat and a scarf. His hair was combed forward, hiding the bruise on his forehead, and had been freshly trimmed; it no longer reached past his shirt collar. The cut on his lip was still faintly visible but the swelling under his eye had gone down. All in all, he was perfectly presentable. She'd been worried about his appearance; she realized that now, and it bothered her that she had.

"These are for you," he said, handing her a small bouquet of flowers.

She accepted them with thanks and stopped herself from saying, "You shouldn't have." Instead she told him they were lovely and invited him to take off his coat. As he did so, she asked Morgan to find a vase for the flowers. "That was so thoughtful of you," she said, taking his coat and hanging it in the hall closet. "Thank you."

Under the coat, Ryan wore a clean gray blazer with the sleeves rolled up, in the style Rose remembered from *Miami Vice*, a clean white T-shirt, and jeans. Had he borrowed the outfit, she wondered? She led him into the living room and introduced him to her guests.

"Everybody, this is Ryan. Ryan, you remember Charles? And Jason. And this is Lee, Jason's girlfriend." In the flurry of introductions Rose realized she still didn't know if Ryan's last name was still Albertini. It didn't matter—and she was hardly going to stop to ask him now, in front of everyone.

"Welcome," Charles said, offering a firm, man-to-man handshake. "Good to see you, son. How've you been? How's life treating you?"

There was no simple answer to this, so Rose hurried to introduce Bernie and Richard, who were next at hand. Bernie peered at Ryan, trying to place him, and then said, "Are you a friend of Jason's?"

"He's a friend of the whole family," Morgan said. "I've known Ryan since I was five!" She had found a vase for the flowers. The best one in the house: Waterford crystal, cut in a starburst pattern. It had belonged to Rose's grandmother and was almost never used. She set it down on the coffee table with a flourish. Rose tried not to appear anxious.

Bernie seemed doubtful, but she smiled and held out her hand. "Well, it's nice to meet you, Ryan."

Jason was pleased to see him but admitted he didn't remember him, much to his sister's annoyance.

"Oh, come on," she said, "you gave him your troll doll, remember?"

"I had a troll doll?"

"Yes. I can't believe you don't remember."

"You were very young," Rose said. "Ryan, this is Garnet, who teaches at the university. And this is Lauren."

Garnet nodded, withholding judgment. You could see he was skeptical: a stranger who'd once been part of Charles's family unbeknownst to him? It was unlikely.

Lauren had no such reservations. "Hey, Ryan," she said, taking his hand and giving it a friendly squeeze. "Nice to meet you. I love your jacket. It's very retro. Can I ask where you got it?"

"Value Village. It was given to me but I think that's where they got it."

"I shop there all the time," Lauren said. "They have great deals."

Rose introduced Marie and Jeff. Marie came forward and gave him a hug. "I'm just so happy to meet you! I've heard so much about you."

"You have?"

"All good things," she said. "I'm so glad you came."

Jeff stood apart, frowning. "You were the babysitter's son, right? That's how they knew you?"

Ryan blushed and Rose said, "His mother took care of the children when they were small. Ryan was part of the family, weren't you, Ryan?"

"Was I? Yeah, I guess maybe I was."

The introductions were over; Morgan broke the brief silence that followed. "What do you think, Mom, should we eat now that everybody's here? I'm starving, aren't you?"

24.

SHE HAD DECIDED TO PLACE RYAN NEXT TO HER, AT
the end of the table. It would be a bit of a squeeze. The solid oak dining table, inherited from Grandma Morgan when she moved into
a home, comfortably seated eight. Now there were twelve—two at
each end, four on either side. Her grandmother, who never had less
than a dozen people at any kind of dinner, would have approved.

She had left the table setting to Morgan, who wanted to do it,
and the result was stunning. She had retrieved the ceramic pumpkin
from the storage cupboard and filled it with hydrangeas, chamomile,
and rusty orange mums. She had scattered dried leaves from the
back garden on a quilted table runner Rose hadn't seen in years, and
added the Blue Mountain pottery squirrels dating back to the 1980s.
The scented candles they kept over the fireplace, but always forgot
to light, danced and flickered in the Mexican ceramic holders Rose
had picked up at a street market for next to nothing. It was a hodge-
podge of colour—a "feast for the eyes" Garnet said—and it worked.

As they made their way into the dining room, Rose gave her
daughter a hug. "It's beautiful! Thank you."

Once everyone was settled, Rose asked Jeff to say grace. As the
only self-proclaimed Christian in the group, it usually fell to him

to perform this ritual, and he took it seriously. After instructing the others to hold hands and bow their heads, he closed his eyes. "Let us sing for joy to the Lord," he said, "let us shout aloud to the Rock of our salvation. Let us come before him with thanksgiving and extol him with music and song. Lord, we are grateful for friends and family, for food and shelter, for the opportunity to come together and share in Thy bounty. For all of this and more, we thank You. Amen."

"Amen," everyone agreed, and Garnet added, "Let us be grateful for the people who make us happy."

"*Ce sont les charmants jardiniers qui font fleurir nos âmes,*" Lauren said and added, almost apologetically, "Marcel Proust. It's the rest of the quote."

Charles was delighted. "You speak French," he said. "How lovely."

"I did my undergrad in French at McGill," Lauren said. "Before I switched to women's studies. I was pretty fluent back then but I've lost most of it living out here."

"That's the problem, isn't it?" Charles said. "We call ourselves a bilingual country but we're not. We should make more of an effort." Charles was unilingual himself, but he enjoyed pointing out occasional cultural flaws in his adopted homeland.

For the next few minutes there was little to be heard above the clatter of plates as the food was served out and distributed around the table. Jason appointed himself sommelier of the evening and uncorked three bottles of red, a Pinot Noir, and a bottle of Chardonnay.

"Let's have a toast," Marie said when the glasses were filled. "To the chefs!"

The others cheerfully echoed "To the chefs!"—clinked their glasses, and got down to the serious business of eating. Conversation, as it does when friends gather to break bread, centred on the food. If Rose had worried (and she had) that there might be too little turkey to go around, or that two packages of cranberries weren't enough for twelve people, she needn't have. They could have fed a multitude with what was laid on tonight; she foresaw a fridge bursting with leftovers.

She was keeping an eye on Ryan, hoping he was getting enough to eat. God knows when he'd get another meal like this; he was probably unused to such—what would you call it? Such *largesse.*

"Ryan, you don't have any turkey... Here, let me serve you some."

He put up a hand to stop her. "It's okay, Mrs. Addams, I don't eat meat."

"Oh, dear, I didn't know."

"It's okay," he repeated. "I'm fine. There's plenty here I can eat."

"I'm a vegetarian, too," Lauren said. "I think it's a very healthy way to eat. And kinder, too, don't you think?"

Ryan tried to brush it off, saying he didn't like to judge people one way or another. Lee offered that kindness didn't really come into it; as long as animals were well cared for when they were alive and killed mercifully, that was all that mattered.

"Really?" Lauren was doubtful. "So if your mother was in a home and they took care of her and killed her *mercifully,* you'd be okay with that?"

"More than okay," Lee said, reaching for a dinner roll. "I'd help them do it."

Rose intervened before Lauren could manage a comeback. "Well, there are lots of vegetables, Ryan, and plenty of cranberry sauce. I don't know if you remember but you used to love it."

Ryan said he didn't remember the cranberry sauce but did remember being impressed that Charles was the one who did most of the cooking. "You still do that, Mr. Addams?"

"I do," Charles said. "But maybe not for much longer."

Rose frowned. What the heck did he mean by *that?*

"Are you planning to abandon your culinary responsibilities?" Garnet asked. "Along with everything else? What do you say to that, Rose? Are you going to keep him barefoot and chained to the stove?"

"Hardly," she responded. "Bernie, what about you? You haven't gone vegetarian on us, have you?"

"No," Bernie answered. "Everything's lovely, really. I'm just not up to much these days." She held out her glass and waited for

Richard to top it up. She might not be up to much when it came to eating, but Rose noticed she was making good headway through that bottle of Chardonnay.

"This is the first time she's been out socially since the last time we were here," Richard said. "I keep telling her she has to get out and mingle. It's no good staying home and moping, is it?"

"Quite right," said Garnet. "The time of life is short, Bernie. Make the most of it."

There was a slight slur in his words that nobody but Rose seemed to notice. Was it possible he'd been drinking before he came, in spite of his vow to abstain? Now he directed his attention at Ryan, whom he'd been regarding with a certain amount of suspicion since the meal began.

"Tell us, Ryan," he said, "where did you go to school, if I may ask?"

"Oh, I didn't," he said. "I'm probably the only person you know who didn't go to college."

The others were silent. It felt like a reproach, although there was nothing accusatory in Ryan's manner. On the contrary, he seemed to feel that he'd discovered something unique: by joining the group tonight he was giving them a chance to mingle with the hoi polloi.

"You're wrong," Jeff responded. "I didn't go to college. I went to work in a bank the summer I finished high school. Someone suggested I take some night school courses in accounting so I did and eventually I wrote the CPA exam and got certified. Never spent a minute in a college classroom."

Jason was impressed. "That's amazing. I didn't know that."

Jeff shrugged. "It wasn't uncommon back then."

"And you were always good with numbers," Marie added.

"I was. I scored ninety-nine per cent in each of the four sections of the test."

Garnet pretended to be shocked. "Not one hundred? I would expect you to get perfect, Jeff."

"Ninety-nine *was* a perfect score. It's the highest mark they give." He turned to Ryan. "So you see, not everyone needs a university degree to get ahead. Some of us have done very well without one."

Now that *was* a reproach.

"Who wants more turkey?" Rose blurted.

"We've only just started, Mom," Jason said. "But I'll take more stuffing if you can pass it down."

"Now, Jason," Marie said, passing the stuffing to him, "tell me—how's that case going you were working on last time I saw you? The one with the woman trying to take her kids out of province."

"We're making headway. The appeals court has agreed to hear the case at the end of November."

"That's wonderful. It's been going on for months, hasn't it?"

"Years, actually. It'll be four years next month. It was my first case when I got hired as an associate. I never thought it'd drag on this long. But that's family law for you."

"So you're a lawyer," Ryan said. "That's great. I remember you always liked to argue."

"Did I? I guess I did."

"He's their youngest associate," Lee said. "They hired him straight out of law school."

Ryan wanted to know if Lee was a lawyer, too; Lee laughed and said she wouldn't have the patience for it, and Jason explained that Lee used to be a nurse and was now a health coach at Korus Life, one of the biggest wellness centres in the country.

"What about you, Morgan?" Ryan said. "Can I ask what you're doing these days?"

"You can ask but it's pretty boring. I'm thirty-six years old and living with my parents."

She said it cheerfully enough, but Rose felt the need to add a clarification. "Morgan's been working on her PhD. She's just taking a break at the moment."

Jason opened his mouth to say something and caught a look from Rose. He shrugged and let it go.

But Lee couldn't resist making a comment. "So when are you going back, Morgan? Have you arranged for an extension on your thesis?"

"I haven't thought about it, actually."

"Don't you think you should? What happens if you miss your deadline?"

Rose was secretly pleased to see that Morgan ignored the question. Evidence, perhaps, that her daughter was coming over to her side. She was feeling light-headed and wondered if it was the wine that was causing it. She'd had a glass earlier in the day while she was helping Charles with the pies—her job was to roll out the dough, under his supervision. And then, after boiling the cranberries and leaving them to set, she had nothing else to do for the rest of the afternoon, so she had another glass of wine. And another.

Now her voice sounded strange in her ears, about an octave higher than usual. She took a deep breath and told herself to calm down. But when she spoke again her words came out breathless and slightly strained. "Has everybody got enough wine?" she asked. "Bernie, you have to try the sweet potatoes. Lee made them. They're delicious. And these corn muffins—Richard, did you say they were gluten-free? You'd never know—they taste fantastic!"

Jason was giving her a look. "Mom?"

"What?"

"Everything okay?"

"Everything's fine! I'm just enjoying the dinner."

"It's delicious," Marie said, and the others agreed. The sweet potatoes and honeyed carrots especially seemed to be going down well. Even the much-maligned Brussels sprouts, that Rose had roasted with garlic and Parmesan, were quickly disappearing.

Best of all, no one so far had brought up *the book*. Marie wouldn't—she knew it was a sore point for Rose—but considering the way it had been the focus of attention during the Labour Day meal, it was only a matter of time until Bernie or someone else thought to ask, "So how's the Myra Hindley book coming along, Charles? Have you started writing?"

But Bernie was saying very little tonight. She'd been picking at her food and now sat fork in hand, staring into space, with her mouth turned down at the corners in a mournful pout. It was an unkind thought but with her frizzy bangs and snub nose she resembled a Yorkshire terrier who was being punished for peeing on the carpet.

Rose made an extra effort to be nice. "So tell us, Bernie, where are you and Richard going for Christmas? Have you made your plans yet?"

"I think I should let Richard answer that," she replied. "Don't you, Richard?"

"Now, Bernie, let's not make a big thing of it. You promised." He seemed embarrassed; the rest were puzzled.

"Come on," Garnet said, "out with it. What's the big secret?"

With everyone waiting on his answer, Richard had no choice. His cheeks were flushed—he wasn't used to being the centre of attention, not in this group, anyway. He looked around the table, hoping for a way out.

"It's all right," said Rose. "It's none of our business."

"Richard is going on his *honeymoon*." Bernie might have announced that her brother was taking a trip to Mars; the reaction from the others would have been the same. For a moment nobody said anything, then Marie blurted, "You're joking!" Hearing how it sounded, she quickly added, "I mean, it's just such a surprise."

"Yes!" Rose said. "I had no idea you were seeing anybody, Richard. Congratulations!"

This was the cue for the others to offer their best wishes. Charles proposed a toast, which seemed a little premature but at least was a way to get through the initial shock.

Now that the secret—if it was a secret—was out in the open, Richard relaxed. "Thank you, everyone," he beamed, "it all happened so quickly. I only had time to tell my sister. And I only told you last night, didn't I, dear? Believe me, she was as surprised as you. But she's happy for me, aren't you, Bernie?"

Was she? It was hard to tell; she looked pretty grumpy, to be honest. Although that could be because of the menopause. And the wine. "Well," Bernie said, "when your fifty-five-year-old kid brother decides to all of a sudden run off and get married, it's a bit of a shock to the system."

Richard took her hand and gave it a reassuring squeeze. "Darling, I am not running off, you know that. Bev and I will be gone for three weeks and when we get back we'll be as cozy as three peas in a pod."

"Is that her name?" Rose asked, being very careful not to make eye contact with Marie. "Bev?"

"It's Beverly," Richard said, "but she likes to be called Bev. She thinks it's friendlier and I agree. She's a wonderful woman—I feel very lucky to have met her."

"You should have brought her," Charles said. "We'd all like to meet her."

There were murmurs of agreement around the table: yes, of course, she'd be more than welcome. And so on. Lee said she thought it was wonderful that Richard was taking this great step, "moving out of your comfort zone," as she put it.

Richard seemed not to quite grasp her meaning and said that he and Bev wouldn't actually be moving: Bev would continue to live in her apartment and he'd go on sharing a house with Bernie.

"Really?" Lee said. "You're getting married but you're not going to live together?"

"We'll have meals together, and, well, you know . . ." His cheeks reddened again at the implication. "But she's been on her own since her husband died twenty years ago, and she has two cats that mean the world to her. And, well, you know me and cats." Richard was allergic to cats—"deathly allergic" was the way he always put it, as if the mere flick of a tabby's tail would put him in the ICU.

Bernie had never expressed an opinion one way or the other. Now she said, "I loathe cats." It was not so much what she said but the way she said it that made Rose think Bernie loathed more than Bev's cats.

25.

IT WAS BEGINNING TO LOOK AS IF THIS WAS GOING to be one of those rare dinners where things went relatively smoothly. No one, so far, had mentioned the Hindley book, and nobody was pressing Ryan for personal details. Maybe they were being polite. Or maybe they were more interested in finding out more about Richard and the mysterious Bev. Rose certainly was.

"How did you two meet?" she asked him, trying not to sound as desperately curious as she was.

Before he could answer, Lauren suddenly stood up, gripping the table. "Oh, god, I'm sorry, I'm doing it again. Excuse me." Rose got up to accompany her but Lauren waved her off. "It's okay, Rose, I know where the bathroom is."

Ryan turned to Garnet. "Is your daughter sick?"

"My daughter? I have no idea. I haven't seen her in more than a year. As far as I know, she's as healthy as a horse."

Managing, just barely, to control her amusement, Marie informed Ryan that Lauren was Garnet's partner, not his daughter.

"Oh, like in business," he said. "I get it."

"Well, no . . ." Marie began, but an indignant Garnet interrupted.

"That adorable young woman is my betrothed. My *inamorata.* My paramour."

Feeling the need to interpret, Rose added, "They're together."

"Really? Wow."

"You might well say 'Wow' young man. *And* she's having my child. So stick *that* in your pipe and smoke it."

There was an uncomfortable silence.

"So Ryan," Morgan said, trying to ease the tension, "where are you living these days? Are you on the North Shore?"

"I have a tent. It's quiet and I like it." He took a sip of water—Rose noticed he hadn't touched his wine—and added, "I'm kind of a loner, you know? I spent three years in Nepal and I got used to being on my own."

"Nepal?" Rose said. "You were in Nepal?"

"Oh my god," exclaimed Morgan, "that's so exciting. What were you doing there?"

"Learning the language. I wanted to go to Tibet but I met a monk when I was in India and he was headed to Kathmandu. I ended up travelling with him and staying with him in Pokhara. That's, like, the second largest city in Nepal."

Morgan was transfixed. "Did you stay in a hostel?"

"We stayed in a monastery," Ryan said.

Jason wanted to know if he thought about becoming a monk, and Ryan rather shyly confessed that he did, for a while. "But it wasn't for me. I mean, they were great and I learned a lot but, I don't know, I guess I wasn't ready."

"What did your parents think?" Marie asked. "About you maybe becoming a monk? Did you talk to them about it?"

"*I* wouldn't," Lee interjected. "If I was making a life decision, like, the last thing I'd do is talk to my parents."

"Maybe," Rose said, "it depends on the kind of parents you have." She turned to her son. "You'd talk to us, wouldn't you, if you were thinking of becoming a monk?"

Jason laughed. "I promise you, Mom, if I ever decide to give it all up and go into a monastery, you'll be the first to know."

"After me," Lee said, with a smile. But she meant it.

"Of course," he said. "After you."

Morgan was getting irritated. "You all make it sound like it's some kind of joke. I think it's wonderful, making that kind of commitment. It sounds so, I don't know, so life changing. Did it change you, Ryan? Spending time in the monastery and all that?"

Ryan didn't answer right away. Was he uncomfortable with the question? All this attention . . . Before Rose could say anything, he admitted that yes, it did change him, actually. "When I came back, I just kind of hated the way it is here. I mean, all the stuff everybody has. The way everybody works so hard to get more stuff. It made me feel kind of sick." He looked around the table and smiled. "It sounds weird to say it, doesn't it? It sounds like I'm against everything, and I'm not. Like, I think this house is great and you're all so friendly and all. But it's just not for me."

"And yet you feel entitled to take advantage of the hospitality we offer." Garnet was obviously still upset. The "daughter" comment had struck home.

"We?" Rose was annoyed. "I didn't know this was your home, Garnet. I thought it belonged to Charles and me."

"I'm just making an observation," Garnet said. "This young man . . ."

"He has a name," said Morgan.

"This young man, *Ryan,* claims to have rejected the material world. And all I'm saying is it seems a little disingenuous to claim to be above our mundane strivings while still enjoying the fruits of our labours."

"Garnet, you're being rude. Ryan is here as our guest. As are you, as a matter of fact. And if I'm forced to choose—" Rose stopped. She was angry and close to tears and not altogether sure what she'd say next. Wordlessly, she appealed to Charles, whose role was to step in at this point and come to her rescue. But he wasn't picking up on her cues. He continued to eat and said nothing. In fact, he'd hardly said a word since making that toast to Richard. Morgan was right: he was definitely "off" these days.

Garnet seemed to realize he'd overstepped. "I'm sorry, Rose, I didn't mean to upset you."

"It's Ryan you should be apologizing to," said Morgan.

Ryan had stopped eating and was watching this exchange with interest. "You think I'm a hypocrite," he said.

A non-question, directed at Garnet. Who cleared his throat and began to search for a way to back down gracefully. "I put it badly," he said, with a smile that was meant to be ingratiating.

Ryan shook his head. "No, it's okay, you're making a point." He looked around the table. "Actually, I had this discussion with my dad, about three years ago. He said kind of the same thing."

Rose saw a way of redirecting the conversation. "How is your father, Ryan? We only met him that one time but we liked him, didn't we, Charles?"

"We did?"

"Yes. He came to get Ryan . . . he was taking a job in Seattle. Remember?"

Charles was staring at her blankly. She wanted to throw something at him. She *would h*ave thrown something at him if they were alone. And if it weren't Thanksgiving.

"He's fine," Ryan said. He turned to Garnet. "Did you ever read *The Way of a Pilgrim?*"

"Oh! I've heard of that book," Morgan said. "It was a central theme of *Franny and Zooey,* which I read back in high school. But I thought Salinger made it up. I didn't know it was a real book."

"Did you read it in the monastery, Ryan?" Marie asked.

"I actually read it when I got back. Someone left a copy in a place where I was staying, and I carried it around with me and read it three or four times. It made me want to try it. Live the life of a pilgrim—like, not be attached to anything."

"So it's an experiment?" Garnet asked. There was a note of censure in his voice, despite his desire to be cordial.

"It started that way, I guess. I wanted to try living like a *bhikkhu,* someone who lives by begging."

"And is it working? This experiment of yours?"

Ryan smiled. "I'm here, and I'm still alive."

"But surely you want more than that. More than just to be alive."

"Do I? I'm not sure. Maybe."

"Well, I think you've had a really interesting life," Morgan said. "It makes me want to drop everything and travel."

"You've already dropped everything," Charles snapped.

Rose thought he was overtired. He'd been up since six preparing dinner; perhaps she shouldn't be expecting him to do it on his own so much. Perhaps, at this late stage of the game, she should learn to cook. "Well," she said, "I suggest we drop this conversation. Who's ready for dessert?"

"Great segue, Mom," said Jason. "Here's to less talking and more eating."

"Hear, hear," Richard said, and the others agreed. It was Thanksgiving, after all.

Lauren returned to the table looking better than when she left. It was time for another toast. Rose raised her glass. "We usually go around the table and say what we're thankful for. Shall we do that? I'll start: I'm thankful for my family."

Morgan sighed. "You *always* say that, Mom."

"Well, I'm always thankful for them. For you."

"You should come up with something else," Jason said. "Just for a change."

"Good idea," said Charles. The pilgrim discussion seemed to have brought him back from wherever his mind was wandering. "Go on, Rose, surprise us. What else are you thankful for?"

She thought about it. What else was she thankful for? "Well, I guess I'm thankful that I'm here. That I'm not dead yet. My parents are gone, my sister . . . all my original family. So many people gone. It's sad . . ."

There was a pause.

"Well, *that* was depressing," Jason said.

"Yes, well, you asked for it." In an effort to make amends with Garnet, she turned to him. "You're next. What are you thankful for?"

Garnet put down his utensils, dabbed at his lips with his napkin, and prepared to make a speech. "I am likely the most grateful man at this table," he began. "I have been gifted, at this relatively late stage in my life, with another chance to be something I never quite managed earlier: to be a good father. Lauren, my dear, thank you for that. I will not let you down." His voice trembled a little, right at the end. Rose thought, my god, he's going to start crying.

Charles, always uncomfortable with "scenes," hurried to forestall any further display of emotion. "Lauren, it's your turn. What are you thankful for?"

Lauren didn't answer right away. She sat in silence, head down. The others, assuming she was thinking, were prepared to give her a moment. Just as Rose was about to suggest they move on to Richard, who was next in line and might possibly say a little more about Bev, Lauren gave a gasp and bent forward, clutching her stomach. "Oh my god!" she exclaimed. "I think I'm bleeding."

Richard was first on his feet, pushing his chair against the wall and helping Lauren to her feet. "Hang on. I've got you!"

"Stay calm, darling!" Garnet said. "Keep breathing!"

The chair was soaked in blood, more than Rose thought possible. "We need to call your doctor! Where's my phone? Jason, do you have your phone?"

Morgan already had her phone in hand. "I'm calling 911. Lauren, you need to lie down."

They led her into the living room, Richard on one side and Marie on the other, and stopped in front of the Barcalounger. For a brief moment Rose wondered if Charles would protest. He didn't, of course.

"Here," he said, removing the newspaper he'd left on the seat, "sit down and put your feet up. Don't try to talk. Are you in pain?"

Lauren nodded, and Lee, who was helping to settle her in the chair, asked for acetaminophen. "*Not* aspirin. It'll cause more bleeding."

Rose tried to think. "Is that Tylenol? We have a bottle in the bathroom." Jason went quickly to fetch it.

Morgan announced that the ambulance was on its way. "Fifteen minutes, they said. What can I do? Can I do anything?"

Lee asked for a heating pad. Morgan said she had one in her room. "It's one of those wheat-filled ones you heat up in the microwave. Will that do?"

"It'll be fine," Lee said. She placed a hand on Lauren's forehead. "You're going to be okay. Just breathe."

"Am I losing the baby?" Lauren began to cry.

She looked young and fragile. Rose's instinct was to reassure her; she wanted to say no, of course not, but Lee knelt down and told her, very calmly, that she was probably having a miscarriage.

"We don't know that," Rose whispered. "It might just be spotting."

Lauren wasn't listening. Her eyes were closed and her mouth was set in a tight, painful grimace. Jason returned with Tylenol and a glass of water, which she swallowed without opening her eyes. Lee stood up and took Rose aside. "She's hemorrhaging," she whispered. She showed Rose the palm of her hand—it was stained with blood. "We need something—a towel."

Bernie hurried forward, clutching her purse. "There's two sanitary napkins in here—I carry them just in case."

Lee shook her head. No, it had to be a towel. "A large one," she said. "And safety pins, if you have them."

Ryan said, "I'll go!"

"First door upstairs, on the left!" Rose called out. "The thick ones are in the cupboard."

"We have pins, don't we, Rose?" Charles asked.

"The drawer in the kitchen. Where we keep the measuring tape." Rose felt she should be doing more than just standing there giving directions, but doing what? Lee was handling the situation with such competence—well, she was a nurse, wasn't she? Or she had been. Rose knew she should be grateful. Still, she thought Lee shouldn't have said that about the miscarriage; Lauren might indeed be losing the baby, but the bad news, if it had to be spoken, should be delivered by a doctor.

Ryan returned with a stack of towels. "I wasn't sure which ones . . ."

Lee took the towels and asked everyone to leave the room. All but Morgan, who had hurried back from the kitchen with the heating pad. "Maybe you can stay and give me a hand?"

"Of course."

"I should stay . . ." Garnet began, but Lee was firm.

"Better if you don't. Just give us a few moments."

"Are you sure?" Rose asked. "I can stay, if you need me."

"It's okay, Mom," Morgan said. "We can manage."

Reluctantly, Rose agreed. She shepherded the group back into the dining room, and tried not to feel she was being shut out. Marie read her mind, as usual. As she went to take her seat at the table, she stopped to give Rose a hug, saying, "It's going to be okay. They don't need us right now and that's a good thing, right?"

Rose nodded. It *was* a good thing. And there was her daughter, who generally felt faint at the sight of blood, stepping up to the plate like a trouper.

They took their seats but nobody wanted to eat.

"Would it be too much to ask," Garnet said, "to open the bottle of Scotch, Rose? I think I could do with a drink."

"I think we all could," Rose said, and sent Jason to the kitchen for it.

26.

BY THE TIME THE TWO MEDICS ARRIVED, LAUREN had been fitted with a large bath towel securely pinned in place. Garnet, fortified with two ounces of Highland Park single malt, stood guard beside her. While one young man checked her vital signs, his partner took down a brief history: Why did you call us? What happened? How long has she been bleeding? They took Lauren's blood pressure and checked her pulse. When one of them clipped a small device onto her index finger, Lee told Rose they were checking her blood oxygen levels.

"If it's low," she said, "they'll start her on high-flow oxygen with a face mask. And they'll start her on an IV with a saline solution."

The reading, according to the medic, was 96 percent.

"Is that good?" Garnet wanted to know.

"It's normal," the medic replied. He applied a tourniquet to Lauren's upper arm and explained what was going to happen next. He spoke to Lauren but the information was for them all. "We're going to insert a catheter. You'll feel a little bit of pain, but it'll settle down once we secure the IV line. So, I need you to make a fist. Can you do that?"

Lauren complied, keeping her eyes closed, while the medic searched for an appropriate vein. As he inserted the needle, Garnet winced and looked away. For a moment, he looked worse than Lauren.

"Everything okay?" the medic asked.

"Feels cold," Lauren whispered.

"Good. That means it's in the vein."

While he taped the IV in place, his partner turned to the others. "We're going to transfer her to a stretcher," she said, "and take her to the hospital. We'll keep her warm with a thermal blanket and elevate her legs." Then, to Lauren, she said, "You're going to be fine. We're going to take you to the ER. There'll be a doctor standing by to take care of you. Do you understand what I'm saying?"

Lauren nodded, eyes closed.

"Good. Is there anyone that should be notified? Is your mother here? Or your father?"

She didn't ask about Lauren's husband. The father of the baby. Maybe it was obvious. Or maybe they just didn't do that anymore. Ask about the father.

Lauren shook her head. No, there was no one to notify. No one she wanted to tell.

"All right." The woman turned to the group. "One of you can come with us in the ambulance, but I'd suggest the rest of you wait till she's been treated."

"I'm coming with her," Garnet said.

"Fine. Maybe you can gather up her things. They'll want her ID, if you have it."

Rose went to fetch Garnet's coat and Lauren's purse, jacket, and boots. When she returned Lauren was lying on the stretcher, wrapped in a blanket. She was pale but alert; Garnet was gripping her hand for support—more for his, Rose thought, than hers. He might need medical treatment himself by the time they got to the hospital.

Marie took her aside. "Maybe somebody should go along to keep an eye on him," she suggested. "He looks like he's going to faint."

Jason, overhearing, said he and Lee would go. "We won't get in the way. We'll just be there in the waiting room in case he needs anything."

As the medics packed away their equipment and prepared to leave, Lauren reached for Rose's hand. "I'm sorry," she said, in a voice just above a whisper. "I ruined the dinner."

"Don't be silly, you didn't ruin anything."

"I did. I feel awful."

"Think of it this way: nobody in this room is ever going to forget how they spent *this* Thanksgiving. Right?"

Lauren managed a weak smile and closed her eyes. "I guess you're right."

"You're going to be fine. Garnet's going to be with you, and we'll come see you as soon as you want us to."

The departure of the ambulance signalled the end of the evening. Jason and Lee left for the hospital. Bernie was experiencing hot flashes and wanted to get home. Morgan offered to give Ryan a lift downtown, and, to Rose's surprise, he accepted with enthusiasm. "That would be great, if you don't mind."

Rose put together a selection of leftovers and insisted he take them with him. "You'll be doing me a favour. There's far too much food here—we'll never get through it all." When Ryan hesitated, she added, "Please, take it. If you can't use it, maybe somebody else can?"

He took the two large shopping bags she handed him and slung one over each shoulder. "Thanks. They won't go to waste."

Charles shook his hand and told him to feel free to come by any time. "I'm always here, and I can use the company. Tell your father hello for us next time you talk to him."

So now he remembers, Rose thought. *What on earth is going on in that head of his?*

Marie stayed behind to help out in the kitchen, so Charles and Jeff retreated to the living room to watch football. Charles loathed

American football, and Jeff wasn't a huge fan either, as far as Rose knew. But at least with the television on they wouldn't have to talk.

Half an hour later, Rose turned on the dishwasher and collapsed on a stool by the counter. "I'm exhausted. How did I do it when the kids were small? All those birthday parties and school lunches and kids needing to be fed every twenty minutes."

"Yes, well, you weren't dealing with emergency 911 calls in the middle of dinner," Marie said helpfully. "And none of those children were homeless."

"What do you think? About Ryan? What's your opinion, now that you've met him?"

Marie finished wiping down the counter, folded the dishcloth, and hung it over the kitchen spout. "I think there's more to him than meets the eye. And I also think . . ."

"What?"

Marie grimaced. "I'm not sure I should say. I could be completely off base."

"Go on, tell me. Oh, come on, Marie, you have to tell me now. What do you think?"

"I think there's just a teensy bit of chemistry there, between Morgan and him."

"You do?"

"Just a bit. I sensed something, that's all. Don't look so shocked. You didn't see it?"

Rose shook her head. No, she didn't. She was sure Marie was mistaken. Morgan was just being kind, is all, offering to drive him—well, not home, perhaps, but to his tent. Which *was* his home, actually. And nobody but her seemed to find that strange.

"He's not what we thought he was, is he?"

"How do you mean?"

"Well, we had him pegged as this poor homeless guy, someone who needs a helping hand. I thought he must be on drugs. Why else would a young man end up living on the street? You don't think about it being a choice, do you? And now it turns out he's something of a mystic. I'd love to know the rest of his story."

"Speaking of stories," Rose began.

"Yes! Richard—what the hell was that all about?"

"What do *you* think it's all about? This Bev thing, I mean. Is it real?"

Marie shook her head. "You could have knocked me over with a feather. Was I rude? I hope I wasn't. I was just so startled."

"We all were. I've known Richard Maclean for more than twenty years and I've always believed he was gay. It just shows you how wrong you can be about people."

"Oh, we're not wrong about that. He's definitely gay. Maybe she is, too. Who knows? Best of luck to both of them, I say. I hope it works out."

"Me, too. But one thing's for sure . . ."

They said it together: "Bernie hates her guts."

When the call came from Jason later that evening, the news was what they expected: Lauren had lost the baby. She was being kept in the hospital overnight to be monitored; she was still bleeding and in pain. Jason passed the phone to Lee to fill in the gaps.

"She's up in the gynae ward," she said, speaking above the noise of the street traffic. It was almost midnight but the hospital was in a busy section of town. Rose could hear a siren wailing in the distance. "They'll probably take her into surgery to remove the rest of the tissue. She's doing okay but she's still in shock."

"Will they . . . will there be . . ." Rose wasn't sure how to ask it.

"A funeral? I don't think so. She was fourteen weeks. They don't require you to have a burial until twenty-four weeks, but she might want to have the baby cremated. She doesn't have to decide right away. She shouldn't, actually. She shouldn't have to think about any of it."

Rose asked about Garnet, and Lee passed the phone back to Jason. "He's being amazingly stoic, Mom. He's talking to the doctors and asking sensible questions. He hasn't sounded like a dweeb all night."

Rose said good night, hung up, and relayed that information to Charles. "Jason says Garnet is being a rock. I'm astonished. I assumed he'd collapse in a heap."

"You underestimate him," Charles said. "We all do. But now and then he can surprise you."

She thought about what Garnet had said earlier that evening, when he spoke about being thankful. "He's going to be sad. I think he was really looking forward to the baby."

"I think you're right." He stood up and stretched. "I'm going to turn in. Coming?"

"In a bit. You go ahead."

She wanted to wait up for Morgan, who hadn't returned from driving Ryan home. To his tent. It was almost midnight. She tried calling but it went straight to voicemail, so she sent a text instead. *R u on your way back? Call me!* Ten minutes later she sent another text, then tried calling. Again, straight to voicemail. Morgan's phone was turned off. Or the battery was dead. Which was unlikely; her daughter was obsessive about keeping her cell phone charged. She waited another twenty minutes, watching the news with the sound turned down, then gave up and went to bed.

This was the downside of having Morgan staying with them: Rose turned back into a worrywart. She'd always been a worrier, convinced the axe was going to fall at any moment. She told herself she was being ridiculous. Morgan was thirty-six, for god's sake, she wasn't a child. Back in Toronto she might stay out all night and Rose would be none the wiser. But it was hard to break old habits.

Once in bed, she couldn't sleep. She was exhausted but her mind wouldn't relax. Charles, who almost never worried about anything, was sound asleep. If he did worry he was able to tuck it away when he needed to. The ability to compartmentalize—that was the secret. It's what hit men did, according to a study she read in *Time* magazine. They detached themselves from the deed and then, once it was done, they didn't think about it until they needed to. The researchers who carried out the study looked at contract killers who worked for the IRA. They saw their victims as targets, not people. Which was why they could shoot someone point blank in the head and still be good husbands and fathers. It was a gift. Charles would make a good hit man, not that he'd ever kill anybody. But he had that capacity of detachment; he could walk away and not look back. He'd done that with his first marriage; more recently, he'd done it with his career.

Unable to sleep, she decided to name all the people she knew who'd make good hit men. Turns out there were quite a few. Besides Charles, she could think of Julie, who'd once had her cat put down because she was moving; Jeff, Marie's husband, if only because she sensed a certain *froideur* in his manner, a kind of coolness befitting an assassin; and her first boss, whose name she'd forgotten but whose wife died unexpectedly and who turned up for work, very cheerful, the next morning. Oh, and there was Cyndi, Ryan's mother. She had that quality in spades.

Poor Ryan. It was no surprise he'd become a kind of pilgrim, forever searching for—what? For something. Marie was right; he wasn't the kind of homeless person they'd envisioned. But he was certainly adrift and it was most likely because of his mother. She abandoned him when he was five, and there was no sign she'd reappeared since then. Rose tried to remember: had Ryan said anything about her? They'd talked about Greg, his father, briefly. And then Ryan had changed the subject—started talking about that book. *The Way of a Pilgrim.* And there was Morgan getting all interested in his life, and Marie thinking there was some kind of spark there.

It was preposterous. First of all, Morgan was . . . well, she was Morgan: educated, bright, attractive. Until recently, Rose would have called her driven. Determined to succeed. And Ryan—okay, let's clean him up. Get his teeth fixed, a decent haircut, some better clothes. Do all that and what do you have? A not-bad-looking young man with soulful brown eyes. Who doesn't work. Doesn't have a place to live. Is absolutely *not* driven.

Sorry, Marie, it doesn't add up. You're wrong.

27.

ROSE SLEPT LATE THE NEXT MORNING, THE BEDSIDE clock read 9:10. Shouldn't she be at work? It took a moment for the fog to lift when she remembered: it was a holiday; she didn't need to be at work. She could go back to sleep if she wanted to, which would be lovely except that she could hear voices from the kitchen. This meant that Morgan was up having breakfast with her father, and Rose really wanted to know what, if anything, had happened last night. She put on her dressing gown and slippers and padded downstairs.

"Hey, Mom, have a good sleep?"

"I did. What time did you get home?"

Morgan checked her phone. "Twenty-five minutes ago. Dad's made waffles, do you want some?"

"You were out all night?"

"I was, actually. Don't look so shocked. I wasn't robbing a bank or anything."

Charles fetched a plate from the cupboard. "Sit down, Rose. I've got another batch ready to go. Go on, sit, I'll serve you."

Obediently, Rose took a seat and considered the best way to put the question. It was going to be tricky: she needed to ask her daughter about her whereabouts without sounding critical, judgmental, or even all that interested. Luckily, Morgan beat her to it.

"I know what you're wondering, Mom, and you can relax. We sat up talking all night."

"You and Ryan?"

"Mm-hmm. We went to this all-night vegetarian place on West 4th."

"I know that place," Charles said, spooning batter into the waffle-maker. "It's been around for years. They used to do terrific huevos rancheros."

"They still do. Ryan had that and I had the scrambled tofu."

"So," Rose asked, "what did you talk about?"

"Oh, everything. Me, mostly. He's a terrific listener. He always was, even when we were kids. I remember that about him."

"You couldn't possibly remember that," Rose said. "You were a little kid yourself."

"Well, I do. You'd be surprised what I remember. I remembered Jason giving Ryan the troll doll. I can't believe Jason doesn't remember that. He *loved* that doll."

"Memory's a funny thing," Charles said. "We remember what we want to remember. If it doesn't resonate with us in some way, we forget it. Which is why I remember every detail of England winning the World Cup in 1966."

"And can't remember to put down the toilet seat when you're finished," Rose added.

"Exactly. You've proven my point." He lifted the lid of the waffle-maker and tested them with a fork. "Almost done. Do you want one waffle or two?"

"One'll do me, thanks." She turned to Morgan. "So you were talking about yourself?"

"Mm-hm. Most of the time. Although I did get a chance to ask him about himself. You know he was mugged a couple of weeks ago? Some kids beat the shit out of him. He ended up in the hospital."

"That's terrible! Did he call the police?" Then she remembered the sight of his injured face when she found him walking the pug.

Morgan shook her head. "He didn't want to. He knows one of them—he says the kid has a really hard home life. He doesn't want him to go to jail."

"So he's turning the other cheek," Charles said. "That's very commendable, but a little naive, don't you think?"

"Maybe. He doesn't look at it that way. He says it's all about practicing non-attachment. It's what they teach you in Buddhism." She waited while her father served out the waffles, one for her and one for Rose, thanked him, and continued. "He's had a really interesting life."

Rose wanted to know how interesting, and Morgan said that, for starters, he got married when he was only nineteen.

"Married! He has a wife?"

"Not any more, it was annulled. It was never consummated. He was involved in some kind of religious cult—well, his mother was, and he lived with her on a farm up north. She left after a year or so but he stayed. He said the people there felt like family, and he hadn't really had a proper family, you know? But they were a *very* strange bunch."

Charles said that cults usually were. Morgan agreed. "This one, though, was really off-the-wall. They believed the world was going to end in the year 2012 and only married people were going to be saved."

Rose was intrigued in spite of herself. "Where on earth did they get that from?"

"Paul's letters to the Corinthians. He said it was good for people to find a mate instead of suppressing pent-up urges. Or something like that."

"Better to marry than to burn, 1 Corinthians, 7:9," Charles informed them grandly. "I've always thought that was the most sensible verse in the Bible."

"But he didn't say only married people were going to Heaven," Rose said. "He wasn't married himself. At least, I don't think he was."

"No, Ryan said they got that a bit twisted," Morgan said. "Anyway, he turned nineteen—"

"Who, Paul?"

"Pay attention, Dad. We're talking about Ryan. He turned nineteen and they set him up with this older woman—"

Rose interrupted to ask how much older, and Morgan said she thought there were maybe twenty years between them. "That was part of their thing, putting young and old together. Young men married older women, older men married young girls. It was pretty sick, actually. Anyway, Ryan and his wife never had sex. Her husband had only just died and she was still grieving. He felt sorry for her. He said he'd just lie in bed with her and hold her—comfort her, you know? And eventually, she told him the farm was not a good place for a young man and he should leave. And so he did."

"My god," said Rose.

"Yeah, pretty strange, eh?"

"Very." Rose wanted to know more about Cyndi. "So she came back into Ryan's life after all?"

"Yes, but not in a good way. She just turned up one day when he was twelve and living with his grandmother." She paused in order to concentrate on pouring syrup from the jug onto her waffle. "She had some kind of custody order so his grandmother had to let him go. Ryan said it was really weird, he didn't even know her. He didn't see his grandmother again for years."

This time it was Charles' turn to say, "My god. The woman's a sociopath."

"Ryan doesn't see it that way," Morgan said. "He just says she's a lost soul and he feels sorry for her but he can't let her into his life."

"Has he tried?" Rose asked.

Morgan said he had. In between bites, she reported that each time Ryan had connected with his mother it turned out badly. She would call him from wherever she was living and give him a sob story about being broke and needing money for rent. Ryan would manage to scrape up the cash and send it to her. And then she'd drop out of sight again. "The last he heard she was back in Montreal, living on the street."

"Is she . . . you know, is she doing drugs?"

Her daughter smiled. "No, Mom, of course not. She's working as a certified dental assistant."

"Oh well, if you're going to be sarcastic . . ."

"I was teasing! I'm sorry, I haven't slept. Yeah, I think she takes oxycontin or something. Ryan didn't really say. I don't think he likes to talk about her all that much. Anyway, from the sounds of it, he doesn't want to reconnect with her. He says their relationship works best from a distance." Morgan smiled, "Kinda like ours, right, Mom?"

Rose didn't see the similarity but wasn't about to argue the point. She was more interested, anyway, in Morgan's side of the conversation. Had she confided in Ryan about her plans? Charles had promised to have that talk with her but it still hadn't happened. Although god knows he'd had plenty of opportunities. The two spent most of the day together—Morgan hardly went anywhere except for her daily run, and he was always back from the village by 3:00, 4:00 at the latest. Waiting for the right moment, he said. There'd been her friend Kim's wedding, and then a baby shower for one of the others—Caitlin, she thought, she was the pregnant one. Morgan had said she didn't want to see any of them ever again. Well, she seemed to have recanted. They'd all be married soon. And having babies. And there was Morgan breaking up with Ian. And spending all night in a diner, talking with a homeless person. Nothing against Ryan but at this rate Rose was unlikely ever to be a grandmother.

"So what else did you and Ryan talk about?" Rose asked. "Besides his marriage and the cult and all."

"Oh, you know, I just filled him in on what I've been doing. I told him about Ian and the wedding. He wanted to know about my dissertation so we talked a lot about that. And he read my aura."

"Really? What did he say about it?"

"He said there is a lot of red, which means I'm very grounded. But he said it isn't as bright as it should be, which means I'm stressed. Or maybe I'm coming down with something. It was interesting. I recorded it on my phone. I'll play it for you later, if you want.

Okay, I'm done. The waffles were great, Dad, thanks." Morgan took her plate to the sink, rinsed it, and placed it in the dishwasher. "If nobody has any objections, I'm going to bed. If I'm not up by two, call me, okay? I told Ryan I'd go to a meeting with him tonight and I want to get some writing done before then."

"What kind of meeting?"

"Oh, just a meet-up he's organized, Mom. I'll let you know more when I get back."

So Ryan was organizing meet-ups. And reading auras. Was there no end to his accomplishments? Rose waited till Morgan was out of the room and then put the question to Charles: is it possible for a homeless person to organize a meet-up? Charles said there was no law against it and Rose said it wasn't a legal question; it was one of logistics. "I mean, how do you get the word out if you don't own a computer, you don't have a phone—you don't even have a place to sit down and work?"

Charles looked at her and shook his head. "My darling, try to think outside the box. You've heard of the *library?* You know, that place where you work surrounded by books and computers and free access to the internet? Students write their papers there all the time. They can't all afford Macbooks."

"Yes, alright, there's no need to be sarcastic. You're sounding just like Morgan."

But it made sense. All that time Ryan spent there, reading books, keeping out of the rain. The library was as good a place as any to network. Rose hadn't seen him there in a while, but she stopped checking after she met up with him in the park. She forgot about the far section, away from the windows, where they kept the bank of computers. He might very well have been using those all along. Something else: Morgan said she was going to do some writing. Was she picking up where she left off? Finishing up her thesis?

"Do you think she's going back to school?"

"Do you want her to?"

"I want her to do *something,*" Rose said. "I don't want her to end up—you know."

"Reading auras?"

No, she didn't want her daughter to end up reading auras. She should never have invited Ryan to Thanksgiving dinner. If she had it to do over again, she wouldn't.

After breakfast she put in a call to Garnet. It went to voice mail and she wondered if perhaps he was still at the hospital. She thought Jason would know, but when she texted him he wrote back that he and Lee had left around two in the morning, when it was obvious they were going to keep Lauren in overnight. Her phone rang shortly after that: it was Garnet, sounding tired but relieved.

"She's doing fine," he said. "Her blood pressure's back to normal. She still has some pain in her abdominal area but they've given her something for it. She was awake half the night, poor thing. It's ridiculously difficult to sleep in these places—the bells never stop ringing."

Rose wanted to know if they were going to be discharging her soon. Garnet told her they were keeping Lauren in for another night. "To monitor the situation. Must run. I want to be there when she wakes up."

He hung up before she could ask about the baby: was it a boy or girl? Would there be a funeral? Better not to ask, maybe. It was hard to know.

28.

AS MORGAN TOLD IT OVER DINNER THE NEXT NIGHT, the meeting Ryan organized sounded more like an encounter session than a formal meeting. Morgan said it was a mix. A couple of ministers, someone from the Sikh temple on the North Shore, even a city councillor.

"Ryan seems very well-connected for a homeless guy," Rose said.

"I don't see why that should make any difference," Morgan said. "He's chosen not to live like we do. That doesn't make him any less able to make connections, does it?"

In the wrong. Again.

"Sorry. So what was the point of the meeting?"

"Have you ever been in a room filled with people who really and truly want to do good?"

"Well, I used to go to church every Sunday. It's been a while, but, you know . . ."

"I don't mean that. Anyway, church people aren't really there to *do* good, are they? They're there because they think they already *are* good. It's not the same thing."

Rose wasn't going to argue; she wanted to hear about the meeting.

"This group, they meet twice a month in the basement of the Westside Church on Homer."

Rose felt vindicated. "So it *is* a church group."

"No, not really. It's called *sangha*, a Sanskrit word meaning 'community'. There's people from all different faiths. Two Muslim women there wore the *niqab*, you know? The head scarf that just shows your eyes."

"I thought it was called the *burka*," Rose said. "Or is it the *hijab*? Either way I don't get it."

"What don't you get?" Morgan regarded her with steely eyes.

Rose knew she was treading in dangerous waters, but if she couldn't express herself here, in her own home, to her family—well, where could she? "I guess I don't understand why a woman would choose to hide herself like that in this day and age." She turned to Charles, who was paying attention, for once. "You agree with me, right? Doesn't it seem strange to you?"

"I think it's kind of sexy," Charles replied.

"What? You do not." Even Rose was appalled.

"No, I do. You find yourself imagining what's under that veil. It's like the old burlesque shows where they didn't show a lot of skin, just enough to tantalize."

"Oh my god," Morgan said, "that is wrong on so many levels!"

"I can't believe you're comparing wearing the *burka* to, I don't know—fan dancing," Rose said.

Charles was silent.

Morgan continued. "*Anyway*. It's not a *burka*. The *burka* is the complete covering from head to foot. A *niqab* is a headscarf that just covers the face but shows the eyes. It was a little weird for me at first—I thought they'd just sit there and not say anything but I was completely wrong. They were very outspoken and really knowledgeable. They run a shelter for Muslim women who've had to leave their homes. And they're trying to set up a place for Muslim teens to come and talk about drugs. They were really impressive."

"Sally Rand," Charles said.

"I beg your pardon?"

"That was her name, the woman who danced with the ostrich feathers. Sally Rand. I haven't thought of her for years." Morgan waited for her father to go on but he just said, "That's all. Carry on."

"Well, it was pretty informal. There was no set agenda. We went around the circle and people talked about what was happening in their communities, and what they're doing about it. Or trying to do. Oh, and that kid was there, the one that beat Ryan up. Ryan invited him and he came."

Most of the talk the night before, she said, had been about a young woman who died of an overdose earlier in the week. "I didn't get at first why they were talking about her in particular," Morgan said, bending down to pick up a napkin that had dropped. "I mean, people OD every day. It's terrible. Ryan says it happens so often we stop thinking of them as individuals—they're just another statistic. He wants to set up an honour wall. Like they did with the people who died of AIDS, you know? A memorial."

Morgan had taken her parents to visit the AIDS Memorial the last time they were in Toronto. It was set up in a park within walking distance from their hotel. Fourteen concrete pillars. What hit you was the number of names engraved there. Thousands of names, beginning in the early 1980s and continuing to the present. There, Rose found the name of a friend who died in 1990. Long before they were keeping people alive with a cocktail of drugs, turning AIDS from a death sentence into a chronic, but manageable, disease. He was thirty-four when he died . . . the same age as Jason. It was all too sad.

Ryan, it seemed, had started a Facebook page in memory of the men and women who had died of drug overdoses in the city. "But what he wants," Morgan said, "is an actual wall somewhere downtown, with pictures put up in frames and all. And some detail underneath each one saying who they were and when they died. That's why the councillor was there. They wanted to pitch the idea to him and see if he can get it through council. They've got a petition going with about a thousand signatures."

Charles said he thought it would be a hard sell, considering the way people look at drug users. "It's not like the AIDS epidemic, is it? It's not a disease in that way."

Well, this was the wrong thing to say. Morgan got very huffy and told him he was misinformed, that drug addiction was absolutely a disease; it was an epidemic and needed to be treated as such. "You can't just go around saying, well, it's not *my* kid who's dying, it's nothing to do with *me*."

Charles tried to defend himself. "I'm not saying that!"

"You can't just bury your head in the sand. You can't just hope it'll go away."

"Morgan—"

"I'm sorry, Dad, but you sound just like the councillor last night."

"Why? What did he say?"

"A lot of bullshit about how we don't want to send the wrong message about drugs. And he said he wasn't sure it would be helpful to remind people of all the ones they weren't able to save. He said it might be counter-productive."

"Well," Rose said, "he might have a point. It might seem like praising people who made bad decisions—"

"Oh my god! I can't believe I'm hearing this—you two are so uninformed! You think becoming addicted is a choice—like choosing to wear a blue shirt rather than a white one. You really think that?"

"Of course not," Rose said defensively.

"Well, that's what it sounds like!" Morgan pushed herself away from the table and stood up. Her cheeks were blazing. Rose hadn't seen her so angry since she was a teenager. It was a little frightening, to be honest. She wanted to tell her to calm down but she knew from experience that was always the worst thing to say to her daughter when she was upset. It was the worst thing to say to any woman. At any time. So trust Charles to say it.

"Calm down, honey, you're getting yourself into a state."

Morgan turned and flounced out of the dining room; a moment later they heard the front door slam.

"Now you've done it." Rose couldn't help feeling just a little smug. She was the one who generally locked horns with their daughter; Charles enjoyed a more conciliatory role. He was the peacekeeper, the one who kept things on an even keel. It wasn't such a terrible thing to see him getting the pointed end of the sword for a change.

"I don't understand," he said. "What's she so upset about?"

"She thinks we're dinosaurs. And she's right. We're out of step with things these days. We don't get it."

"What is there to get? Can't a man have a difference of opinion with his daughter without it blowing up into a full-blown ruckus? I'm not even sure what we were arguing about."

"Drug abuse, Charles. You said it wasn't a disease and I said it's a choice. We're probably both wrong—what do we know?"

It was almost seven. It would be dark very soon. If Morgan had gone for a walk she'd be back before long. She'd have calmed down by then and Rose would apologize; Charles probably wouldn't—he wasn't big on apologies—but he'd go out of his way to be kind, make her a cocoa or something.

They finished their meal in silence. Rose was thinking about Ryan, about what Morgan had said about the meeting he organized. He had invited that young thug, the one who put him in the hospital. That was surprising enough but what was really astounding was that the kid had accepted the invitation. She was beginning to think that Ryan, formerly known as the homeless guy who stands outside the grocery store, was something of a wizard.

The *Encyclopaedia Britannica* is one of the few online authorities Rose trusts implicitly, so she looked up what it had to say about *sangha:*

A Buddhist monastic order, traditionally composed of four groups: monks, nuns, laymen, and laywomen. The sangha is

a part—together with the Buddha and dharma (teaching)—
of the Threefold Refuge, a basic creed of Buddhism.

It went on to say that "sangha originated in the group of disciples who renounced worldly things to wander with the Buddha".
After he died they stayed together as a community, continuing to
wander, living off charity.

It reminded her of the old stories she heard in Sunday school
of Christ and his disciples roaming around Galilee, Samaria, and
Judaea. When she was eight, a friend of her mother's told her that
Christ walked a total of 21,525 miles during his ministry, the equiva-
lent, almost, of circumnavigating the globe. She thought at the time
that He must have been in very good shape; since then, she'd had
reason to doubt her mother's friend. Not that He was in good shape
but that He did so much walking. Her mother's friend was a fun-
damentalist and they were given to exaggeration. This particular
woman—what was her name? Hummer? Hammer? something like
that—she took everything in the Bible literally: the world was created in seven days; Adam and Eve were the first people; Christ was
born of a virgin, died and went to Heaven, and was due back any
day. "So be prepared," she told Rose. "You're sitting there doing
something you shouldn't and *bang!* Christ comes back and catches
you in the act."

Wouldn't He have known anyway? If He really was up there
watching He'd already know you were letting Robbie McNulty
copy your homework or lying about going to Disneyland next summer. There'd be no hiding anything from Him, if He existed.

That was the big *if,* though. If He existed. By the time Rose
met Charles she was pretty sure He didn't, but she was too super-
stitious to come right out and say it. Charles had no such scruples.
He'd grown up in an Anglican household, gone to a Church of
England school, and knew his scripture as well as anybody. And
the moment he was able to do so, he discarded it all in the name
of secular humanism. His hero was Terry Jones of Monty Python
fame. Charles said Jones was proof you could be moral without

God and funny without being mean. He liked Jones so much, in fact, he forgave him for being Welsh.

As a lapsed Christian, if that is a thing, Rose had no difficulty with her daughter being attracted to Buddhism. In theory, anyway. What she worried about was where it might lead. A little lost, lacking purpose or direction, Morgan was a prime candidate to be swept up by some sect.

Since attending Kim's wedding, Morgan had seen almost nobody. Rose assumed she still stayed in touch with her friends but she never met up with them. She said she wanted to travel, but she made no plans. And she had no money to go anywhere at the moment. Shortly before Thanksgiving she signed up for yoga classes at a local gym but found it too crowded and stopped going. And now that the rain was here, she wasn't likely to continue to do her daily run. Rose was worried about her.

There were studies, she knew, that showed that many people leave one cult only to join another. Ryan had been a member of a cult when he was in his teens; who's to say these meet-ups he'd organized weren't just another way to recruit vulnerable people? They were meeting to "do good," Morgan said. And maybe they were. It could still be a front.

The problem was, there was nobody to ask. Charles would laugh it off; tell her she was being an alarmist. Jason would do the same; he'd be sympathetic, she knew that, but he'd assure her she was getting worked up over nothing. Even Marie would probably say the same. As for Morgan—well, confiding her suspicions to Morgan was not an option. She already thought her parents were unenlightened yokels. Rose could only imagine her reaction if they suggested *sangha* is a cult. Keep it to yourself, she thought. You invited him here; you brought them together. You only have yourself to blame.

29.

"WHAT WILL WE SAY TO HER?" MORGAN SAID, AS SHE backed the car out of the drive. "I mean, what is there to say?"

Rose and Morgan were on their way to see Lauren. It had been two weeks since the miscarriage. Rose called every other day just to see how she was doing, but this would be her first visit. She didn't like to push; Lauren didn't appear to want to see anyone.

Garnet had informed Rose that Lauren was sleeping a lot and watching Netflix on her phone. "I'm worried about her," he told her one afternoon when he stopped by on his way home from a committee meeting and seemed happy to have an excuse not to hurry home. Charles offered him a Scotch and after some hesitation he accepted.

"I'm not likely to get pulled over at four on a weekday afternoon. And if I do, I'll plead senility. These young constables assume anyone over fifty is a dotard."

"Dotard," Rose said. "Haven't heard that word in a while."

"I'm not surprised. The Queen's English is becoming extinct. In a generation or two we'll be back to communicating in grunts. Make it a large one, will you, Rose? I'm feeling in need of a tonic."

The situation as he described it was disturbing: Lauren wouldn't talk about the miscarriage, and he was at a loss how to comfort her. "She's obviously hurting," he said, "but she won't let me help. She won't discuss it. She says she's fine, gets quite angry when I press her on it. So I don't. But it can't be healthy, can it, being on her own all day?"

No, it wasn't healthy, thought Rose, but there wasn't much to suggest except the old clichés: give it time, let her heal, she'll talk when she's ready. Or she won't.

Garnet finished his drink and declined a second. It was getting dark; Lauren, he said, didn't like to be alone in the evening. "It's not that she wants me around, particularly. She just doesn't want to be alone. A cat would serve the purpose just as well." He stood up and stared out the living room window. The streetlights had come on, and the sycamore trees guarding the driveway were bathed in an amber glow. "I've asked her to marry me, you know."

They didn't know. Charles, for one, was appalled. "You don't mean that," he said. "She's—well, she's too young for you. You're old enough to be her grandfather."

"Not quite, old man. But yes, there's certainly an age difference. I give you that. The thing is, I love her. So what am I to do?"

He didn't seem to want an answer, which was just as well. Rose saw him to the door and watched as he got into his car and backed out of the driveway. For the first time, she felt a pang of compassion for the old rogue. He was a scoundrel in many ways—Maeve would say he was getting his just deserts—but there was no denying he cared for Lauren. And he cared about the lost baby. He might not be willing to admit it but he was hurting as much as Lauren.

When she called the next morning, expecting the usual response, Rose was surprised to hear Lauren sounding quite cheerful. "I'm feeling better," she said. "I'd love to see you. Morgan, too, if she can make it."

Morgan was happy to come along, as long as she could do the driving. She said it was about time; she was getting ready to just drop in unannounced if she didn't get an invite. Now that they were on their way, though, she was uneasy about making conversation. "I don't want to say the wrong thing," she said, turning onto the main road. "I don't want to be one of those people who say 'Oh, you'll get over it, you'll have other kids.' That kind of thing."

Rose was focused on watching on the road. She was a terrible passenger. Whenever Morgan or Charles was driving, she felt anxious and out of control. She forced herself to look away; reaching out, she patted her daughter on the shoulder. "We'll just say what's in our hearts: We're so sorry, there's nothing we can say to make things better, it's just a very shitty thing to have happened. That's all."

Morgan gave her a quick glance; she was slightly shocked. Rose seldom swore, especially around her children. But she agreed. "You're right, Mom. It's a shitty thing and I'm sorry."

When they arrived, Lauren was alone in the house, wearing a shaggy floor-length bathrobe that must have belonged to Garnet. Rose had suggested they pick a time when he'd be at work. If Lauren was going to open up about things she'd be more likely to do so without Garnet hovering by her side, hanging on to every word. She let them in, took the packages of tea and candied ginger and set them on the kitchen counter.

"You remembered," she said, referring to the ginger. "Thank you, that's so sweet."

"How are you?" Morgan asked. And then, "Oh, I'm sorry, that's a stupid question."

"No, it's okay. I'm all right, really. I'm not bleeding anymore and I've stopped taking painkillers. Should I make some tea?"

"I'll make it," Rose said. "Why don't you two go sit down and I'll bring it in?"

Relieved to have something to do, she bustled around the kitchen, filling the kettle with water and retrieving cups and saucers from the cupboard. She found a package of chocolate digestives in the cupboard by the sink and a tin of Walker's shortbread. Tea and cookies: she might be preparing a tea party for Morgan and her dolls. A sudden, unexpected burst of laughter emanated from the other room—Lauren or Morgan, she wasn't sure. A good sign, surely. She was young, after all. There'd be other babies. Other opportunities.

Exactly what you aren't to say, she reminded herself. Morgan was right: those clichés might have worked for a previous generation but they were not helpful now. Maybe they never had been. Rose's mother had miscarried twice, once before Rose was born and once when her sister was a toddler. It was never talked about. Rose only found out long after her mother was gone when an elderly aunt came to Morgan's christening and mentioned her mother's "lost babies." Two of them, the aunt said, but it was all right. "I told her she'd have others and she did. You and your sister. She told me she wasn't going to mope, she just wasn't going to think about it and I said, 'Good for you, Claire, that's exactly the right thing to do.' And it was."

Was it? Rose wasn't so sure. This was the woman, after all, who tried to kill herself the summer Rose was twelve. Her father said it had been an accident, a mistake. She was ill and confused. Completely bedridden, barely able to speak. She hadn't meant to take so many pills. She wasn't thinking straight. Rose and her sister believed that story for a very long time. Because they wanted to, because it was easier. It was years before they admitted the truth to each other, that their mother had deliberately tried to take her own life. A few years after that Rose learned how angry her sister was at her mother for doing it.

"She was depressed," Rose said, needing to defend the mother who'd been gone for decades. "She believed she was a burden. Look at it from her side, how would you feel? She couldn't walk, could barely talk. She couldn't do any of the things a mother was supposed to do. Or a wife."

"She didn't leave a letter," Beth said. "She didn't leave a note saying she loved us or was sorry or anything. She just went ahead and did it."

She wasn't successful. They found her in time, her father and the housekeeper, and rushed her to the hospital. It didn't change the fact, though: she had done it and she hadn't left a note.

In spite of the fact that she'd known Garnet for years, Rose had only been inside this house a few times when he was still married to Maeve. Birthday parties for the children, mostly. And once or twice for dinner, although those occasions were never particularly easy. Maeve was uncomfortable in groups; nowadays you'd say she had social anxiety, but back in the day there were many who thought she was a snob. Rose didn't; she liked her and felt a little sorry for her, being harnessed to Garnet and all.

Maeve had come from money. There were those who said she'd taken a step down by marrying Garnet. Rumour had it that he'd married her for her family connections; that it was her father, a university donor who eventually became chancellor, who saw to it that Garnet was granted tenure long before the usual seven years, and before he had anything published. And when they split, her father's lawyer took Garnet to the cleaners. Afterwards, Maeve took pity on him and gave him back the house. Sans furniture, bedding, area rugs, and his mother's good china.

Garnet could be very morose about the china when he'd had a few drinks. "Royal Worcester in the Pompadour pattern. A setting for twelve. Plates, cups, saucers. Hand-painted. Absolutely irreplaceable. They belonged to my great-grandmother and they're worth a bloody fortune."

It didn't seem such a loss to Rose, considering how infrequently they had anybody to dinner. She, on the other hand, could have really used a good set of china. "Did you use them?" she asked. "I don't remember seeing them."

Garnet stared at her as if she'd suddenly lost her mind. "Use them? My god, woman, you don't *use* Royal Worcester! We're talking about heirlooms, something that's passed from one generation to the next."

"Well, that's all right then. Maeve will give them to your daughter. Or your granddaughter. They'll stay in the family."

"That isn't the point! Maeve absconded with a fortune in porcelain and I will never forgive her!"

Rose felt he was overreacting but Charles argued that he wasn't, really, if you looked at it. Garnet had very little money of his own, apart from his salary. If he'd do what everyone was telling him to do, sell the house and move into an apartment, he'd be fine, but he refused. It was a lovely old house, better than he deserved, in Rose's opinion. It sat on a sprawling lot in the tony Shaughnessy neighbourhood, on a quiet street lined with horse chestnuts, lilacs, and oak trees. Built in the English Arts and Crafts style in the early years of the last century, it had kept its structural authenticity: exposed beams, handmade tiles, an open floor plan. It was charming but getting run-down. The kitchen needed upgrading and, as Rose noticed now, it wasn't terribly clean. When Maeve was still in the picture she had a cleaner in once a week; maybe Garnet could no longer afford it. It didn't look as though the place had seen a mop or scrub brush in ages. Well, that's something she could do: she'd mention it to Lauren—tactfully of course—and suggest that she—Rose—come by one weekend and give the kitchen a scrub. It was the least Rose could do, after everything the young woman had been through.

30.

As she carried the tray of tea things into the living room, Lauren, who was lying on the couch, started to get up to help her. Rose waved her away. "Don't get up. We can manage."

Morgan reached for the tray and set it on the coffee table. "Digestives! My favourite."

Rose looked around the room, trying to decide where to sit. There wasn't a lot to choose from. Lauren was lying on the couch, and Morgan had perched herself on a hassock on the other side of the coffee table. There was a stiff-backed dining chair that looked less than inviting, considering it contained a stack of *New Yorkers* somebody had yet to read and a worn-out armchair that Rose recognized from Garnet's first marriage. So Maeve hadn't taken *all* the furniture, after all.

"Here, Mom, take this." Morgan stood up and indicated the hassock, but Lauren swung her feet down to the floor and patted the space beside her.

"Come sit here, Rose. It's really the only comfortable place to sit in the house. I keep telling Garnet he should buy more chairs but he says a man doesn't need more than two chairs to get him through life. Any more than that is self-indulgent."

Rose could imagine Garnet saying just that. Another excuse for being cheap, she thought, but didn't say it. She took a seat next to Lauren, helped herself to a biscuit, and looked around expectantly. "So, what were you girls talking about?"

The younger women exchanged a look, and Rose wondered if she'd interrupted a private discussion. But what could Lauren and Morgan have to talk about that couldn't be shared?

"Actually," Morgan said, "we were talking about Ryan."

"Ryan? What about him?"

"I was teasing her," Lauren said.

"About Ryan?"

Oh god, Rose thought, Marie was right. Something's going on between those two.

Morgan, who'd begun to pour the tea, smiled and said nothing.

"Well, come on," Rose said, "what about Ryan?"

"I was telling Lauren about Ryan reading my aura, and I just happened to mention—"

"That he said you were sexy," Lauren said.

"He didn't say sexy. He said I have a strong sacral chakra. Which means I have the capacity for an active sex life. That's all."

"Yes, but that's not all he said."

Morgan began to laugh. "Are you trying to get me in trouble? I don't think my mother wants to hear this stuff."

Morgan was right—she didn't. But Rose was determined to present herself as a modern, emancipated woman. She would not be pigeonholed. "Don't be silly," she said. "We're all grown-ups, aren't we? We don't have to play the mother–daughter role at this stage."

"We don't? Well, that's a switch."

"Go on. What else did Ryan tell you?"

Morgan helped herself to another biscuit and sighed. "Okay, if you're sure."

"I am."

She wasn't feeling sure at all, but it was too late now to back down. If Morgan and Ryan were having a—relationship, she might as well hear about it first-hand.

"Ryan says my chakra is blocked. He says it's not in harmony with the rest of me, and it's keeping me from feeling sexually fulfilled."

"Oh."

"And he said he could unblock me."

"*Oh.*" Rose took a moment to digest this. "How would he do this?"

"That's what I wanted to know," Lauren said. "It sounds like a pretty good pickup line."

Rose was thinking the same but of course she couldn't say it. Morgan, though, didn't take offence. "He didn't go into the details," she said, "but I think it's about working on being more creative. Maybe taking art classes or joining a dance club. That kind of thing."

Rose tried not to show her relief. "That sounds not a bad idea. Are you considering it?"

"Maybe. He also said I should talk with Ian."

"About . . .?"

"About this imbalance thing. He says it sounds like Ian has the same problem."

"He doesn't even know Ian!"

"Calm down, Mom, he wasn't being critical. He was just trying to be helpful."

"Do you really think you should be taking advice from someone who lives in a tent?"

"I thought you liked Ryan."

"I do like him. I just don't see him as a qualified therapist, that's all."

If they had been alone, or even at home with Charles, there's no telling how much further things would have gone. Rose knew she was saying all the wrong things but she couldn't seem to help herself. She'd reverted to her mother-knows-best role, and Morgan was beginning to get annoyed. Thankfully, it occurred to them both that they'd come here to spend time with Lauren and arguing like this was inappropriate and not very helpful.

"I think we should change the subject," Morgan said.

"Yes, you're right. How are things, Lauren? With you and Garnet? Is he being, you know, helpful?"

"He's being Garnet," Lauren said, with a smile. "And that's fine. I quite like the old coot."

Rose was shocked. Garnet *was* an old coot, but it sounded awful coming out of the mouth of the woman he was proposing to marry. Making a great effort to sound nonjudgmental, she reminded Lauren that she'd once said she didn't like him very much at all.

"I did say that, didn't I? I don't know. I guess I've changed my mind. Did he tell you he's asked me to marry him?"

It was Morgan's turn to be shocked. "Not really, Lauren! You've got to be kidding."

"I'm serious. He's bought a ring and everything."

"You're not going to do it, though, are you? You're not going to go through with it." She looked at her mother for support. "You think it's a bad idea, don't you? You don't even like Garnet. You wouldn't want to see Lauren marry him."

Rose started to say it was none of their business but Lauren interrupted her.

"Don't worry, you two, it's not going to happen. I'm pretty sure he only said it because he feels guilty. You know, about the baby and all."

"Why should he feel guilty?" Rose said.

"He thinks it was his fault. That I—you know. The miscarriage."

Rose was at a loss, as was Morgan. It was understandable that Garnet would be upset about losing the baby but why would he feel guilty?

"I don't get it," Morgan said. "It had nothing to do with him, right? It wasn't anybody's fault—that's just crazy."

"We had a fight," Lauren said.

Rose paused, her teacup halfway to her lips. "A fight? When?"

"That day. Before we came to your place. We had a really bad argument and he hit me."

"He *what?*"

"Well, I hit him first. And then he hit me back. It was a kind of reflex, I think. He didn't mean to do it."

As if that explained things. Morgan was staring at Lauren as if she couldn't quite believe what she was hearing. "He hit you? Like, punched you in the face?"

"Slapped," Lauren said, adding that it hadn't been all that hard, but she lost her balance and fell, and that was what Garnet was upset about. "He thinks the fall caused it. I don't think it did but, well, I guess we'll never know."

Rose had nothing to say; she was trying to process this. Whatever she thought of Garnet over the years, physical violence never came into it. He could be pompous and irritating, and ridiculously sentimental, but violent? Maeve had never mentioned it. Not that she'd be likely to confide in Rose even if that were the case. Maeve saw Rose and Charles as Garnet's friends, not hers. And Charles had never hinted at anything like that. She knew he'd never stand for it, if he knew. Over the years he'd had plenty to say about men who took out their anger on women. On this point, he and Rose presented a united front.

They sipped their tea in silence and avoided looking at each other. It was just so . . . shameful, that was the only word for it. On his part. To think they had a friend, a close friend, one they'd known for years, who would do something like this.

Lauren was the first one to speak. "Look, I know it sounds awful. But really, it's not as bad as you think."

"No?" Morgan said. "Because I think it's pretty bad." Her speech had a strained quality as if she were close to tears. Or angry.

Lauren had nothing to say to this. She set her cup down on the coffee table and began twisting a slim silver band she wore on the ring finger of her left hand. Rose didn't remember seeing it before and wondered if Garnet had given it to her.

As difficult as it was, Rose wanted to restore a sense of balance to the conversation. Whatever had happened, Lauren mustn't be made to feel she was in the wrong. She wasn't to blame; she was the victim. "Can I ask what the argument was about?" she asked. "Unless you'd rather not talk about it."

"No, it's okay, I'm happy to talk about it," Lauren said. "I mean, not happy, exactly, but . . . it was just so stupid. He caught me smoking."

"And he hit you?" Morgan was in no mood to be placated. "That's a pretty lousy reaction, if you ask me."

Lauren shook her head. "No, it wasn't like that. He caught me smoking and he got upset. You know, because of the baby and all . . ." She stopped. It was the first time she'd said it that afternoon. The baby. The almost child.

Rose put her arm around her. "It's all right, you don't have to explain anything."

Morgan reached across the coffee table to take her hand. "I'm sorry, Lauren, I didn't mean to be a bitch. I was just—well, shocked, you know? I'm sorry to make you feel bad."

Rose suggested they change the subject but Lauren said no, she wanted to explain. She said it was complicated and she didn't want them leaving today thinking Garnet was a monster. Morgan appeared to have already made up her mind about that, but Rose wanted to hear something that would restore the man in her eyes. He was Charles' friend, after all; she owed it to her husband to at least try to be open-minded.

"I really did try to quit," she said, referring to the smoking. "I got it down to one or two a day which I thought was great, but even that was too much for Garnet. So I hid it. I'd smoke outside when he was on campus—well away from the house."

Rose couldn't help herself. "You shouldn't have been smoking. You know that, don't you?"

"I know, I know. It's awful. I get it. But I can't seem to quit. Anyway, Garnet was off that day because of Thanksgiving and I was dying for a smoke, so I took a chance when he went upstairs to change. For the dinner, you know? And he caught me."

She said Garnet was furious. He dragged her into the house, so as not to make a scene in front of the neighbours, and began shouting at her. She was putting her health at risk, putting the baby at risk—his baby, he said. His child. Lauren retorted that it wasn't his baby, was it, and he told her that it might as well be because she probably had no idea who the father was, which is when she slapped him.

She didn't mean to, she said. "I was just so fed up. And he slapped me back. And I fell. He felt terrible. He helped me up and I thought I was okay. But then at dinner I started to feel sick and—well, you know what happened. But I still don't think it was the fall."

"He shouldn't have slapped you," Morgan said.

"And I shouldn't have slapped him. We were both in the wrong. But we have a pretty complicated relationship. Sometimes—well, it can get a little violent."

31.

AS THEY DROVE HOME, ROSE TOLD HERSELF SHE should have made her excuses right then and left. It was pretty obvious when Lauren said what she did that the next words out of her mouth were going to be things nobody wants to hear about an old family friend. She should have stood up, said something like, "Well, as long as you're okay," and headed out the door. But she didn't.

That time back in the garden, when Lauren said they didn't do it, she and Marie had wondered what they did if they didn't have sex? Well, now she knew. And she really wished she didn't. And now, for the rest of her life, every time she thought of Garnet she'd be stuck with this unpleasant, sickly feeling in her stomach.

Morgan obviously felt the same. After driving for at least a kilometre without speaking, she finally said, "So. Was that weird or what?"

Rose acknowledged that it was pretty weird all right. More than that, it was upsetting. It was like something out of a novel. A bad one. Garnet and Lauren, it seemed, had a kind of role-playing thing going on. They pretended, when they were alone, to be father and daughter. Garnet, as the father, would set certain rules: no leaving food on your plate, no talking on the phone past ten at night. Lauren would do something "against the rules," and he'd have to punish her. Sometimes the punishment was a time out; she'd have to stand in a corner with her face to the wall until he allowed her to come back into the room. More often, though, he spanked her. Lauren said she'd been spanked when she was a child and found it arousing, even back then.

"I like it," she said. "I always have. I used to go out of my way to get my dad mad enough at me to spank me. It was really the only time he paid attention to me."

Smoking was definitely against the rules she and Garnet had agreed on. When he caught her with a cigarette, or smelled traces of smoke on her person, she got "a good licking," as he liked to call it. This time, though, he was really angry, which led to her breaking one of the cardinal rules: she was not allowed to hit him.

"We established that in the beginning," she said, oblivious to the discomfort she was causing her audience. "He's the dad, he doles out the punishment. I'm Daddy's little girl and I have to just take it. I have no power in the situation—it's what we call giving up our agency. I've done it by choice. When I slapped him, I wasn't staying in character. And he was so shocked he just hit me back."

There were other things, Lauren said. "He tucks me in at night and reads me stories. He's a great reader, you know, he's got such a soothing voice it puts me right to sleep. And when we're watching TV I sit on his lap and he tickles me. I never did that with my father; I'm making up for lost time."

Inwardly, Rose was shaking her head. There were so many things wrong with this relationship she hardly knew where to start. Lauren was a feminist, or so she said. She majored in women's studies, goddammit. She didn't seem like someone who'd enjoy being abused, but certainly that's what this was. Wasn't it?

Morgan wanted to know if her other relationships had been like the one she had with Garnet; Lauren said no, Garnet was the first. "I've always fantasized about having a kind of Daddy for a partner," she said, helping herself to another biscuit. "But the guys

I knew were always too young. And they didn't want to do it. They just wanted to have sex. And that spoils it for me. You can't have sex with your father—that would be incest."

"So," Morgan said. "No sex, only spankings. And stories at bedtime."

Lauren started to laugh. "It sounds crazy when you put it that way. It probably is crazy, but it's not hurting anybody, is it? There's lots worse things we could be doing."

Which was true. It's just that it was Garnet, someone they knew. Someone who'd been, let's face it, part of the family for years.

Morgan turned into the driveway and stopped the car. "Are you going to tell Dad?" she asked.

"Do you think I should?"

"No, I don't. Absolutely not. And not Jason either. I think we should just try to forget she told us about it. I really don't want to think about it."

"Me neither. Although, when you think about it, she's right: there are lots of worse things they could be doing. It's just play-acting, isn't it?"

Morgan glared at her. "If you're about to tell me that you and Dad have something like that going on, I don't want to hear it. I mean it, Mom, keep it to yourself. Please."

"Don't be silly," Rose said. "Your father and I have a perfectly healthy sex life. There's nothing kinky about it."

"Good," Morgan said. "I'm glad to hear it. And I don't ever want to talk about it again." She started to get out of the car and then stopped, her hand on the door, and turned to Rose. "Oh my god," she said, "I just remembered. What Ryan said at dinner—when he came for Thanksgiving. Remember? He thought Lauren was Garnet's daughter! Mom, he was right!"

In spite of what Morgan said, Rose couldn't help feeling she had a responsibility to discuss this with Charles. Even though she was pretty sure his first reaction would be disbelief. Unless he knew already. In which case he'd be defensive. None of our business—she could imagine him getting very huffy, very high-and-mighty. What two people do in the privacy of their own homes, etc., etc.

And if he did agree to discuss it, he'd blame Lauren. Who knew anything about her, really? She'd got herself pregnant (even Charles would use that phrase) by some person unknown and latched onto Garnet as an easy target. And then, after everything he'd done for her, she took it upon herself to gossip about their sex life. She could only imagine how the conversation would go:

She: "I need to talk to you about Garnet."

He: "What's he done now?"

She: "He's in an abusive relationship."

He (frowning): "He is? With who?"

She: "Lauren."

He: "I don't understand. Are you saying he's beating her up? That doesn't sound like him."

She: "It's more complicated than that. They have this—this *thing,* this game they play, I guess you would call it. Lauren told us about it when we went to see her after the miscarriage. Morgan knows—she was very upset about it."

He (sitting down on the bed, taking her hand): "I suppose you'd better tell me about it. What did Lauren say?"

This was unrealistic. She was making him far too sympathetic, too willing to listen. Garnet was his friend; he barely knew Lauren. He liked her well enough but if it came to choosing sides, well, obviously, he'd choose Garnet. So really, Morgan was right; there was no point in involving Charles in this.

There was also the possibility that he'd say it was no worse than their own little game they played, back when the children were young. She smiled, thinking about it: Tony and Tanya. Strangers meeting in a bar. Once every couple of months they'd book a hotel room and hire a sitter for the night. Rose would go down to the hotel bar alone and order a drink. Charles would wander in, a stranger looking for a good time. He'd sit down beside her and strike up a conversation.

"What's a pretty little thing like you doing all on her own?" he'd say. His pickup lines were always pretty dreadful, but she liked that. It reassured her: Charles hadn't had much practice picking up women and that was a good thing.

She would be standoffish at first, not wanting him to think she was that kind of woman. "I'm waiting for a friend," she'd tell him, giving him the proverbial cold shoulder.

Not to be deterred, he'd offer to buy her a drink, then introduce himself: Tony, a dentist from Seattle. Or Tony, a car salesman from Montreal. And once, very daringly, Tony, an importer of ladies' lingerie, from Calgary.

He'd buy her a drink, and then another, and eventually she'd thaw and introduce herself: Tanya, who owned her own hair salon. Or Tanya, a teller with the Royal Bank. Once, just to confound him, she said she was a rocket scientist; he didn't miss a beat.

"I'm an astronaut," he said, putting his arm around her. "We'd make a great team, don't you think?"

It was silly, but it was fun. And by the time they got back to the hotel room they were like teenagers in heat. Without the curfew.

When was the last time, she wondered? One of their birthdays—his fortieth? Now that she thought about it, yes, it was Charles' fortieth. He didn't want a party. When she asked him, he said he wanted a date night. If possible, in the same hotel. So she put the surprise party on hold and went ahead and booked a hotel room, asking for their "romance package." That, she knew from before, came with a bottle of chilled champagne waiting in the room and a complimentary breakfast. And a view of the ocean.

Over Morgan's protests, she arranged for the girl next door to babysit. "I'm almost eleven," Morgan said "I'm getting my certificate this summer. I don't need a babysitter."

"You may not," Rose said, "but your brother does. And he'd never listen to you, you know that."

"It's not fair. You're treating me like a child."

Resisting the urge to reply that she was, after all, a child, Rose offered a bribe. "Be nice for Debbie and you can stay up and watch *Saturday Night Live.*"

"And Jason can't?"

"And Jason can't."

"Deal."

The wheeling and dealing was all for nought: the night was a flop. First of all, there was a screw-up and the romance suite was given to somebody else. The clerk at the front desk apologized but could only offer a medium-priced room on the third floor, facing the street.

"We have three conventions registered this weekend," he said, "so we're short of available rooms. It has a king-sized bed if that's what you're worried about. And I'll have a bottle of champagne sent up, on the house."

The bar was noisy and crowded; Charles couldn't secure a seat next to her when he arrived and when he finally did manage to sidle up to her, his pickup lines were drowned in the roar of dozens of conventioneers having a night on the town. They finished their drinks and headed up to their room, to discover the "champagne" that was waiting for them was a bottle of Asti Spumante, not chilled. Charles made a foray down the hall to the ice machine, and they drank it with ice, which was refreshing if not terribly satisfying.

Charles, usually the more upbeat of the two, was disappointed. He said he was going to write the manager and give him a piece of his mind. Rose suggested they go to bed, and when they did, they were interrupted by phone calls, twice. For some reason, Debbie, the babysitter, failed to understand the meaning of "emergency use only" and gave the kids the number of the hotel. The first call came shortly after they stumbled into bed: Jason was calling to demand that he, too, be allowed to stay up and watch *Saturday Night Live.* The second call was from Morgan, wanting to know where they kept the Ouija board. *Saturday Night* was boring, so she and the babysitter were going to have a seance.

Rose asked to speak to Debbie. "If Morgan isn't going to watch TV, I'd rather she went to bed," she said. "You can play UNO or Crazy Eights but no spooky stuff, understand?"

Debbie said she understood and Rose hung up the phone. "You should have let me give you a surprise party," she said. "I'm going to go brush my teeth and go to sleep."

Charles protested but Rose headed to the bathroom. By the time she came back to bed, he was asleep. She woke him up and they finished the Asti Spumante, and had sex. Good, healthy, conjugal sex.

No violence involved. No spanking.

32.

ROSE USED HER LUNCH HOUR TO CARRY OUT HER weekly task of scrolling through Wikipedia, occasionally making edits, deletions, and additions. It was a self-imposed task; she wasn't paid for it. None of them were, the volunteers world-wide who took the time to fact check. One of them, Steven Pruitt, had been named one of the web's most important influencers by *Time* magazine. A bit of an oddball, but a legend, thanks to having made more than five million edits and written some thirty-five thousand articles. For free.

Rose's contributions were miniscule, compared to Pruitt's; still, she'd made some significant additions to several of her favourite wiki sites, such as the "Workhouse" and the "Home Children" pages. Currently, she was working on expanding the page on *Redemption*, the historical fiction novel by Leon Uris. It was one of her favourite books, and she'd been appalled to discover it merited no more than four lines in Wikipedia.

Julie Mitchell stopped by with a box of cookies: dark chocolate pumpkins with orange Smarties for eyes. It was an unexpected gesture, which she immediately downplayed. "I made too many," she said, "and we don't get a lot of kids these days. I thought maybe you could give them out. Or eat them yourself."

"Well, thank you. They look delicious." Rose almost added, what's the occasion? But then she remembered: the Outstanding Service Awards. Julie had been nominated and the deadline was Friday. Did she know Rose hadn't voted yet? The voting, which was carried out online, was supposed to be confidential, but maybe she'd found a way to hack into the website. Or maybe she was just covering all bases.

"That young man you recommended hasn't called me. Does he still want the job?"

"I'm not sure. I think so."

"Well, if he does he'd better get a move on before we post it."

Rose started to say she'd let him know but Julie didn't wait to hear it. When she left it occurred to Rose that the job had been her idea and there'd been no talk at any point of posting it. Job postings were sacred territory; they involved minute scrutiny on the part of HR. Julie, of course, knew that. She was asserting her authority, as usual.

At 5:00 she switched off her computer and was getting ready to leave work when Marie called to see if she wanted to get together for a drink. "Or a bite to eat. I can do either."

"I don't think so," Rose said. "I promised Morgan I'd get back by six. She's handing out treats, but she has something on this evening so I said I'd get home and take over."

"You're sure you're all right? Jeff's doing door duty, I can get away if you need me."

She thanked Marie and reassured her that she was fine. "I'll have a glass of wine and watch something on Netflix once the kids are gone. It'll be okay, Marie. Thanks for thinking of me."

It was good of Marie to call. She was the only other person on the planet, besides Charles, who knew how Rose felt about Hallowe'en. For years she'd avoided anything to do with it but she was stuck after the kids were born. Until they were in their teens it was one of the big days of the year, after Christmas and their birthdays. It couldn't be ignored.

Now, with the new subdivision going in across the road, there was a brand new batch of youngsters going door-to-door, ringing the doorbell and demanding treats. She could turn out the lights and hide in the dark, of course. She'd done that, once or twice in the past. But it made her feel worse, somehow, huddled on the sofa with the curtains closed, straining to hear the TV. And with Morgan at home she had no choice: she had to carry on the charade that October 31 was no different from any other day. Except for being Hallowe'en. The day that she, as a sixteen-year-old obsessed with punishing herself, had chosen as his birthday. The son she would have had. Forty weeks to the day she got pregnant. She couldn't be sure, of course, but she was. Just as she was sure it would have been a boy.

She kept track of the birthdays; every year, she added a year. Eighteen: graduating from high school. Twenty-one: old enough to vote. And now: forty-four. Eight years older than Morgan. He would have had children, most likely; Rose would be a grandmother.

Driving along the darkening streets she thought how appropriate it was that she had chosen Hallowe'en, the night when the living connect with the dead, as his birthday. A scattering of children were out already, making their way from door to door, chaperoned by dads and older siblings. Disney princesses, superheroes, vampires, zombies. Not as many ghosts and witches any more. It was all about the brand.

When Jason and Morgan were little she made their costumes: Superman for Jason one year, a floppy-eared rabbit for Morgan. She thought about the first time she held Jason in her arms, his face bruised and battered from the forceps. Looking like a miniature prizefighter. Was this her son from years ago, the child who never was? Could be; an astrologer once said he had a very old soul. "He has the finger of God in his chart," she told Rose. "It's kind of a big deal."

Rose was suitably impressed although she had no idea what it meant. She looked it up in the library, in the Religion and Spirituality section. This was before they had the internet, when you went to actual books to find out things. The books weren't terribly helpful, being written by astrologers for their colleagues. Something to do with planets in sextile creating a third at their inverse midpoint. Math was never her strong point. She let it go.

Morgan was waiting at the door when she got home, relieved to see her. "These kids are really ungrateful," she said, handing Rose the pumpkin bowl containing the treats. "They check out everything you give them and if they don't like it, they hand it back. One little jerk told me his mother said he wasn't allowed to have chocolate. What the hell is she doing letting him go trick-or-treating, then? We weren't like that, were we, when we were kids?"

"I don't remember you ever turning down chocolate," Rose said. "Did he say what he wanted instead?"

"Fruit roll-ups. But not strawberry. I told him we didn't have any fruit roll-ups and he asked for money instead. Can you believe it?"

By now Rose was laughing. Kids—what can you do? "What did you tell him?"

"I told him to go fuck himself."

"Oh, you didn't!"

"No, I didn't, but I was really tempted. I don't know how you can stand the kids in this area. They're spoiled rotten."

Rose didn't think they were so bad but she had little contact with any of them. There were a couple who used to come to the door selling Girl Guide cookies and she always bought a few boxes to take to work. Now, though, the Brownies and Guides did their selling outside the grocery store, with their mothers standing by to make change. Rose continued to buy but it didn't feel as personal, not knowing the girls.

Morgan paused to check her hair in the hall mirror, which was when Rose noticed she had changed out of her usual Lululemon gear and was wearing new jeans, knee-high boots, and a silk wraparound top. And if Rose wasn't mistaken, she was wearing makeup.

"You look nice," she said. "Are you meeting up with a friend?"

"It's *sangha*," Morgan said. "Ryan's group. I invited Lauren to come with me."

"It's tonight?"

"Uh-huh. Why, is that a problem?"

"No, it's just that—well, I was thinking I'd like to go one of these nights. If that's all right."

"Really?"

"It sounded interesting, when you were telling us about it. I thought, you know, maybe there's something I could do to help."

Morgan was taken aback, but said she was sure Ryan wouldn't mind if she wanted to come along.

For a moment, Rose was tempted. It would be a way to get out of Hallowe'en. But that would mean leaving Charles to deal with the trick-or-treaters on his own. "I'll go next time," she decided. "Just let me know ahead of time, okay? Do you want to take my car or your dad's?"

"I'll take yours, if you don't mind. I told Lauren I'd pick her up."

"Right. Well, have fun."

Morgan grimaced. "It's hardly *fun*, Mom. We're going to be discussing setting up a drop-in centre for Muslim teens."

"What about the memorial wall?"

"Oh, that's going ahead, didn't I tell you? Ryan took the petition to city council and they approved it."

"They did? That's wonderful."

"Yeah, he's something, that guy. Okay, I'm gone. Tell Dad not to wait up."

Speaking of Dad, where was Charles? He was usually the one doing door duty on Hallowe'en. Plus, he got a kick out of seeing the children in their costumes. When their own kids were young he used to get dressed up himself and greet the doorbell-ringers draped in a toga, or something equally outrageous. Morgan found it all terribly embarrassing. "Nobody else's father dresses up," she used to complain. "Why can't you just be normal?"

Morgan picked up the car keys and said, "Dad is downstairs, going through boxes of old newspaper clippings. I think it's got to do with that book. He's been down there for almost an hour."

Rose handed the pumpkin bowl back to her daughter and asked her to hang on while she checked on Charles.

"Mom, I'm in a rush!"

"I won't be long, just let me see what he's up to." She found him sitting on an old wooden bench surrounded by boxes, most of them unopened. "What's up? Morgan says you've been down here for a while."

"Yeah, I guess I have."

"Is everything okay?"

He didn't answer right away.

"Charles? Are you all right?"

"I don't know. I think so. I came down here to do something but now ..." He looked up at her and laughed. "I can't remember what I was going to do. I took down all these boxes and for the life of me I don't know what I was planning to do with them."

"Move over." Rose sat down beside him and took his hand in hers. "Morgan said she thought you were getting started on your book."

He brightened as it came back to him, why he'd come down. "Right—I wanted to find the box of clippings, the ones I kept from the newspapers. I stored them down here years ago, but now—" He waved his free hand in the direction of the boxes, randomly stacked and mostly not labelled. "I did a terrible job of filing these things. I got used to Bernie taking care of things when I had my office. I don't think I know where to start."

Rose had an idea. "Maybe Bernie would be willing to come and help you sort this out."

"Do you think so? Do you think she'd do that?"

"She might. She adores you. I think she'd be happy to help."

"I'd pay her, of course. That's a brilliant idea, Rose. Brilliant!"

"Mom!" Morgan was calling from upstairs. "I have to go."

"Coming!" Rose stood up. "Leave that for now, okay? Morgan's heading out so we need to take care of the trick-or-treaters."

"Where's she going?"

"Another one of those meetings Ryan organizes. She said he got his memorial wall passed. City council approved it. Isn't that amazing? He made a presentation and they bought it."

Charles furrowed his brow, trying to think.

"You don't remember? He wants the city to put up a wall honouring the people who've died in the opioid crisis. She told us about it. Remember?"

"Morgan told us?"

"Two weeks ago, at dinner. You made that comment about Sally Rand. The fan dancer."

"Why would I talk about Sally Rand?"

Rose gave up. "Never mind. Come upstairs and give out the treats and I'll get supper started."

As they headed upstairs the doorbell rang; the sing-song chant of children at the door: "Trick or treat!"

"Sally Rand . . ." Charles said. "I haven't thought of her in years."

33.

IT HAD BEEN A RELATIVELY MILD FALL SO FAR, APART from the rain, but the temperature dropped overnight. By morning, ominous storm clouds had gathered, unleashing a powerful blizzard that practically closed down the city and made commuting impossible. Rose opted to work from home but was forced to give it up when the power went out shortly after eleven. With no electricity and no internet, she tried to use the Notes app on her mobile but soon quit in frustration.

Morgan came downstairs at lunchtime. She had spent the morning composing an email to her advisor asking for an extension and managed to send it just before everything went dark. This was good news to Rose; it meant she wasn't necessarily dropping her dissertation work altogether.

"There's no power to boil water for tea," Rose said, "but there's water in the fridge if you want a cold drink. I filtered it this morning."

Morgan retrieved a glass from the dishwasher and filled it to the brim. "It's good you're drinking more water. You're supposed to drink eight glasses a day."

If Rose drank eight glasses of water a day she'd never be off the toilet. As this comes under the heading of what young people call too much information, she kept it to herself. "How did the meeting go last night?"

"It was okay. Actually, I think it was really good for Lauren. She thinks the Muslim women's shelter could make a good research project. You know, for her thesis."

"And what about you? You said you've asked your professor for an extension?"

"I did."

"How long an extension did you ask for?"

"Six months, maybe more."

"That seems a pretty long time. What will you do in the meantime?"

"That's a good question."

"It *is* a good question," Rose said, "which is why I asked it."

"Okay, Mom, don't start freaking out."

"I am not freaking out—"

"Um, you are, actually. And it needs to stop."

Rose took a deep breath. "So I'm not allowed to have a conversation with my daughter about what she plans to do with her life?"

Morgan rolled her eyes. "Oh, god, here we go."

"What?"

"You do this all the time. You go from zero to sixty in, like, five seconds. I give you a tiny bit of information and you zoom off into the future before I've even thought it out."

That was exactly the problem, thought Rose: Morgan only gave out tiny bits of information, leaving Rose to assume the worst. To be fair—and Rose really, *really* wanted to be fair—Morgan had been very open about the situation with Ian. But that was unusual; as a general rule, Morgan operated on the assumption that the less her mother knew about her life the better.

"I suppose you'll tell your father, if he asks," Rose said.

"Oh, for fuck's sake!"

"Don't swear. And anyway, it's true, isn't it? You pounce on me whenever I ask a perfectly normal question but he can ask you anything."

"Except he doesn't. Dad lets me live my life. I wish you'd do the same."

"Okay, fine, I will."

"Fine."

They were both close to tears but neither was going to give in, not at this stage. Sooner or later one of them would apologize and the other would say there was no need. There would be hugs and it would be over. Except it wouldn't be, really. It would be lurking in the darkness, with all the old hurts, the misunderstandings, the grievances. Lying in wait till the next time. Nothing was ever resolved between them. Rose had begun to think it never would be.

Morgan put her glass in the sink and stomped upstairs to her room. Just as she slammed her bedroom door the power came back on. Let there be light, Rose thought; better than that, let there be peace.

As is so often the way in this part of the world, the blizzard blew itself out overnight, changing to rain by morning. By noon most of the snow was washed away. Rose took advantage of the fact that she'd already decided to work from home and called Marie to see if she could come by.

"Oh, do!" Marie said. "I've written my character into a corner and it's going to take an act of God to get the poor bugger back home safely."

"I don't want to disturb your writing."

"No, please, disturb me. Maybe if I leave it for a few hours he'll work it out himself."

"Does that happen often?" Rose wondered.

"Not really. But there's always a first time."

When Rose arrived Marie ushered her upstairs to the cozy, book-lined room Marie liked to think of as her study, although she did most of her writing downstairs on the kitchen table. It was a beautiful sunlit space, furnished with an old pine desk that had been stripped down and varnished by a previous owner and a vintage sofa right out of *Little Women.* Rose loved the room; when she asked Marie, ages ago, why she didn't write there, her friend had been typically self-deprecating.

"It's all those books," she said, "written by real writers. They intimidate me to the point where I get stuck and can't write."

"But *you're* a real writer," Rose said. "You've written over twenty books. And you've won prizes."

"I'm a children's writer. There's a difference."

Rose pointed out that J. K. Rowling and Roald Dahl had done all right, writing stories for children. There was nothing to be ashamed of.

"I'm not ashamed," she said. "I love writing for kids and wouldn't have it any other way. But when I'm in the middle of trying to create, I don't need Virginia Woolf looming over me, rolling her eyes and being critical."

"Is that what she does?"

"Oh, I'm sure of it. Trust me, when she was alive she was a major eye-roller."

This morning, with the sun hidden behind the clouds and the skies threatening yet more snow, the room was cooler than usual. Marie suggested they sit downstairs by the fire. But Rose wanted to be away from Jeff, who had a habit of wandering into rooms and joining discussions, uninvited. So they drank their tea upstairs in glorious solitude, sharing the patchwork quilt Marie's mother had made for their tenth anniversary, while Rose talked about the argument with Morgan.

"I'm the last person who should be giving parenting advice," Marie said, "but mother–daughter relationships are complicated. Everything you read says so. It's what happens, Rose, don't let it get to you."

Rose sighed. "I don't know. I think I need to be more tolerant. I miss Morgan like crazy when she's away at school, but when she's home we're always snapping at each other."

"Have you ever read Rainier Maria Rilke's *Letters to a Young Poet*? There's a passage in there where he talks about the relationship between parents and their children. It's quite beautiful. Hang on, I'll find it. I've got it here somewhere."

While Marie rummaged through her bookshelves, Rose relaxed against the sofa cushions, enjoying the sense of peace she always experienced in this room. The house backed onto a ravine and the view from this particular window revealed only a great, grey expanse of sky. You could be anywhere and nowhere, floating in delicious isolation. Marie and Jeff had lived here for thirty years; Rose hoped they would never feel pressured to sell.

"Found it."

Marie pulled out a slim paperback volume that had been tucked behind *Roget's Thesaurus*. She thumbed through the pages, found what she wanted about a third of the way through. "It's in the fourth chapter. Rilke's in Germany and he writes about being ill, and about the weather. He advises the young poet to find solace in nature and not worry about finding answers to life's questions. 'Live the questions,' he says. Isn't that beautiful? Let's see . . . He goes on a lot about sex—"

"That sounds interesting."

"Yes, but where's the part I'm looking for?" Marie skipped a few pages and then said, "Ah, here it is."

Avoid contributing material to the drama that is always stretched taut between parents and children; it uses up much of the children's energy and consumes the love of their elders, which is effective and warming even if it doesn't comprehend. Ask no advice from them and count upon no understanding; but believe in a love that is being stored up for you like an inheritance and trust that in this love there is a strength and a blessing, out beyond which you do not have to step in order to go very far.

"It's quite lovely," Rose said. "I'm not sure I completely understand it but I like it."

"I think he was talking about the importance of staying connected to your parents even as you grow apart from them in wisdom and experience. He was writing from the perspective of a child but it works both ways, don't you think?"

Staying connected. That was the hard part. "I'm not sure I'm good at it. Connecting."

"Sure you are. Look what you've done with Ryan, looking him up after all those years and inviting him to come for dinner."

That wasn't quite the way it happened—it was Ryan who did the looking up, after all. But she did seek him out, didn't she, and made him feel like part of the family.

"That might not have been such a good idea," she said.

"Because of Morgan?"

"I guess. I mean, I wanted him to come for Thanksgiving. I felt sorry for him. I thought he'd come to dinner and then maybe I'd help him get a job at the library or something. I didn't think he was going to . . . take over."

She was exaggerating and she knew it. Ryan hadn't taken over—yet. But she had the distinct feeling that he was going to, if she let it happen. "There's something about him," she said. "I can't put my finger on it exactly but there's *something*. I wish I knew what it was—what's making me so uncomfortable."

"Maybe you just don't feel comfortable with his influence on Morgan. She does seem pretty taken with him."

"Maybe. I don't know. I think it's more than that."

"What does Charles think? Have you talked to him about it?"

"I tried," Rose says, "but he just tells me I'm overreacting. And maybe I am."

Marie stood up, letting her half of the quilt fall to the floor. "I know you love this room but it's freezing up here at the moment. I vote we head downstairs, light the fire, and crack open a bottle of wine. What do you say? Deal?"

"Deal."

34.

ROSE DROVE HOME THINKING ABOUT WHAT SHE *hadn't* said to Marie: she'd said nothing about Garnet and Lauren. The reason being, she wasn't sure what to do about it. Or even what she should think.

Marie would be horrified if she knew, Rose was sure of that. Well, she was pretty horrified herself. Not so much about the spankings, which weren't really that shocking and didn't seem to cause any real damage. It was more what it said about the two of them. There was Lauren, who could, as Marie had said, get any young man she pleased, preferring a relationship with a man old enough to be her grandfather—yes, grandfather, Garnet, admit it. And Garnet pretending Lauren was his little girl—well, it made your toes curl just to think about it.

Which Rose tried not to do. But she couldn't help it. Garnet had been part of her life for almost thirty years, ever since Charles applied for the position at the university. Garnet was on the hiring committee. They took an immediate liking to each other, and Garnet, whose father-in-law was the chancellor, was influential in getting Charles hired. They still saw each other at least once a week. They had a standing lunch date on Saturdays and they got together for coffee a couple of times a month. It was stretching it to say Garnet was like family, although he was, sort of. Her children called him "Uncle Garnet" when they were little and Jason was still very fond of him. Morgan, however, generally avoided him by the time she was in her teens.

"He gives me the creeps," was the way she put it back then. Alarm bells had sounded. When Rose pressed her to say if there was ever a time when Garnet had, well, behaved improperly towards her, Morgan was emphatic. "Yuck—no! Don't be disgusting."

"You'd tell me, wouldn't you? If he ever tried to touch you or anything."

"Stop! There's nothing like that. My god, Mom, why would you say that?"

"You said he gives you the creeps—"

"He does," Morgan said, "but it's not anything like that. It's just all that Shakespeare stuff. He's always talking like he thinks you should be paying to listen. I bet he thinks up things to say before he comes over and then waits till he can use them."

Out of the mouths of babes. And teenagers.

The traffic, which had been slow enough, came to a halt just before the entrance to the Stanley Park causeway. Friday afternoon, what could you expect? She'd taken Denman hoping to avoid the crush of cars leaving downtown, but she should have headed out sooner. She would have, too, if Marie hadn't inveigled her into having a second glass of wine. Now it was almost four thirty and the congestion was at its worst.

She leaned back in her seat and gazed out the passenger window. All those lucky people walking along the sidewalk, doing their shopping, picking up fresh bagels and bread. West Enders: people who'd stayed on this side of the bridge and didn't have to make the commute. Living on the North Shore was lovely as long as you never had to leave it.

An urgent blast of the horn from the driver behind her alerted her that traffic was moving again. Rose stepped on the gas and inched forward, and went back to thinking about Lauren. And Garnet. Was this father–daughter play-acting something new, or had Garnet behaved like this all along? Both of his ex-wives had been younger than him, although not as young as Lauren. Maeve was twenty when she married him, ten years younger than Garnet. And Belinda, the second wife, was in her early forties, making her almost twenty years his junior. Neither of them seemed like the type who'd enjoy playing Daddy's girl. But then, neither did Lauren. So who knew?

Well, Charles did, of course. He had to. He and Garnet were thick as thieves: they finished each other's sentences, they laughed at the same jokes, they shared the same interests. There was no way Garnet would keep this kind of thing from Charles. And if it wasn't new—if it was a pattern of behaviour going back to his marriages—Charles would know.

If that were the case, Charles should have told her. So why didn't he? Was he trying to protect her? That would be out of character. More likely Garnet asked him not to. There had always been an edge between Garnet and her . . . an underlying tension rooted in rivalry. Garnet was the old friend, the mentor. But Rose had married Charles—she was the wife.

"You're going to love him," Charles told her before introducing her to Garnet. He seemed unaware that this was just the kind of statement guaranteed to have the opposite effect. He probably did the same with Garnet. But she did like him more than she expected. Garnet wasn't quite so full of himself in those days—Maeve kept him grounded. He could be gallant and quite charming at times, and he went out of his way to seek Rose's advice on marital matters, especially when his own marriage began to founder.

But they were never close; they didn't confide in each other. That call she'd made back in September, asking for his help in keeping Charles busy, was pretty much the only time she reached out to him in that way. And what did it get her? Nothing. Charles was annoyed with her for assuming he needed a project. And Morgan agreed with him. The only family member who wasn't jumping down her throat these days was Jason, and that was probably because he wasn't around enough to find her irritating.

As the traffic finally streamed onto the causeway and over the bridge, she fretted about what, if anything, she should do. Because there was that fall: Garnet had slapped Lauren hard enough to fall down. And it may or may not have caused her to lose the baby. That was abuse, wasn't it? And if he did it once, he'd do it again.

Lauren had said the play-acting got "a little violent, sometimes," which left Rose wondering if the slap on the face hadn't been the worst of it. Were there other things? Were the spankings only the—how do you say? The tip of the iceberg? If it really was consensual, all this play-acting, why had Lauren chosen to talk about it? She must know how terrible it looked, an older man abusing a young woman—a young *pregnant* woman, in fact. Did she expect someone like Rose to do something about it? Take some action. Call the police?

That would be a bit extreme; she could hardly call up and report a case of inappropriate spanking. Maybe she should call a women's shelter—an abuse hotline. You could do these things anonymously, call one of those support groups, see what they thought. They'd know if there was anything to be done.

Or maybe—and it came to her just like that—she could stage an intervention. She'd invite Lauren and Garnet over for dinner, and maybe have Ryan come, too. It was the kind of thing he'd be good at, she thought. And between them—Rose, Morgan, Ryan, and Charles—they would confront them about their relationship. Charles would have to be put in the picture, of course. If he didn't know about Garnet—and she was pretty sure, now, that he didn't—he was going to take some convincing. The thought of the discussion that lay ahead exhausted her. But Lauren had confided in her for a reason. She wanted Rose to do something. It was a cry for help.

The house was dark, apart from the lamp next to Charles and the light from the TV set. It was after five, but nothing emanated from the kitchen to indicate dinner was being prepared. When Charles was teaching he finished early on Fridays and it became customary for him to fix dinner on that night. These days, though, he seemed to have lost his passion for it; he hadn't cooked a thing since Thanksgiving.

She found him sitting in front of the TV, the book about Churchill on his lap. He set it aside when she came into the living room and put the TV on mute. The book was a prop, obviously; he'd been watching golf being played somewhere in the southern US.

"How was your visit with Marie?"

"Fine," she said. "Haven't you finished that yet?"

He looked up at her, startled. "What?"

"You're still reading that book," she said. "I'd have thought you'd have finished by now."

He looked down at the book as if he was surprised to see it there. "Was I reading this? Funny, I don't remember picking it up."

She sat down beside him, picked up the book and studied the cover. Churchill as a young soldier, newly arrived in South Africa at the beginning of the Anglo-Boer War. "He was actually pretty good-looking," she said. "When he was young."

"Does that surprise you?"

"A little. You always just think of him as that old bulldog—you know, in the Karsh photo." She handed Charles the book. "So what do you think? Are you going to finish it? I've renewed it once already, should I renew it again?"

It was not a particularly long read, just over three hundred pages. The kind of book Charles would normally devour in a day or two. He'd taught himself to speed-read when he was at university and it had served him well over the years. So it seemed strange to find him struggling with this one.

"I could buy you a copy," she said. "A little pre-Christmas gift."

He shook his head. It was against his principles to buy books when they were available through the library. "Leave it with me," he said. "I'll get through it. Another week and I'll be done."

"Is Morgan around?" Rose asked. "I think we should talk."

"She went out earlier. I told her to take my car. She said she was meeting up with Ryan."

"Again? What's with this sudden fascination with the guy? Do you think there's something going on between them?"

"I don't know. Does it matter?"

"Probably not. No, I guess it doesn't."

"She's a big girl, Rose. Let her live her life."

Let her live her life. That was almost exactly what Morgan had said to her: *Dad lets me live my life.* Rose wondered if Morgan had been talking to her father, telling him about the argument. She wasn't going to ask. In a day or two, when enough time had passed, they'd make up. They always did.

"Are you hungry?" she said. "Should I get supper started?"

"I'm all right. Morgan made me a sandwich earlier."

"We could go out to eat."

"We could." There was little enthusiasm, the way he said it.

"We should!" she said. It was the perfect solution: she always found it easier to initiate a difficult conversation in a noisy, crowded restaurant, lubricated by a half-bottle of Merlot. There was less opportunity to argue—Charles especially never wanted to create a scene. "We haven't been out for dinner in ages. Why don't you call Besante's and make us a reservation and I'll get changed?" Rose waited for a response. When he continued to sit, staring at the TV, she found herself getting angry. "Charles, would you at least answer me?"

"What?"

"I'm asking you to call Besante's and get us a table."

"Oh. Right." He stood up and began searching for his phone.

"It's right there," Rose said. "On the coffee table."

"Yes, okay." He picked it up and then said, "What's the number?"

"It's in your phone."

He nodded and began searching his contacts. "It's all right," he said, "you don't have to stand over me like that. Go and get dressed."

She was struggling to get into a pair of slim-fit trousers she hadn't worn in a year when Charles came to the door of the bedroom.

"Besante's is full," he said. "They can't fit us in till nine."

"That's too late."

"I know. That's what I told them."

Rose gave up fight with the pants and slumped down on the bed. These pants fit perfectly when she bought them. How had she gained so much weight?

"Do you want me to try somewhere else?" Charles said. "Or we could order pizza."

"I'm fat," Rose said.

"No, you're not. You're curvy." Seeing her expression, he added, "In a good way."

"If you say Rubenesque I'll throw my hairbrush at you." Garnet had called her that once, shortly after Morgan was born and she never forgot it.

"He meant it as a compliment," he said remembering Garnet. "You had spectacular breasts."

"I was breast-feeding," she said, "and I hadn't lost the baby weight."

"Well, I thought you looked wonderful. And so did he."

He sat next to her on the bed, put his arm around her, and nuzzled her cheek. "Let's order pizza," he said. "It'll take forty minutes to get here. There's a lot we can do in forty minutes."

Rose laughed and gave in. "There's a lot we can do in *ten* minutes. Why don't you help me off with these pants for starters?"

35.

SEX WITH CHARLES HAD ALWAYS BEEN GOOD BUT in some ways, now it was better. No fear of getting pregnant, for one thing. And they knew each other so well. He knew where to go and where not to, and so, she supposed, did she. He'd long ago learned to avoid her nipples: no rubbing, tweaking, or playful pinching. Better yet, no touching. They were ridiculously sensitive; she'd finally, after a few years of tensing under his touch, asked him to leave them alone. Charles, for his part, didn't have any no-go zones, but that was likely because he was a man. He was happy to be touched anywhere and responded with enthusiasm and gratitude. They might have their differences—they *did* have their differences—but all was forgiven when they were in bed.

. In the cozy aftermath of lovemaking, Rose made a spur-of-the-moment decision. "I need to talk to you," she said. "About Garnet."

"What about him?"

"He's in an abusive relationship. He's abusing Lauren."

He looked at her, as if he was trying to work out whether or not she was joking.

"It's not a joke," she said. "She told Morgan and me about it, when we were over there the other day. He spanks her. And he hit her, and it might have caused her to lose the baby."

"He hit her?"

Rose nodded. "Yes. I don't think he meant to, but she fell and then later, that's when she had the miscarriage." She waited while he lay on his back and stared up at the ceiling. It was obvious that all this was news to him; he needed time to digest it. After a moment, she said, "So what do you think?"

"I think it's none of our business."

"What do you mean?"

"I mean what I said. What people do in the privacy of their own homes—you know what I'm saying. It's none of our business."

"But these are our friends!"

"Which is precisely why we shouldn't go poking our noses into their private lives. Did Lauren ask you to get involved?"

"Well, no, not exactly."

"Okay, then."

"But I'm sure she wants me to do something She wouldn't have told us about it if she didn't want us to do something."

Charles sat up and gazed down at her with affection. "Sweetheart," he said, "I love you, but you have a tendency to stick your oar in where it isn't wanted. My advice is to stay out of it. You'll only make things worse." He reached for his jeans and began to put them on just as the doorbell rang. "It's probably the pizza guy," he said. "I'll get it."

Saved by the bell, Rose thought. Literally. Well, what had she thought would happen, bringing it up like that without any kind of preamble? She hadn't really expected Charles to buy it, not at first, anyway. She'd give it a day or two and try again. Let him have some time to mull it over—

"Rose!" Charles was calling to her from the bottom of the staircase. "Get dressed and come downstairs. We have a visitor!"

A visitor? At this time of night? Could it be Garnet? He did drop in occasionally on his way home from work. Had Lauren decided to move out? Well, if he came here looking for a shoulder to cry on, he'd come to the wrong place.

She got up and pulled on a pair of pants—not the slim-fits, she wouldn't be wearing those again for a while—and a T-shirt, and headed downstairs.

Charles was standing at the foot of the stairs, brimming with excitement.

"Who is it?" she said.

He waited until she was on the ground floor and then, without saying a word, ushered her into the living room. The room was still in semi-darkness, and for a moment she couldn't quite make out the figure standing by the fire. A young man, but . . .

"Ian! Oh, my goodness!"

"Hey, Rose, how are you? It's good to see you." Ian came forward and embraced her. "I hope I didn't give you a shock, turning up like this. I'm sorry."

"Don't be! It's lovely to see you—"

"He's been trying to reach Morgan," Charles said, "but she won't answer his calls."

"I've been texting and calling her for weeks," Ian said. "I just want to talk to her—I want a chance to sort things out."

"Oh, Ian," Rose said, "I'm so pleased to see you. We both are, aren't we, Charles? We were so upset when Morgan told us—well, when she said you'd broken up. Come, sit down, you look exhausted."

And he did. He had the pale, bleary-eyed look of someone who hadn't slept for at least a day or two. His blond hair was pulled back in a messy kind of ponytail and his clothes had been slept in. A far cry from the tidy, pulled-together young man who visited them at Christmas.

Charles offered to get him a drink, but Ian said thanks, but he'd prefer water. "Or juice, if you have it. I've been drinking on the plane all the way from Toronto."

"Are you hungry?" Rose said. "I can fix you a sandwich."

"I'm really sorry to barge in on you like this," Ian said, sinking into the sofa. "I just got desperate to see her. And then when I got this letter—well, I figured I had to get out here."

"What letter?"

Before Ian could respond, the doorbell rang again. From the kitchen, Charles announced that he'd get it. "That has to be the pizza guy," he said. "Hang on, Ian, I'll bring you some juice in a minute."

"Oh, jeez, I'm sorry, I've come in the middle of your dinner. I was going to go straight to a hotel but I thought I'd take a chance and see if Morgan was in—maybe we could talk tonight. So I just came right from the airport. Is she here?"

Rose felt terrible having to confess that Morgan was out, and probably not going to be back until late. "She's with a friend," she said, hoping he wouldn't ask for details.

But he did. "Is it Ryan? Is that who she's with?"

"Well, yes, but—you know about him?"

His frown turned into a sneer. "It's why I'm here. I plan to punch the crap out of him, first chance I get." Seeing her reaction, he added, "It's okay, Rose. When I got the letter I planned to murder him. So I've scaled it down."

"What letter?" Rose said. "Did Morgan write you a letter?"

"Oh, yeah, she wrote me a letter all right. Get this: she doesn't answer my texts, won't call me back, and then, out of the blue, she writes and tells me she's going to Sri Lanka! With that bastard! Sorry, Rose, I'm just really tired." He tugged at the front of his shirt and gave a quick sniff. "I'm sorry, I must stink. I've been travelling for twelve hours. The only flight I could get was through Winnipeg and then three hours in Calgary." He stood up. "There's a motel at the bottom of the street. I'll go check in and try to get some sleep. I'm really sorry for dropping this on you. I feel like a jerk."

Rose made up her mind. "Sit down," she said, "and take off your jacket. You'll have some pizza with us, and then you can go upstairs and take a shower and change. I'll make up the bed in Jason's room—you are *not* going to a motel."

Ian looked relieved but apprehensive. "Are you sure? What's Morgan going to say when she gets back?"

"I don't know and right now I don't particularly care. You're our guest, Ian. And please stop apologizing. There's no need for it." She spoke firmly and pleasantly but inside she was fuming. How dare her daughter treat Ian so shabbily! What had gotten into her? To refuse to return his calls? And to send him a letter like that? She was ashamed—ashamed of her daughter, something she'd never experienced before.

Charles entered the room bearing pizza and orange juice. "I hope you're hungry," he said. "I ordered two large pizzas."

Rose gave him a quizzical look. "You did? We always order medium size."

Charles grinned. "Well, I guess I had a premonition we were getting an unexpected guest. Go on, Ian, help yourself. There's plenty to go around."

She waited until Ian had finished his second slice and was helping himself to a third before asking about the letter. "It's none of my business, of course . . ."

Ian put down his pizza, reached into his coat pocket, and pulled out a crumpled envelope. Its contents had been read several times, that was obvious. He handed it to Rose and said, "Go ahead, read it. There's nothing personal in it. Unfortunately."

It began: "Ian." Not "Dear Ian" or even "Hi, Ian." Just "Ian."

"Read it aloud, if you want. Charles should probably hear it, too."

Morgan had written it in the careful, almost childish script Rose remembered from her school days. It seemed rather sweet that she'd taken the time to write it out by hand rather than use the computer, but the contents were anything but sweet.

"Ian," she read aloud. "I've had two months to consider next steps, as, I'm sure, have you. It seems obvious to me that the best thing is to move on as cleanly as possible, and in order to do that

I think it's only fair to let you know I've made some major, life-changing decisions."

Rose looked up. "She has?"

"Go on," Ian said, morosely. "It gets better."

"These decisions don't involve you but I should tell you I've met someone who's shown me how shallow my life is and maybe always has been. As someone who's shared that life for the past couple of years, you need to know how dissatisfied I am with the path I've been on. I've decided to join my friend Ryan on his journey of discovery and will be leaving shortly for Sri Lanka. Please pack up my books, papers, and any clothes I left in Toronto and send them on to my parents' place. I don't care about the furniture—the two bookcases, the papasan chair, the duvet and pillows and the glass side table—but please hang on to Issy for me till I can pick her up myself. She's valuable and I don't want her shipped."

Rose looked up. "Issy?"

"Isadora Duncan," Ian said. "It's a bronze statue from Kensington Market. I gave it to her when we first started going out."

Rose thought that was a good sign, her daughter wanting to hang on to something Ian gave her. She continued reading: "Let me know the shipping cost and I'll send you an email transfer. I'm not expecting any mail but if anything comes that looks important you can forward it to Mom and Dad. Please DO NOT open it. Regards, M." Rose turned the page over—there was a PS: "You haven't asked me about the ring which I left in the top drawer of the night table so I'm assuming you found it."

Ian was right: it was impersonal. Cold, even. And Sri Lanka—when had Morgan decided on that? She turned to Charles. "Has she said anything like this to you?"

Charles shook his head. For once, he was as disturbed as she was, and was taking it seriously. "Nothing. Is there a date on the letter?"

"It's not dated," Ian said, taking the letter back from Rose and folding it into the envelope. "I got it two days ago, so I figure she must've written it sometime last week. What I want to know is, who is this guy Ryan? She never mentioned anyone by that name. Do you know him?"

Rose hesitated; it would have to be said but she hated having to admit that she not only knew Ryan, she'd introduced him to Morgan. Although not, obviously, with the intention of having him ruin her life.

Charles spoke up. "He's a friend of the family. Morgan went to school with him."

"So she knew him at college?"

"No, not then," Rose said. "When she was little. His mother was our babysitter. Our nanny."

Ian shook his head. "I don't get it. Did they go out together?"

"Oh, no!" Rose realized she'd spoken too forcefully, and she tried to put a softer spin on it. "He lived with us for a while, when the children were small, and then his father came and got him and, well, that was it. Wasn't it, Charles? We didn't see him for years."

"We had him here for Thanksgiving," Charles said, adding that Rose had invited him.

"Out of the blue?" Ian said. "You just called him up and invited him for Thanksgiving?"

"Well, no, not exactly." She attempted a laugh that didn't quite work. "That would have been a little weird, don't you think? No, actually, I ran into him. By accident. And I just thought—he didn't seem to be living anywhere, exactly—"

"He's homeless? Is this guy a street person?"

"Oh, I wouldn't call him that," Charles said, turning to Rose for confirmation. "Would you? He's more of a wayfarer, don't you think?"

A wayfarer. It wasn't a bad description, when you thought about it. "Yes," she said, "you could call him that." She smiled at Ian. "He's traveled all over. Nepal, India . . ." She stopped, having run out of places Ryan had mentioned, and then added, "He lived in Montreal for a while."

There was a silence. Ian seemed to be trying to digest what they'd told him. He chewed the last of his pizza, staring gloomily at nothing in particular.

"Ian?" Rose said. "Dear? You're very quiet. Are you all right?"

"No," he said, "I'm not. I don't understand what's got into her. She meets this—this homeless guy from her past and decides to run off with him? Why would she do something like that? What the hell's the matter with her?"

Rose didn't have an answer to this, and she was pretty sure that whatever she said next wasn't going to make Ian feel any better. It didn't help that he was tired and probably jet-lagged; what he really needed was some rest. Also, he was right: he did stink, a little.

"Why don't you take your bag upstairs," she suggested, "and leave it in Jason's room? I'll put fresh sheets on the bed while you have a shower. And when Morgan comes in I'll let her know you're here."

Ian protested that he didn't want her to go to a lot of trouble, but his heart wasn't in it. He stood up, thanked them for the pizza, and headed up the stairs.

Once he was out of earshot, Rose picked up her phone and called Morgan.

36.

"WHAT DO YOU MEAN, HE'S HERE? HERE, AS IN Vancouver?" Morgan was every bit as shocked as Rose thought she would be; in fact, she sounded outraged.

"Yes, here as in Vancouver."

"In our house? What the hell is Ian doing in our house?"

"Well, at the moment he's having a shower—"

"Mom! Are you kidding me? You've invited Ian into our house and now he's having a shower? What. The. Hell!"

"Okay, can you quit swearing, please? He's flown in from Toronto and it was one of those ridiculous routes, you know—Toronto, Winnipeg—Calgary, I think. Or was it Edmonton?"

"Mother."

"What?" There was a pause. Rose could imagine her daughter taking a deep breath, making an effort to speak without shouting. She waited.

"What, exactly, is he doing here? Besides taking a shower."

"Well, he's come to see you, obviously."

"Obviously. What does he want?"

Rose wasn't sure she should be speaking for Ian, and she said so.

"Fine," Morgan said, "put him on. Oh, I forgot, he's in the *shower.*"

"There's no need to be sarcastic. I'm just letting you know what's happening. Don't shoot the messenger." She was trying to inject a lighter note but her daughter wasn't buying it.

Again, a silence.

"Morgan? Are you there?"

"I don't want to see him, Mom. There's no point."

"But he's come all this way."

"I don't care. I have nothing to say to him. Everything I wanted to say I said in a letter. He can go back home and wait till it arrives."

"It did arrive," Rose said. "That's why he's here. Because of what you said about Ryan and going to Sri Lanka. Why Sri Lanka, Morgan? Where did that come from?"

"He *read* you the letter?"

Rose admitted that, in actual fact, she'd read the letter herself.

"Let me get this straight," Morgan said, sounding even more infuriated than before, if that was possible. "Ian gave you a letter I wrote to him—a *personal* letter, from me to him—and told you to *read* it?"

Rose began to say that it wasn't actually that personal, but Morgan stopped her. "When Ian is out of the shower, please tell him I don't intend to discuss any of this with him. I made things very clear when I left but he doesn't seem to understand plain English. I'm sorry he's come all this way for nothing, but that's on him. I'm not taking responsibility for his stupidity. Call me when he's gone, okay?"

"I've invited him to stay the night," Rose said.

She expected an outburst from the other end of the phone, but Morgan was very quiet. Rose could hear voices in the background, and the muted strains of a guitar. Somebody asked Morgan something and she said, "Yes, all right . . . I have to go. I'm sorry Ian's involved you in this but I am not coming back as long as he's there. Let me know when he's gone."

Charles, waiting to hear what Morgan had said, could see that the conversation hadn't gone well. "She's not pleased," he said, after Rose hung up.

"No, she's not pleased, in fact she's mortally pissed off."

"At us?"

"At Ian and me, mostly," Rose said. "But she's always mad at me so there's nothing new about that. She says she's not coming home until he's gone."

The question now was what to do about the young man upstairs using their shower? Charles said it was obvious: he'd have to spend the night somewhere else. Rose wasn't so sure. They could hardly disinvite him, after being so adamant that he should stay. It would be unthinkably rude. Besides, if he left, what were the chances of him and Morgan ever getting together? Once he was out of the house it would be too darned easy for her daughter to just avoid him completely. Until Ian, despairing and resigned, got back on a plane to Toronto.

Rose wasn't going to let that happen. Morgan had her own reasons for not returning Ian's calls—and for writing that letter—but now that he was here she should hear him out. He'd come all this way; at the very least, he deserved a meeting. She went upstairs, put clean sheets, a blanket, and a couple of pillows on the spare bed, and called Morgan back. "I can't kick him out, it's the middle of the night."

"It's ten to eight," Morgan said. "He's a big boy—he can go to a hotel."

"Can't you just come back and talk to him? Just see what he has to say?"

"And what purpose would that serve?"

"Closure. It would give you both closure." She waited; Morgan said nothing. "He doesn't seem to think it's over, your relationship. I get the impression he thinks it can be fixed."

"Oh, yes, that's Ian all right. Mr. Fix-it. Everything can be fixed. Well, he's wrong. If you want him to stay the night, fine, feel free to take his side." And she hung up.

Charles was heading into the kitchen with the leftover pizza. "Should we save this for Morgan? She might like it for breakfast."

"I'm not sure she'll be here for breakfast. She's really upset."

"She'll calm down. Give her time and she'll come to her senses. They're meant for each other, those two. She'll see that."

It was the first really sensible thing her husband had said in a while. Everything he had done and almost everything he'd said for the past two months was odd, and if not odd, then at least out of character. Quitting his job without talking it over with her first. Deciding to write about Myra Hindley, and then not lifting a finger to get started. She hated to say it, but she was beginning to think that when he walked away from the university he was doing more than just leaving the place where he'd worked for most of his life; he was walking away from who he was. The man he'd been as long as she'd known him. Engaged. Interested in the world. Well, at least now he was showing some interest in Morgan's love life. That was something.

Charles returned from the kitchen and caught Rose re-reading Morgan's letter, which Ian had left on the coffee table.

"He asked us to read it," she said. "I don't think he'd mind me reading it again."

Charles shrugged, and switched on the TV.

"It's too early for the news," she said.

"I'll keep it on mute. I just want to see what's on."

Rose ran her eyes over the contents. *I've decided to join Ryan on his journey of discovery.* What on earth was that supposed to mean? Was she going to become a wayfarer, like Ryan? It was one thing to take a break from her studies, even to decide not to get married. But this—it didn't sound like Morgan at all.

"Charles, did you know about this?"

"Know about what?"

"About this. Any of it. Morgan getting calls from Ian and not returning them. And deciding to run off with Ryan. Did you know about that?"

"Of course not. When I talked to her she said she needed some space, that's all. She said she wanted to look at other options."

"When was this?"

"The other day. You asked me to talk to her and I did. She didn't say anything about flying off to South Africa."

"Sri Lanka."

"Right."

So he *had* talked to Morgan after all. And hadn't thought to mention it to her. Making a Herculean effort to keep her voice down, Rose asked why he hadn't told her about this earlier. Why had he waited till now to bring it up?

"I guess it slipped my mind," he said. "I'm sorry, love. But you know now, right?"

When Ian came downstairs, showered, wearing a clean shirt, Rose told him what Morgan had said on the phone. He nodded, as if he'd expected something like that, and then asked if she was staying with Ryan.

"I don't know," Rose told him. "I don't think she could be—he lives in a tent."

"A tent," he said. "I see."

"It's a little strange, I know," Rose said, "but he's just made this lifestyle choice not to be tied down by, well, material things. Isn't that right, Charles?"

She looked to her husband for confirmation but he was having one of his "moments," as she was beginning to think of them. He gave her a blank stare and then, instead of contributing to the conversation like a normal person, he asked Ian where he'd got his shirt.

Ian glanced down, as if to check what he was wearing. "This shirt? I'm not sure. I think Morgan bought it for me."

"I thought so! It looks exactly like something Morgan would have picked out. Don't you think so, Rose?"

She studied the shirt: it was a plain white V-neck, short-sleeved without a logo. There was absolutely nothing remarkable about it.

"I don't know," she said. "Maybe."

"There's no maybe about it!" Charles was positively cackling with glee. "Is it one hundred percent cotton?"

Ian was beginning to show signs of consternation. "I guess so. It's just a shirt, Charles . . ."

"She has excellent taste," Charles confided. "I've got one just like it upstairs. And who do you think bought it for me?"

Ian took a guess. "Morgan?"

"Exactly!"

It's hard to say where things might have gone from this point, but luckily Ian stood up and asked if he might be excused. He'd been up for almost twenty-four hours and he was ready to drop. Grateful for the distraction, Rose assured him they were fine with him heading up to bed. "If you need anything," she said, "anything at all, just let us know."

Rose kept her temper until she heard the bedroom door shut. Then she turned to Charles and demanded, "What the heck was *that?*"

"What?"

"That ridiculous—" She struggled for the right word. "*Non sequitur* about the shirt. 'One hundred percent cotton'—what on earth were you going on about?"

In a voice reeking of injured innocence, Charles claimed he was making conversation. "Why are you so mad?"

"You sounded insane," she said. "You sounded like a crazy person."

"Fuck you!" he shouted.

"Charles!"

"You heard me—fuck you. What right do you have to call me crazy? If anyone's crazy in this household, it's you."

Rose was dumbfounded. He never spoke to her like this. Never had, in all the time they'd been together. Before she could manage a response, he pushed himself out of his chair and came over to where she was sitting, looming over her like an avenging angel.

"You're the crazy one," he hissed, pointing his finger in her face. "You go around poking your nose into everyone's business, upsetting Morgan, making accusations about Garnet, about my friends." She tried to interject but he wasn't listening. "And Ian—what's he doing here, anyway? Did you invite him? Did you tell him to come?"

"No, of course not—"

"What's Morgan going to do? Where's she going to sleep tonight? Did you think of that? No, of course you didn't. You never think—you never think of anyone but yourself."

Rose was too stunned to react; it was so sudden, and so out of character, she couldn't take it in. This wasn't Charles. And if it was, it wasn't the Charles she knew.

"Where's this coming from?" she asked, when he paused long enough to let her speak. "What's gotten into you?"

He began to pace the room, the words tumbling out now as if he was talking to himself. As if she wasn't sitting there on the sofa, watching him in alarm. "Maybe I'm just coming to my senses. Maybe I'm just seeing things for what they are—the hypocrisy, the lies. It's all a sham. A fraud. A hoax." He stopped. He reached the bottom of the staircase, and stood there, leaning slightly against the bannister, as if for support.

"Charles?"

"What?"

"What's a sham? What are you talking about?"

"Us." He shook his head, as if it was all too much to explain. "I'm tired. I think I'll take a nap."

Mystified, Rose watched as he mounted the stairs, slowly, clinging to the handrail. After a few minutes, she crept upstairs and peered into their bedroom. Charles was lying on top of the bed covers; his eyes were closed and he was snoring lightly. Quietly, Rose adjusted the blankets to cover him, leaned down, and kissed him on the forehead. Then she turned out the light and went back downstairs.

37.

IT WAS NOT A RESTFUL NIGHT. WHAT WITH EVERY-
thing that had happened, Charles' outbursts, the argument with
Morgan, her daughter spending the night in a tent, she had lain
awake most of the night, worrying. She did finally fall asleep and
awoke, exhausted, to the shrill chirping of the dawn chorus, well
before sunrise. Charles was still asleep and she didn't want to wake
him. She got up and shut the window, taking a moment to gaze out
into the dim expanse of the back garden to see if she could make
out the birds making all the damn noise. Weren't they supposed to
wait until *after* the sun came up to herald the day? Climbing back
into bed, she saw there was a text waiting for her on her phone.
Ian had sent it a few hours ago, presumably while they were asleep.
*Thanks for the hospitality, Rose, but I feel bad about getting you and
Charles involved in this. I'm going to check into a hotel and give Morgan
a day to think about things. I'll be in touch.*

She got out of bed again and went to check: sure enough, the
spare bedroom was empty. There was no sign of Ian and the bed
hadn't been slept in. She sent a text to Morgan: *Just letting you know,
Ian's checked into a hotel. You can come home. xox*

When she woke up again, the sun streamed through the window and Charles' side of the bed was empty. She could smell coffee brewing and the potent aroma of cooked bacon. Charles was making breakfast—a very good sign, she thought. She checked her phone and sure enough, there was a text from Morgan saying she'd be back later in the day. *Busy working with Ryan,* she wrote. Whatever that meant. But she was coming home, which was all that mattered. And once she was home, Rose was sure she could convince her to sit down and talk to Ian. He was such a lovely young man. Surely Morgan would realize that once she saw him again.

She put on her bathrobe and made her way downstairs to the kitchen. Given how things had ended last night she was relieved when Charles looked up from the stove and greeted her with a grin. "Good morning, my angel! Did you sleep well?"

"Very well. How are you?"

"Never better. I hope you're hungry. I've made eggs Florentine. We're out of prosciutto so I used bacon instead. Take a seat, and I'll serve you."

Rose did as she was told. Whatever had brought on that irrational tirade appeared to be over and done with. Did he even remember flipping out on her? She watched while he put two tomato slices on a plate, seasoned them with salt and paper, and spooned sauce over each slice. With infinite care he placed a couple of poached eggs on top of the tomatoes and sprinkled a handful of crumbled bacon on top.

"There you go, my dear," he said, setting the plate down in front of her. "*Bon appetit!* Or should I say, *buon appetito!*"

"Aren't you eating?"

He shook his head. "I'm having lunch with Garnet. I'll be fine."

"You're sure?"

"Absolutely. The sun is shining, Liverpool is number two in the league, and I'm married to the sexiest woman in the world. I'm a very lucky man." Charles leaned down and planted a quick kiss on her cheek.

After breakfast, Rose took the newspaper into the living room, switched on the gas fire, and settled down to do the crossword. They had cancelled their daily subscription a while back but kept the Saturday delivery for the pleasure of turning actual pages and sharing the sections between them. You could read the same news on your phone, of course, but you couldn't share it in the same way.

Charles sat across from her, reading the sports section. The Churchill book lay on the floor beside him. Careful not to sound as if she was passing judgment, Rose asked if he'd finished it yet.

"No, not yet," he said. "You can take it back when you go into work on Monday. I don't think I'll finish it."

"Is it not very interesting?"

"I guess I'm more interested in his latter years."

"When he was prime minister."

"Yes. He was sixty-five when the war started, and he thought his best days were behind him. He thought he was a has-been. But the best was yet to come." He put down the paper and sighed. "I could do with a good war," he said.

Rose smiled. "Couldn't we all!" She waited a little, then decided to go ahead and get it over with. "Charles, about last night," she said. "Can we talk about what happened?"

"With Ian?"

"No, I mean, what you said to me. You were so angry."

"I was? What did I say?"

He seemed truly puzzled and she wondered if there was any point in continuing.

"You said I was crazy—you said everything was a sham. You really don't remember?"

"That doesn't sound like me."

"I know," she said. "It was weird."

"Well, I'm sorry. I guess I was upset but I didn't mean to take it out on you." He stood up and checked his watch. "I'd better be off. I'm meeting Garnet at noon." He kissed her on the cheek and smiled. "You know I don't think you're crazy. I think you're wonderful. Who else would put up with me?"

Twenty minutes into struggling with the cryptic crossword, Rose gave it up. She couldn't concentrate. She kept thinking about Ian, shuttered away in some drab motel room, waiting for an opportunity to talk to her daughter. She thought about calling him but, really, what was the point? She had nothing to offer him at this point— nothing new to say about Morgan.

The person she wanted to talk to about all of this was Marie. Unfortunately, it was Saturday and Marie would be headed to her writers' group. They met the first Saturday of every month, an afternoon event that usually stretched into the early evening. No point in calling her, Rose thought, but she could send her a text: *Big news. Ian's back in the picture! Call me ok when ur meeting's done.*

It was peaceful, sitting there by the fire, not having anything pressing to do. Rose closed her eyes and drifted into a kind of reverie somewhere between sleep and wakefulness, and when the phone rang she was still half asleep.

"Rose?" It was Garnet, sounding more than a little pissed off. "Is Charles there with you?"

"Isn't he with you?"

"He's supposed to be. We agreed to meet at noon and I've been waiting for the past hour. I've tried to call him but he isn't picking up."

Rose checked her phone: 12:53. Charles had left two hours ago. "Oh my god, Garnet, do you think he's been in an accident?" Charles, involved in a head-on, somewhere on the Upper Levels highway. Thrown through the windshield, lying in a ditch, unconscious and bleeding.

Garnet abruptly changed tack. "It never occurred to me," he said. "I just assumed he got busy with other things—I didn't think about—good Lord, Rose, we must find him."

She tried to think. "Call the hospitals, will you? See if he's been brought into emergency. I'll call Jason."

Her son was always the cool head in a crisis. And he was a lawyer. He'd know what to do, whom to call. And if the police had to be notified, he'd be the one to do it. She could barely hold the phone steady to dial his number, her hands were shaking so badly.

Pick up, she thought, as the phone began to ring. Pick up pick up pick up.

"Hey, Mom, what's up?"

"It's your father," she began, and had to stop to catch her breath. Her voice was trembling and Jason, hearing it, was alarmed.

"What about him?" he said. "Has something happened? Is Dad okay?"

She took a deep breath, told herself to calm down. "He's missing," she said. "He left the house two hours ago to meet up with Garnet, and we can't find him. He didn't get to the restaurant and Garnet says he's not answering his phone."

Jason wanted to know if she'd tried to call him, and Rose realized she hadn't.

"I'll call you back."

She hung up and called Charles' phone. After four rings it went to voice mail; she hung up and called Jason. "No answer," she said. "I just got his voice mail. We have to go look for him!"

"Okay, Mom," Jason said, "you stay put. Tell me where he was going and I'll trace the route and see if there's any sign of him."

She heard Lee in the background, probably asking what was wrong, and she heard him tell her, "It's Dad, he's gone missing."

Rose gave Jason the name of the restaurant and promised to wait until she heard back from him. "Garnet's calling the hospitals," she said. "Should I call the police? Do you have to wait twenty-four hours or something?"

Jason said there wasn't a waiting period, that was just a myth, ("I'm a lawyer, Mom, trust me") but she should wait till he got back to her and then they'd call them together. He said there was probably a logical explanation and Rose desperately wanted to believe that was the case. When she hung up the phone, though, all she could think about was what he'd said last night. All that anger, so terribly unlike him. Coming to his senses, he'd said. Did he mean he was done with her? Done with being married?

Waiting for Jason to call her back was torture. She paced the living room, started at every sound, convinced it was Charles pulling into the driveway. She called his cell every five minutes, silently urging him to pick up. It went to voice mail each time. She left a series of messages until the robot on the other end told her his mailbox was full.

Garnet called to say he'd tried all three hospitals in the city and there were no reports of anyone matching Charles' description being brought into the ER. Just to be sure, he'd called the police non-emergency line to see if there'd been a car accident in the past couple of hours.

"So far so good," he told Rose.

"You think so? But he could have driven outside the city. He could be lying in a ditch somewhere out in the bush—"

Garnet interrupted to say he was heading home to pick up Lauren and then he'd be coming by, "to provide emotional support. Can't have you dealing with this on your own. Time to bring in the troops."

Rose started to say she wasn't on her own, that Jason was going to be turning up any minute, but Garnet wasn't listening. After offering further assurances that all would be resolved by the end of the day, and whatever she did she wasn't to "get into a state," he hung up.

Thinking she might find a clue of some kind, she went up to their bedroom, rummaged through his drawers, checked the pockets of his shirts, pants, and bathrobe. Aside from a few scraps of paper with to-do items scribbled on them: pick up milk, bananas, dry cleaning, lunch with Garnet—she found nothing useful. No sign that he'd made arrangements to do anything out of the ordinary that afternoon.

Back downstairs, she sat on the sofa and thought about calling Morgan. Better not just yet, she decided. Why have both her children running around looking for their father when he might walk in the door any moment? She picked up the Churchill book from the floor where Charles had left it. *Hero of the Empire.*

"You're *my* hero, Charles," she murmured. "Please be all right."

38.

When she did finally hear a car pull up to the house she had a moment of relief followed by intense disappointment when she saw it was Jason, and he was alone.

"Nothing?"

He shook his head, his mouth set in a tight, grim line as he came up the stairs into the house. The brilliant sun that had shone all morning had disappeared behind clouds; it felt cool and damp, as though it might rain. Jason wore a short-sleeved T-shirt and jeans; he'd obviously set off right after talking to her without bothering to put on a jacket.

"We'd better call," he said, meaning the police, and she felt her heart rate increase. For a moment she was unable to think; she reached out to Jason, put a hand on his arm, and he wrapped her in a hug. Then he steered her into the kitchen and told her to sit down. "I'll call them, Mom. Just sit and try not to panic."

She sat and waited obediently while he called 911 and spoke to the dispatcher. From time to time he checked with her to be sure of the details: "He left, what, three hours ago, Mom?"

Rose glanced at the kitchen clock: 2:55. "Almost four," she said. "He left just after eleven."

Name: Charles Raymond Addams

Age: 64

Height: 5'11". Six feet, if you were to ask him.

Glasses? No.

Hearing aid? No.

And then, "What was he wearing?"

She tried to think. She didn't actually see him go out the door, but he would have put on his winter coat and his leather gloves. Charles never trusted the weather forecast: it had been calling for sun all day but he knew how quickly that could change. Dark shoes— Oxfords, you'd call them—and those khaki pants she bought him from Eddie Bauer. The ones with the expandable waistband.

Jason relayed that information and then had another question for her: "They're asking if he's ever done this before? Left like this?"

She shook her head: "No, never. I always know where he is. Always."

"It's okay, Mom," Jason said, "we'll find him."

The dispatcher asked something else and Jason replied, "No, definitely not!"

"What?" Rose asked. "What is it?"

Jason, listening, put up his hand—"Hang on, Mom"—gave the dispatcher Charles' cell phone number and a description of the car, and then said, "Um, just a minute, I'll ask. They want to know if Dad has any favourite places—you know, where he might like to go. I thought of the beach and the park where we used to play soccer but I drove by there and he's not there."

"There's the coffee shop in the village. He goes there weekday afternoons. But it's Saturday and he was supposed to be meeting Garnet downtown."

Jason passed that information on to the dispatcher, thanked her, and hung up. "They're putting out a missing persons alert," he told her. "And they have his license number so if they see him they'll pull him over. They'll find him, he can't have gone far."

Rose wanted to know what the dispatcher had asked earlier and Jason winced, either in embarrassment or distress. "She asked if he was suicidal, and if he had any mental health issues. I said no, of course not. You heard me. He doesn't have any mental problems, right?"

Rose said no, too quickly, reassuring herself as well as her son.

Jason stood up, restless. "I should be doing something—I'm going to head out and try the beach again. Did you call Morgan?"

"No, but I will. I was waiting to see—well, you know."

"I'll call her, Mom." As he opened the front door to leave, he asked, "Are you okay here on your own?"

Rose said she was and then remembered she wouldn't be on her own. "Garnet's coming by with Lauren. They should be here soon, I think." Satisfied that she didn't need him to stay with her, Jason hugged her again and reminded her to keep her phone charged, just in case.

Rose could hear the wind picking up; it was too cold to be walking around without a jacket. "Jason, you shouldn't be out dressed like that! Take your dad's windbreaker."

Jason retrieved the jacket from the hall closet and held it up for inspection. "I'm going to look pretty goofy in this. It's too baggy in the chest and too short in the arms."

"Never mind, no one's going to see you. Go on, put it on and zip it up. At least it'll keep you warm."

Jason did as he was told, zipped up the jacket, and inspected himself in the hall mirror. He did look pretty goofy, she had to admit. Charles was two inches shorter than his son and a good thirty pounds heavier.

"Lee would kill me if she saw me in this."

"She's not going to see you in it and, anyway, it's an emergency."

He left, promising to call if he had any news at all, and she said she'd do the same. Rose closed the door and went into the kitchen to pour herself a glass of wine. Her hand was trembling. She had to put down the bottle and take a deep breath. Calm down, she told herself. He's all right. He's going to be all right.

Morgan called, sounding upset. Jason had called her with the news and she was on her way back to the house. "What do you think, Mom? Has he gone off somewhere?"

Rose said she didn't know, couldn't think. She was close to tears at this point and Morgan hurried to reassure her.

"We'll find him," she said. "When we get back we'll put it on Facebook, okay? We can use that picture I took when you guys came to see me in Toronto. The one in front of the CN Tower. It's a good one." It *was* a good a one—one of the few showing Charles wearing a suit. "We'll put it on Instagram, too," Morgan said, "and Twitter. We'll post it everywhere. People will share it. We'll find him."

Rose was unsure. All this social media stuff . . . what if he'd just taken it into his head to worry her—worry them all? Wasn't it likely that he'd walk in the door any minute, cool as a cucumber, affecting astonishment that he'd caused so much distress "Let's wait," she said. "Wait to see what the police turn up. It might be nothing."

"Are you sure? I mean, if anything's happened . . ."

"I know. But I'd feel better if we give it just a few more hours."

Morgan agreed and said she'd be back soon. "Ryan's with me... Do you mind if he comes over?"

What could she say? "No, of course not."

Ryan spoke up; she hadn't realized she was on speakerphone through Morgan's Bluetooth.

"Are you sure it's all right, Mrs. Addams? I don't want to cause trouble or anything."

Rose assured him he wouldn't, and hung up, thinking once again about the—what was the word? The *ubiquity* of this young man. Ever since stalking her in the parking lot (because that was, after all, what it was), he'd been hanging around like a bad smell. And Marie was right: the attraction, of course, was Morgan. Well, if her daughter wanted to throw her life away on a homeless vagabond, it was up to her. Rose had other things to worry about, just at the moment.

Garnet and Lauren arrived just before four, bearing wine and take-out food from Samir's Bombay Restaurant. Nobody felt much like eating, but Rose appreciated the gesture and the wine was good: a French Merlot and a Napa Valley Chardonnay. Lauren set the food out in the kitchen. Garnet, after ascertaining that everything that could be done was being done, poured them each a glass of wine.

For once, he was serious without being pompous, sympathetic without being patronizing. He didn't try to cheer Rose up or offer false hope, and she was grateful for that. He did say, though, that in all the long years he'd known Charles, he'd known him to own an indomitable spirit, and believed him to have a cheerful nature. "I've always thought it was a gift, the way he can live in the present and not let the past trouble him. He doesn't fixate on things—doesn't let them overwhelm him."

Rose desperately wanted to believe this was still the case. As much as she tried to push it aside, that question from the dispatcher, the one about Charles' mental health, nagged at her. He had tried to kill himself once, according to Liz; was it possible his demons had resurfaced, now that he was no longer working? What did she really know about his state of mind these days?

There was a time when they talked about everything. When did that stop? You'd think, him being retired and all, there'd be plenty of opportunities for discussion these days, but in fact the situation was reversed. The more time they spent together, the less they seemed to say. It was as if for the bulk of their married life, they'd squeezed all the important conversations into the spaces between work and family and now the pressure was off, so was the sense of urgency.

It was beginning to get dark. If they didn't find him soon . . . she couldn't finish the thought. Garnet reached over and patted her knee. "They'll find him, Rose. It'll be all right. Trust me."

When her phone rang they all jumped to attention. It was Jason. He'd spoken to a police officer who asked for a picture of Charles and an article of his clothing. "I can't give them this jacket. I've been wearing it. I'll come by the house and get another one."

"Do you want something to eat?" Rose said. "We have Indian food. Quite a lot, actually."

"Save some for me," he said. "I need to check in with Lee, but maybe we'll join you."

Lauren, keeping vigil by the front window, called out, "Somebody's here!"

Rose rushed to the front door. Her car had pulled up in the driveway and Morgan and Ryan got out. Before they reached the steps Morgan called out, "Any news?"

Rose shook her head, and went on to tell her about the police wanting a photograph of Charles and an article of his clothing.

"They're taking it seriously then," Morgan said. "Good."

"It's time to get the word out," Lauren said, adding that she had two thousand followers on Instagram and more on Facebook. Which was news to Garnet.

"You do? How is that possible?" Lauren chose not to reply.

Ryan volunteered that he, too, had quite a few followers on Facebook. "Well, not me so much but sangha," and Morgan added, "Which *is* you." Ryan acknowledged that this was true. "I usually post about meetings and petitions and stuff, but this is important humanitarian information. We should get started."

"Let's work on this in the kitchen," Morgan said. "I'll get my laptop—Mom, can Ryan use yours?"

"Of course. Lauren, what about you? Do you want me to set you up with Charles' desktop computer?"

"No, thanks, I can use my phone."

"Well, help yourself to whatever you want to eat. If you need anything—"

"Thanks, Mom, we're fine," Morgan said.

Having been dismissed, Rose was left with no option but to remain with Garnet in the living room where he was working his way through a second glass of wine and brooding. "Did she really say two thousand followers?"

Rose tried to make light of it. "Beyonce has 150 million, apparently. Last time I checked. It's what they do, Garnet."

"Young people, you mean."

"Well, yes. I mean, not just young people. But mostly."

He was quiet, mulling this over. "I'm too old for her, Rose."

"No, you're not." She was determined to be gentle. "But she's too young for you."

He nodded, cleared his throat, and nodded again. "Right," he said. "That's that, then." He turned to her and gave a rueful smile. "No fool like an old fool, that's what they say, don't they?"

"They do," Rose answered. "But they're not always right."

39.

The rest of the evening, and the night that followed, was the longest she'd ever experienced. Jason came by, alone, to check on her, stayed long enough to confer with Morgan and the others about their social media postings, and agreed to spread the word on Twitter. Then he left, to "prowl the neighbourhood," as he put it. This was because of something the police told him, that the majority of people who wander off are found within a kilometre of their homes. Rose thought this was unlikely but she was grateful that he wanted to keep searching.

The Facebook and Instagram posts were brief, but touching: "My Dad is missing," Morgan's read, and went on to describe her father: "6', 210 lbs., with blue-green eyes, and a full head of dark brown hair, greying at the temples." She went on to say "He is smart, well-spoken, and friendly, but a little confused at the moment. He's never gone off without telling us so we are VERY worried." It signed off with a link to the local RCMP detachment, and included the phone number of the missing persons department.

Ryan posted something similar on his sangha page, referring to Charles as a "dear friend and fellow Pilgrim," which is not how Charles would describe himself, Rose was sure. Still, it was the kind

255

of wording meant to appeal to sangha followers. And who's to say Charles wasn't a pilgrim, in his own way?

Lauren's Instagram post was shorter—just his name, his photo, and the words "MISSING @rcmpmissingpersons." When she showed it to Rose, she could see it had already been shared several times, as had the Facebook posts. Which had been "liked" several times with added messages of support and "thoughts and prayers."

Lauren offered to set up an Instagram account on Rose's phone.

"I'll probably never use it," Rose said.

"It doesn't matter. If you only use it this once to let people know about Charles, it'll be worth it, right? It can't hurt."

At seven she heard from Marie. Her meeting was over and she was in the car, eager to learn what had happened with Ian. When Rose told her about Charles, she was horrified—Rose could hear it in her voice. "Oh, Rose, I'm so sorry! What can I do? Do you need anything? I'm coming over—I'll be there in half an hour."

Rose said she didn't need anything but she was so relieved to know Marie would be with her she started to cry. "Sorry," she said. "I'm a bit of a mess at the moment."

"Well, no wonder. Do you have any idea what's happened?"

"I don't. We had, well, kind of a fight last night, but he was okay this morning. He didn't even remember it. And now the kids have all these messages on Facebook and the police are looking for him—"

She couldn't go on. It was overwhelming, thinking of all the possible explanations for his disappearance, none of them good. She tried to keep from picturing the worst one: Charles unconscious, maybe dying, trapped within the wreckage of his car. Hadn't he been complaining about the brakes not so long ago? When was the last time the car was serviced? She'd always left it to Charles to take care of those things, oil checks, antifreeze, replacing the air filter. He was proud of the care he took to make sure both their cars ran smoothly; surely he wouldn't leave something like brake pads to chance.

And he was a careful driver. Rose had been pulled over a half dozen times over the years for speeding, but not Charles. "Never had a ticket," he boasted. "Not for speeding, not even for parking." It probably helped that he didn't own a car until he came to Canada, at which point he was in his late twenties and past the crazy driver stage. Still, a clean driving record is not to be sniffed at and it paid off: year after year he qualified for the lowest insurance premiums in the province.

Garnet, more subdued than she'd ever seen him, was beginning to fade. Rose told him he didn't have to stay but he said he wanted to keep her company until Marie arrived. He called the hospitals again, just to check, and once again told her, "So far so good." Apart from that, he didn't say much. Lauren was occupied in the dining room with Morgan and Ryan; she seemed oblivious to Garnet's misery. Or perhaps she simply didn't care. When Marie arrived, Garnet stood and prepared to leave. Lauren glanced up, saw him standing in the doorway, but made no move to go. He waited, uncertain of his next move, looking rather foolish.

"Are you coming, my love?" he said.

"You go. I'll get a lift later."

"Are you sure?"

"Go *on.*" There was no mistaking the irritation in her voice. If she'd been playing the role of "Daddy's girl" with Garnet up to now, she wasn't any longer. Morgan caught her mother's eye and raised her eyebrows. The game, such as it was, was over.

"You'll let me know, won't you Rose, when you hear anything?" he said. "He's my best friend—my oldest—" He stopped, unable to continue.

"I know," Rose said. "Thank you for being here." And then, surprising both of them, she embraced him. He hugged her back, his face close to hers; Rose felt his shoulder blades through the soft tweed of his jacket and detected, underneath the scent of his aftershave, a faintly unpleasant, grassy odour. What can only be described as an old man smell. He was seventy, six years older than

Charles, not yet frail, but slipping into old age. And very soon, if what she saw tonight was any indication, he would be on his own. She waited while he got into his car and drove off, then went back into the living room to join Marie.

"You can't help feeling a little sorry for him," Marie said. "Lauren's done with him, and I think he was really excited about that baby. Even if he wasn't the father."

Rose agreed. "Charles said he was devastated. He practically cried on his shoulder."

Mention of Charles brought them back to the matter at hand; they went into the dining room to check on the others. Morgan, Ryan, and Lauren were gathered around the dining table, poring over four sheets of paper, Scotch-taped together, forming a square. As Rose and Marie joined them, Morgan explained they were conducting a planning session, with a view to organizing a search party first thing in the morning.

"We may not need to," Morgan added, as Rose started to object, "because of course we're hoping they find Dad before then. But we thought it would be good to be ready, just in case."

"Of course," agreed Marie. "Show us what you're thinking."

"It was Ryan's idea, really," Lauren said, and nudged him. "Go on, Ryan, you explain it." There was something in that nudge, and in Lauren's voice, that spoke volumes. Rose and Marie flicked their eyes at each other, then turned their attention back to the table.

Ryan explained that they had used Google Maps to find the location of the house, and then zoomed out to show a five-kilometre area around it. They printed that out, then repositioned the cursor to an area outside the first map and did the same. When they were done they had a fairly complete map of the city. Ryan was now using a compass to draw ever-expanding circles, using the house as the centre point.

"You kept my old geometry set," Morgan said. "Lucky thing, eh?"

"What are the circles?" Rose asked.

"We're going on what the police told Jason, that most people who go missing stay somewhere close to home. The circles are a kilometre wide, right? We'll start with the area within the first circle and then move outward, once we've covered that ground. We can change the centre point," Ryan said, "if we find more information. Like, if somebody says they saw him downtown or something. But it seems like a good idea to start here."

It sounded like a logical approach to Rose, assuming they were right, and Charles hadn't driven out of town. "It's good. I just hope we don't have to use it."

"Me too," Morgan said. "This is just in case. Oh, and Ryan found something out—he talked to a psychic!"

Ryan explained that through his sangha website he found a woman in California who specialized in locating missing persons. After meditating on Charles' photograph, she informed them that Charles was definitely alive. As to where he was, she couldn't say, but she did offer that she saw mountains in the distance. Considering that three-quarters of the province was mountains, this wasn't very helpful, but Rose was grateful.

"Well, that's amazing," she said. "It gives us hope, anyway."

"Where there's life there's hope, Mrs. Addams." It was a cliché, but the way Ryan said it, it sounded like a profound truth.

Rose wanted to know if she and Marie could do anything, but Morgan said there wasn't much more that could be done except keep an eye on the news. Just in case. "We've got this covered, Mom. I'll let you know if Jason calls or if anyone posts anything important on Facebook. You should go into the living room and try to relax."

Marie agreed. She brought out a small bottle of gin, some tonic water, and a couple of limes. "Times like these," she told Rose, "call for something stronger than wine. You go check the news; I'll make us drinks. And put your feet up—you look ready to drop."

Rose did what she was told. As much as she wanted to keep busy, keep herself distracted, she was dead tired. Sleep was out of the question—how could she possibly fall asleep not knowing where Charles was, what was happening to him? But she needed to breathe again; she had to find a way to loosen the tightening in her chest. She could hear Charles' voice in the back of her head, admonishing her: "Good lord, woman, calm down! Get a grip— you're getting yourself all worked up over nothing."

Please, God, she thought, let it be true.

They sat on the sofa together, sipping their gin and tonics, watching the local news channel with the sound turned down. Rose didn't seriously expect to see anything to do with Charles, who'd been missing for all of—she checked her phone—nine hours and twenty-eight minutes. She kept her phone charged and always by her side, made sure the ringer was on, and checked it regularly. Unable to stop herself, she kept dialling Charles' phone, hanging up when it went to voice mail.

Glancing towards the kitchen, Marie asked about Ian. "Can you tell me what happened? Are they getting together?"

Speaking *sotto voce,* so as not to be overheard by the others, Rose filled her in on the details of Ian's arrival and Morgan's response.

Marie was dismayed. "So she doesn't want anything to do with him?"

"Nothing. At least, that's what she said. He's staying in town until he has a chance to talk with her. So . . . I guess we'll see."

Together they gazed towards the kitchen and sighed, simultaneously.

Rose's phone rang. "Oh, my gosh, it's *him.* Ian. What should I do?"

"Answer it," Marie said. "You have to answer it, Rose. Tell him what's happening."

"Ian?" Rose said. "I can't talk. I have to keep the line free. Charles is missing."

"I know," he said. "I just saw the posts. What can I do? I want to help—what do you need?"

"Nothing," she said. "I can't think of anything."

"I'm coming over. I'll be there in twenty minutes."

"No—wait—"

It was too late. He had hung up. "Oh, my god, he's coming over!"

"Now? Call him back—you have to stop him."

Rose redialled but it went to voice mail. "He's probably calling a cab."

They regarded each other in silence. Finally, Marie said, "You have to tell her."

Rose stood up and squared her shoulders. "Come with me. I need backup."

40.

MORGAN TOOK IT PRETTY WELL, ALL THINGS CON-
sidered. Apart from blurting out a mild expletive, she merely
shrugged and accepted the inevitable. If he was going to come
though, she said, he needed to understand she had more important
things on her mind at the moment. She was not going to get into
a discussion about their relationship. That, for the time being, was
off-limits. "And he'd better make himself useful. We're getting all
these messages on Facebook and Twitter. We need to share the load."

"I'm sure he'll be happy to help," Rose replied, relieved there
wasn't going to be a scene. "He thinks a lot of your father—he's
probably as worried as you are."

Morgan rolled her eyes in disgust. Like Virginia Woolf, she was
a major eye-roller.

Back in the living room, Marie shared Morgan's Facebook
post and posted a link to it on Twitter, where she had hundreds
of followers. Unfortunately, she wasn't optimistic her tweets would
be helpful. Most of her followers lived outside of Canada, either
in the States or in Japan. She was enormously popular in Japan,
and called it the Anne-of-Green-Gables effect. Misty, her most

popular heroine, had red hair and pigtails, and was as imaginative as Montgomery's Anne, although more pugnacious.

"Should we call the media, do you think?" Marie asked. "This website says it's never too soon to contact police and the local media. You've contacted the police, what about calling one of the radio stations?"

Rose thought about the possible consequences of Charles, a very private man when it came right down to it, learning that his name and personal details had been discussed on air. He'd hate it and he'd blame her. It would be no use arguing that she was desperately worried, that it seemed the right thing to do—he simply wouldn't forgive her.

"No," she said, "I don't think so. Not right now, anyway. Maybe if he's not back by morning . . ." She stopped.

Marie squeezed her hand, "He will be. I know it. And the psychic said it, too, didn't she?"

"She said he was alive—she didn't say when he'd be back. Or *if* he'd be back."

The gin was loosening her tongue. Hard liquor always had that effect on her, which was why she generally stuck to wine. Gin, vodka, rum and Coke, they all made her feel the need to confide her troubles to the nearest sympathetic ear. And what was troubling her now, what had bothered her from the beginning, almost more than the worry that Charles had met with a catastrophe of some kind, was the fear that he hadn't.

"What if he's left me, Marie? What if he hasn't had an accident or got lost? What if he just decided he's had enough—that he doesn't want to be married anymore? At least, not to me?"

Marie dismissed this with a wave of her hand. "That's ridiculous, Rose, and you know it. Why would Charles do something like that? You've been together forever—he loves you, everybody knows that. You're just upset."

Rose was determined to have her moment. "No, it's more than that. I'm a terrible wife. He does most of the cooking, I hate housework, I hate sports. He used to ask me to watch soccer with him and I refused. Last night he said it was all hypocrisy. He called our marriage a sham. And I told him he sounded insane. 'You sound like a crazy person.' That's what I said to him. Can you believe it?"

"Of course I can believe it. I've been married almost as long as you. I've said worse things to Jeff a dozen times over the years. It's what we do. We snap at the people closest to us because they're there, they're close at hand, and they can take it. If Charles was going to leave you it wouldn't be because you told him he's crazy. Or because you won't watch soccer. He'd have to have a better reason than that."

"Maybe he does."

"He doesn't!"

"No, he probably doesn't. But I almost wish he did. At least then there'd be a reason for all of this."

Rose had finished her drink and was down to a single, melting ice cube. Marie suggested a top-up and Rose didn't have the energy to argue; whether it was the gin or the support from her friend, she was feeling a little better, a little more hopeful. There was an explanation—there had to be. People like Charles didn't just up and disappear. Did they?

While Marie was in the kitchen, mixing their drinks, Jason called to say he'd scoured the immediate neighbourhood but there was no sign of his father's car. "You're probably right, Mom, if he was driving in traffic he likely got at least as far as downtown. I'm going to head home but I'll be back first thing in the morning. And I'll let you know if I hear anything before then."

"Anything," Rose said. "Anything at all."

"Anything, Mom. I promise."

Ian arrived just before ten, apologizing for the lateness of the hour. "I couldn't get a cab, so I walked. How are you? Has there been any news?"

Rose shook her head. "No. Nothing." His eyes darted around the room, looking for Morgan, and she put a restraining hand on his arm. "She's in the kitchen but, Ian, she's not alone. So please don't, you know, don't do anything silly."

"I won't," he said, "I promise. I just want to talk to her. And anyway, that can wait. There's more important things right now."

Relieved, Rose led the way into the kitchen; Ryan was hunched over Rose's laptop, Morgan and Lauren were tapping messages into their phones. They looked up, briefly. Rose made the introductions, then left them to it.

"How did it go?" Marie whispered.

"She wouldn't even look at him. I just don't understand why she's so angry with him. The way she talked about it before, it sounded like a mutual decision."

"It never is, though, is it?" Marie said, and patted her hand. "Never mind. It's up to them now. They'll figure it out, or they won't."

Towards midnight, Jeff called, wanting to know if there had been any developments, which was his way of letting Marie know it was time to come home.

"It's been a long day," Rose said. "You had your writing group and you always say you're exhausted after that. Go home and get some sleep."

"I couldn't possibly sleep," Marie said, "but I can't think what else I can do here to help. I'm pretty useless at the moment."

Rose gave her a hug and told her not to be silly. "You could never be useless. Just being here tonight means so much. You're a good friend. I don't say that often enough, but I should. You are a *very* good friend."

"As are you, my dear. I'll go, but promise me, the minute you hear anything—*anything*—you'll call me, right? Promise?"

Lauren and Ryan were reluctant to leave, so Morgan suggested they stay the night. Half-heartedly, she extended the invitation to Ian, which he accepted with an eagerness Rose found pathetic. It was clear that Morgan had the upper hand; more than that, she was enjoying it. But Ian was right. Now was not the time to think about such things. Although Rose did need to figure out where everyone was going to sleep. And that could be awkward.

"None of us are planning to go to sleep," Morgan said. "We'll hang out here in the living room with you. And just, you know, wait."

Rose nodded. It was fitting, after all, that she should have them sit up with her. Keeping vigil. A phrase of comfort, with intimations of quietly waiting, being still—maybe praying? Should they pray for Charles to be found? Rose hadn't prayed for years; would it be hypocritical to start now? And whom would she pray to?

Ryan sat cross-legged on the floor, head bowed, fingering the string of beads he wore on his right wrist. He looked up at her and smiled. "Would you like to chant, Mrs. Addams?"

Those luminous brown eyes of his, they had a kind of mesmerizing effect. Morgan had succumbed, as had Lauren; Rose was determined to resist. "I think we need to keep focused, Ryan. We need to be concentrating on Charles."

"We are," Morgan said. "We've done everything we can do for the moment. All we can do now is wait."

Ryan was still watching her, waiting for an answer.

"Will it help Charles?"

"It will help you," he said.

She gave in. "I'm willing to try. Do I have to join you on the floor or can I sit on the sofa?"

"You can sit wherever you're comfortable."

Rose perched herself on the sofa and waited for instructions. Morgan and Lauren sat on the carpet on either side of Ryan, closed their eyes, and waited. Maybe it was something they did in the sangha meetings, Rose thought; they appeared familiar with the procedure. Ian, after a moment's hesitation, joined them, sitting as far away from Ryan as he could.

"Close your eyes and try to clear your mind," Ryan said. "We'll begin the mantra and when you're ready, you can join in."

It occurred to her that this might be a prelude to a kind of hypnotic trance. Feeling uneasy, Rose closed her eyes, bowed her head, and waited. Ryan began to chant something in a foreign language and Morgan and Lauren did the same. To her ears it sounded like *nam mee-yoho rengay kee-yo*. Whatever it meant, it was simple enough, and after a few moments she joined in:

Nam mee-yoho rengay kee-yo.

Nam mee-yoho rengay kee-yo.

She couldn't have said how long this went on—it might have been an hour, it might only have been fifteen minutes. When Ryan stopped, the others quieted down, except Rose. She kept chanting and when she, too, fell silent and opened her eyes, she was surprised to find her cheeks were wet. Morgan got up and sat next to her mother. "It's okay, Mom," she said, putting her arms around her, "it's going to be okay." Rose nodded, unable to speak.

Lauren handed her a tissue. "It had that effect on me, the first time. I just found myself sobbing like crazy."

Rose wiped her eyes with the tissue and then blew her nose. "So it's normal? But why? I don't get it."

"It's got to do with your chakras, the ones in your throat and your heart," Ryan said. "That's where you hold in emotions that you don't want to let go, that maybe you don't even know are there. Chanting releases those emotions. It helps you let go of negative feelings and lets the body relax."

"It reminds me of what my mother used to say. There's nothing like a good cry. It always makes you feel better." Rose grabbed another tissue.

"When I was thirteen I cried every night," Morgan said. "Cried myself to sleep. Over nothing. Every single night."

"I never knew that," Ian said, sounding aggrieved. "You never told me that."

"You never asked. I don't remember you ever asking me anything about my childhood. And if you weren't going to ask I wasn't going to tell you."

Ian said nothing. Rose felt a wave of sympathy for her daughter. We all need to be heard, she thought. And sometimes we need our partners to read our minds. Charles had always been especially good at that, reading her mind, sensing what she was feeling before she said it. She stood up. It was beginning to feel cold, sitting there in the living room. She switched on the fire and offered to make cocoa.

"I'll make it," Ian said, standing up, "if nobody minds. It'll give me something to do."

Rose expected her daughter to object, but she didn't. Instead Morgan asked if anyone was hungry.

Lauren stood up. "I could eat something. We could heat up the rest of the food in the fridge. We hardly ate any of it."

"Good idea," Rose said.

Morgan stood, stretching her arms overhead. "Just relax, Mom. You, too, Ryan. We can manage."

Left alone with Ryan, Rose searched for something to talk about. He seemed content to sit in silence—comfortable in his own skin—that was the way she'd describe him. "So," she asked, "what do you think of Ian? I mean, what you've seen of him so far?"

"He seems like a nice guy," Ryan replied. "But that doesn't really matter, does it? It's what Morgan thinks of him that counts." He was right, of course.

"Can I ask you something?"

"Sure."

"Don't you ever get lonely?" It was a personal question, maybe even rude. But it had been on her mind for ages.

"Sometimes," he said. "When I'm around a lot of people."

Was he teasing? There was a glint in those dark brown eyes of his that suggested he was playing with her, just a little. "My turn," he said. "Can I ask *you* something?"

"Of course."

"Did you always want to work in a library?"

She considered the question. Morgan asked her this once, and she gave a flippant answer, said she wanted to be a ballet dancer when she was six, an actress when she was twelve, and a missionary when she was fifteen. All of which were true, and satisfied her daughter at the time.

"I always wanted to be around books," she said. "Maybe because the one thing I remember about my mother was that she loved reading. When she was ill and couldn't walk, that was about all she could do. Before she was sick, she used to take me to the library every Saturday, and leave me in the children's section while she went upstairs where they had the adult books. I loved every minute of it. It felt so safe, you know?"

Ryan nodded, and she saw that he understood it completely. The safety, the comfort that can be found where books are kept.

"I studied English at university, and it was sort of expected that I'd teach. But I didn't want to; I don't have the patience for it. I got contract work at the university library and eventually worked my way through a master's in Library Science and, well, here I am."

"And you like it?"

"I do."

It was on the tip of her tongue to ask, What about you, Ryan? What did you want to do, when you were younger? But she didn't say it. He had been abandoned by his mother when he was five, handed over to a cult when he was twelve. It was likely—*very* likely, she thought—that all he'd ever wanted to do was survive.

41.

IT WAS STILL DARK WHEN JASON CALLED WITH important news: the police had found Charles' car. It was parked on the side of the road not far from the university campus. The keys were in the ignition; Charles' wallet and phone were on the front seat.

"And your father?"

"He's not in the car," Jason said. "The police say there's no sign of an accident. No blood or anything, the car's fine. As soon as it's light out they're going to start searching the area. I guess they're bringing in a dog. Or maybe a couple of dogs. It's that area where it's all trails and bush. They're thinking he maybe wandered into the forest and got lost."

Rose was bewildered. Why would Charles drive all the way out to the university? For what? She made up her mind. "We need to go there. We need to find him."

Jason didn't argue. "Do you want me to come pick you up?"

"We'll drive and meet you," she said. "Morgan will come with me. And Lauren and Ryan. And Ian, he's here, too. We'll form a search party."

"Sounds good," he said. "But we won't be able to see anything until it gets light. I'll text you the cross street and meet you there at, say, seven-thirty, okay?"

Now that she had a plan, Rose was revitalized. There hadn't been a catastrophic car accident—Charles was not lying in that ditch—he was somewhere on campus and she, together with the others, would find him.

It was early, not yet five, but she promised Marie she'd call her the moment she heard anything. Marie picked up on the first ring—like Rose and the others, she hadn't slept. "Oh, thank heavens! Let's get out there now and start looking!"

But Rose repeated what Jason had told her, "Jason said we should wait and meet him at 7:30, when it starts to get light."

"Ok, it makes sense. He's right. Besides, Jeff has to eat, I'm afraid. It would take a nuclear war breaking out to keep him from having his breakfast. Jeff and I will grab something to eat and head over."

"No need to hurry," Rose replied. "We aren't heading off until dawn. For now, we're getting gear together for the search: flashlights, a couple of blankets. I've got Charles' overcoat and gloves, a second pair of shoes, and warm socks. If he's been out all night, exposed to the elements, he'll be soaked and frozen."

"Whistles!" Marie added. "I was on a search and rescue website during the night, since I couldn't sleep, and they said everybody should have a whistle. I can bring a dozen."

"Where are you going to get a dozen whistles?"

"The book launch—*Misty and the Whistling Porcupine*. We gave them out as favours. I have a whole box of them."

Rose wondered if she should call Garnet but Lauren said not to. She said he wouldn't be able to walk very far and might be more of a hindrance than a help. "Better to wait until we find Charles," she said, "and then call."

The car, Jason told her, had been found parked on a side road leading into the forest. With the help of Google Maps, Ryan was able to print out a map of the area, and made copies for each of them. "There are trails," he said, "but you can see there's miles of bush. And this time of year you can get fog, so it's really important to stick to the paths." Rose said he sounded like he knew the area, and he confessed to having spent a summer there, just off the trail that led to Spanish Banks. "I wanted to get out of the city, so I took my tent and hiked out there. I had to keep moving around so as, you know, not to get caught, so I got to know the place pretty good."

"You sound like the perfect guide," she said. "We'll follow you."

By the time they reached the university forest, the first pale rays of sun were emanating from the eastern sky. The day promised to be cool but clear. No rain in the forecast, thank goodness. Rose was shocked to see the car planted at the side of the road, just as Jason had said, but with nothing to protect it. She'd assumed the police would have cordoned it off with yellow tape and those orange traffic cones. "Where's the yellow tape? And where are the police, anyway? Shouldn't they be here?"

Jason was waiting for them. He walked over while Lee waited in the car. He was wearing a fluorescent vest over a white sweatshirt. "The police are on their way, so we should wait for them. As for the yellow tape, they generally only do that for a crime scene and no crime's been committed, right?"

"We don't know that! Charles may not have had a car accident but something has happened to him and who's to say at this point there wasn't a crime?" Knowing he was somewhere in this area, cold, alone, even frightened, she was impatient to start the search. "Do we have to wait for the police?" she said. "I think we should get going and they can catch up. We have maps. And whistles."

"I really think we should wait, Mom," Jason answered. "The police have their protocols in situations like this."

"Fuck their protocols! My husband is lost and we need to find him and you're telling me I can't go look for him. Well, that's fine, you can stay here and wait for the protocol police—I'm going to go find your father!" She took her whistle out of her pocket, slipped it over her neck, and grabbed a flashlight from the car. As she turned to leave, Morgan took hold of her arm.

"Mom, wait! You can't go off by yourself."

Rose was fighting tears and angry with herself for losing control. This was not the time to get emotional—there were bigger issues at stake. "I'm not going off by myself! Marie's coming with me."

Marie stepped up to her side. "If Rose is determined to set off, I'm going with her," she said. "Don't try to stop me," she told Jeff, who was obviously perturbed. "Rose is my friend. And yours, by the way, just in case you've forgotten. She needs our support."

Jason was vacillating; Rose could see that. Any moment now and he'd give in, agree to start the search before the police arrived. Well, she wasn't going to wait. She turned to Marie. "Ready?"

"Ready!"

She gave the others one last chance. "Are you coming with us?"

"I'll go with you," Ian said. "Let me grab a flashlight from the car."

"You're not helping, Mom," Morgan said. "Please, this is silly—"

She would have said more but Lauren suddenly interrupted, "Is that a bear?"

A figure stepped out of the shadows and ventured towards them. Not a bear, not even an animal. It stopped, just for moment, getting its bearings, perhaps, and then nodded in their direction. "Hello."

It was the way he said it—politely, as you would greet a stranger, or a neighbour you've run into at the grocery store. He didn't shout, didn't show surprise—shock—even relief. Just a mild "hello" and a nod.

As she explained it to Marie when they were talking later, Rose temporarily entered some kind of a dissociative state.

"I felt completely detached from everything," she said, "from myself, my surroundings—everything. It was just such a shock."

"You were white," Marie said. "I was afraid you were going to faint."

"I almost did. And Charles, he was fine."

He was. His hair was tousled, with a tuft sticking up at the back, and his clothes were rumpled, as if he'd slept in them. Which he probably had. But his demeanour was eerily composed. She embraced him, timidly, not wanting to upset him, and felt him pat her, several times, on the back. The way you would comfort a child.

"What are you all doing here?" he said.

"Looking for you," Morgan said. "Where were you, Dad? Where did you go?"

Disconcerted, Charles frowned, and glanced back at the entrance to the forest. "I guess I went for a walk . . . Should we go back to the house?"

He started to walk towards the car, then suddenly stumbled and slumped forward. Rose gripped his arm and Jason hurried to support him on the other side. Together they half-walked, half-carried him to the car and got him into the back seat. As Rose climbed in beside him, Lee asked about his blood sugar.

"He has hypoglycemia, doesn't he?" Lee said. "He probably needs to eat."

"Oh, my god," Morgan said, "do you think that could be it? Could that be what happened?"

"It could be," Lee said. "Did anybody bring juice?"

"The bag's in the trunk of my car," Rose said, handing Morgan the keys. It was the first thing she thought of when they were packing a lunch. A half a cup of fruit juice, the doctor had said—always keep some on hand.

"We have sandwiches," Lauren reminded them. "Egg salad and tuna. Which would be best, do you think?"

"I don't think it matters," Lee said. She poured some juice into the top of her thermos and handed it to Rose. "Put it to his lips. See if you can get him to swallow some of it."

Once again, Lee was taking charge of a medical situation, and once again Rose was grateful. She held the cup to his mouth and tipped it slightly, urging him to take a sip. Charles' eyes were closed and he didn't respond, but she managed to get a small amount of juice into his mouth. The tip of his tongue appeared, tasting the liquid on his bottom lip; encouraged, she coaxed him to drink a little more.

"Hypoglycemia is probably what caused it," Lee said. "His blood sugar dropped; he got confused, and ended up not knowing where he was."

Lauren volunteered that she had an uncle who went into a coma because of it. "He lived on his own," she said, "and he practically died."

Lee ignored her, broke off a small piece of sandwich—egg salad on white bread, his favourite—and handed it to Rose. "Try to get him to eat this," she said. "Not too much at a time, we don't want him to choke."

Very gently, she fed him the sandwich, a bite at a time, interspersed with sips of orange juice. His eyes remained closed and his eyelids, pale and translucent, fluttered occasionally, like the trembling of a small, frightened bird. This was new, a transformation of a kind. She had that sensation again, of being outside of herself. She was looking down on the two of them and saw there'd been a shift in their relationship and that it had been coming for a long time. She hadn't seen it. She, who was never able to live wholly in the here and now, had been engulfed in the present and hadn't seen it coming.

Morgan sat on the other side of her father, holding his hand. She had taken a blanket from the trunk of Rose's car and settled it firmly around her father's shoulders. "Should we take him to the hospital?" she said in a whisper.

Rose looked to Lee, but for once she seemed uncertain. "I'm pretty sure he's in shock," Lee said, "but if he comes out of it in a hospital that could be upsetting for him."

Jason, who had been on the phone to the police, said they suggested taking Charles to the ER just to check his vitals. "They also said you can take him home and monitor him. So maybe that's the best bet?"

Charles opened his eyes. "No hospital," he whispered. "I just want to go home."

That settled it. They would get him home and into bed. His hands were cold and she thought of the gloves and warm socks they'd brought. Marie fetched them from the other car. Together they managed to remove his shoes and socks—which were, as she feared, soaking wet—and manoeufvred his feet into the socks. That was as far as they got. His feet had swollen during the night and the shoes they brought were useless.

"We should have brought wellies," Marie said. "Rubber boots."

Charles, in the meantime, drifted off again. Rose worried that they wouldn't be able to get him into the house, if he was asleep when they got home.

Ryan said, "We'll carry him. Jason and me and Ian. We can manage it, right?"

"Yeah, of course," Jason said. "We'll carry him upstairs and get him settled in bed."

"We'd better come with you," Jeff said. "You might need an extra pair of hands to get him into the house. He's a big guy."

42.

THEY DROVE BACK IN A CONVOY, JASON AND LEE leading the way, Rose and Charles in the back seat of Charles' car, with Morgan and Ian in front; Marie and Lauren in Rose's car; and Jeff and Ryan bringing up the rear. It was a Sunday; there wasn't much traffic. Even so, the drive took almost an hour, as Morgan was driving slower than usual, not wanting to jostle her father. She kept checking on him in the rear-view mirror, and asking her mother if he was all right.

Eventually, Rose got impatient, "He's not going anywhere, Morgan, and he's fine. But he needs to get to bed so please just concentrate on driving, okay?"

It was the kind of comment that would normally have ignited sparks between them, but Morgan only mumbled, "Sorry," and accelerated, slightly.

After that, no one said anything. Ian tried to initiate conversation with Morgan a couple of times but finally gave up and stared out the passenger window in silence. When Rose met Morgan's eyes in the rear-view mirror it was impossible to read her expression. Her daughter was as sombre as she'd ever seen her but whether it was anger with Ian or worry about her father, Rose couldn't tell. Probably a combination of both.

Charles dozed on and off as she held his hand and squeezed it reassuringly. "Not long now," she said. "We're almost home."

He nodded. "I'm fine. I just need to lie down for a bit."

By the time they arrived at the house, he'd fallen asleep again. Rose nudged him awake and managed, with Jason's help, to get him out of the car and onto his feet.

"What do you think, Dad?" Jason said. "Can you make it up the steps?"

Charles seemed to think he could, with some assistance. Jason took hold of his right arm, Ryan supported him on the left, and together they made their way up the stairs, through the front door and into the hallway. Rose was waiting with a dining chair. Charles lowered himself onto it with a soft groan and shook his head. "I'm winded," he said. "There's no way I'm getting upstairs."

"What about the sofa?" Morgan said. "You could lie down there till you get your strength back."

"My chair," Charles responded. "Get me to my chair and I'll be fine."

It made sense. "It reclines almost flat," Rose said, "and we can adjust it to suit him." Rose was glad she had had it shampooed after Lauren's miscarriage.

"Perfect," Jason said. "Okay, Dad, deep breath—one, two, three—up!"

It was only a matter of a few steps from the hallway to the living room, but nobody dared breathe until Charles was safely deposited in the recliner. Morgan was ready with the blanket. She waited while Rose and Marie removed her father's jacket, shoes, and gloves. They adjusted the footrest, then draped the blanket over him and tucked it firmly around his torso. There was nothing else to do, now, but give Charles time to recover.

"We should go," Marie said. "You need some sleep. Unless you want us to stay?"

"Oh, no, you should go," Rose said, giving her a hug. "Thank you so much, Marie—and you, too, Jeff. Thank you! I just appreciate your help so much!"

It was nothing, Jeff insisted, but you could see he was relieved to be heading home. "Be sure to call us if you need anything," and Marie seconded that. "We're only a phone call away," she said. "I know you have the kids, but—you know."

Taking no offence, for once, at being called a kid, Morgan wrapped them both in a hug and thanked them.

"You'll let us know, won't you, if your mom needs anything?" Marie said.

"I will. Don't worry, we'll take good care of them both."

Rose noted that Jason and Ryan looked almost as drained as Jeff, and told them to go home and get some sleep. Belatedly, she remembered that Ryan didn't have a home to go to, and started to amend her suggestion. "I mean, sorry, Ryan, you're welcome to stay here."

"It's all right, Mrs. Addams, I'm fine."

Before he could say any more, Lauren took hold of his arm and announced that he was coming back to her place.

"Your place?" Ryan was taken aback by the suggestion. "Um, I don't think . . ."

"You need somewhere to sleep," she said, "and this place is full up." She glanced pointedly at Ian who was standing there looking uncomfortable.

"I could go back to the hotel," Ian said. "I mean, if that's what you want?"

The question was directed at Morgan who pretended not to hear it. Instead she said she was going to stay downstairs in the living room and keep an eye on her dad.

Once again, it was up to Rose to settle the issue. "Ian, why don't you go upstairs and have a nap? I'll stay downstairs with Morgan. And Jason, if you and Lee could give Lauren and Ryan a lift, that would be great."

"Of course," Jason said. He gave her a hug and said he'd call her later to see how his father was doing. "If anything changes, you'll call me, right?"

Lee hugged her, too, which was a first. "He'll be okay," she said. "He just needs to sleep." She stepped back and studied Rose for a moment. "You do, too, Rose. Try to take a nap, okay?"

Rose said she would but the truth was she was too wound up to sleep. She was experiencing a kind of euphoria and felt spirited and alert. She made a pot of coffee and while it was brewing she paced the kitchen, unable or unwilling to settle. Charles was safe. He was not lying in a ditch, he hadn't been hurt in a car accident; he hadn't left her. He was hypoglycemic and that was a small, small thing to what might have been.

She took her coffee out the back door and stood on the patio. Copper-coloured leaves blanketed the ground beneath the magnolia trees; their bare branches carved graceful patterns against the light. The hydrangeas Lauren had admired were done for the year, of course, but they'd come back in the spring.

Rose held the ceramic mug against her lips and closed her eyes. She felt the pale November sun warming her forehead, her cheeks, felt the movement of unsettled air playing through her hair. She felt the concrete patio slabs pressing up through the soles of her runners, and she felt the weight of the moment, the certainty of her existence. It was real and it was fragile and she was grateful. Namaste. She opened her eyes and went back into the house.

Morgan was curled up on the sofa, watching her father sleep. She gave her mother a rueful smile and told her she felt that if she took her eyes off him he might just disappear. "It's so scary," she said, "when you think what might've happened. What if we hadn't found him?"

In actual fact, they hadn't, Rose thought; he found them. But yes, it was scary to think about how it might have turned out. "I'm glad you're here," Rose said, plumping herself down on the sofa next to her daughter. "You and Jason. And Lee."

"And Ian?"

"Well, yes. I am glad he's here. I think the two of you need to talk."

Morgan said nothing and Rose wondered it if was wise to continue. Still, her daughter had brought him up.

"Maybe you're not ready to get married," Rose said, "but I would hope you'd stay friends. I just feel bad that you're shutting him out."

"He had an affair."

"Ian? You're kidding!"

"I'm not kidding. He had an affair and he lied about it. He started seeing his old girlfriend and when I called him on it he said they were just meeting up for coffee. He said she was in a bad relationship and needed someone to talk to. And when I got upset he said I was being paranoid. He said I was imagining things."

"Oh, honey." Rose put her arm around her daughter and drew her close. "I'm so sorry. Why didn't you tell us?"

"I didn't want you to hate him. When he finally told me he asked me to forgive him and I thought I could. But I couldn't. So I left. I thought if I came home I could figure things out but the more I thought of it, the more I felt betrayed. And then I just made up my mind it was over."

"And now you're going to Sri Lanka," Rose said. "With Ryan."

Morgan looked a little sheepish. "Well, no. That was the plan— it was my plan, when I wrote the letter."

"And now you're not?" Rose couldn't keep from sounding hopeful. Was it possible Morgan had come to her senses, finally? Was she going back to school?

"It doesn't look like it. I talked to Ryan about it the other night and he thinks I might be looking at it the wrong way. He thinks I'm looking for my calling in life. My purpose. He says I need to learn to be happy in the present and forgiveness is a big part of that. I need to forgive Ian."

Gently, so as not to jinx the conversation, Rose said, "And can you?"

"I don't know. I'm not really the forgiving type."

Neither was I, Rose thought, when I was your age. But you learn.

"If you're going to stay down here," Morgan said, "I think I'll go upstairs and get some sleep. Do you mind? Will you be okay?"

"I'll be fine. And honey, thanks for confiding in me."

"No problem."

"One thing, before you go. Can I ask you something?"

"Sure, what is it?"

"Lauren and Ryan," Rose said. "I was just wondering. Is something going on between those two?"

Morgan frowned. "Going on? What do you mean—you think they're attracted to each other?"

"Well, yes. I mean, she does seem attracted to him. Don't you think?"

"No, I don't think, actually." She stood up and stretched. "Ryan's gay, Mom, and Lauren knows it. There's nothing sexual going on there. Trust me."

Garnet called at midday, relieved to hear that Charles had been found but concerned about his state of mind. Lauren had told him he'd been "practically unconscious." "Whatever that means," he said. "I mean, one is either conscious or not conscious. Is he aware of his surroundings?"

"Off and on," Rose said. "He woke up earlier and had a bite to eat and now he's sleeping again."

"And this all happened because of his blood sugar, I gather? I had no idea it was that serious—he's never mentioned it."

"He didn't think it was that important. Neither of us did. But we know better now." There was a pause, and then she said, "How are *you*, Garnet? I mean, how are things with you and Lauren?"

He cleared his throat. "Well, she's brought that young man to the house. I suppose you know that."

"I did hear her say something like that . . ."

"She gave him the guest room. I mean, really! What does she think—I'm operating a flophouse for homeless drifters?"

"It did seem a little strange," Rose said. "Is he still there?"

"I have no idea. I'm not at home at the moment. I'm calling from Bernie's. She very kindly offered me a room for the night. I told Lauren to have her hobo out of the house when I get back. If she knows what's good for her, she'll do as I ask."

If she knows what's good for her . . .

Rose was alarmed. "Garnet, you wouldn't hurt her, would you?"

"What are you talking about?"

"If Lauren doesn't do what you say, you're not going to hit her, are you? You mustn't, Garnet—I can't let you do that."

"*Hit* her? I've never hit a woman in my life. Good god, Rose, what do you take me for? You think I go around hitting women?"

"You said 'if she knows what's good for her.'"

"Well, yes. If she wants to continue to live under my roof—free of charge, I might add—then she can't be dragging home every Tom, Dick, and Harry she takes a liking to. I deserve *some* respect, after all."

"So if Ryan *is* still there when you get home . . .?"

"Then I'll insist that they leave," Garnet said. "Good riddance to bad rubbish. But I certainly won't *hit* anybody."

The rest of the afternoon was quiet. Rose did a little tidying up, mainly in the kitchen, packing up last night's leftovers and storing them in the fridge. When Charles was ready for a proper meal she could offer him butter chicken and naan bread, along with chickpea curry and his favourite, palak paneer. There was pasta in the freezer; she could thaw that and serve it to Ian and Morgan for dinner, along with a salad. Assuming, of course, that Ian was going to be staying for dinner. He might, if Morgan allowed it, but considering the circumstances, maybe he shouldn't. He'd had an affair and lied about it. He'd behaved badly; there was no denying it. And Morgan wasn't one to forgive easily—she said so herself.

Finished with the kitchen, Rose went back into the living room and stretched out on the sofa. Jason had left a message on her phone, asking about Charles. She texted him back: *All's well, Dad seems okay, thanks for all your help*

He got back to her right away: *Lee says you're a superstar, Mom! And she's right. Love you.*

Around four o'clock Morgan came downstairs to check on her father and see about borrowing the car. She was taking Ian back to the motel so he could check out, and then they were going to get something to eat.

"We have food here," Rose said.

"I know, but we need to fight and I'd rather not do it in front of you and Dad."

"Does it have to be a fight?"

"It does." She bent down and kissed Rose on the cheek. "Don't worry, Mom, and don't wait up. This may take a while."

It wasn't the most auspicious beginning but it was something. She watched her daughter leave the room, heard Ian tumble down the stairs and out the door, calling out "Goodbye and thanks" as he hurried to catch up with Morgan. Lord, Lord, Lord, how exhausting it is to be young.

43.

AT SIX ROSE SWITCHED ON THE READING LAMP NEXT to the recliner. Charles' eyes flew open and his eyeballs darted in their sockets, terrified, almost. "What? Where am I?"

"It's all right," she said, and stroked his cheek the way she did when the children were little. "Go back to sleep, hon, it's okay. I'm here." He gave a soft grunt, closed his eyes, and was quiet.

She went into the kitchen and took the leftovers out of the fridge. She'd heat them up now, she thought; if Charles wasn't ready to eat, she certainly was. When she came back into the living room, he was awake and sitting upright. "What day is it?"

"Still Sunday."

He shook his head. "So I slept all day?"

"On and off. You needed it. How are you feeling?"

He didn't hesitate. "Ashamed. I'm embarrassed and ashamed and I'm sorry."

"Oh, Charles—"

"No, I am. I'm sorry for causing you all that worry. You and the kids. Everyone. All that fuss."

"You're safe. "That's all that matters."

He reached for her hand and pressed it to his lips. It was a touching gesture and so out of character, for him, that she wanted to cry.

"What do you want to do? Are you hungry?"

"I could eat."

"Right. You stay here. I'll bring you a tray."

As hungry as she was, Rose was too keyed up to do more than nibble at her food. She sat on the sofa while Charles polished off the butter chicken and palak paneer and waited for the right moment. She wanted to talk about what happened, when he was ready. So much of it had been her fault—she hadn't been paying attention. She'd been focused on so many other things—Morgan . . . Ryan . . . even Garnet and Lauren. She had missed what was going on right under her nose.

Lee was right: low blood sugar was serious, even dangerous. There was a kit you could get, she'd said, by prescription; first thing tomorrow morning, Rose would get Charles to call his GP and make an appointment. They'd get a handle on this hypoglycemia thing. Together.

When he had finished eating, Charles leaned back in his chair and smiled. "That was wonderful. Thank you."

"Do you want to talk about what happened? Are you up to it?"

He considered for a moment, gathering his thoughts. "I was driving," he began, "and I got it into my head I was going to work. I thought I had a class." He shook his head. "It sounds crazy, I know, but I just drove out to the university like I used to, and then at some point I couldn't remember where I was going. I pulled over and stopped the car. And I think I sat there for a while."

"You left the car," she said. "The keys were in the ignition, your wallet—everything was there."

"Yes . . . I don't know. I remember thinking I'd like to walk down that trail, the one that overlooks the beach. Remember? We used to take the kids there, when I first started teaching."

She remembered. It was a peaceful trail bordering an ecological reserve, shared by hikers, cyclists, and horseback riders. And people walking their dogs, off-leash. It was the dogs that made her decide to stop coming. They were not only off-leash, they were often aggressive. "Is that what you did? You went down that trail?"

"I did, but I must've got turned around. I didn't recognize it from when we walked there."

She said it was a long time ago and he agreed. He said he walked for a long time and eventually found his way to a clearing overlooking the beach, not the area he remembered, but one supplied with a bench and a view of the north shore mountains. "It was so peaceful. There was no one around; I could have been alone in the universe. I was worn out from walking. I couldn't think what to do next and there didn't seem any reason to go anywhere, so—I didn't."

"You just sat there?"

"I guess so. I know I lay down and went to sleep and when I woke up it was dark. I thought, if I stay here I can watch the sunrise over the ocean."

"But the sun *doesn't* rise over the ocean."

He laughed. "I know. Just as well I didn't wait to see it. And I was hungry. I figured I'd better find my way back. So I headed back along the trail and I guess it was a shorter trail because I was suddenly on the road and you were all there. I thought I was imagining it, seeing you all."

"We were getting ready to go look for you," she said. "Jason thought we should wait for the police, but I was so worried I was going to go on my own. And Marie said she'd come with me. And Ian."

"You called the police?"

"We had to, Charles. We didn't know where you were. We looked everywhere. We had no choice."

"All that fuss," he said. "I'm so sorry."

She didn't want him to be sorry, not while she was feeling so terrible about her part in all this. "It's my fault—I should never have let you leave without eating something. We can't ever let your blood sugar drop like that again."

"It wasn't the blood sugar," he said. "It probably triggered the whole bloody episode, but there's more to it than that."

"What do you mean?"

Charles took a deep breath. "I haven't been completely honest with you about why I left the university."

Well, she knew that. She never really believed him. "I knew there had to be more," she said.

"There was."

She waited. He seemed to be working out in his head what to say, how to continue. Maybe he needed a push. "So what was it? Why did you just up and make a decision like that, without talking it over with me? It doesn't make sense."

He rubbed his forehead, frowning in concentration. "I should have told you, months ago, but I didn't want to worry you. And I need to warn you, I don't think you'll like what I'm going to say."

"Try me." She waited. Be calm, she thought. Don't overreact. Whatever he said, whatever he'd done, it could be fixed. Everything can be fixed eventually, can't it?

"So, you're right," he said, "it wasn't the student. It was something that happened earlier that morning: I got lost on my way to my office."

"What do you mean? You got lost driving?"

"No, I got there all right, but after I parked the car I stood there and—I didn't know which way I was going. I had to ask somebody to direct me to Buchanan Tower. I remembered the name of the building—I just had no idea where it was."

"But that's what Lee said can happen. Did you eat that morning? I can't remember. If you don't eat, you can get confused. It was the hypoglycemia."

He shook his head. "It wasn't the first time this had happened. It was the first time I blanked out completely, but it had been happening for over a year. I would set off for a meeting and not be able to find the room. Or I'd forget the name of a committee chair. Someone I'd worked with for years."

He was becoming agitated. He pushed himself out of the recliner and began to pace the room. "I knew there was something wrong. I couldn't concentrate. Couldn't remember what I was supposed to be doing. That first-year survey course, how long have I been teaching it—fifteen years? I *wrote* that course, Rose—I know it like the back of my hand. And there I was, wracking my brain trying to remember the date of the Protestant Reformation. Looking it up on Wikipedia, for Christ's sake. When I was marking papers, I had to get my TA to do the bulk of it. The words weren't making sense. I thought maybe I needed glasses but I had my eyes checked and they're fine."

Again, the results of low blood sugar. It could all be explained. And it could be fixed. "I wish you'd told me. We could have got on top of it, made sure you were eating regularly."

He stopped pacing, came over to her and sat down beside her. "I didn't want to worry you. I thought maybe it was exhaustion . . . maybe I just needed some time off. It was better over Christmas when I wasn't teaching. I felt less stressed and I was able to read a couple of books. We took that trip down the coast and I was fine. I really thought it was over and done with. But it wasn't."

She reached out for his hand and he gripped it tightly as if she were his lifeline securing him to the present. Keeping him anchored—not letting him drift out to sea. How did she not know? It was shameful, to be with someone for almost forty years and not sense such a thing. Such a disturbance. What the hell was she doing that she hadn't noticed? "I'm sorry," she said. "I knew something was wrong. I should have asked more questions. I shouldn't have let you deal with this on your own."

"No, I'm the one. I'm the one who's sorry. I've let you down."

"But now we know," she said. "Low blood sugar. We'll get you onto a strict regime, we won't let it get out of hand."

He looked directly at her and she knew, just then, that he'd been right: she wasn't going to like what he was going to say next.

"It's more than that, Rose. Progressive cognitive decline. That's the diagnosis."

"What are you talking about? I don't understand—you've had some kind of diagnosis? When?"

"In June. When we came back from California."

"But why would you do that? You were fine on that trip. I remember."

He admitted it was because he'd been fine on the trip that he decided to see his doctor. Maybe it was stress, he thought. Maybe the solution was to scale things back, drop a class or two, turn the committee chair duties over to somebody else. At the very least, he was hoping it might be something physical.

Which was what his regular doctor, his GP, suggested. It could be a thyroid abnormality, she told him . . . a vitamin deficiency . . . a problem with his blood pressure. She gave him a battery of tests and that was when it came up that he had hypoglycemia. But when he went back to see her, she said she was referring him to a neurologist.

"She said she didn't think low blood sugar explained everything," Charles said. "She said if there was anything else going on they needed to rule it out. The neurologist is a friend of hers. There's usually a six-month waiting list but she got me in the following week."

"You saw a neurologist?"

"I did. He carried out some cognitive tests for memory and problem solving, and he did more blood tests. In the end he scheduled me in for a CT scan and an MRI."

Rose was disconcerted. "You did all this, had all these tests, and you never told me?"

"I didn't want to worry you . . . I was still hoping it was something that could be fixed. A tumour or something."

"You were hoping you had a tumour?" It sounded bizarre but it made sense: a tumour could be removed. A tumour was fixable.

This wasn't, unfortunately. His own doctor gave him the news on a Friday afternoon, just days before the beginning of the fall term. She didn't try to sugarcoat it, for which he was grateful. "It's a one-way street," he told Rose.

"She didn't say *that!*"

"Not in so many words. But there's no cure. And it doesn't end well. I'm sorry, but that's just what it is."

She didn't want to say it but it had to be asked. "Alzheimer's?"

"It's early days but . . . yes. Probably."

Now she didn't know what to say. What could you say to something like this? Eventually she asked if the doctor had any advice. "Did she prescribe pills or—I don't know. Anything?"

"There are support groups. She gave me a list. She said it's important to take regular exercise, eat well, keep positive. The usual. And she made me promise to tell you."

"And you didn't. God, Charles, why on earth didn't you tell me?"

"I wasn't sure how you'd take it."

"How did you think I'd take it?"

"Well, I guess I thought you'd get upset."

"You *thought* I'd get upset? Well, *of course* I'd get upset. I *am* upset! But you should have told me."

He agreed. Yes, he should have. And now he had. And there was nothing for it but to keep on going. "Keep buggering on," he said, quoting Churchill. "He was right, you know. There's nothing else you can do with something like this. You just have to keep on going."

Until you can't. Neither of them said it but it was there, hanging in the air between them. Until you can't keep going. And then what? Rose had no idea.

44.

THE FIRST HURDLE IS ACCEPTANCE. IT TAKES TIME to absorb the information. Charles has had two months to assimilate it all so he's ahead of her on the acceptance journey. If that's the right word for it. People say that now, don't they? They refer to any troubling event in your life as a journey. Well, it isn't helpful and it takes all the joy out of the word.

So, here she is, on a journey to acceptance. Made more difficult by the fact that he waited so long to tell her. *I didn't want to worry you.* When she pushed him on that—why didn't you want to worry me?—he added, almost as an afterthought, that he assumed she'd overreact. "You know what you're like," he said. "You let things get to you."

She doesn't think this is the case. Not in the least. *Some* things get to her, certainly. Mechanical things, for the most part. The time the car broke down when she was heading up north to see her sister. She couldn't get reception on her cell phone and there wasn't a garage for miles. *That* kind of thing puts her into a panic, yes.

But when it comes to dealing with a crisis, she's steady as a rock. She thinks about that time when Jason was six and he fell out of a tree and Charles was out of town at a conference. She was the one who called 911 and sat with her son on the lawn, holding a cold compress to his forehead, reassuring Morgan that her brother would be fine, keeping him warm until the ambulance showed up. The medics, when they arrived, complimented her on staying calm and not moving him. As frightened as she was, she did everything right.

It was only afterwards, when Jason was given the all-clear and sent home from the hospital with a cast on his arm, that it hit her, what might have happened. How many times had she told him not to climb that tree? Obviously, not often enough. A supracondylar fracture, the doctor said. Very common in children under the age of seven. It could have been worse; he could have broken his neck. Been paralyzed for life. But he wasn't. Broken bones heal, tumours can be removed. Things can be fixed. But not this. There is no fix for what is happening to her husband.

How could she not see it? What did she miss? Before he quit work, before he began to lose track of conversations, behave oddly— were there hints that his behaviour was changing? She can only recall one: the scene in the hotel restaurant on the last night of the California trip. The server had mixed up their orders and Charles had gone ballistic. Reamed her out, right there in front of everyone. So embarrassing. And so out of character. Rose thought he was tired; it had been a long day with a lot of driving around, visiting wineries in Napa. When they left she gave the young woman an extra large tip and apologized. And nothing like that happened again.

But since then, all those discordant notes, she should have caught them, she should have had an ear for them. She should have been listening.

Charles says it doesn't matter. It wouldn't have made a difference, he says. He wasn't ready to talk about it until, well, until he was. Getting lost the way he had, spending the night in the forest, it was his clarion call. "If I'm going to go through this," he says, "I want you there with me. I don't want to do it alone."

There's just one sticking point: he doesn't want the children to know. Not yet, he says, and he has his reasons. Jason has an important court case coming up; he doesn't want to create a distraction. And Morgan is going back to Toronto. With Ian. Not to get married and maybe not to live together. But they've had their fight and come to an uneasy truce: she will finish her thesis and submit it; he will take a break at the end of this film. After that, they are planning to travel. To Sri Lanka? Maybe, Morgan says. We'll see. He says he's willing to go wherever I want. And Ryan says—

"We're still quoting Ryan?" Rose asks, but Morgan doesn't take offence—

"Ryan says everything we need is here and now, but sometimes travel can bring us to it. Especially if we look at it the right way."

"And what way is that?"

"Give up your expectations," Morgan replies.

"So everything's good between you two?" Rose means Morgan and Ian, not Morgan and Ryan.

"No, not really. They say you should forgive and forget. I've forgiven him, but I haven't forgotten."

"Forgetting is much harder. Practically impossible. I wouldn't worry about it." Rose comes back to the present, with Charles and her life. "What about our friends? Can I tell Marie? Will you tell Garnet?"

Charles considers, weighs the pros and cons, asks her to give him time. He's only just coming to accept this himself, as is she. "Right now, let's keep it to ourselves. We'll know when the time comes."

It's not how she would do things, if it were up to her. But it's not. First thing Monday morning, she makes an appointment with the specialist, for both of them this time. Again, not a long wait: the nice young woman who answers the phone says she can fit them in on Friday.

For the rest of the week, Rose works from home; aside from a couple of meetings which can easily be moved back, there's very little that can't be done on her computer. Julie Mitchell copies her on an email to the library's board of trustees, thanking them for the Outstanding Service Award, and Rose sends a "reply all" congratulating her. Julie gets back to her with thanks and lets her know that Ryan has been in to see her and will start work, part-time, the following week. "He lacks experience," Julie writes, "but he's intelligent and seems keen so I think I've made a good choice."

"You have," Rose replies, "as always!" And hopes Julie misses the irony.

On Thursday she drives Morgan and Ian to the airport. Rose wants to come into the terminal with them but they tell her not to—parking is expensive and, anyway, they're just going to head to the gate. Morgan wraps her in a hug while Ian lugs the suitcases out of the trunk.

"Don't worry about us," she says. "We'll be okay."

"You'll let me know what happens, won't you? With the two of you? I want more than just a postcard from Sri Lanka."

"I will," she promises. "Take care of yourself. And take care of Dad."

Rose waits while they make their way through the sliding glass doors and is rewarded with a final wave good-bye before they disappear into the throng. She's kept her husband's confidence and has let them think the "incident," as they're calling it, was due to his blood sugar levels. It feels wrong. If they do go off traveling somewhere, it may be a long time before they're back. And who knows how things will be with Charles at that point? She has a sudden urge to hurry after them, confess the truth of the situation to Morgan, let her know what's really happening with her father. But the security guard tells her to move on, move her car out of the drop-off lane, and she complies. It was a selfish impulse, she thinks. Dropping that kind of information on her daughter would only create difficulties. Morgan would likely change her mind about leaving, and Charles would feel betrayed. And anyway, until they see the doctor, they don't really know just how bad things are. Charles thinks he knows—he's made it pretty clear—but he might be wrong.

The appointment with the specialist is for one o'clock. They set off in plenty of time but Rose, who's driving, gets lost. Her phone is telling her to take a side street to avoid construction, but she thinks she knows better and ends up in an unfamiliar part of town, twenty minutes away. Charles finds it funny: "*I'm* the one who's supposed to be confused," he says. By the time they arrive at the doctor's office, a surprisingly small, unpretentious suite of rooms above a sporting goods store, they're running late and Rose is flustered. The young woman who greets them is likely the same one who answered the phone. She's friendly and remembers Charles from his previous visit: she calls him "Professor" and says she's reading the book he recommended.

"Now remind me," he says, without batting an eyelash, "which one was that again?"

"*Vanished Kingdoms.*"

"Ah, yes, and are you enjoying it?"

Rose can tell he doesn't remember the book, or at least doesn't remember recommending it, but he's getting skilled at covering up. She thinks he's been doing it for a while—not with her, perhaps, but at work and out in public. It must be exhausting. No wonder he decided to quit.

The doctor is young—they're all young these days—and pleasant and kind enough but a little reserved, and she's grateful for that. He speaks to them in measured tones that offer a weird sort of comfort. It's a condition, it's not treatable, but it can be managed. Memory aids, medication to slow or delay the symptoms, home care if they need it. It may be a year or longer before it comes to that; the process of decline varies with the individual. And decline means, what? That, too, can vary. Best to take it day by day. There'll be good days and not-so-good days; focus on the good ones.

When Charles tells him he's no longer teaching, the doctor nods gravely and makes some notes in his chart. "That's probably a good move," he says. "The stress of trying to keep up with routines and other people's expectations can have a negative effect. But you want to replace it with something you enjoy. Do you play golf? Or tennis?"

Charles says no, but he's writing a book. Planning to, that is.

Another nod, another note in the chart. "That's fine. But you might want to take up a sport of some kind—even walking." He looks at Rose. "Something you can both do together."

She nods—yes, they'll think about it.

"Tell your friends," he says. "Let them support you."

Twenty minutes and they're done, on their way out the door. He didn't hurry them out, he would have spent longer, talking to them, answering their questions. But once she's had the word, the definitive diagnosis, there doesn't seem much more to say. He tells them to call if they have questions, the nurse will put them through. "You'll think of things," he says. "Things will come up. Most of what you need to know you'll get from the support group. But I'll be here if you need me."

In the car on the way home, Charles insists on driving. "What the doctor said, about telling our friends. He's right," he says, "and you were right. I guess we should let them know."

"Yes. We should. How do you want to go about it? Should we call them?"

"Let's have them to dinner. Invite everyone and we'll tell them together."

Rose remembers Thanksgiving and what Charles said about cooking. She suggests potluck, thinking it would be easier, but he says no, he wants to cook. He wants to show them he can still do it. He suggests Friday, two weeks from now. Rose checks her phone. November 22nd. Black Friday.

"Perfect! Don't you think? We'll tell our friends that night and then call the kids the next morning. So everyone will be in the loop."

"What's the occasion?" Marie asks, when Rose calls, and she, unwilling to outright lie, says they have an announcement to make.

"You're not moving, are you? Please say you're not moving."

Rose assures her they're not moving, apologizes for being in a rush, and hangs up. It feels disloyal not to confide in Marie, but she'll know soon enough.

She calls the others and the guest list swells. Bernie says Richard will want to bring Bev; Garnet, surprisingly, is coming with Lauren and Ryan.

"He's been staying here," Garnet says, "helping out, you know? It makes sense, really. It's a big house, and I have to tell you, Rose, it's getting to be too much for me, keeping up with all the things that need to be done. He's going to be paying rent, too, once he starts working."

"You're okay with all this?" she asks. "I mean, you weren't happy about Lauren bringing him home, as I recall."

"No, I wasn't. But he's not such a bad sort, is he? I do think he has some growing up to do, some maturing if you will."

"You think so?"

"I do. He's never really had a father figure, has he? Until now."

Is Garnet saying he's going to be a father to Ryan? Like he's been to Lauren but without the spanking? If you believe Lauren. Rose isn't sure that she does, anymore. She likes her—quite a lot, actually. She just thinks Lauren has a little trouble with the truth.

The night of the dinner, they take their usual seats around the table, with the addition of Bev, Richard's fiancée, who turns out to be attractive, soft-spoken, with delicate features. Rose had expected someone more solid in appearance: ruddy cheeks, opinionated. She's pleasantly surprised and happy to welcome her into the circle. And Ryan, of course, he's one of them now. That being the case, Rose asks Jeff if he minds, just this once, if someone else asks the blessing.

"Not at all," he says, adding that prayer is an act of communion. "It's meant to be shared."

She turns to Ryan. "Will you say grace for us tonight?"

Ryan asks them to join hands. He bows his head, closes his eyes: "Thank you, all living beings, for giving us this food. May it nourish us so we may nourish others. Amen."

"Amen." Rose lifts her head and surveys the room. This is it. These are their friends and this is their life. Marie was right; they're at the stage where everyone is going to die or get divorced. They probably aren't going to make new friends—their adventures will be limited. Without realizing it, they've come to the end of something.

It isn't an unpleasant thought. It is actually rather comforting.

Acknowledgments

I BEGAN THIS BOOK WITH A DISTINCT AUDIENCE IN mind: women like me. Older women, who have raised their children but are still, at least in their own minds, involved in their children's lives. Women who've been married to the same man for decades and believe there are no more surprises. Women who see the world changing around them, who are part of it and like to think they're adapting beautifully, but often aren't. First and foremost, I want to acknowledge all those friends and colleagues who, for better or worse, inspired *Rose Addams*.

Novels aren't written by committee but the writing of fiction can be enriched by the thoughtful feedback of one's peers. I discovered this to my delight over a period of 18 months as I met with the members of the Coquitlam Writing Group once a week and offered up a new chapter of *Rose*. Their comments and observations helped to keep me on track and provided fresh perspectives on the narrative. I'm grateful to them all, especially Ted Yabut Jr. and Lisa Hislop who took the time to beta read the manuscript. Without this group, I'm not sure *Rose* would have seen the light of day.

Speaking of which, kudos to NeWest Press for once again taking a chance on me. In particular I need to thank Matt Bowes who heads up a terrific team of people who really care about books—and writers; production coordinator Meredith Thompson whose patience and attention to detail is phenomenal, and my editor, Eva Radford, who had the (sometimes unenviable) task of proofing and copy-editing these pages and gently persuading me to make changes where needed. Eva is a marvelous, instinctive editor; she has the rare ability to suggest revisions, modifications, and rephrasing without ever "getting in the way". Thank you, Eva.

Finally, I have to acknowledge my family—Sarah, Jesse, June, and Logan—four people who keep me supported, amused, and interested in life. And humble. Because that, after all, is why we have children.

MARGIE TAYLOR GREW UP IN THUNDER BAY, ATTENDED Lakehead University, and began her radio career there. As a CBC Radio host and producer, she hosted regional and national radio programs, and appeared on arts and entertainment programs across Canada. She's the author of three novels: *Harrow Road*, *Displaced Persons*, and *Some of Skippy's Blues*, as well as a collection of humorous essays, and a compilation of book reviews. Currently, she lives in Port Moody where she teaches EAL and is working on a novel based on the life of her mother.